Dragons of the Past

Book Four
of
The Dragons of Nibiru

Lorna J. Carleton

Published by
Nibiru Press
3858 Brown Road, Suite 207
West Kelowna, BC V4T 2J5
Copyright © 2022 by Lorna J. Carleton
All rights reserved.

ISBN 978-1-7775448-0-5

First Edition May 2022
First Canadian Printing May 2022

Illustrations by Danielle Hebert

Also by Lorna J. Carleton

The Dragons of Nibiru

Dragons of Earth

Dragons of Remini

To Dieter,

my special Prince Deet;

I love and miss you.

CHAPTER 1

Unexpected Happenstance

"*Lazarus!*" cheered Jager. He held Celine's hands tight, gazing into her deep green eyes with electric intensity. "I *know* I can do it. With the Lazarus spell I can bring your father back to life!"

Celine, incredulous, could only stare back at her soulmate, her mouth half agape in wonder. "Oh! Oh, my goodness!" she finally cried, and wrapped him in a superhuman embrace.

They parted, laughing, then began a joyous dance around the rocky chamber. After a turn or two about the space, Celine brought them to a sudden stop.

"We've got to get tell Fianna and the others!" She flicked away a joyful tear. "It's almost unbelievable!" She brought the young man's hands to her cheeks. "Are you sure you can do it?"

Jager, just as excited, reached up, took her slender

hands in his and squeezed. "Yes, Pumpkin, yes. I am sure. Absolutely sure."

She flung her arms around his neck and they embraced again, as fiercely as before. A few breaths later, she pulled away and led him at a fast trot back up the tunnel toward the main chamber of Vin's cave-home. Once light filtering down the tunnel showed they were near the exit, she sent an exuberant mental call to her Dragon Companion.

"Fianna!" came her mental shout. "Fianna! I have fantastic news!"

"What is it, Little One?" the Dragon responded. "What has you so excited?"

"We can bring my father back!" laughed the girl, breaking into another dance of joy. "Jager can bring Dad back to life!"

"Oh, my," gasped Fianna. "That is wonderful. But, how is it possible? I have never heard of such a thing. You must tell me. I sense you are at Vin's home; we shall be there shortly, after taking leave of my parents. We have had such a lovely visit!"

"You're right, we're at Vin's. Come soon!" Celine gave Jager's arms — wrapped around her midriff as he stood behind her — an excited squeeze and snuggled into him. Just as elated, he kissed the top of her chestnut-brown head. The pair scanned the skies in the direction of Dragon Hall, looking for their winged friends.

Minutes later, Fianna and Vin touched down close to the Humans and shared their delight in the fabulous news.

"We'll need to get back to Remini right away," announced Celine.

"Indeed, I agree," said Jager. "So our first task is to head for the Cynth Pedestal and open the shield so we can call West or the Major, explain our plan and ask to be taken there. We can't just hop on the next shuttle to Remini, you know."

"Of course!" laughed Celine. "Silly me. I'm so excited, I didn't even think of that. Ha!"

The boy and girl clambered up into the Dragons' saddles and soon the four spiraled down to land at Dragon Hall. Jager already had the great staff Omaja unsheathed and in hand as he leapt from the saddle. Rushing to the Cynth Pedestal at the center of the gathering place, he held Omaja high and assumed the prescribed position for the magical rite to come. Celine joined him, and Fianna and Vin flanked them on either side.

When his friends were all settled, Jager's mellow voice rang out strong and clear, chanting the shield-manipulation spell. He completed the precisely-worded final phrase, and the four saw and heard...nothing.

Omaja remained silent.

Not a fizzle or twinkle burst from the staff's tip — much less the dazzling blue-white flash they all expected.

The mystic pedestal was just as puzzlingly inert. No warm glow, no resonant hum, bone deep. Not a glimmer or squeak.

Confused, Jager scrutinized the staff, but found it undamaged. Vin circled the pedestal twice, searching for any clue to its stillness. None was to be found.

"Hmm," grumbled Jager. He pulled out his handheld and scrolled rapidly through several screens. "Maybe I mis-performed the incantation. Let's see..."

"No," he continued after a bit, shaking his head. "Looks like I was spot on with the wording, but let's try again. He took his stance, cleared his throat, raised the staff, and repeated the chant — just as the spell-book required, and just as he had before. And just as before, both Omaja and the Cynth Pedestal remained silent.

"What's wrong?" cried Celine, wringing her hands. "Jager, what's happening?"

"I...I don't know," replied Jager. Again he rested Omaja against the pedestal, opened his handheld and scrolled through screenshots. "Yesterday I saw some things in a couple of cave drawings that piqued my interest," he explained. "I'm thinking they might help explain what's going on. "There was a curious depiction of the Unification Ceremony that didn't quite fit with how I believed it must work. It also didn't show life after the shield was in place, so I snapped an image of it to study later."

Jager held up his handheld so the others could see the painting he was referring to, then went back to studying it closely. Celine looked on, over his shoulder.

"Nothing," he said. "I don't see anything here to explain what's happening."

"Not yet, anyway. But back on *Asherah* I made sure to download everything in her database on the Ancients' magical spells, so maybe there's some explanation there. I'll check that now." He pored over another long series of images, then stopped and looked up from the screen, silent.

"What is it?" asked Celine. "Did you find something?"

"Oh, yes, Pumpkin," he groaned. "Yes, I did find something...but geez, Pumpkin. I...uh...have some bad news."

"*No!*" cried Celine, pulling away from him. "Oh, please, no!"

Celine's sudden despair came as a wrenching, physical and emotional discomfort to Jager, Fianna and Vin. When Jager finally managed to draw her close and comfort her, the sensations eased. It was an example of a new phenomenon the four had noticed over the past few hours. In addition to their new ability to hear each other's ments, now they also shared any negative sensations or emotions. They were all troubled by this new situation, but hadn't yet had an opportunity to discuss it.

"I am so sorry, Celine," said Jager. And then he was shaken by a chilling new realization.

"What is it?" Celine demanded. She sensed he was holding something back, and withdrew in a huff.

"Unfortunately, sweetie, things just got a lot more complicated. But do not worry, all is not lost. We'll find a solution." He gave her one of his best spirit-smiles, hoping it would help. It didn't appear to, though; the girl's frowns and anxiety deepened.

"Apparently," he continued, in as sensitive a voice as he could conjure, "even West is not aware of what I just learned. If she were, she certainly would have mentioned it."

"What? What is it?" wailed Celine, losing control. *"What did you find?"*

"Uh, well...," hesitated Jager, trying to maintain a positive tone despite the message he had to convey, "It's just that the Homeworlds Shield can only be opened for a single day, and only once in twenty-three days."

"*NO!*" shouted Celine. She backed off a step and planted herself, hands on hips, defiant. "That cannot be true. In the first days after the shield went up, we passed through it several times, trying to locate the Remini Dragons. There must be a mistake. What you read isn't true. It can't be!"

"I'm so sorry, Celine," replied Jager softly, sending her a reassuring mental "hug" and reaching for her hand, "but unfortunately it states right here that the shield can only be penetrated until midnight of the second day after it is acti-vated. Then another twenty-one nightfalls must pass before the shield can be penetrated again. I'm so sorry."

"It's not fair," she growled, jerking her hand from his. "Why is the universe always against us?!"

"Now, now, Little One," soothed Fianna, her Dragon voice as velvety as she'd ever mustered. "Do not despair, dearest friend — for there is always the tube-chute."

Celine signed heavily and counted to herself under her breath. "Thank you, Fianna," she said. She knew she was being difficult, acting more like her petulant sister than she'd care to admit. She swiped away fresh tears. "Sorry for my outburst, but I'm just so anxious to help my father. I feel so guilty because it's my fault he's dead. And if he can be brought back to life, well..."

"That's not true!" interrupted Jager sternly. "Soader killed your father, not you. Please, don't be silly and blame yourself for what another did. No good ever came of that. All right?"

She nodded sheepishly.

"I understand how you feel, dear friend" Fianna said qui-etly. She stroked the girl gently with one of her ivory wings. "This is just one more obstacle, but it is one we can overcome by sticking together and working as a team. And we *shall* overcome it, as that is something you and I, and all of us, are very good at doing."

Celine sighed heavily and hung her head in shame. "Yes, I know. You're right," she said. "Again, I'm sorry for my neg-ative remarks, everyone." The girl took a few deep breaths, raised her head, and forced a small smile.

"There, that's the spirit," cheered Jager. "Besides, all's not lost! As I mentioned, I have another idea." Celine managed another small smile, to everyone's relief.

"Let me try my comm pickup," said Jager with a wink. "Normally, it would not reach as far as Remini, but somehow it did when we first put up the Homeworlds Shield, remember?" Celine nodded and widened her smile a bit. "So," continued Jager, "perhaps it will work again. The major might not be on Remini at the moment, but if the comm pickup works, maybe I can reach one of the other *Asherah* crew who happen to be within the boundaries of the Shield."

"*Oh!*" exclaimed Celine, excited once again at the prospect of reviving her father. "What a fabulous idea, Jager! Try it! Please, try it right now!"

Jager reached up to his lapel, where he always pinned his comm pickup, in uniform or not. He'd learned months ago that one always had to be prepared. And once again, he was glad he'd been meticulous in following his academy training.

"Major Hadgkiss, Major Hadgkiss, this is Ensign Cornwallis. Please come in, Major Hadgkiss," he called. His friends huddled close about him, attention fixed on the tiny device and breathless with anticipation.

But no reply came. Jager tried again, first for the major, then for other Fleet crewmembers he'd recently seen on Remini. Still no reply greeted the group's anxious ears.

Celine wanted to scream, but knew she needed to keep her emotions in check. She brought all her frustrated energy into the present, clenched her fists and searched for something else to talk about. *Anything* else.

And almost at once, she found something. "Well, Fianna, you're right," she said. "There is still the tube-chute." Instantly the girl felt better, calmer. Jager sensed what she was doing and gave her one of his mental hugs, proud of her. She hugged right back.

Celine's calmer outward manner still concealed inner turmoil, but she went on. "Jager and I could use the 'chute, but that would mean you and Vin would have to come too." Now feeling fully in control of herself, she continued. "I know you both would do it without a second thought, but your wedding is so close, and none of us can miss *that!*"

Celine looked lovingly at Jager and the others before going on. "Also, Fianna — and all of you — I'm terribly sorry for my earlier behavior. I was being selfish and unnecessarily dramatic. I just didn't want to wait until after the ceremony to go save my father. With such wonderful friends as you, I can see I'll survive until we can again penetrate the shield. Besides, it's always better to make a well-planned trip than a last-minute, hasty one. My father is safe in a stasis unit; he'll be fine a while longer. Right, Jager?"

"Correct, sweetie."

"My dearest Companion," said Fianna, "I do not think that you will have to wait until after our wedding to get to Earth."

"Nor do I," added Vin, with a wink at his mate.

"I don't understand," said Celine, with a frown at her grinning friends. "What do you mean?"

Vin turned to Jager. "Does your new discovery regarding the Homeworlds Shield also affect Remini? And if not, would you be able to get through to the planet as soon as you leave Nibiru?"

"Ah, good questions," replied Jager, "I was wondering the same things myself. I'll see what information I can find." He quickly skimmed through a flurry of files on his handheld. "Hey!" he shouted. "Good news. Only communications to and from Nibiru and Pax are affected by the shielding. Has something to do with protecting their pedestals — Cynth and Talyth — which lie at opposite ends of the shielded zone. Anyway, it appears that Mentors can access Remini and the other Dragon worlds whenever they wish. Nice, eh?"

"Yes! Yes, it is!" laughed Celine, suddenly all smiles again. "Thank you, my clever Jager." She hugged him and planted a big, wet kiss on his cheek. She leaned in for a second kiss, but abruptly pulled away. "Oh, Vin!" she exclaimed. "I did it again. I'm so sorry. You asked Jager a question and I barged right in. Please forgive my rudeness."

"You are forgiven," laughed Vin, his eyes twinkling. "Excitement and good news are so needed in times such as these. They diminish the shadows for all of us. Jager, I thank you for the promising news."

"My pleasure," replied Jager. "That's just one reason I make a great Companion."

The friends had a good laugh, then Vin spoke again. "As Fianna and I suggested moments ago, dear Celine, you and Jager need not wait until after our traditional wedding to head to Earth."

"Okay," said Celine, "but, again: What do you mean?" She had an inkling of what he implied, but wanted to hear it from him, directly. "Jager and I cannot travel the tube-chute without you and Fianna. Besides, there's no need to use it. And, to tell you the truth, I'm grateful for that. The chute is not my favorite mode of transportation." She smiled at Jager, having used one of his little sayings. "And it will only be a few days after your wedding until we can use the shield-manipulation spell. That's not too long to wait, considering everything that's happened of late. *Or* what's *about* to happen, come to think of it."

"True," replied Vin, "but I do not know if you are aware that it is customary for Nibiruan wedding celebrations to continue for a fortnight after the ceremony. Longer, following a royal wedding. Our people would never forgive us if we were to depart before or during the festivities. Especially because this will not only be a royal wedding, but a double wedding as well. Double royal, in fact! So, I can see the celebrations continuing for weeks. And yet another reason for their extension occurs to me: One of those to be wed is soon to assume the throne.

"Thus, it is paramount that the celebrations take place. They are vital to affirming important relationships and traditions — including the integration of the noble Remini clans as true and treasured members of Nibiruan society. As part of this affirmation, Fallon and some of her friends are to participate in the marriage ceremony.

"So you see, young Celine, traveling the tube-chute is our only viable option at present. And be assured that we Dragon folk have no hesitation in the matter. We will accompany you, and bring you home safely and swiftly. And that is that.

"I would say we should call the vortex and depart this very night," Vin continued, "but the hour is now too late. Tomorrow will do, though; tomorrow will do."

"Oh, Vin, thanks for explaining," said Celine, with a small bow of respect. "I don't know what to say. But it's certain you've changed the way I view the whole situation. And I thank you for your gracious offer, but there is no way you two can miss out on your own *wedding*. And no one can say what will happen once we leave Nibiru. I would be too worried we might not be back in time.

"Furthermore, I do not want to miss out on your wedding either. As I've already said, I was being silly and selfish a while ago. My father's body is safe, and a couple of weeks will not affect his revival. Even a month or more. Isn't that correct, Jager?"

"Yes, Pumpkin, that is correct."

"My dear Celine," replied Vin. "I see your reasoning and admire and appreciate you for it, but in my opinion, you were not being silly or selfish. You were reacting as anyone would — or should — in a similar situation, when it relates to someone dearly loved. Look how silly Ahimoth and I get when it comes to anything regarding Joli or my lovely Fianna." He gestured with a smile and nod towards Fianna, who smiled back.

"That is nice of you to say," said Celine, pursing her lips. "Thanks, Vin. Thank you very much."

"Also, my friend," Vin continued, "you are correct, our magical wormhole cannot be altered to ensure the safe passage of a Human traveling alone. A Human must be a Companion, traveling with his or her Dragon, in order to traverse the tube-chute safely. The only exception is a Human who has had the Dream, of course, as both you and Jager have. But that is only to reach Nibiru, not to leave it. Meaning that neither of you would survive the trip without one of us accompanying you. That is how it has always been and will always be. But if Fianna and I bear you and Jager, you would arrive at the terminus undamaged. So that is what shall be done."

"Ah. All right, Vin," said Celine softly. "I thank you and understand all that you have explained, and appreciate your offer, but you will not have to do so, for we can lower the shield and be transported to Remini by Major Hadgkiss or the Mentors after your wedding and all the traditional festivities have taken place."

"I am sorry for my rudeness," interjected Fianna. "But as Vin stated, he and I will not be attending the upcoming nuptials." Fianna perceived Celine's instant objection, but continued. "Ahimoth and Joli will still be married, so the disappointment for all of Nibiru will not be as great. Their union will be a wonderful and noble event to celebrate."

"No, no, no," said Celine, pacing and wringing her hands, "You have to be there. It is to be the most momentous — and first! — double wedding of royalty ever to take place on Nibiru. You *must* attend. Besides, there is a cave-wall painting that depicts the moment."

"Do not worry, Little One," said Fianna. "The events portrayed in our treasured paintings are not to be enacted if doing so would be illogical. The creators of the images did not mean them to cancel our free will and good judgment. Besides, our dear family and friends will understand why Vin and I had to postpone our ceremony. They will be disappointed, of course, but they would consider it a travesty if they learned that Vin and I had declined to assist you in your newest and most important quest. You have done so much for our people that they all will consider it an honor to help you at this time and in this circumstance. The welfare of families is one of the highest priorities of our people.

"That is also how my parents and Vin's parents will see it, I assure you. Besides, in our hearts, my dear Vin and I were wed in the gracious ceremony you helped to create at the Mentor's home. Furthermore, our nation will still be able to celebrate the joining of my brother and his lovely Joli. And, my friend, it remains entirely possible that we will be able to return to Nibiru by the appointed wedding day.

"True, we will miss out on any more of the traditional pre-wedding ceremonies, but because it is to be a double reached the outside ledge, the others had already stepped inside. The pair followed, and Celine disembarked and moved to Jager's side.

"Ah, perfect timing, Fianna," said Vin, bowing deep. "Welcome to my home. I hope it is acceptable to you, Princess." Fianna surveyed the interior for several moments, then went back outside, took in the view from the entry ledge, and stepped back in.

"What a splendid view," she said, a bit stiffly.

Vin shifted his weight nervously, anxious that she be pleased with their future home. He watched as Fianna moved about, examining the space as closely as a kingfisher does a newly captured trout.

Celine giggled. The performance reminded her of Lye, the old nanny-Dragon who had been in charge of the clan's nursery until her recent passing.

"It is a lovely cave," said Fianna at last, with a slight head tilt and upturn of the snout. "I believe it will make a fine home. Thank you, Vin."

Vin grinned wide — a huge grin, even for a Dragon. "All right then, everyone," he announced, "let us go examine those paintings, and see why they have both you and Orgon so excited, Jager. There are also some other newly revealed depictions I want to look at. No doubt they will be deeply interesting in themselves, but our ancestors' magic, which has obscured them from our sight so long, fascinates me."

The Dragon spun around and strutted down the tunnel into the mountain. Everyone followed, their grins echoing his.

As they traversed the hard-packed, ancient floor, light-orbs lining the walls came to life, lighting their way. Vin kept up a quick pace, leading the group past paintings they'd already scrutinized, deeper into the cavern toward the most recently revealed works. At last, he signaled the group to stop, and lined them up facing a floor-to-ceiling mural. Jager and Celine, still perched in their saddles, shone the light-orbs they carried up high so all could see clearly. Everyone looked, and after a few moments' contemplation of the scene, they all gasped in the same breath.

The enormous, vibrantly colored painting before them spread over nearly a hundred meters of both walls and ceiling. It depicted Dragons of diverse types, among stars, spaceships, witches, people of various races, and unusual creatures. It seemed it must be meant to convey multiple stories, all linked to a central image. Jager and Celine agreed it would take quite some time to interpret it all, and come to an understanding of its meanings.

"Wow!" exclaimed Jager, eyes wide. "This wasn't here yesterday. Truly amazing! Look there," he pointed, "it's me, and I'm holding Omaja! And you Celine, you're beside me. Oh, and to the left, it's you, Vin! And Fianna. You're flying over a planet, a pretty, green one. And there — there with you are Ahimoth and Joli, and a little golden Dragon, too, close behind. And another bluish Dragon too, but smaller than you, Vin."

Reluctantly they moved on from the fascinating mural, hoping to discover other newly revealed works. They soon came upon a depiction of the Unification Ceremony they had recently taken part in. Then there were the weddings of Ahimoth to Joli and Fianna to Vin — set to occur in the near future.

As they moved from image to image, they marveled that each had been rendered on the stony walls thousands of union, I believe all will be forgiven. Particularly when it is made known that there is good reason for us to be late — if indeed we end up being late at all."

Celine threw her arms around Fianna's neck. Tears of happiness and relief trickled down her cheeks. She turned to Vin and gave him a happy hug, and then the Dragons returned the Humans to Fianna's cozy cave-home, before heading back to Dragon Hall to speak to the king and queen.

CHAPTER 2

Hidden Thoughts

As Fianna and Vin flew toward her parents' home, Fianna mulled over her concerns about the upcoming talk with the elder Uwattis. The princess loathed the idea of disappointing her parents, and the good Dragon folk of Nibiru — especially in light of all that had transpired in recent times. Yet in her heart she feared that traveling off-world might not be the wisest choice at this time, whether it would assist Celine or not.

She could not yet put her feelings or assumptions into words. Nor could she explain the ever-present darkness that had shadowed her since she last left Earth. But there was one thing she was thankful for: Her doubts and dark forebodings had begun to lift at the very moment she had decided to help Celine and Jager navigate the tube-chute again. She'd felt the lightening of spirit at once. She had mented Vin her decision, and was thrilled and further comforted when he expressed his full support.

As Fianna and Vin neared the royal home, they spotted King Neal and Queen Dini seated in their colorful garden, much as they'd left them not long before. Now the king's brother Orgon the Wise had joined them, and a deep discussion was in progress. The younger Dragons, not wishing to interrupt, skirted past the garden, out of sight. They landed in a neighboring meadow and strolled back toward the royal residence. Arriving at the front of the large, lushly flowered estate, they admired the brilliant colors and scents, waiting patiently. It wasn't long before Fianna's parents sensed her presence nearby — and her desire to converse with them.

"Daughter!" called the king, "Come, join us! Your uncle is here; we are discussing some new cave paintings he discovered today."

"Thank you, Father," replied Fianna, entering the garden with Vin close behind. "Hello, Mother. Hello, Uncle," Fianna gave each elder Dragon a polite bow, as did Vin. "Our Companions have also seen paintings today, in Vin's cave-home. They were most excited at what they saw, though I have not heard the details. I am curious!"

"It is nice to see you, dear niece," said Orgon, "and you, Vin. And yes, I was telling your parents of the newest images which have appeared on the cavern walls near Dragon Hall, in addition to those in Vin's cave. We are living through events foretold in our oldest prophecies; we must take great care to understand what is being asked of us by the Ancestors and Ancients."

"Undeniably so, Uncle," agreed Fianna, with a nod of respect.

"I must take my leave now," said Orgon. "I am pleased to have seen you both, brief though our visit has been." The elderly Dragon thanked his host and hostess, then added,

"Neal, I shall speak with you later this evening about what I have proposed."

"Yes, please, brother," replied the king. "That will allow me time to ponder your wise counsel."

After Orgon took flight, the senior Uwattis turned to their daughter, concerned. Her return so soon after their early-afternoon visit that same day suggested a serious conversation was about to ensue. And serious it most definitely was. The king and queen did not hold back their disappointment at Fianna's decision to postpone the lavish wedding, preparations for which were already well under way. But once they'd heard her entire explanation, they gave her and Vin their full support — just as Fianna had assured Celine they would. The regal couple agreed that the princess's purpose was just and her reasoning sound; she could not be expected to act otherwise, and the good people of Nibiru would see it that way as well.

"Daughter," said Neal, "as you must have guessed, it is too late to conjure up the vortex tonight. Nor have you and the others rested for such a trip. But we will address the council in the morning and have everything ready so you may begin your journey tomorrow night."

"Thank you, Father, Mother." Fianna gave her parents hugs, then she and Vin left to find Ahimoth. The exuberant prince and Joli could be heard boisterously playing with Alika and other fledglings in Linglu Glade. Tamar, the nanny, had begun to round up the youngsters to return to the Nursery Chamber, so Fianna and Vin's timing was perfect.

Ahimoth and Joli, upon hearing Fianna and Vin had postponed their wedding and why, at once decided to postpone theirs, too. No matter what Fianna said, Ahimoth refused to change his mind, and soon he and Joli left to speak with the king and queen.

A few minutes after they trotted off, Fianna and Vin decided to follow, to lend any support the two might need. Fianna didn't want to disappoint her parents or the clan, but truthfully, she was glad to have Ahimoth and Joli join them. She knew the darkness pressing upon her meant she would need plenty of love and support to weather whatever the future held for her.

Naturally, the king and queen were disappointed to learn the weddings might have to be delayed, especially after they and the council had announced the date and set the grand preparations in motion. But King Neal came up with a bright idea that he was sure everyone would find acceptable.

Dragons, especially Nibiru Dragons, are deeply devoted to their traditions, so any change in protocol can create upsets and even rifts. To guard against that possibility, Neal decided the *pre*-ceremony celebrations should simply be continued until the happy couples returned from their important journey. That meant, he concluded, that not only would the celebrations not be cancelled, but technically they would not even be postponed. They would simply be extended, with the ceremony moved forward in time accordingly.

He reasoned that because Dragons love to celebrate, the change shouldn't create much of an issue, if any. The good people of Nibiru would be quite happy to enjoy the extended festivities until the prince, princess and their prospective mates returned and the ceremony could commence. Besides, he announced, the fact that Fianna would be crowned as their new ruler would give the clans even more to rejoice in, celebrate and look forward to. He believed the council would readily agree that there was no shortage of things to keep the people happy. No, there was much to support pushing forward the wedding day, if that should prove necessary.

"Thank you, Father," said Fianna, planting a gentle kiss on his golden cheek.

"Yes, thank you Father, Mother," said Ahimoth with a bow.

"Thank you both," replied King Neal. "Your mother and I will take our leave of you now, and present the new plan to the council. We will return as soon as we are able, and relay their decision on the matter."

Hugs were exchanged, and Fianna, Vin, Ahimoth and Joli left for Fianna's cave-home, where Celine and Jager waited, anxious for news. Once in flight, Fianna mented Celine to say they'd arrive soon to relay all that had transpired. As it happened, the young Humans were drying off after a swim-race when Fianna called; they scanned the skies in the direction of Dragon Hall, and soon spotted the approaching Dragons. Warm greetings were exchanged, and the group was deep in discussion almost at once.

"My parents have gone to speak to the council," explained Fianna, "and soon they will tell us whether we have their official support."

No sooner had Fianna spoken than word came from her father, confirming the council's agreement with the new plans. She relayed the happy news to the others.

"Oh, Fianna," gasped Celine, wrapping her friend in a loving hug. "You're the best."

"It is the least we Dragons can do for you, Companion," replied Fianna. "The council and our families agree that you and Jager are now treasured members of our fold. Adjusting the wedding plans to allow for a possible delay was a group decision. Even though Ahimoth and Joli could elect to remain behind and have their own ceremony, everyone is happy to allow them to join us. That is good, because Ahimoth is adamant about going along; I really have no say in it. I believe he would even defy the council, if they had disagreed!" She grinned at the ebony Dragon. "I do not think my brother will ever again let me out of his sight; he takes his name's meaning quite seriously," she laughed.

"I most certainly do," agreed Ahimoth, taking a bow. "Brother of Death, at your service."

"But, but..." said Celine, her cheeks now wet with tears of joy.

"There will be no argument, Celine," said Ahimoth, planting a foreleg and ruffling his wings — a mannerism of his regal father's. "As you know, one of my most serious duties is ensuring my dear sister's safety. So, if she must travel to Earth and beyond, then I shall do the same."

"And I, in my turn, will not permit my Ahimoth to go anywhere without me," chimed in the lovely Joli. "So, there will now be enough Dragons in your company to ensure the magic remains strong and your travels are both safe and successful."

Thank you, thanks to all of you," gushed Celine, her face one enormous grin. "I feel terrible to be interrupting your wedding plans, but I truly appreciate your willingness to help." The girl had more to say, but she sealed her thoughts and feelings away. The group exchanged looks. Celine need not say anything more — they all had similar thoughts and sentiments.

Celine glowed inside, thankful and relieved that all four Dragons would return to Remini with her and with Jager. A deep, dark apprehension had been pressing in upon her since they'd left Earth. It had intensified in the past couple of days. She had managed to seal away her concerns, even from Jager and Fianna, but she knew she could not continue for long.

The girl sensed deeply sinister developments taking place all across the universe, and knew what they meant for her and for Jager. She worried whether she was prepared to participate in what would come — or if she truly even wanted to. Soon they would have no choice but to face whatever the darkness held; to do so was their destiny. It was why the Mentors had nurtured them; she and Jager were vital instruments, essential to the defeat of the evil Volac Forces.

Celine swallowed, ashamed. She knew their roles in the Mentors' plans were of far greater importance than her quest to revive her father. And deep down, she knew their roles were the true reason they must leave Nibiru at once. She sighed, happy for the moment that she had managed to keep her concerns hidden.

Still deep in thought, Celine was startled into the present by Jager, who had decided to lighten the mood. He'd challenged the others to a game of tag; all four Dragons raced skyward, with Celine and Jager clinging tight to their Companions' saddles. In no time, everyone was laughing and living in the moment, thoughts of evil beings and dark, deadly masses forgotten. Momentarily, at least.

After an hour of hard flying, Ahimoth decided to change the game and challenged Vin to "who's the best Dragon at this." The friends laughed harder than they had in weeks, as Ahimoth failed at his own challenge.

As night drew near, the Dragons decided to speak with the king and queen one last time, to learn if their help might be needed in the preparations for the next evening's vortex ceremony. Goodbyes were said, and Celine and Jager and were once again alone.

CHAPTER 3

Concerns

As Fianna and the others began their descent toward Dragon Hall, they were surprised to spot the king and queen beside the Cynth Pedestal. Orgon the Wise stood with them, in what appeared to be an intense conversation. Fianna and the others set down as silently as they could, then moved quietly off to the side to await an opportunity to speak.

Neal paced back and forth, then stopped to face Orgon. "You are correct, dear brother," he said. "With new paintings appearing daily, it is hard to know when and how we must act on our newfound knowledge. Nevertheless, I believe in my bones — indeed, deep within my heart and soul, that our children traveling to Earth for a few days will not much matter in the larger scheme of things. Besides, as I earlier proposed, we need not cancel or seriously postpone the weddings. And the entire council agrees. You agreed yourself, when we voted earlier today. So I do not understand your present concerns.

"Furthermore, our dear daughter has assured me they should not be gone longer than a week. As you know, Orgon, many of our traditional wedding preparations may go forward without the bride and groom present. And I feel that our children and their mates will indeed return in time for their nuptials. I say we have nothing to fear."

"Yes, I agree, dear brother," replied Orgon, folding his green wings. "What you say is logical and wise. My concerns are no more. I believe I would have pursued the same course myself, had you and Dini not returned from your long captivity, to rule as wisely as you do this day."

"That is good to hear, Orgon," said Neal. "Very good indeed. It is important to me to have your support in this matter."

"Have it you do," replied Orgon. "The more I think on it, the more I believe the newest paintings, discovered but a short while ago, support your children's plan to travel to Earth at this very point in our world's history. In fact, I now believe such a journey is expected."

Fianna and the others exchanged looks, but remained silent.

"Ah, Ahimoth. Fianna," said Neal, turning his attention to his children. "As you must have heard just now, the possible postponement of your weddings caused some angst among our great council, as it would be a divergence from our long traditions, steadfastly observed. But as your wise mother so astutely pointed out to the council, there is no prophecy or mandate in all Nibiruan tradition which states precisely when you should be wed.

"We explained that your trip will mean but a slight

adjustment to convention. Perhaps no adjustment at all, since you say you may well return quickly. Allowance should be made for the possibility, though, to ensure that it will be a *double* wedding, as foretold in the prophetic cave images most recently revealed. The council has seen the wisdom in her words, as has your uncle here. And so you have the blessing of us all, in your honorable intent to aid your dear Companions in their quest."

"I cannot thank you enough, Father. Nor you, Mother," said Fianna. "It means a great deal to both Vin and me to support our Companions. As it does, I believe, to my brother and his soon-to-be bride. We shall return as quickly as we are able. Ahimoth will not leave my side; of this I am sure, for his name, by tradition, dictates so. I appreciate your granting him leave to accompany us."

"Dear daughter," replied the king. "Your mother and I are honored by your loyalty to your friends. As our new leader, with such a fine mate at your side, and such a loyal and loving brother, I know you will restore our cherished home to the wonderful haven it once was. I know this by how well you follow your mind's eye — in tune, as it is, with your loving heart." Fianna bowed to her father but remained silent, sensing he had more to say.

"I also thank you for asking our permission to follow your plans. That was no mere gesture, but the act of a true leader. We both know that you will do what you believe to be right, regardless of permissions. And that you asked us out of respect. We know that if we had not granted our blessing, you would have acted as a true leader, without hesitation, and taken your Companions through the chute. The council believes the same, and respects you for it, just as do your mother and I."

Fianna bowed once again, now smiling broadly. She hugged her parents tight, and Ahimoth did the same.

"Thank you again, Father," said Fianna at last. "I will leave it to you and Uncle to prepare everything for the opening of the vortex tomorrow night. And now it is late, so I wish to bed down for some rest. I am sure the others wish to do the same."

"Yes, daughter," replied Neal. "All shall be in readiness at the appointed time. But for now, a good night to you all!"

The four watched as the royal couple entered their home and Orgon headed for his; then they too exchanged goodnights. Joli left for her parents', while Ahimoth headed back to Vin's cave, and Fianna and Vin left for hers.

Upon arriving at her home, Fianna and Vin found Celine and Jager talking under their favorite tree near the river. The Dragons joined them to chat for a bit before retiring, and to watch the slow-moving river and the many fish jumping in the pools along its banks.

"Fianna, I must thank you again for what you're doing for me," said Celine. "I cannot properly put my feelings into words. In fact, I haven't really even had time to consider what it will mean to have my father alive again. I must confess, I've not been myself the past few days, but now I'm feeling better and better. Once this is all over, I look forward to spending undistracted time in your fine company; with all of you. And, most important, to attending your wedding."

The talk continued until Vin and Jager decided it was time to leave. Jager wanted a look at some of the newest paintings Orgon had mentioned, before it grew too late. "See you tomorrow, Pumpkin," he said, hugging Celine close and giving her a kiss. He and Vin were soon aloft; Celine and Fianna watched until the night sky enveloped them.

Just as in times past, the two curled up without a word. Snug beneath their tree, both were yet mindful that Fianna and Vin's marriage would soon bring such nights to an end. "It's awfully hard to believe that so much has happened, and in such a short time," said Celine. She shifted her weight to get more comfortable.

"Truly," replied Fianna. "I have thought much the same."

The two friends continued to talk for quite some time, until both knew sleep was mere moments away. After a whispered goodnight, Fianna fell sound asleep. Celine, now alone with her thoughts, remained wakeful despite her fatigue, troubled by images she could not keep at bay. She called to Jager, hoping to find him still awake.

"Yes, Pumpkin. I'm here. Having difficulty sleeping, too. What's keeping you up tonight?"

Celine didn't want to talk about her father, or the huge black mass that haunted her — despite knowing that in the past, discussion of such things with Jager had always helped. Intuition told her to keep her apprehensions to herself, for the time being at least. So she found another subject to bring up. "I've been thinking about all the wonderful things we've accomplished or been part of lately," she lied.

"I see," he replied. He knew she was evading the truth, but also that he must be patient and gentle if he wanted her to reveal what troubled her. Otherwise, her pride would likely get the better of her, and she'd continue to hold back.

"Mm, yes. Smart to be putting attention on all that. One of those wonderful things, if I might add to your list, is being able to hold you in my arms for real, instead of only imagining it. I'd say that's at the top of my list!"

Celine sent him a mental smile, glad he couldn't see her slight blush at his words. She realized she was becoming less and less sensitive on the subject, but sometimes she still felt a bit of embarrassment.

Jager sensed her flicker of discomfort, and gently shifted the subject. "Number two, if I were counting, would be the fantastic honor of meeting Fianna and the others. Oh, and becoming Companion to Vin, and flying with him! Incomparable. And helping you save Nibiru, for sure. Can't help but be proud of that."

Celine giggled at the images Jager now relayed — memories of one of the silly times they'd shared with the Dragons. He continued to list favorite events: "Meeting Fallon and the other Remini Dragons was right up there. And remember when West said it was paramount to keep the Dragons safe? I guess we definitely succeeded there, when we put up the Homeworlds Shield. My, we *have* been busy, haven't we?" They both laughed.

"Let's not forget you meeting Omaja and becoming Holder of The Staff. And wow — we met the twin brother we didn't even know you had! That was huge. What a surprise, seeing Jaecar for the first time, sitting on his throne!"

"Ha!" laughed Jager. "That's putting it mildly. I had to feel my legs and grab the chair arms, to make sure I was still sitting up in the gallery with you! We'll have to go visit him soon."

"I'd like that," said Celine. Finally, she felt relaxed, near ready for sleep. "And you got to meet my family. I hope Mom and the others are doing well."

"I'm sure they are. Dino probably has things under control. That reminds me of all the cadets, and Bonafede and

Dorte. Oh, and we mustn't forget that I managed to send Soader to RPF113. A great moment, eh?" They laughed some more. "And that reminds me: You and Fianna handled the Brothers quite admirably. I was so proud to hear how you managed it."

"Thanks!" Celine said, then let out a yawn.

"Not to dampen things, sweetie, but we mustn't forget we've got to prevent Scabbage from following through with his plans. I expect he's going to be considerably more difficult to handle than he's been so far. But then, we're also stronger than we were just weeks ago. Stronger as individuals, and stronger as a united force."

Celine smiled. Somehow Jager instinctively managed to comfort her, without knowing exactly what bothered her. "I agree," she said. "It will take a great deal of effort to defeat the High Chancellor. From all of us. Major Hadgkiss included. And...my father."

"Without a doubt," replied Jager.

Despite all the good that had transpired, she still struggled against the dread that preoccupied her. And now, without warning, it intensified to the point of palpable pain in her chest and a pounding in her head. With an effort, she pushed away the anxiety and pain. She mustn't let Jager perceive it. Not for the moment, anyway. "I think I can sleep now," she said.

"Me too," said Jager, with a yawn. "It's a good thing. We've got a long trip ahead. And truthfully, it's not one I'm looking forward to. A good rest will help."

"To be honest, I'm not looking forward to the tube-chute either," confessed Celine. "I'm more apprehensive than any time I've traveled it, and that concerns me. You are right, though, as always. We should get some sleep. Love you. Night."

"Love you too, Pumpkin. Sweet dreams."

Celine sighed, relieved to have kept her dark thoughts and memories from Jager. Since early that morning, a premonition had plagued her. One that repeated over and over: it was imperative she go immediately back to the Mentor's hidden outpost. Jager's realization regarding Lazarus could not have come at a better time, she thought. And then she rolled over and fell quickly into sleep.

CHAPTER 4

Surprises

The next morning, both Fianna and Celine noticed a change in the darkness that had haunted them since their recent arrival on Nibiru. To their great relief, it had faded considerably. Both guessed the welcome transformation might have to do with their upcoming return to Earth. Although both appreciated the respite, they remained apprehensive; there were still so many unknowns. Not wishing to discuss the matter or worry those they loved, they simply kept their thoughts and feelings about it hidden. Hidden so well that neither was aware the other was doing so too.

The two were still stretching the sleep out of their limbs when Vin and Jager arrived, bearing the news that the council wished to speak to Fianna. She and Vin headed toward Dragon Hall, where they would join Ahimoth and Joli at the ceremonial plaza.

Celine and Jager watched the Dragons wing away, then

challenged each other to their usual swim match. They raced across the river and back. They left the water and fell, out of breath, on the bank, peals of laughter coming in choked spurts. Adding to the merriment was the fact they'd reached the shore at the exact same moment. Just as they had in their previous three challenges. The happy couple hugged, then retreated to the cave for a quick breakfast. During the post-meal cleanup, Vin and Fianna returned.

The Dragon princess explained that when they had arrived at Dragon Hall, not only had the council been present, but so had almost the entire clan. Somehow, they'd already heard why their prince and princess would miss out on most, if not all, of the pre-wedding celebrations. Apparently, all was forgiven. Later, many were heard bragging about the true dedication and selflessness of their young royalty, in their willingness to aid their Companions in time of need.

"I hope you and Jager understand," said Fianna. "It is important we Dragons spend as much time as we can with our fold before our departure tonight, partaking in pre-wedding festivities. We would be honored and delighted if you two would join us."

"I would be the one honored," said Jager, making a deep bow. "Thanks for asking."

"Me, too," added Celine, and she and Jager quickly climbed into their saddles. Within moments, the contented friends were soaring towards the celebrations, which were already boisterously underway.

For several hours the companions participated in a celebration of what the Dragons called Memory Day. Once he'd learned what was going on, Jager explained to Celine that on Earth, they called such a party a wedding shower or bridal shower. There was a difference here on Nibiru, though.

Memory Day was for both the bride-to-be and the husband-to-be as well. The affair involved gift giving, enjoying plenty of tasty foods (and then even *more* tasty foods), and the telling of stories, both true and imagined. Seeing as Vin, Ahimoth and Joli had been away from home for many years, most of the tales and jokes centered on Fianna, but the others didn't mind her being the center of attention. They even contributed stories and jokes themselves. Often did the charming Fianna's cheeks blush pink that day. All in all, it was a lovely day, with great times and fun had by all.

When the time for the noonday feast arrived, the six friends congregated at a spot close to the edge of the gathering, which had spread to cover almost the entirety of Linglu Glade.

"Hey, everyone," said Jager. "How about we all enjoy the feasting for a bit, and then Celine and I can show you the newest paintings we discovered yesterday? While there, I'd also like to show you the ones Orgon spoke about earlier. They're particularly curious."

"Great idea," chimed in Vin, who never passed up a meal if he could help it.

"All right," agreed Fianna. "I think it will be acceptable to step away from the celebrations for a short time. I will join you as well."

Nibiruan pre-wedding feasts are not small events. Yet another lavish spread of food was being placed out on many tables. The spread looked and smelled wonderful; soon the close-knit group were happily stuffing themselves, enjoying each other's company and chatting with guest after guest after guest.

After a while, when they could not swallow another

morsel, Vin groaned. "I do not know about you, my friends, but I am well and truly finished." His obviously over-satisfied belly bulged as he rested back on his haunches. The others laughed; they too had eaten a bit to heartily of the delicious offerings. "I could use a nap," Vin moaned. "But how about if we all go to my cave to see the new paintings Jager was talking about, before it gets too late. Then I will kick you out — politely and respectfully, of course — and sleep until tomorrow."

They all laughed again, knowing none of them would get such a rest; instead, they would be traveling through the tube-chute in just a few hours.

"Good idea, Vin," replied Jager. "The paintings I want to show you are different than any of the others, and I need some help with details of the interpretation."

"I'm in," said Celine. "Fianna, are you still interested?"

"Ah, um...yes, yes," replied her friend, who suddenly seemed like a different person.

"Excellent," said Vin. He glanced at Fianna, sensing her apprehension, but not mentioning it, for the moment.

Ahimoth looked to Joli, arching a questioning eye ridge. She nodded, and he smiled. "Joli and I would love to join you," he said. "But we Dragons should be quick about it, for again, we should spend as much time as possible with our clan before departing."

Vin winked at Fianna, then let slip a tremendous burp that had everyone laughing again. He bowed his appreciation to a cook standing nearby, then raised a foreleg so Jager could scramble up into the saddle. The Dragon made a small bow to Fianna, then leapt up into the air, with Ahimoth and Joli close behind. The Dragon princess and Celine held back and watched their friends fly off.

"What is it, Fianna?" asked Celine, sensing her friend's hesitations.

"Ah, Little One," replied Fianna. "You are too perceptive!"

"Please, tell me what's wrong; you have me sort of worried."

"It is nothing of grave importance, my friend. It is more a matter of my just being a silly Dragon."

"You can never be just a silly Dragon, Fianna. You are one of the noblest people I've ever met," declared Celine. But her concern for her friend was undiminished. "Please tell me what is bothering you."

"All right. I will try to explain." The Dragon took several slow, deep breaths. "It is because...um...Vin's cave is...um.... Oh, I am sorry, I shall just say it. Now that Vin and I are to be wed in the Nibiru fashion, Vin's cave will soon be my home. Today will be the first time I will see it. It is an important step in the binding of two Dragons.

"Mere weeks ago, only you were in my life, and now I am to be mated. And then, adding to that, I will be crowned ruler of an entire people and their planet. And all during a difficult time — not only for Nibiru, but for the entire universe. It is much to comprehend. My life has changed so, and in such a short time. I feel a bit...a bit dizzy from it all."

"Oh, I see," nodded Celine sagely. "If it is any help to hear it, I believe it is normal and understandable to feel as you do. I agree — your life has changed drastically, and in very major ways. I too would find it overwhelming if I were to experience such things.

"Actually, do you know what? I can relate to what you're facing in many ways. My life's also been turned upside down.

But Fianna, no matter what happens, please know that having you in my life has made it wonderful. Even despite all the terrible things we've endured together. Sharing my days with you makes me glad to be alive. It is a life I would never change."

"And that is why you are a Companion," smiled Fianna. "You are wise beyond your years. Thank you for listening to a fool of a Dragon. Since that day I first met you at my cave-home, life has been a wonder and a joy as well. We have made memories I will hold dear all the days of my life. You have made me a better Dragon; one who may now lead this world's good people. Thank you, dear friend. I know, though, that life is not always wonderful; often there is a plenitude of bad mixed in with the good. But I can choose to what I give my attention; I need not dwell on the bad, nor like it."

"My exact thoughts," murmured Celine. She could not help thinking of the dark mass that so often haunted her. "It will all work out, Fianna. You will see. You will make a wonderful leader, and a wonderful partner to Vin. He's one lucky Dragon." She patted the Dragon's side. "Now! Ready to go check out your new home?"

Fianna sighed one last time, then ruffled herself. "Yes, I suppose I am," she said, with a smile only a tiny bit rueful.

The two soon found themselves on the ledge outside Vin's cave. Even though Vin had been absent for years, held captive on Earth by the wicked Soader, his parents had kept his home clean and ready, in hopeful anticipation of his return. They never permitted anyone else to use it, let alone take up permanent residence there. The cave was enormous, with more than enough living area for several Dragons of Vin and Ahimoth's size. It would be perfect — quite comfortable for Vin and his soon-to-be bride. When Celine and Fianna

years in the past, only to appear now, for reasons they did not fully grasp. The more they saw, the more they became immersed in their own thoughts and conclusions — and fears.

The group came to the entrance of a side tunnel, branching off from the main tunnel they had been following. Celine and Fianna elected to follow it, while the others continued down the main passage. A hundred meters or so down the side tunnel, a glint from the wall to their right caught Celine's eye. "Just a moment," she said to Fianna. "What's this?" She raised her light-orb, fully illuminating a painting — a familiar painting. Recognizing it, the pair gasped.

"Jager!" Celine excitedly mented. "Come quick!"

Jager, Vin and the others rushed to join them. As they took in the painting Celine had illuminated, each gasped in recognition. The mural included an icon they all had seen before, in Fianna's cave: the symbol of purity, truth and abundant survival. It was an image of a young man and woman facing one another, kissing, their arms interlocked. A purple halo shone above their heads in the shape of a horizontal figure "8" — the ancient symbol for infinity. A larger infinity symbol also embraced them, encircling their waists.

At the feet of the kissing pair sat two small children, embraced by yet another infinity halo. One was a blond-haired blue-eyed boy dressed in rags, with bloodied knees and hands; the other was a little girl with long, chestnut-brown hair and piercing green eyes, similarly dressed. Close beside the pair were two Dragons — one white, one blue — with two shiny eggs at their feet. Near the eggs lay a large staff, clearly Omaja. This last detail was new — the staff had not appeared in the version of the painting all had seen previously.

The mural included another significant feature, new to

the group. Arranged all along its borders were depictions of Alika, Fallon, Remi, Mia, Dino, the Mentors, and — surprisingly — Celine's father. Jaecar was shown as well, as were Father Greer, several Lyran cat-people, and others. Perhaps most surprising were depictions of King Neal, Orgon and other Nibiru and Remini Dragons, as well as Narco, Choy and two more of their Kerr Dragon race, all flying above what appeared to be a crowded, roiling battlefield.

Deathly silence filled the cave. All stared at the elaborate work, transfixed.

At length, Vin ended the breathless hush. "The prophecies have always mystified me," he said, his great head tilting from side to side, "but this painting reaffirms what my heart has told me: We — the six of us — belong together. We are stronger *because* we are together. We are meant to use our united strength to bind and protect our families and our worlds."

"You speak truth," replied Fianna, softly.

"All I can say is, wow!" exclaimed Jager. "Life is amazing. I can scarcely believe what I'm seeing. So many of the cave images we've seen — this one and many others — portray circumstances that have taken place without influence or action from any individual. They just came to pass naturally. It's like Mother Nature and her mysterious ways."

"Mother Nature?" asked Celine.

"Yes, that's what Earthers call, um...well, I guess you could simply say 'life.' It's a way of personifying Nature as a creative and controlling force. It helps to explain things like an unexpected storm, or a beautiful animal. Or a lovely girl from Erra, for that matter."

"Oh," said Celine, "I like that explanation. Seems

appropriate for some situations. And yes, it suits what we see in these paintings. For the longest time, I didn't tell you anything about the paintings in Fianna's cave-home; I didn't want to inadvertently influence what they seemed to foretell. But as you can see, a number of events we've been through — events shown in the paintings — have occurred regardless of anything Fianna or I did. I believe it's all Mother Nature at work, guiding and controlling events." She smiled at Jager, who gave her the thumbs up for using 'Mother Nature' as he'd explained the term. "For example," she explained, "Omaja chose you to be his Holder. That was the way of the universe: Mother Nature. Although we found it — or maybe it found us — neither Fianna nor I had any idea what the staff really was."

"Interesting indeed," replied Jager. "And yes, Mother Nature appears to have an influence in these paintings. Vin, do you know of any more paintings that appear to depict events further into the future?"

"I am not sure," said Vin, "but we should look farther along. Follow me."

Vin led them back to the main tunnel, then deeper into the mountain. Soon they flanked another enormous painting, similar to the one they'd just witnessed. This mural depicted a grounded Fleet ship with Major Hadgkiss, Commander Zulak and other crew nearby. Numerous Dragons, including Neal and Orgon, spiraled high above. Strangely, Soader appeared in the painting, standing beside Celine — and holding her hand! At the sight of it, Celine cringed, shuddered, and gulped twice.

"It's all right, Pumpkin," soothed Jager. "I get the feeling things shown there are not quite as they appear to be."

"It's horrible!" wailed Celine, turning away from the

painting.

"It will be all right, sweetie. Again, I don't think what we're seeing there is as simple or awful as it looks."

"What is it, then?" asked Celine, more than a little agitated by the image. Deep shivers continued up and down her spine; flashbacks seared her mind.

"It will be all right, Celine. I'm sorry, but I've been such an idiot — again!" groaned Jager. He smacked his forehead with his palm. "I can't believe I missed it!"

"What are you talking..." began Celine. Then she caught Jager's mental image.

"Oh, my!" she gasped. "Can you? Is it? Oh my, that *does* explain this painting, doesn't it?"

"I think so. I'm quite sure I can..." Jager paused, frowned and grew silent, deep in thought. Then he burst out: "Yes, I can! Without a doubt, I can."

Fianna and Vin perceived the Humans' conversation and mental images, and gasped aloud themselves.

"What a great idea, Jager," said Fianna and Vin.

"Well, I should have thought of this before. I can't believe I didn't," said the young man, rolling his eyes in exasperation. "I could have saved us *so* much trouble and worry."

"It's all right," whispered Celine. "You've thought of it now."

Ahimoth, unable to perceive the Humans' ments and feeling left out of the excitement, abandoned all Dragon manners and broke into the conversation. "What is it? What is going on?"

"Well," said Jager, attuned to Celine's thoughts as he spoke, to be sure she was okay with what he was about to say,

"Soader's body is still at TS 428 — the soul transfer station on Earth's moon. So is a quasi-spiritual form of me. Both might come in handy... But I digress. I believe we can use Soader's body in a couple of positive ways. First, we could use it under my control, impersonating him. Use it to lure out Scabbage so we can catch and dispose of that maniac once and for all."

"Wow!" exclaimed all the Dragons together.

"I want to be a part of this plan," said Ahimoth, his already considerable grin spreading even wider.

"And I shall take part as well. Most definitely," announced Vin, beaming just as widely as Ahimoth.

"Agreed and understood," answered Jager. "With Scabbage out of the way, we will have a much better chance of defeating the Volac Forces. I feel badly that I didn't think of this earlier; we might have been able to use the body to rescue all those women and girls imprisoned in the labs. What a dummy I was. It would have saved a lot of difficulties if I'd just been thinking clearly."

"It's okay, Jager," soothed Celine. "We're thinking of it now. It's not too late to use the body as you suggest. Besides, hitting on this right now is perfect timing. We can use it to deal with Scabbage, and then whatever other ideas you were talking about just now. I'm surely interested in hearing those!"

"Me too!" Ahimoth laughed. "Brilliant! I must say, Jager, you are clever, for a Human." Everyone joined in a good laugh at the comment, and at Jager feigning offence at the prince's joking poke at Humans as inherently dimwitted.

"Well, dear friends," said Fianna in a stately tone. "I believe we should rapidly conclude our studies here, then go partake in some more of the festivities being held in our honor." The lovely white Dragon paused, gazing at Vin and grinning. "However," she smiled, "while there, we should do our best to refrain from eating anything at all. We have a tube-chute journey to make tonight, and I scarcely need to remind you how uncomfortable such a trip can be, even on an empty stomach!"

Everyone laughed at Vin; he wore an indignant look and patted his belly, still overstuffed from their last round of celebrations.

"Most definitely," they all agreed, laughing.

"Wisely spoken, our future leader," replied Vin with a bow. "Yes, my gluttonous appetite could give me trouble. I gladly promise to abstain from further stuffing for the rest of the day."

"I promise the same, dear sister," added Ahimoth with a grin. "One thing, though, before we leave," he continued. "I am confused as to how all these paintings could possibly be here. They do not seem to align with many things we were taught as fledglings. Perhaps, as Jager earlier suggested, Uncle could counsel us on what he believes they mean. He may know something that would shed light on why these paintings have now appeared, and what they may imply. And, most interesting to me, why have they only appeared to us at this particular time?"

"That is a good idea," replied Fianna. "Perhaps we can ask him before we go to take our rest. I know he was studying these very walls yesterday, so he is likely to have some wise words to share regarding his perspective."

"Wise words from a wise Dragon," chuckled Ahimoth. "Once again, sister, you have demonstrated yourself a better choice to lead our great people than me. In my view, at least."

Fianna smiled her warm Dragon smile.

"Most definitely," agreed Vin, grinning until he noticed Ahimoth feigning hurt feelings. "Oh, oh, I am sorry, Ahimoth. I did not mean that you would not make a good leader. That is far from how I feel. I…I was just trying to show Fianna my support." Vin's blue cheeks were nearing a nice blush of violet.

"Ha!" laughed Ahimoth. "Have no fear, Vin, no fear. I saw exactly what you were doing, and would do the same under similar circumstances. I have no doubt of your faith in me, for are we not the best of friends?"

"Yes, indeed we are," replied Vin with a nod — the sort of nod one sees among friends who have suffered and survived great challenges together. "Yes, indeed we are."

The group all cheered, in a great release of the tension that had been building since Jager's realization about using the Lazarus spell.

"I'm continually amazed by the universe we live in," said Celine, walking with the group up the long passageway. "I never grow tired of the wonders I see. These drawings encourage me to fight on even harder, to save all that is good and decent, and for everything worth loving and cherishing across the galaxy."

"I am similarly inspired," professed Fianna. "The images will aid us in our future endeavors, especially if Uncle's perspective lends us further insights." The white Dragon cleared her throat. "Companion, I must tell you something now, regarding…"

A deep baritone interrupted Fianna, from up the tunnel, along their path to the entrance. "Hello," said Orgon the Wise. "I am sorry to startle you, but our king and queen request your presence. The time has come for your mother's favorite pre-wedding activity.

"And I am curious to hear your thoughts, now that you have gazed again upon the precious ancient walls of our people." Orgon paused to look over the closest of the images and smiled. "The walls," he continued, "that foretell the future and have once again revealed what is to transpire, now that you all have safely returned home."

"Thank you, Uncle," said Ahimoth. He passed the elder Dragon and continued up the tunnel. "And yes, we see that the prophecies do not stray from the truth: that we all have our parts to play in what is to come. Even as you most certainly do, according to what I observed in the last painting we examined today. Perhaps you can find an explanation for it, and for the other new images that have recently come to view. Then I hope you will join us in visiting our parents."

Orgon looked taken somewhat aback. He could be heard mumbling as he walked on, deeper into the mountain, pausing to examine each painting he came to. The friends grinned and followed Ahimoth out into the sunshine.

The group spent a few hours partaking in the clan's celebratory activities, before excusing themselves. The soon-to-be queen wished to speak with her parents, and all were in need of a few hours' rest.

The Dragon princess was surprised to find the king and queen facing the council, all arrayed before the Cynth Pedestal in serious deliberation.

Neal signaled for a pause in the proceedings and addressed the new arrivals. "My dearest Fianna and Ahimoth," he said, his forearms spread in greeting. "We were just discussing the meaning of the prophecies most recently revealed in the paintings, in Vin's cave and in others throughout our valley. It appears, daughter, that your decision to invite the Dragons of Remini to our lovely home was anticipated by the Ancients."

He swept his wings wide to include all in attendance, then continued. "All those present here, and, I am certain, all the Dragons of our world, support me in what I am about to say." He bowed to his daughter, just as Orgon glided in to land a few meters away.

"Fianna," Neal went on, "your gracious mother and I, and our council on this grand evening, wish to make the matter official and affirm that you are shortly to be crowned our new ruler. And to announce to all that you will be Queen of Nibiru. There is no time for a coronation before your departure, but we ask that you would, upon your return and in conjunction with your wedding, ascend the throne as our beloved queen."

Though somewhat surprised at the announcement, Fianna and the others remained quiet, reflecting on several of the murals they'd most recently viewed. Suddenly, their meaning was clear. The assembled Dragons waited quietly for Fianna's response.

But no response came. Ahimoth, sensing his sister's discomfiture, gave her a secret wink, then whooped and trumpeted long and loudly. Fianna mented him a thank you, collected her thoughts, and addressed the gathering with a speech that would be remembered for years to come.

"Father, Mother, Council, Uncle — this is indeed a gracious and grand surprise. I am truly honored and humbled that you consider me, young as I am, to be ready to assume such an enormous responsibility.

"As a Nibiruan, and a member of the royal family of this wonderful world, I shall never take my reign or my duties lightly. I promise with my loving heart, mind and soul, and with every bone in my body, that I will seek to emulate the sterling leadership that has inspired me since I was a fledgling, playing in the Nursery chambers beneath Dragon Hall.

"I thank every one of you standing before me today, for helping a once-naïve youngster to become the Dragon that I am here and now." She bowed long and deeply to each Council member, her parents, and her uncle. Then, to everyone's surprise, she bowed as well to her brother, then Vin, Joli, Jager and — longest and most deeply — to Celine. Each returned her gesture in turn, most with tear-moist eyes and faces alight with smiles of joy.

Fianna moved close to Neal's side; "Thank you, Father. I know this is a special evening, but with your permission, I wish to take my leave. It is late; before braving the tube-chute, I desperately need rest. As do my brother and the others. I am sorry, but it is so."

"No apologies necessary, daughter," replied Neal. "Your uncle and I will ensure all is in readiness for your departure when the moon reaches its peak." With a bow, he continued. "You make us all proud, Fianna." Goodnights were exchanged, and Celine and Fianna were soon curled comfortably beneath their favorite tree, watching water bugs skim the backwaters at the river's edge. The pair chatted for a short while, then dozed.

CHAPTER 5

Heartbreak

Later, as the moon neared the crest of the sky, Fianna, Celine, Vin and Jager gathered in Dragon Hall, expecting the prince and his mate to join them momentarily. They stood in silence, watching the others who paced the majestic courtyard, eager to participate in the upcoming incantation; their colorful scales glistened in the firelight.

Fianna and Vin began a conversation, so Celine grabbed Jager's hand and moved off to visit with Fallon, whom she had spotted across the court.

"Hello!" Celine began, careful to observe the decorum so important to Dragons of any race. "I am Celine, Companion to Fianna, and this is my mate, Jager." Like Fianna, Fallon was a princess, deserving of respect.

"Greetings, Celine, Companion to my friend Fianna," replied Fallon, bowing deep. "I am called Nimu Fallon Roark, Princess of the Dragons of Remini."

"It is a pleasure to meet you, Princess Nimu Fallon Roark of the Dragons of Remini," responded Jager and Celine. All three bowed.

Soon a lively dialogue was underway, with a few of Fallon's friends joining in. Celine and Jager were surprised to discover the youngsters were anxious to get back to Remini.

"Ah, but Fallon," remarked Jager, "I think you ought to grant your father and your sage council their intelligence. Their long years have graced them with wisdom, and they believe they are doing what is best for your people."

"True, they are aged," replied Fallon, somewhat grudgingly. She snorted and scuffed at the stony floor.

"You misunderstand me," said Jager. "Facing one's enemy directly is not always the best way to win a battle. Neither is it necessarily cowardly to retreat, if one does so to protect one's people. By the sound of what happened to the other factions on your planet, your folds were no match for the army of Humans intent on your destruction. If your king and council thought it best to come to Nibiru to save your people, it would seem unjust to fault them; they had the elderly and young whelps to consider, among other things."

"Yes, you speak truth," said Fallon, "but we left as cowards. We struck them not a single blow, dealt them not one fire blast."

"Fighting, my dear Fallon," continued Jager, "and destroying one's enemy is not always a physical thing. With you and your fold safe, your enemy will be disappointed they could not strike a blow against you, let alone kill you off, as was their intent. It is a disappointment that will fester and grow to a gaping hole in their hearts and their society. A blinding hatred that will lead them to fight amongst themselves. In the end, it will be their downfall. I guarantee it.

"This is how Human events have transpired throughout my planet's history, century upon century. Lust for revenge or dominance, desire for restitution of wrongs, real or imagined, recent or long past — these have proven the deadliest destroyers of societies. And sadly and unfortunately, such things still happen on Earth to this day.

"These emotions and motives are more injurious than any physical conquest. They fuel only negativity for both 'winners' and 'losers.' They keep wars brewing, wounds and resentments fresh. So much so that cities and homes, the innocent, the children, the elderly, *all* suffer needlessly, on both sides. All grow sad and unrighteous, as does the entire society.

"Such attitudes never make any faction a winner — never. So do not cling to the role of victim; neither in your thoughts nor your actions. It is one of the most insidious destroyers of the peoples of any world. It always has been and always will be. To take it on is the beginning of the end for any person, group, race or civilization.

"Dear Fallon, take responsibility for what happens to you. Make strong, controlled efforts forward. Always forward. If you do this, wars will be won, lives and souls will be saved. Do not fall into the traps only selfish, arrogant people promote, such as attempts to avenge wrongs against their ancestors. They are not paths to happiness — not now, not ever."

"Oh?" perked up Fallon, as did her friends, and several young Nibiruans — including Alika — who had gathered to listen.

"Yes. I speak from the heart, and from a reality that is truthful," affirmed Jager, pursing his lips. "This is how it has been through thousands of years of wars and strife. And not only on my own home planet. Do not think it would be any different for your Dragons of Remini. I believe your father and council wise in their decision, and I am glad for it. And then there is this: If not for their choice, I would never have met all of you!" He grinned warmly at the numerous Dragons now gathered round.

"Your leaders' wise counsel will make it possible for you and other young Remini to grow up knowing love and happiness; far better to experience and express than hatred and all-consuming lust for vengeance."

Fallon huffed and stomped. "Celine!" she said, "Is he always so full of words that make you mad, because they are so wise and true?"

"Ha!" laughed Celine. "More than I'm willing to admit to him." They all had a good laugh and chatted for a few minutes, but stuck to less tension-filled topics. Before they knew it, it was time to make final preparations for the evening's big event. Fallon and her friends said their goodbyes and joined their families, happy to have met two more good Humans.

Celine and Jager returned to where they'd left Fianna and Vin. The pair were nowhere in sight, so the young Humans mented them. "We will be there soon," answered Fianna, and within minutes, the two Dragons arrived, their saddle-bags stuffed with the items Celine and Jager had packed earlier. Omaja was secure in his scabbard, tucked neatly aside Jager's saddle. The four gathered beside the Cynth Pedestal to watch events unfold.

Celine felt the same relief she perceived in Fianna: relief that with this new adventure, they would once again side-step final goodbyes. Celine leaned down to hug her friend.

Then the two sat silent, enjoying their closeness and watching the courtyard fill with a rainbow of Dragon colors.

Before long, Ahimoth and Joli joined the gathering before the mysterious wall where the tube-chute vortex would soon appear. As they moved to the front of the watching crowd, the first trickle of water began to flow down the wall's shiny surface. The rivulet grew quickly into a small waterfall; faster and faster, the streaming waters plunged from high above, down into a beautiful pool of shimmering, multi-colored swirls.

"Wow!" exclaimed Jager, holding Celine's hand tight. "Breathtaking!"

"It surely is," smiled Celine.

"Looks as if things are almost ready," commented Jager. "But where is Orgon? I wanted to know what he thought of the newest paintings in Vin's cave."

"I see him coming now," announced Ahimoth.

"Oh, good," said Celine. She and the others looked upward to watch the elder spiral down toward them, his beautiful green wings catching the moonlight as he came. In seconds, he set down lightly a few meters away.

"Hello, Uncle," greeted Ahimoth. "We are eager to hear what you have to say about the paintings we pointed out to you earlier."

"And rightly so, nephew," replied Orgon, nodding his head as the wise seem often to do. "Indeed, there is no denying my tremendous interest in them. Clearly, these are momentous times; our stories have always been a focus of our culture, and now more than ever we appear to be living them."

The elder turned to Jager and Celine. "Young man, I find it strange that you and your uncle appear on our walls, as does your father, Celine. Especially when one considers his unfortunate passing. Throughout our history, the Ancients have had our deepest respect. They have always been considered most powerful, and their magic strong, for their depictions in our tunnels have never led us astray. Thus, Jager, your magic must indeed be strong as well — for the Ancients say Celine will soon greet her father, returned to the world of the living."

"Thank you for your kind words, sir," replied Jager. He and Celine bowed respectfully.

"It is also of great interest," continued Orgon, "that there is so much more to consider in the paintings now. Truly, these are unprecedented times. First, images of you both appeared upon our prophetic walls — and then you yourselves arrived among us. This can only mean that the prophecies of long ago will come true in our time. I do not fully understand why, but for some reason the two of you, as well as your families, are at the center of Nibiru's future. Strange, very strange indeed."

The elder Dragon took a pause in his sermon, eyes distant, as though he had retreated deep into thought. Eventually, he addressed the Humans once again. "It seems that events to occur far from our sheltered and shielded homeworld, and involving the two of you, shall determine Nibiru's fate. Even to the extent of determining whether our beloved planet is to continue in existence. A fearful matter; one I do not like. Not at all." Worried murmuring arose from some who'd gathered close to listen.

"We Dragons pride ourselves on the wisdom and knowledge we glean from our prophesies," continued the revered elder. "As well as the outcomes we can achieve through their use. Our beliefs and traditions bind our culture. That others

— people not of Nibiru — seem now to be responsible for our lives disturbs me. It is not something I easily understand, appreciate or accept. However, I trust the wisdom of the ancient painters of the prophecies. I do believe that you all shall return to us, with your chosen tasks completed. I look forward to that day. May it come soon."

Celine and Jager thanked the Dragon elder, and bowed again in respect.

"Thank you, Uncle," said Ahimoth. "We appreciate your wisdom. I, too, believe we shall be rejoined shortly, and together celebrate success." The two Dragons bowed deeply to one another, then Orgon stepped aside for the approaching King Neal.

"My father will lead the ceremony!" announced Fianna, scanning the crowd with regal regard. Then she mented her friend. "Are you ready, Celine?"

"Yes I am. Are you, Jager?"

"Yes sirree," grinned Jager, though he did not look forward to the turbulent trip ahead.

Now the Dragons crowding the courtyard began a rhythmic hum. Meanwhile, one of the elders placed a bundle of dried leaves and twigs in a small pit close to the vortex and set it alight. He fanned the fragrant smoke toward the small group as King Neal gestured for the crowd to quiet their humming and attend.

"Fianna, princess, and Ahimoth, prince," his voice was firm and strong. "Your mother and I, and all the fine people of Nibiru, wish that you and your mates were not leaving us again this day. Nonetheless, we understand your reasons, and as parents and a people, we are honored you have chosen to support your friends — appropriate in any event, but especially so, in light of their inestimable service to our nations. It is understood and acknowledged that as you set out once again, the prophesies are being — and will be — fulfilled.

"But before you depart, I, along with your mother and our revered council, wish to make a momentous announcement." King Neal turned from Fianna and her company to face the gathered Dragon throng within the hall and perched on the soaring ledges above.

"Dear peoples of Nibiru. Kinspeople of Remini who now share our world. It is with the deepest respect for you all that I present Albho Fianna Uwatti who will, not many days hence, be our sovereign queen." He gestured for Fianna to join him; she advanced to the front of the ceremonial ledge.

At first there was a hush, followed by a few stunned whispers. Then Ahimoth began to cheer; his strident trumpeting reverberated off the high courtyard walls. And within moments, the entire crowd joined in.

After a boisterous minute of song, King Neal raised his wings, commanding their attention. At once there was silence. "Thank you! Thank you every one, for your loving welcome to our queen soon-to-be. There is no time for a coronation this day, clearly, for she and her company must leave us now, for a brief time. But upon their return, and before the royal wedding takes place, Fianna shall ascend our throne, crowned our beloved sovereign."

All remained silent, anticipating words from the queen-to-be. Her blushing cheeks returned to their accustomed snow-white. She cleared her throat, bowed, and addressed the multitude. "Thank you, Father, Mother, Council, and good people all. I am honored beyond telling at the opportunity to be your queen. To serve such an honorable, loving people is a blessing and a privilege. Every day I sit upon your throne, I will reign with the same respect you have shown me, and more. Thank you, thank you, for guiding and assisting me to become the Dragon I am today.

"I am truly thankful that today you grant me, and my brother and our mates, gracious blessing in our quest to assist Companions Celine and Jager. I shall never forget your unwavering support. I look forward eagerly to greeting you all upon our return." Fianna bowed long and deep to the crowd's robust cheering, which went on for several minutes. When quiet had returned, she retired to Vin's side; her mate stood tall and proud.

King Neal raised his wings; all gave him full attention. "Thank you, daughter, for your dedication to your people's service. We shall be honored to receive it, and know we will prosper under your wise, kind rule."

The crowd cheered once more, as long and as loudly as before. When the cheering flowed into a glad chant, the king took it as a cue to bless the travelers and so move the whole proceedings forward.

"Dear Fianna, Ahimoth, Vin and Joli, we know in our hearts and in our blood that you will return safe and sound, for so the prophetic paintings have shown us. Fly strong, return whole. We love you all. Our thoughts will be with you through every moment until your return."

The crowd's chant resumed, louder than before. As their voices intensified, they flared their wings and stomped their feet to reinforce the rhythm of their words. Even young Alika joined in, standing as close as he could — until Tamar, Orgon's mate and the young Dragon's guardian, insisted he move back to within her reach. Normally youngsters such as Alika would be in the Nursery during an event of this sort, but Tamar had thought it would be a good learning experience for the older fledglings to partake in the ceremony, especially because it involved the prince and princess. Their history was in the making.

Celine glanced at Jager; the furrows in her tired face deepened. He responded with a nervous smile. "No worries, Pumpkin," he mented. "It's unfortunate we must travel the chute again so soon, but for you, I'd do it a hundred times. Just to see your smile."

She sent him a mental kiss, and the two scrambled up into their saddles. "Fianna, we're ready," whispered Celine, hugging tight to the Dragon's back. Jager, his knuckles white, did the same with Vin.

Without a look back, the Dragon princess leapt skyward; Vin and the others followed in close pursuit. The crowd's chanting intensified, their excitement uncontainable. High above Dragon Hall, Fianna whirled around and dove, the others following her lead in an awe-inspiring, high-arcing line. They plunged straight downward into the vortex's swirling mass of colors to vanish, one by one, in a spectacular procession. The gathered Dragons looked on in awe, but their chant continued, its rhythm unbroken.

Only little Alika ceased the chant. When the last Dragon, Joli, had entered the vortex, he slipped away from Tamar; he raced through the crowd and across the ceremonial ledge. His golden scales glinted in the moonlight as he maneuvered among the towering adults. When the fledgling neared the vortex, Neal sensed what he must be about to do; the king spread wide his wings in attempt to block his passage, but Alika out-finessed him with a quick side-step and fake lunge. He slipped past and dove off the ledge, following Fianna and the others into the mouth of the vortex. The throng's chant ceased, replaced by a collective gasp of horror. No Dragon so young could survive the tumultuous wormhole with so few to assist him.

Then, just as unexpectedly, young Fallon and two of her friends also broke from the crowd, charged for the vortex and dove in, close on Alika's heels. Another collective gasp went up, then cries of "Oh no!" and a loud, *"Fallon!!! Nooooo!!"*

Before anyone could react further, the vortex itself vanished with a loud clap. All that could be seen was the meager trickle of falling water that had preceded the vortex's arrival. The waters twinkled merrily in the full moonlight, as if there were no cause for worry on all of Nibiru.

The gathered Dragons stared, speechless, at the empty space where the vortex had been, then looked frantically back and forth amongst themselves, at an utter loss for what to do.

"Please, everyone," King Neal broke the silence. He gently raised and lowered his wings to comfort the crowd. "Please, please, wonderful people, be calm. We must be level-headed and work together to help our loved ones. They need us desperately to keep them safe."

Queen Dini glided up beside her husband and spoke with quiet, calming resolve. "Yes, that is good, that is good, my friends. Be calm, take heart," she reassured them. Sweeping her wings slowly, she looked from one Dragon to the next, meeting the eyes of all she could, with a warm, matriarchal smile. The effect was almost magical; but as the tension that had filled the hall subsided, Dini struggled to hide her own horror at what had just occurred. She fought the same sort of bleak and helpless heaviness that had assailed her, and nearly caused her death, when her own children had been thought lost, not long before. She could not allow the dread to consume her. Not when her people needed her most.

"There now, Aliya," said Dini, speaking to a senior close by. "Come closer, dear friend. You too, Eadie. Good. Good." She addressed the whole gathering. "As you are all aware, our loved ones now need our help more than ever, if they are to pass safely through the tube-chute to their destination. We must continue to contribute our magic: to resume the incantation and maintain it until the dawn. If we do not, the young ones are all too likely to be lost to us forever. We are their only hope."

Recognizing the truth in what she said, the Dragons nodded, resumed their positions, and looked to Dini for the signal to resume the incantation.

"Good, good, very good, everyone," said the Queen. "Let us begin..." she continued, and began to raise her wings, the signal to commence the chant.

"If I may, Your Highness," came a deep voice: Orgon. He stepped up to stand beside the queen. "I would be honored to lead our people in the incantation."

Iridescent colors gleamed and shimmered on Dini's elegant head and neck as she turned to the elder Dragon and nodded affirmation, granting his request.

Orgon swept his wings upward, paused, then brought them downward: the signal to begin. As one, the assembled Dragons resumed the incantation, at the exact point they had left off. Although their bodies trembled, their voices were strong; the ancient words rang loud, rang clear.

The close-knit Dragon folds of both Nibiru and Remini shared a common fear: that their loved ones might not survive the treacherous wormhole. The unanticipated burden of guiding and protecting the youngsters who'd joined them might be too much for Fianna and the others. At the back of every mind lurked the horrifying image of the tube-chute spitting the travelers out into the vastness of space, rather than bearing them safely to their destination. Their deadly earnest chanting echoed through the night.

With dawn's arrival the chanting ceased. The exhausted Dragons embraced and went their separate ways, praying silently that they would see the moon rise that evening, the sign that the travelers' passage had ended safely. Should the moon fail to rise, it would mean their worst fears had come true.

Eventually, only one Dragon remained before the Cynth Pedestal: King Haco Quade Roark, leader of the Dragons of Remini. He stood transfixed, every fiber of his azure-blue body still, his eyes staring intently at the spot where the vortex had manifested. Then he resumed a quiet chant, and offered a fervent prayer to the Ancients, beseeching them to return his Fallon — his only living family — safe and whole.

THE FOLLOWING EVENING, THE DRAGONS' worst fears were realized: the moon did not rise above Nibiru. Its absence marked the second time in known history when the tube-chute had failed. Soul-wrenching, mournful cries echoed for hours through Dragon Hall and down the river valley below it. Loud among them were the piercing wails of the tormented King Quade.

CHAPTER 6

Malfunction

Split seconds after they plunged through the vortex and into the tube-chute, Celine and Jager cast spells to encase Fianna, Vin and themselves in bubbles of breathable air and calm. The strong bubble wall would shield them from the worst of the chute's turmoil and smooth their progress through the time-space wormhole towards Earth. Joli, accomplished in the ways of magic, called up a bubble for herself and Ahimoth. In no time, the six travelers flowed along expertly with the rowdy current.

Suddenly, the Dragons perceived piercing, terrified mental screams, coming from behind them. Swinging their heads round to discover the sounds' source, they saw Alika, then Fallon and her two friends, all spinning out of control in the chute's liquid-and-air currents. Something had to be done for the youngsters, and fast — lest they smash into the chute's margins and tumble out into the cosmos, never to be seen again.

"Celine!!!" Fianna's mental voice screamed out. "Behind!"

A full second before the girl received her friend's mental words, she picked up the Dragon's mental image and knew to spin around and draw her incant-baton. A blazing light shot from the wand's tip, straight towards baby Alika. At once he was enclosed in an impenetrable bubble of calm air. The tiny fellow continued to tumble, though, his golden-hued limbs and wings flailing frantically. Fianna instinctively mented to the little Dragon, attempting to calm him even though she knew analytically he couldn't hear her. But to her relief, he tumbled less until he was once again upright.

Jager also heard Fianna's ment to the hysterical youngsters, and almost at once he had his incant-baton in hand; flashes erupted from its tip, and Fallon and one of her friends were enwrapped in bubbles similar to the one Celine had sent round Alika, and now cast to the other of Fallon's companions.

Dragons are normally only able to ment close family members, chosen mates and Water Dragons. But, to their great surprise, Fianna, Vin, Ahimoth and Joli found they could communicate mentally with Alika, Fallon and her friends. And they were just as surprised to learn that Ahimoth and Joli could now ment with Celine and Jager, even though they were not linked as Companions. For the moment, neither the Humans nor the mature Dragons questioned this unexplained new extension of their abilities — they simply put it to use to aid their unexpected fellow travelers in the tube-chute. It would be some time before they would have a chance to ask the Mentors about it, and learn how it had come about.

"Alika, it will be all right!" shouted Fianna's mental voice. "Hang on! We will help you. Vin, are you able to maneuver alongside him?"

"Yes, Princess," replied Vin. "I believe I can." The large blue Dragon stopped swimming along with the currents of liquid and air and braked. In no time, the current carried little Alika up close to him. When the youngster was alongside, Jager cast a new, larger bubble to encase the bubbles already in place around Vin, himself, and the baby. Seeing what Vin had done, Joli pointed it out to Ahimoth and suggested they do the same to help Fallon's struggling young friends. Ahimoth agreed, and the pair slowed to allow the Reminis to catch up to them. At just the right moment, Joli cast a bubble around Ahimoth and the Remini closest to him, then another around herself and the other adolescent.

Meanwhile, Fianna had slowed as well, and brought Fallon alongside so Celine could encase the three of them in a fresh bubble. The four youngsters, now somewhat oriented and their initial terrors calmed, mented heartfelt thanks to their elder Dragon rescuers.

With the fledglings stabilized and protected as well as could be expected, the elder Dragons, Celine and Jager established secure and private mental communications with one another, so Alika and the others wouldn't be frightened at anything they might overhear.

"Is everyone okay?" asked Celine, her eyes darting from one friend to the next. All answered straight away — for the moment, they were fine. "Good," she replied.

"Something terrible must have happened back on Nibiru for these fledglings to be here!" cried Ahimoth, head swinging back and forth, examining the youngsters. "Can anyone make any sense of it?"

"No, my dear brother," Fianna's mental voice replied softly, calmingly. "I see no logic in it either."

"Nor, do I," spoke Vin, just as softly.

Fianna continued, "I do so hope all is well back on Nibiru, but I do not believe we should question the fledglings about that; not for the moment, at least. Perhaps once we are all safe on Earth, we can ask them what happened to cause them to enter the vortex."

"That would be the wiser course, yes," agreed Vin.

"All right, my sister," said Ahimoth, regaining his composure. His sister's efforts to calm him were working. Joli, close behind him, also lent her support in a private ment between them.

"Thank you, Ahimoth," said Fianna. "It is unfortunate that, due to the nature of the tube-chute, we are unable to turn back. If we could, we might return the youngsters, sparing them the dangers of the passage. And allaying their parents' fears for them too, no doubt. Our clan's magic is strong, but I know of no spell that can re-open the vortex until the moon has cycled. There is no choice but to continue with the flow of events in which we find ourselves. To embark on such a journey with so few to carry such a heavy burden is frightening, but survive we must. And we must dispose of all negative thoughts and believe in ourselves, so that we may succeed."

"Sound counsel," replied Ahimoth. "The task we face is difficult, but no viable alternative exists. We must forge on. Difficult, but not impossible." The Dragon looked at the baby Alika, so tiny next to the mature Vin.

"I concur with Fianna," said Celine. "The only real option open to us is to head on to Earth. Joli, are you able to maintain your bubbles for the entire trip?"

"Yes. Yes, I am certain that I can," she replied. "I am strong, and Ahimoth and I have established a mutual rhythm which makes us all the stronger. With him by my side, I can make it to Earth. So please, lead the way."

"Thank you, Joli. I am pleased to hear it," mented Celine. "I have faith in both you and Ahimoth. Please, maintain regular communication with the little ones, in case they have questions or need assistance. We are fortunate that, for some reason I do not yet understand, you Dragons are able to hear the fledglings' mental voices."

The elder Dragons now repeated much of what they had just privately discussed, opening their menting so that Alika, Fallon and the others could perceive them and be reassured, and apprised of the elders' plans. The youngsters became more composed at once, apparently confident the older Dragons and their Companion Humans had matters well in hand.

Thank you for explaining all this, said Fallon. "And please, do not fear — Nibiru and your loved ones there are safe. I am sorry for what my friends and I have done. It was impulsive, not planned ."

Ahimoth and the others sighed with relief; then the Nibiru prince replied: "Thank you, Fallon, for this reassuring news. But, as I am certain you are well aware, your actions warrant stern response, whether they were planned or not. We shall continue this discussion later, when you are all home and safe."

For several hours the group battled the difficult ebbs and flows of the wormhole. Without incident, fortunately. All were growing weary, though — especially young Alika.

"Celine, do you think giving Alika his own separate bubble

would help him?" asked Jager.

"That's a great idea," she replied, drawing her incant-baton. "I'll do the same for Fallon, too."

Sure enough, the individual bubbles within the larger one relieved the near-exhausted travelers of some of their burden. It meant more work for Celine and Jager, for now they had more bubble spells to maintain. And more air-replenishment spells to execute, too. Despite the strenuous circumstances, though, they were happy to do the work. It kept everyone alive and safe.

Ahimoth and Joli saw the impact of the extra bubbles the Humans had created, so Joli enchanted individual bubbles for herself, Ahimoth, and the young ones who traveled at their sides. At once the older Dragons felt a merciful easing of the constant strain and exertion required to fight the chute's roiling and difficult currents. Although still at exhaustion's edge, everyone's spirits improved, and their hopes of arriving on Earth seemed more real. Hours later, now weary beyond words, the travelers' optimism waned, while their prayers for an end to the ordeal waxed.

As the hours passed, Ahimoth grew more and more concerned for the weary baby. "Alika, you are doing so well," he praised. "It will be another hour or so before we reach Earth, but we will make it. I know you can do it. I believe in you."

The young Dragon's response was cut short when he was suddenly thrown into a headlong, gasping tumble within his protective bubble. Next, he let out a screech of fresh panic when the tube-chute began to buck and roll beyond anything he'd experienced yet. Fianna and Celine felt the jolts and jars, and saw the reason for the turbulent manifestation: up ahead of their little group, an errant asteroid had grazed the chute, ripping a gaping hole in the tube wall as it passed. The chute's magical time-space "fabric" began to realign almost at once, returning to its natural form — but not quickly enough. The travelers were rapidly approaching the tear. Fianna sent out a warning ment to all the adult Dragons.

Instantly the four threw themselves into heroic efforts to stop their forward motion. Jager and Celine, unable to provide physical help, summoned up every magical force they could to support the Dragons in their braking efforts, and simultaneously attempted to mend or patch the treacherous hole.

Their efforts proved futile. Fianna and Celine reached the opening. Fianna tried to leap across the gap to reach the intact tube on the other side, but it was no use. She, Celine and Fallon tumbled out into the cosmos, and the bubble that enclosed them all went into a gut-wrenching spin. Fortunately for those inside, the bubble's walls remained intact; had they not, the hard vacuum of space would have killed them in short order.

Vin, whose bubble was still seconds away from the chute opening, panicked at the sight of his love being swept out into the void. He slammed into the side of his bubble, jarring it sideways against the tube-chute wall. The move didn't have the desired effect; a moment later, the bubble spilled out into space, carrying Vin, Jager and Alika within.

It was clear that the bubble protecting Ahimoth, Joli and Fallon's young Remini friends was almost sure to follow shortly. "Ahimoth, I cannot stop us!" screamed Joli, desperately fighting against the chute's turbulent current.

"It is all right, my dear," soothed Ahimoth. "I am here, and will never leave your side. Keep our bubble intact; it should keep us safe once we are past the walls of the tube-chute.

Hang on!"

A split second later, their bubble joined their friends' in the raw blackness of space. The bubble began a wild spin, just as the others had. The Dragons' fevered prayers to the Ancients were heeded, though: the bubble remained sealed. And, just as their friends had managed by now, Joli was able to counter the wild spinning. The whole party — seven Dragons and two Humans, wrapped in conjured bubbles of protection — floated in the void, badly shaken but uninjured. Mental and verbal communications flew between them, until each was assured all the others were safe and whole as they bobbed along.

"So!" said Jager, sounding a bit more confident than he felt, "We survived that disaster. Now I think we should quickly reinforce all the bubbles. I know it'll be difficult to keep all the spells going, but I fear it's imperative."

"Good idea," replied Celine, raising her incant-baton. Jager followed suit, and soon the Humans had reinforced the three main bubbles. Then they cast an additional bubble around each, and Jager improvised a spell to join them all into a sort of bubble-chain to prevent their drifting apart.

Satisfied for the moment, the Humans looked back at the tube-chute, still visible but dozens of meters away. They could see that the gap in its wall was rapidly closing. *Not that it matters much,* Jager thought. *There is no way we could get safely back inside again.*

"I am so glad you are all right, Joli my love," said Ahimoth, his eyes fixed on her; they touched noses through their individual bubbles, which seemed to bobble in unison.

"And I am just as glad to see you well," she replied. She glanced once again at the fledgling by her side, assuring herself of the youngster's well-being. Then she looked all round at the place they'd come to. She was pleased to see that they had arrived somewhere near Sol; its familiar yellow rays shone strongly upon them.

Suddenly, Joli was startled to hear the voice of Dagmar, her revered teacher throughout her youth on Earth. There were a few words, then silence. Though she couldn't quite make out what had been said, the mental voice was unmistakable: it was Dagmar. Now she saw Ahimoth giving her an enquiring look. Thinking the voice might have been nothing more than a fleeting illusion, a mental glitch brought on by stress, she focused her attention on Ahimoth — and on their present perilous situation. Unfortunately, she was unaware that Ahimoth and Vin had heard Dagmar, just as she had.

Celine mented Jager privately: "Jager, I know you just linked our bubbles, but could we perhaps create a larger sheath around the entire group? Like putting us all into one bag? Everyone's exhausted, so the more support we have, the better. From what I can see, we're close to Sol, but that doesn't do us much good. We can't survive out here for long. The bubbles are going to deteriorate, no matter what we do. And we're going to need food and water and fresh air soon."

"You're absolutely right. And I like that big sheath idea. I'll do that right now." He chanted briefly, gestured with his incant-baton, and in a flash an additional bubble surrounded the entire group as they floated like leaves on the face of a dead-black lake.

"Exactly what I had in mind!" said Celine, relieved.

"You're wel — " Jager began; he stopped abruptly, eyes wide. "Celine! Look!" he called, pointing above her and slightly to her left. "Mars!"

The girl spun around to see where he'd pointed. Sure enough, there was the ruddy planet, so clear she felt she could reach out and touch it. "We're so close!" she cried.

"Yes, and it's a good thing," Jager replied, still menting privately. "I hope."

"I think it is," said Celine, "but we're going to have to move fast. Look — you can see where the bubbles are beginning to break down. Being out here in raw vacuum is more than they can take for very long."

"Right," said Jager. "And we've got so many spells going right now it's hard to keep track of which is which, let alone try to keep the sheaths sound."

"Too true," said Celine. "And I hate to mention it, but I'm too exhausted to fight much longer. Can you call West while I focus on keeping everything in place? I bet she can help us out of this mess."

"My exact thoughts, Pumpkin," said Jager, and he at once reached out to the Grand Marshal of the Mentors.

"Jager, Celine! Is that you?" cried West.

"*Yes! Yes!*" they shouted, still limiting the communication to the three of them, not wishing to worry the others.

"We need your help!" called Celine, in the mented equivalent of a yell. "Right away! Please, hurry! The tube-chute was ripped open and we're floating in space. Our sheaths will soon burst."

"Most certainly," replied West. "Do you have any idea of your location?"

"We can see Mars directly to our left as I face the sun," stated Jager.

"Give me a moment," replied West. She quickly ordered

outpost personnel to ready a ship that was in a parking orbit above, then rushed to the transbeam room. She 'beamed herself aboard and made her way to a computer station. "Celine, Jager, I am at a ship's console now. Ah, good — I can see your location from the chips embedded in your medallions. Please prepare; we must finish preparing the ship, then make the jump-shift journey. We should be there within twenty minutes."

Celine and Jager acknowledged her — and hoped against hope that the bubbles would remain intact that long. They relayed the good news to Fianna and the others, making no mention of how perilous their situation still was. Everyone cheered despite their exhaustion, overjoyed at the news of imminent rescue.

Celine and Jager kept the excitement alive as best they could, but both were deeply worried. The bubbles encasing their little band of tube-chute voyagers were weakening by the minute. Death loomed close, and unless West's ship arrived very soon, it would take them all.

Ahimoth sensed their peril, too. Worried that little Alika would catch the dire mood, he distracted the youngster by explaining that the ship soon to arrive was much like the ships that had transported all the Remini Dragons safely to Nibiru. Meanwhile, Jager had begun a riddle game to distract the others.

"Well, Pumpkin," he said aloud to Celine, as they waited for someone to solve the riddle he'd just posed, "if the excitement of these past few weeks with you keeps up, I can't imagine ever having a boring day. Ever. Even if I live into my nineties!" Everyone laughed, then returned to the task of guessing his riddle's answer.

Meanwhile, though they fought to maintain a pleasant,

no-need-to-worry air, Celine and Jager were strained to the utmost to keep the bubbles whole. Finally, they quietly mented Ahimoth and Vin, asking that the Dragons take over the riddle game until help arrived.

The young Humans were very nearly spent when the Mentors' gleaming ship burst into normal space, like a duck popping to a lake's surface after a deep dive. None too soon; they figured the bubbles were less than two minutes from catastrophic failure.

"Celine, Jager," West called, as close to haste as they'd ever heard her. "We shall transbeam you and the others to our cargo hold in twos and threes. Please brief everyone on what is about to transpire."

"Yes!" cried Celine and Jager together. "And thank you, West."

Within moments, a 'beam field arose around Joli and the young Dragon beside her; they vanished like a bursting soap bubble, complete with colorful, shimmering after-effects. Ahimoth and his young charge were next, followed at once by Celine, Fianna and Fallon. As soon as Fianna's feet touched the ship's transbeam platform, Celine burst their remaining bubbles with a flick of her incant-baton. Fianna and Fallon scurried to get their footing and hurried off the platform just as Vin and Jager began to appear.

And now the whole party stood, badly depleted but safe, like puppies rescued from drowning in a lake, long-eared and long-faced. It wasn't long before they began to perk up, though, to stare in thankful wonder at the floating, robed figures of their rescuers. The Mentors moved with exquisite grace, arraying themselves along one side of the ship's hold. Celine and the rest cheered their rescuers, West front and foremost.

Celine rushed forward to embrace the ethereal being, Jager not far behind.

"Well, that definitely wasn't on my agenda this morning," he laughed, letting go of West to hug Celine. Above all else, he was thankful she was safe and uninjured. Though not a religious person by upbringing, he said a silent thank-you to the Ancients.

"That wasn't on my agenda either," giggled Celine, enjoying his embrace and scent. "Thank goodness it all worked out as it did, but unfortunately everyone back on Nibiru will think we must all be dead — the magic was broken, so their moon will not rise tomorrow."

"Yes, I have been thinking the same," moaned Fianna. "It greatly saddens my heart, and fills me with a terrible dread." The Dragon princess bobbed her head and pawed in frustration. "I cannot bear for our parents and friends to think we all perished." She turned to West and bowed. "It is a great pity, Your Excellence, that we are unable to lower the Homeworlds Shield and send word of our safety. I cannot express how much it would gladden my heart to prevent the needless sorrow of all those on Nibiru."

"Fianna," replied the Mentor. "I am very sorry for the agony your people will soon experience, when their moon fails to rise. You are correct, the Homeworlds Shield's ancient magic will not permit its lowering at present, but at the appropriate time, we Mentors may open it."

"Oh?" enquired Jager and Celine together.

"Yes," responded the Mentor. "As you know, Jager, as Omaja's Holder, can use the staff, the Cynth Pedestal and the magic of the Ancients to open the shield at will. But he must be in physical proximity to the Cynth Pedestal to do so — and here he is, in Sol's system, far from Nibiru and the pedestal.

"However, unknown to most is the fact that we Mentors can also penetrate the shielding at certain times. At one-week intervals, in fact; this is what the Ancients' lore specifies.

"Unfortunately, the beginning of the interval is reset any time the vortex is opened — so we will not be able to open the shield until a week from this evening. So, we really have no immediate means of reassuring them."

"It is wonderful to know that you and other Mentors may open the shield at times," said Celine. "I can easily imagine that becoming an important factor in the future." But then she slumped in despair. "That doesn't resolve our current dilemma, though."

Ahimoth realized it was time to share his strength and offer support to those who could use it. He cleared his throat. Everyone turned, surprised at the interruption. "Sorry for jumping in so rudely," he said, with a bow of regret and a quick wink at Celine, "but it occurred to me that perhaps we could send a comm stone through the tube-chute to Nibiru. Just as we did before, with Celine's comm-stone message and spell to preserve our eggs."

"Oh, Ahimoth! Wonderful!" burst out a relieved Fianna. "What a fantastic idea! Our families will mourn until the message gets through — a day or so, I should guess — but it will relieve their woes. Even give them news to celebrate. How clever of you, dear brother!" Ahimoth gave her a huge grin. Joli patted his shoulder and flashed an admiring smile.

"This is good; very good," said West, glowing a deep golden color. "A fine solution. I shall assist you to reach Earth so that you may send the stone. We must act quickly, for midnight will come to Loch Ness in just a few hours. We must reach out to Nessie immediately and brief her on what is planned. There should be just enough time for her to make preparations to open the vortex, but I may be underestimating. No matter, though — if need be, my sisters and I can assist with the incantation. Fianna, would you please contact Nessie?" Fianna replied with a nod, then went blank-faced as she initiated mental communication with her Earthly cousin.

"Good!" said Celine, grinning like a Cheshire cat. "That part is under control. Now we just need to get to your outpost, West, so I can prepare a comm stone. May we go there now?"

"Certainly," said West. "Please prepare yourselves for the jump-shift."

The whole group gave a cheer, their spirits considerably revived. Celine and Jager helped the Dragons to secure for the jump, strapped themselves in, and let West know they were all ready. West acknowledged, then gestured for North, who was piloting the vessel, to activate the jump-shift drive. North nodded, did a rapid final check of her monitors and tapped a contact. The ship answered with a growling hum, then an eerie vibration, and then, in an instant, leapt across a wide expanse of the void.

"Celine, Jager," called out West as the group exited the ship in a bustle of excitement and relief. "We must also notify your mother and Major Hadgkiss that you are safe. They have been quite worried, even though they knew you were safe with your friends on Nibiru."

"Oh, yes. Thank you, West. You're correct; we should do that right away." replied Celine sheepishly, feeling guilty. She hadn't thought to contact her mother for several days. The poor woman must be distraught. "But first we would need to find a way to get a communication through their bunker's protective barrier, would we not?"

"Yes, child, but do not fret," said West. "This outpost is within the boundaries of the Homeworlds Shield. And because the Remini under-world was originally established by the Ancients, there happens to be a spell that permits the under-world's protections to be deactivated and re-activated at will. A spell with which I am familiar. In fact, it is through its use that Major Hadgkiss has been visiting the Remini bunker religiously, each day since your departure.

"He came to visit us out of concern for you two. He is able to use the spell to lower the shield when he wishes; I recorded the spell onto a comm stone for him. He has only to play it, and the shield lowers or is restored, at his reciting of a magical spell I taught him. He has learned his first bit of magic."

"Wow!" exclaimed Jager. "Brilliant! You — all the Mentors — are so full of surprises."

"Yes, you absolutely are!" laughed Celine. She remained contemplative, though, about what she would say to her mother.

The Mentor gave them the equivalent of a smile, but once again they could not help but feel some guilt. Even though they had done nothing wrong, their lives now involved so many actions that caused others worry; they regretted causing such feelings.

"We should see the major late tomorrow morning," continued West. "You can talk to him then." The Mentor's motherly look became questioning when her young students' looks of shame vanished, to be replaced by grins. "May I ask what it is you have not told me?"

"Yes, yes," they replied. Although dog-tired, the two were eager to tell West of Jager's recent realization regarding Celine's father. Jager nodded for Celine to continue.

"We have some exciting news — for *everyone*," she laughed. Jager gave her a wink.

"Oh?" smiled West. "Exciting news is to be desired; please, do not keep me waiting." They laughed some more.

"I think we can revive Commander Zulak," said Jager. "He's been in a stasis tube since moments after he died, and..."

The young man did not need to say more. West had fully divined his intention. The force of her realization washed over the two young people with such pressure that they felt as though they'd been physically struck.

"*Oh, my!*" the Mentor gasped, then went silent for a long moment. "I am sorry for that," she went on. "And Jager, I apologize for interrupting you, but...but, oh my. I should have asked about this long ago. Celine, by this I mean that I should have enquired as to what happened to your father's body. If I had, I might have brought about his recovery weeks ago, and saved you and your family those many days of sorrow. I could have saved all of us the grief and pain. Dear, I am so sorry."

"It's okay," said Celine. She stepped to the Mentor's side and gently squeezed her arm. "When Jager revives my father, that will surely be forgotten. There is nothing to forgive."

"Thank you, child," replied West warmly. Then, as though a switch had been flicked, the ethereal being was all business again. "By my knowledge of stasis units," she said, "your father's body has essentially aged no more than a few seconds since immersion in the tube's Termyles gas and stasis field.

It is unfortunate that you will have to wait until the shield is lowered tomorrow to revive him. I suppose a few more hours will not make so great a difference, though, seeing as it has been weeks since he succumbed to his injuries.

"Besides, I see how much you both need rest. So perhaps a brief wait is a good thing. Moreover, Jager, rest is needful if you are to have the energy to perform your spell and return our Commander Zulak to us. Come, follow me to my office; brief me on what transpired on Nibiru before you go to your quarters for rest."

The pair nodded; their fingers entwined, and they followed West as she floated down a corridor and entered her working space.

The Mentor was already aware the two had performed the Unification Ceremony successfully. The result was an impenetrable barrier around all the Dragon Homeworlds between Pax and Nibiru, and the long, narrow corridor of space between their planetary systems. But she had had no opportunity to discuss the particulars of the event. They explained all they could remember, in great detail. West took particular interest in their description of the conduit or channel that had opened momentarily between Pax and Nibiru, allowing them to see and converse directly with Jager's twin brother Jaecar, as through an open window.

"Most interesting," mused the Mentor. She embraced each of her students. "Interesting and wonderful. It seems I have underestimated you yet again! And, as I suspect you have already realized, the barrier may prove instrumental in winning the war that has come to our doorstep. But enough for now. We travel to Earth in just a few hours, to transmit your comm stone. Rest now. Rest."

The two needed no more prompting than that. They

hurried to their quarters, where they fell asleep the moment their heads hit their pillows. Their rest was dreamless and sound.

While Celine and Jager were engaged with West, the Dragons made their way to their own quarters. The elder Dragons led the way. Alika and the other young stowaways followed reluctantly, heads down and tails dragging, dreading the well-deserved lecture and punishment they were sure was coming.

To Alika's surprise, no lecture or punishment materialized. Instead, Ahimoth showed him where to sleep, and soon the fledgling was in dreamland, sleeping soundly beside the watchful prince.

CHAPTER 7

Communication Breakdown

After a few hours of rest, the Dragons woke, eager to quiet their rumbling stomachs. They quickly made their way to the refectory and enthusiastically dug into the glorious feast the kitchen staff had prepared.

As they ate, Vin and Fianna glanced every few minutes toward the entrance, anxious for Celine and Jager's arrival. Their eagerness to see their Companions didn't slow the feast, though. The hungry Dragons continued dining on every type of fish imaginable.

When he'd satisfied his immediate hunger, Ahimoth turned some attention to the youngsters with a silent glare. Alika felt the sting of the Dragon's gold-and-ebon eyes upon him, and wished he knew a spell that would let him slip through the floor and disappear forever.

Alika began to quiver when Ahimoth unexpectedly jumped up, ruffled himself, and approached. The black

Dragon towered over the youngster, glaring angrily. Alika cowered, wishing even harder that the floor would swallow him up.

"Alika, what were you thinking?" growled Ahimoth. He addressed only Alika, even though Fallon and the others were just as guilty. If not more so; they all were older, and should have known better. In fact, the Nibiru prince considered the Reminians guests, and so felt obliged to excuse them from discipline. He had also heard their account of their actions and motivations, before Alika had arrived with Vin. He was now interested solely in the baby's actions, and how he should address the situation.

Alika remained stooped and silent. He knew it was not the correct time to respond to the elder Dragon's rhetorical query.

Ahimoth stretched to his full height, his shining ebon head mere centimeters from the ceiling. He fanned his enormous wings towards the fledgling, a gesture of scorn. Grumbling, he strutted about the room, then came to stand once again before the tiny Dragon. "Alika, you have endangered all our lives, and terribly worried those who love you. I am extremely disappointed in you. Your actions were most shocking and unacceptable."

The youngster kept his head low, as was proper when being addressed by royalty in such grave circumstances. Fallon's guilt ate at her, seeing how frightened Alika was. She moved to the baby's side; her friends followed suit. All bowed to the prince in support of the baby.

Alika mentally thanked his new friends. He recognized now was the time for him to reply to his prince. "I...I am truly sorry, Prince Ahimoth. I truly am. But it was as if someone else controlled my legs. I could not stop them! Truly, I tried!

And the harder I tried to stop, the faster I seemed to run. I do not know why, sir.

"Please, Your Highness, accept my apologies. I would never intentionally do anything to harm you or our princess. Or any of you. Ever!" The little Dragon angled his bowed head upward just enough to steal a peek at the prince. To his great surprise, he saw that Ahimoth and all the older Dragons looking down at him — and their eyes all registered genuine love and understanding.

Ahimoth drew breath to reply, but stopped short at the sound of Celine's laughter, just outside the refectory. The girl strode into the room, arm in arm with Jager. The Dragons greeted the couple, and waited as the Humans filled their plates at the food service table. Once they were seated, the Dragon prince gave them an account of what he'd learned from the young Dragons. The pair listened intently as they ate, commenting now and then.

"Hmmm. All very interesting," Jager mused, rubbing his chin. He didn't seem at all astonished that Alika, Fallon and her friends all described the same curious phenomenon: they had felt physically compelled to enter the vortex, and powerless to resist.

"Ahimoth," said Jager, "I think what occurred was predicted in one of the paintings in Vin's cave-home." Though he addressed the comment to the prince, he intended that Celine and the others contemplate it too.

"Of course!" exclaimed Celine at once — instantly realizing the rudeness of her outburst. "Oh! I'm so sorry, Ahimoth. I apologize for interrupting."

"It is all right, Celine," replied Ahimoth, with a slight frown and tilt of the head. "We are in a difficult time. Such breaches of communication etiquette are to be expected."

"Oh? Um, thanks, Ahimoth," said a surprised Celine. "But I will do my best to refrain from such outbursts in the future. I greatly appreciate your understanding."

"Apology accepted. Now, please tell us what you were going to say."

The girl smiled. "I was going to say that I know the painting Jager speaks of; it depicts Fianna, Vin, Joli and you flying above a large green planet with three small orange moons."

"Yes, I remember the painting," replied Ahimoth after a few moments of what appeared to be deep thought.

"I do, as well," grinned Jager, in his usual positive tone. "A most interesting painting, at that. But there were more Dragons in the image, if you recall."

"Hmmm. Yes, that's true," smiled Celine, thinking she was the luckiest girl alive to have such a wonderful fiancé. "There was a little golden Dragon, and a blue one smaller than Vin," she added, "about Fallon's size and color." She chuckled, her grin spreading into a full-fledged smile. "I guess the universe *does* work in mysterious ways."

"Yes, it most definitely seems to," said Ahimoth. He turned to scrutinize the still-apprehensive youngsters. "Well, you four troublemakers, I believe your stories, so I will not discipline you. *However*, there will now be *maaaany* rules by which you must abide. You must adhere to them every moment of every day, from this time forward — without fail. Please realize that one wrong move could mean death for one or all of us. I hope that you have learned this by now. Do I have your understanding and agreement?" Ahimoth folded his forelegs and looked sternly at each of the youngsters in turn.

Like a drill sergeant! thought Jager, grinning to himself.

Alika and the others anxiously bobbed their heads several times: the expected response. Ahimoth flashed a quick grin. The youngsters missed it, but Celine and the others caught it and grinned themselves.

Soon everyone returned to the interrupted meal. The positive emotions seemed to make them hungry all over again.

Jager noticed Alika and the other youngsters frequently sneaking glances at Ahimoth, as if to verify that they really were back in his good graces.

When the younger Dragons' bellies were finally full, Ahimoth escorted them back to their beds, then rejoined the others — who were still feasting, though at a slower pace — for a discussion of a strategic approach to their next few steps.

"This is all very interesting," commented Vin, gulping down another mackerel. "I assume the green planet in the painting is Remini, because it now seems Fallon and her friends have parts in whatever is happening. But what do you all think?"

"I think the same," answered Fianna. Up to now, she had been silent, listening intently. "Remini," she continued, "has an older history than that of Nibiru. If any Dragon world other than Nibiru were to be involved in what is happening in the cosmos, I believe it would be Remini. This would also explain why I felt compelled to contact young Fallon, when she was held prisoner in Remini's under-world. It was as though the impulse to contact her was forced upon me and beyond my control.

"At first, I tried to ignore the compulsion, but the harder I tried, the more compelling the impulse. As we know now, it was the correct thing to do; it led to our rescue of Fallon and her fold. It appears that the youngsters, when they jumped into the vortex, were influenced in somewhat the same manner as was I."

"Indeed, that appears to be the case," said Jager. "I believe this leaves us in an interesting situation. And I propose that our first action should be to prepare the comm stone immediately. Then, with West's help, we should travel to Loch Ness, deliver the stone into the vortex, and return here — tonight — for a good, solid rest, in preparation for tomorrow's events."

"I concur," yawned Celine. The others nodded agreement and, echoing her weariness, yawned big Dragon yawns. The girl turned to greet West, who had just stepped through the entrance: "Hello!"

"Hello everyone," replied the Mentor. "Our ship is prepared to transport you to Scotland as soon as you are ready. We are fortunate that Earth is within the boundaries of the new barrier; else this would be a much more complicated affair. And now, Celine, here is a comm stone you may use for your intended task."

"Thanks!" said Celine, cupping the warm purple crystal in her palm. She laid it on the tabletop, then picked up her bodypack from its place on the floor beside her and set it on the table next to the stone. She opened the pack and began to remove items from within, carefully setting them, one by one, in a neat row on the table.

"Here, let me help you," offered Jager, and the two continued the process, all so Celine could perform the little rite required to install a message in the stone.

"Fianna, would you like to give your parents the message?" asked Celine.

"Most definitely. I am so relieved to be able to send word to our loved ones. My heart is full of sorrow, just to imagine their suffering, thinking us all lost. I am thankful they will not grieve for long, and hope they will rejoice to hear my voice, with the message that we are all alive and uninjured."

Celine smiled at Fianna, both physically and through their mental bond, comforting them both.

With all the rite's required items now in place near the comm stone, Jager sprinkled a circle of salt around Celine and Fianna, and set up two dozen white candles to encircle the girl, the Dragon and himself. When all had been placed, they looked like little white sentinels on guard upon a turret. The others stood looking quietly on.

With everything in readiness, the youthful witch took the comm stone in her right hand, sat crossed-legged and began to hum. With her left hand she swirled her incant-baton gently back and forth above the purple crystal, concentrating on the message she imagined Fianna would convey — the words the Dragon would place within the stone.

After a time, the girl opened her eyes, laid the crystal on a piece of white cloth, and nodded for Jager to light the encircling candles. When he'd sparked the last to life, she began to chant.

Still chanting, she motioned to Fianna. The Dragon came close and lowered her snout to just above the comm stone. Celine flicked the incant-baton at the crystal and nodded for the princess to begin her message.

"My Dear King and Queen of Nibiru." Fianna paused to clear her throat, and to mentally ask Celine if she was proceeding correctly.

"Yes, perfectly fine," replied Celine.

Fianna nodded, her long, lithe neck gleaming in the light. She resumed. "Mother, Father, it is I, Fianna. This is not a trick. I am alive and unhurt; so are Ahimoth and the others, including the young ones who so unexpectedly joined us on our journey. Please do not worry, for we are all safe. There was a rupture in the tube-chute, but by great good fortune, we were rescued by friends of Celine. No harm came to us. We will move forward with our mission and return home to you soon. Ahimoth and I love you, and all our good people. Please reassure them."

Chanting once again, Celine swished her incant-baton, and bright rays of light leapt from its tip and into the depths of the stone. Fianna sat down beside her Companion; she hummed along with the chant, and together they watched the candles until, at last, Celine blew them gently out.

As smoke from the last candle wafted upwards, Celine rose, swept up the salt and gathered the melted wax. She placed both in a cloth, tied it closed and set it within her bodypack to end the spell. Next, she slipped the comm stone into a small case West had provided, and clicked tight its clasp. She glanced up to give Fianna a huge smile, only to find that her friend needed more than just a smile.

"Aww, do not worry, dear friend," said Celine, embracing Fianna's neck. "This will work, and everyone on Nibiru will be relieved of their sorrow."

"Thank you, Little One."

Ahimoth, who had been standing quietly by, heaved a huge sigh and thanked Celine and Fianna for their efforts. "I wish to check on the youngsters," he said softly, then headed to the caves. The others chatted a few minutes more before heading to West's office.

"Hello, West. We're ready to go to Earth," said Celine.

"Ah, what good timing. I just finished my task," replied the Mentor with a smile. She stood up from a console and stretched, then exited towards the transbeam room, Dragons and Humans close behind.

To everyone's surprise, Ahimoth was already on the transbeam platform — and he was not alone. Alika, Fallon and her friends were all lined up like cadets awaiting orders. Somehow the fledglings had convinced the prince it would be a great experience for them to see the Water Dragons, the vortex-calling ceremony, and the casting of the comm stone. Joli and the others grinned; they understood the big black's fondness for the young ones. They also identified with his feelings in the matter; they were part of deep, long tradition of love for the young among the Nibiru race.

While the others discussed what would happen next and briefed the youngsters on what to expect, Joli stepped back. Once again, the dear old witch Dagmar was inside her mind, repeating what she had said when the Dragons had been in dire danger, drifting in space — and several times since.

The lovely green began to tremble.

Now the group began to mount the transbeam platform. Joli took a step to join them, but found herself losing control of her movements. Her trembling intensified. Worried and frightened, she turned to Ahimoth. But before she could speak, a wracking shiver ran up her spine — and she found her mind in a different time, and on a different world.

At once, Ahimoth sensed something was amiss. He turned, only to see his love collapse at his feet. *"JOLI!!"* he roared. "Joli!!"

The others turned, and gasped at the sight of Joli, slumped

at the platform's edge.

"It cannot be," whispered West. "It simply cannot be."

"What is it?! What has happened to Joli?" cried Fianna. All rushed to join Ahimoth, bent over their fallen friend. "What is wrong?" exclaimed the princess.

Celine and Jager knelt beside the graceful green head. Celine passed a hand in front of Joli's nostrils. "She's still breathing," she assured.

West glided over and gave Celine's shoulder a gentle touch. "She will be all right, child. She will be fine. I expected this to happen, but not so soon or so suddenly — never mind in this dramatic manner."

"What has happened to her? What is wrong?" wailed Ahimoth, towering over them, his black wings fanned in anxious frustration.

"It will be okay," soothed the Mentor. "Our dear Joli is doing her part in all of this. She will be all right, my friend. But we must keep her body safe until she comes back to us."

"I do not understand!" cried the prince, stomping and snorting.

"There is no time to explain," declared West. "But please, trust me, gallant Ahimoth. Trust me, dear friend. It is a matter of the great workings and mysteries of the universe, and it is all for the good. I can assure you that no harm will come to your Joli. Come, we must take her to Medical at once."

CHAPTER 8

Lost

Thousands of years before the present day, Prince Deet and his people fled to Earth, seeking refuge from the vicious being, Byrne. Byrne sought to eradicate them for no other reason than the fact that they were ethical, spiritual beings. Beings now known to some as the Ancients. For the same reason he had massacred many Mentors, including West's parents. And instructed his wicked minions, the Barbdews Brothers, Lancaster and Dodd, to wreak havoc across the universe.

It was on just such a havoc-wreaking venture that the Brothers had discovered where Prince Deet and his people had settled on Earth: a relatively small continent known as Atlantis. Delighted at their unexpected find, they engineered a great flood, hoping to eliminate not just Deet, but the entire continent, all its inhabitants, and all those living in the thousands of kilometers of tunnels and caves that branched out from Atlantis across much of Earth's northern hemisphere. Some of these caverns housed large cities. Largest and most important were those beneath the region now called Turkey. More than once over the centuries, the Atlanteans had taken refuge in the tunnel network and its cavern-cities. Refuge from evil entities and "gods" such as Byrne and his minions.

One day, a trusted sentinel in Deet's guard warned the prince of the Barbdews' treacherous plan. Deet was able to evacuate his people — this time off-planet, rather than in the tunnels and caverns. He left behind a select few of his most trusted wizards and a trusted group of native Earthers to guard the Atlantean's mysteries and treasures until his people could return. One of these caretakers was Dagmar Bjornson, an ancestor of Joli's teacher of the same name.

Among the treasures Deet left hidden were two ancient spell books: *The Book of Atlantis* and *The Book of Mu*. The very grimoires Celine and Fianna had found and recovered just weeks earlier. At West's direction, the pair had transported the precious volumes to Nibiru and hidden them safe within a secret cavern close by Dragon Hall's sacred Cynth Pedestal.

Just before their latest entry into the vortex, Celine, acting on a premonition, had removed the ancient books from their hiding place and stowed them in Fianna's saddlebags. On arrival at the Mentor's outpost, she had entrusted them to West and the Mentors' ultra-secure vaults.

The young witch later explained that it had been as if the grimoires had spoken to her, asking to be returned to the Mentors' direct care. Everyone would soon learn how correct she had been in her action, and shower her with praise for her keen perception.

When conversing with West and Jager about the grimoires, Celine had also mentioned a strange foreboding regarding Dagmar and Joli. She'd described, in great detail, visions of possible future events involving the two. After some discussion, West suggested Celine and Jager should not speak further of these things until there was more time to discuss them in greater detail.

Now, bending over the unresponsive Joli, thoughts of that discussion ran through Celine's mind — as did the visions she'd seen. She returned abruptly to the here and now, though, when Jager rested a hand on her shoulder. She turned and smiled at him.

"It will be all right," he said, putting an arm around her.

"Thank you," she whispered. They both rose and watched as two Mentors flanked Joli and brought their delicate hands up before them, palms upward. They raised their hands slightly, a gentle lifting motion, and Joli's body rose from the platform. The Mentors nodded to one another, then guided the suspended body out of the transbeam chamber and down the corridor toward Medical. The rest of the Dragons and Humans followed.

As all this transpired, her earlier visions assailed Celine once more. Now, more than ever, she was certain of some intimate connection between Dagmar, Joli and the ancient grimoires.

"Jager," she mented privately, "I wonder if the foreboding I had regarding Dagmar is connected to what's happening to Joli right now."

"Hmm, I wonder," he mented back. "Your assumption seems sound. We should discuss it with West when we can." He locked fingers with her as they walked; their thoughts shifted from Joli to Ahimoth, walking just ahead of them and clearly agitated. Following his floating Joli, he let out a low moan every dozen steps or so.

"Please, everyone," soothed West, "your friend will be all right in due time. This I promise. What you see happening is a result of her having been born on Earth and counseled for many years by Dagmar, a powerful descendent of the Ancients. As you may already have learned, Dagmar is also known to you, Ahimoth and Vin. She was the voice-friend, the mental influence that helped you both during your time of captivity on Earth."

"Thank you for your words of comfort, West," Ahimoth replied. "They soothe me, at least a bit. And yes, it is true Dagmar helped me to escape my prison beneath the world of Earth. Joli explained this when we first met. She also said she assumed or inherited her teacher's powers when Dagmar died. I had thought that only meant that Joli could ment with Vin and me, though she was not kin. But if I understand your implication correctly, West, as well as what I recently heard from my voice-friend, what is now happening to Joli is a result of her deep spiritual connection with Dagmar. And, since she was born there, her connection with the spiritual world of Earth. Is this correct?"

"Yes, generally so, Ahimoth," replied West. "I assumed something like this might happen, but did not expect it so soon. That is why I did not mention it earlier; an error on my part, for which I am terribly sorry."

"I understand," said the prince, hanging his head. "I do not hold you accountable for what is happening to my Joli. I only hope you can help her. And that my love, our friend, will return to us, well and whole. And soon."

"Thank you for your understanding and gracious forgiveness," said West. "I cannot at present help Joli; the magic working within her is ancient and surpassingly strong. Even if I could, to interrupt the process might harm or possibly kill her. I am confident, though, that she will be all right, and come back to us before long."

Ahimoth gave a deep sign and huffed several times, as stressed Dragons often do. "Thank you for your honest words, West." Sighs could be heard from the others as well, Celine among them.

"I am pleased to know you have faith in her recovery," continued the prince, "but I feel useless. Is there nothing I might do for her at present?"

"Yes, dear Ahimoth," said West, "Although Joli does not speak to you, she can hear your words, so let your love know that you are present, that you love her and will be here the moment she returns. Hearing you may aid Joli in her quest and bring her back to you sooner."

West bowed and addressed the group. "I must leave you all for the moment, but I will return shortly. My sisters will attend to young Joli in the meantime. Do not fret." The group nodded understanding and said their goodbyes to the grand Mentor, then stood back to watch and wait while East and South monitored their still-unconscious friend.

"Will she be all right?" asked Ahimoth, already pacing again, unable to wait in silence for more than a few seconds.

"Yes, Prince," replied South. "She appears to be suffering no ill effects; she is simply not present in our here and now."

"What can I do for her?" he pleaded.

"Reassure her, just as West suggested. I too believe she will return to you soon."

Ahimoth eased down beside the bed of straw on which Joli now lay, comfortably curled.

"May we join you?" asked Fianna.

"Yes, sister," replied Ahimoth sadly. "I must tell you, I have tried to ment with Joli many times since this began, but my mate is lost to my calls."

"I am sorry to hear this, brother," said Fianna. She and the others moved quietly to stand or sit in silence close by. They remained that way for several minutes, as if to shroud the black Dragon and his mate in a loving bond of consciousness.

West returned a short while later; she whispered for a moment with North, then joined the small group encircling Joli. "I am glad that you are all here," she said. "As you can see, our friend's condition remains the same. But North assures me Joli is not distressed. That may give you some comfort."

Suddenly, Joli stirred, as if she had been waiting for West's return. Ahimoth jumped up, frantic, his eyes darting between the lovely green Dragon and the Mentor. He hopped from foot to foot, afraid to speak. Joli began to moan, so the others stepped back as West and her sisters moved in. But as they reached her, Joli slowly opened her lovely golden eyes, and with unsteady efforts, raised her head up from the bed of straw.

"J...Joli," whispered Ahimoth. "My dear, are you all right? I am here."

The still-groggy Joli looked up and smiled. "That you are, dear friend," she replied. "That you are."

"Please, Joli, do not stand just yet," said West, holding up a hand to keep the young Dragon from rising. "You gave us a scare, and we want to make sure everything is fine."

East and South examined Joli, and shortly pronounced her to have a clean bill of health. Still, they too advised her to rest for a while before attempting any exertion.

Ahimoth paced, waiting for East and South to step aside. When they did, he rushed forward to give his bride a huge but gentle Dragon hug.

"Oh, Joli," he said, leaning back. "Whatever happened?"

"There is much to tell, dear Ahimoth," she replied, "but first, I have a great thirst."

"Yes, yes, of course," he said, releasing his tight embrace. "How selfish of me!"

"Joli," said West, "I recommend that you rest and avoid exertion for a day or two. For it was very powerful magic which affected you."

"Yes, thank you, I will," replied Joli. "And thank you kindly for assisting me in my difficult time."

"You are most welcome," said West. "I will join you all in the refectory in a few minutes, if I am able. Then perhaps Joli will relate her experience just passed."

"Yes. Yes, of course," agreed Joli. "Once again, my humble appreciation to you and your sisters for your assistance in returning me to my loved ones." She rose gingerly. With the still-worried Ahimoth at her side, she made her careful way toward the exit, and on to the refectory. The rest followed, murmuring among themselves.

"Celine, Jager," said West, walking alongside the pair, "we have a few minutes to spare, but must soon head to Loch Ness."

"Okay," they replied, nodding their understanding and agreement; their faces showed no trace of their true feelings.

"Would twenty minutes be all right?" asked Jager.

"Yes, that will be fine."

On reaching the refectory, Joli headed straight to the

water basin that had been provided for the Dragons. She took several long drafts of cool water, then sighed a satisfied sigh.

The young Humans arrived just as Joli finished her drink. They found the group in better spirits than they'd seen since leaving Nibiru. They chatted among themselves, taking care to give Joli and Ahimoth a respectful space. Jager and Celine were more reserved than the rest; not surprising, in light of Celine's recent premonitions.

CHAPTER 9

Oy Vey

"Vin? Ahimoth?" queried Celine, "Before we head to Loch Ness, and before Joli is ready to tell us the story of what she just experienced, could you possibly let us know what your voice-friend has said to you over the past few hours? It might be of some help."

Ahimoth looked to Joli, who gave him a reassuring smile. "Well," he said, "as you know, over the years of my captivity under Soader, I was regularly comforted by my voice-friend. In time, she saved me from that deplorable dungeon. I will always hold her, and her wise words, in high regard. Since meeting Joli, though, I had not heard Dagmar until quite recently. Our kind friend departed her body just days before that glorious first meeting with Joli; since then, she has been silent until our recent tube-chute misadventure.

"As we floated in space, my voice-friend told me, loud and clear, what I must do. What we all must do, to help the

Aadya Coalition win this war." He glanced reassuringly at Joli again, then at Fianna, before going on. "Dagmar was adamant that I do everything in my power to protect you, dear sister — as my noble name dictates — but to protect our dear Joli as well. She said that Joli's life depends upon my being the great warrior Orgon the Wise trained me to be, in my youth. She said that if I do not protect both you and Joli, there will be grave consequences for Nibiru.

"She also said that if I should fail in my mission, our beloved home, and every Dragon living upon it — including those from Remini — will perish. She said this would come to pass even though the new shield is in place." Everyone looked confused; young Alika gasped, as did Fallon and her friends.

"Well, this is interesting," remarked Vin. "I too have been hearing my voice-friend, strong and persistent, over the past few hours. She has told me we must protect Fianna and Joli at all costs; but, in addition, she emphasized how crucial it is that we locate an artifact which Prince Deet hid on Earth, centuries ago. This treasure, she says, is the answer to our prayers. It will help save us all from future attacks by the Volac Forces, if only we will recover it and learn to use its powerful magic."

"She has been telling me the same," added Ahimoth. "But, more important, she told me to remain by Joli's side." He was already quite close to Joli, but pressed even closer and gave her a gentle nuzzle.

Everyone considered Ahimoth and Vin's words. They stared at one another, more confused than ever.

Joli downed another large draught of water, then spoke. "Teacher said the same to me, and told me to stay always at your wing, Ahimoth. To fly where you fly, and never to let you battle alone. For if I did, she said, you would die under our enemies' fire."

The Dragon prince comforted her with a warm embrace and soothing pats. Seeing West enter the refectory, Joli gently withdrew; West nodded to her — it was time for the green Dragon to tell her story. Joli gathered herself and faced her friends.

"Thank you, everyone, for your patience and gracious understanding," she said. "It must have been difficult and frustrating when I collapsed as I did. You could not know why, nor how to help me. I am sorry for all the worry I caused, and for keeping us from our important duties."

"It is all right, love," assured Ahimoth, nuzzling her once again. "We are just so happy you are all right, and back here with us."

Joli smiled at him, then at the others.

"I should have mentioned," Joli continued, "that before I collapsed, Teacher contacted me. If I had told you this, perhaps you would not have worried so." She paused; Ahimoth mented to let her know it was okay that she hadn't, and encouraged her to go on with her story. She thanked him and did so.

"Since the tube-chute incident," she said, "I have felt Teacher's strong presence. When we were in the transbeam room, I could no longer block her communication; before I knew what was happening, I had left my body and was with her in a sort of non-space. A spiritual world, maybe. It is hard to describe, but she was there and I was there, and we could communicate directly. Teacher explained that she had acted to ensure I completely understood her intentions and those of her family and friends. She and many of her kind are very near and ready to help."

Joli looked questioningly at West; the Mentor responded with a nod. The Dragon turned to Celine. "It is interesting, Celine, but Teacher asked me to relay something to you. She said it was a particularly important message."

Everyone in the group, Dragons and Humans alike, exchanged wondering looks. What could this be about?

Seeing their astonished looks, Joli added, "I too thought this curious. But after hearing what Teacher wanted me to relay, I understood why she had brought me over to the other side — to that 'non-place' I described. One thing she asked me to relay is a riddle for you, Celine. She said it was important for two reasons. First, it would help you choose the correct spell from the ancient Atlantean grimoires. Second, it would tell you where to locate Mutuum, and Prince Deet's personal grimoire and personal incant-baton as well. With these relics, you and Jager will be ready to take on great forces."

"Mutuum? Who's Mutuum?" asked Jager.

"Not quite so much a 'who,' as a 'what,'" answered Celine, quietly. She began to fidget, then paced for a few moments before stopping to explain. "Mutuum is the most powerful incant-baton ever created. One of my magic books explained that it was specifically crafted for Prince Deet by the most skilled wizard alive during his reign. The prince feared his precious incant-baton might fall into the hands of the Brothers or other evil beings, so as a precaution, he hid Mutuum. Just as he hid the great grimoires and other Atlantean treasures. He hid them all before departing Earth with his people, when they came under vicious attack. For day-to-day work, he used a less powerful incant-baton. That would be the personal baton Joli mentioned. Many thought *that* baton was Mutuum. Exactly as he wanted them to think, so the true Mutuum would be safer; hidden far from those who would use it for evil.

"Mutuum is said to be fabulously potent. In the right hands, capable of casting the most difficult of spells. Spells hidden in a special section at the back of the ancient grimoires Fianna and I found. Together, Mutuum and these spells are powerful enough to destroy, I believe, an entire planet. According to what I've read, at least."

"Wow!" exclaimed Jager.

"Yes, wow indeed," said Celine. "Thinking on my feet here, I believe one reason we're supposed to recover Mutuum is to destroy the harvesting station at TS 428 — on Earth's moon. That would thwart G.O.D.'s plans to ravage Earth."

West interjected. "Joli, it is all right. You may explain everything." Everyone looked quizzically at West, then back at Joli.

"Thank you, West," the Dragon replied. "And yes, Celine, destroying the harvesting station would be a good and proper use for Mutuum. But Teacher mentioned that I must keep your focus and attention on a more vital purpose and use for him." The Dragon paused to take another long draught of cool water. "I say 'him,'" she explained, "because he is imbued, in a sense, with a life of his own."

"It is most important to remember," she said, licking a stray drop of water from her lip, "that Mutuum has an essential role in the quest to destroy our enemies. Just as you stipulated, Celine. However, you and Jager must use Mutuum in combination with three *other* things: A spell from Deet's personal grimoire, a spell hidden deep within the pages of the ancient grimoires, and Prince Deet's personal incant-baton.

"This means Jager must cast one spell using Prince Deet's personal baton, while you—simultaneously—cast the other spell using Mutuum. Then, and only then, will the forces of the Aadya Coalition have a chance. Finally, at the time of the casting, the two of you must execute a spiritual linking spell, which West will impart to you at the appropriate time.

"Teacher also stressed that I must emphasize this point: Do not forget that *both* incant-batons are required for success. Their magic, together, links with the Aadya Coalition's powers. All together, they are able to generate enough energy to defeat Scabbage, as well as Byrne and the other Lords, all of whom are bent on destroying this universe."

The room was silent, and remained so for a long minute.

"I was afraid it would all come to this," said Celine, so softly that the others heard only a muffled murmur. The girl could feel the dark foreboding and anxiety that had haunted her back on Nibiru rising up again, demanding attention, threatening to overwhelm her. Suddenly she remembered something West had once said: "It is in your power, child, to quell your own worries." And without another thought, the girl did just that. She stood straight and gave the group a firm look.

"What?" enquired Ahimoth, his Dragon hands held up before him, his shoulders shrugging. "What is going on? Why does the entire room suddenly feel like we've lost this war before it really started — again?"

"Sorry, Ahimoth," replied Celine, still pale despite her new-found resolve. "I'll explain. Unless you would prefer to, West."

"No, you are doing quite well, Celine. Please continue," answered the Mentor.

"All right," said Celine. She gave West a slight nod, to indicate she understood the Mentor's reasoning, and what lay behind her unusual actions of late. It was reasoning that saddened Celine, but she quickly pushed away all other thoughts, to focus on what currently faced her and those she loved.

"Because," Celine continued, with a heavy sigh, "Mutuum was crafted for an Atlantean. He can only be used by a descendant of the Ancients. Fortunately, Jager and I are so descended. But, as I've mentioned, Prince Deet hid Mutuum thousands of years ago. That brings us to the biggest difficulty: how to find him. If what Joli is saying is correct — that we must recover and use the ancient incant-baton if we are to win this war — life just became a million times more difficult for everyone."

"What? How could that be?" asked Ahimoth, his Dragon hands once again in the air. "I remember how difficult you said it was to find the ancient grimoires, but you and Fianna found them — and almost entirely on your own. Even though you had to battle Soader and his demented mutant Dragon. It was just the two of you. Now we are all here, and in this together." He swept his wings in a wide arc, to indicate everyone in the room, and the entire Mentor facility as well.

"Yes, that is true, dear Ahimoth," replied Celine softly. "But there are a couple of challenging barriers in place, meant to prevent Mutuum from ever being found." The girl paused, sighed, and shrugged. Jager gave her a reassuring smile and mented her a kiss; she returned the mental kiss and thanked him.

"The first difficulty," she said, "is that Mutuum can only be located by traveling..." she paused again, took a deep breath and looked at each member of their little group. Their loving looks gave her the strength to continue, to say what she needed to say. "By traveling back in time. As avatars, into past-time bodies that are spiritually compatible."

Celine paused again to take in their reactions before going on.

"So, as you can surmise," she said, "as I assume you already have, by the looks on your faces, there are numerous difficulties ahead for us, one and all."

"Indeed," whispered Ahimoth.

"Yes, indeed," said Jager, "but please, Pumpkin, go on."

"Thank you," said Celine. She paused for a sip of teala, feeling she had the resolve to continue without hesitation. "Yes, things are getting more difficult. Which is saying a lot, because almost everything up to now has been difficult beyond anything imaginable. But, saying that, our new first step is to locate Mutuum. And to do that, we need to discover when and where we must travel. Once there, we must quickly find suitable bodies, take control of said bodies and manipulate them so we can find Prince Deet. Then we need to be present with him at the precise moment he mentions the two separate hiding places of Mutuum and his personal incant-baton. And, of course, we have to accomplish all this entirely without being noticed."

"Oy vey," said Jager.

"Indeed," replied Celine with a frown — though now she felt more confident, ready to further explain what was needed. "And, as I imagine you're all thinking," she said, "all of this will be made more difficult by the fact that we must share our 'borrowed' bodies with their hosts, without the hosts' being aware of our presence. It's not the same as a soul transfer, because the host remains in the body, and must not be harmed by our intrusion. On top of all this, during the time we are acting as avatars, we will have to cast spells without using an incant-baton. And when our work is finished, we must memory-wipe the hosts."

Ahimoth's eyes grew wide; he and the others remained silent, waiting for Celine to clarify and expand on her surprising comments. All were fully aware that she was talking about magic far beyond what most of them could grasp.

Celine cleared her throat. "I realize all this is rather difficult to comprehend," she said. "And it is unfortunate that we need to do any of it; it is an extremely problematic mission. Our chances of success are slim for many reasons, but we have no choice but to try. And at once.

"So, I will need a great deal of help if we are to succeed. Traveling back in time will be dangerous enough, but the journey will be far from over when we've accomplished that. Because once back in the present, we will have to go find Mutuum in the here and now. As well as Prince Deet's personal grimoire and incant-baton." Celine paused. Everyone could see her shoulders sag and face sadden. "And I, at present," she whispered, "feel overwhelmed. I'm unsure we can accomplish any of this, never mind all of it."

"Double oy vey!" exclaimed Jager.

"Whatever 'oy vey' means, I feel the same," sighed Celine. She straightened up and tried to shake off the newest pang of despair before continuing. "As I mentioned before, we need to be especially careful not to tarnish the timeline. To do so could create catastrophic consequences across the universe. Especially because our involvement in present-time issues affects numerous worlds. We cannot, no matter what, leave actual advanced technology behind — not even suggestions or memories of it. So we must prepare beforehand to prevent any such event.

"All this is in addition to our primary mission. We will need to have specific magical skills to hand, without access to our incant-batons and grimoires."

"Triple oy vey!" said Jager.

"Exactly," said Celine. "Then, on top of all that, there could be geographic difficulties. Years ago, the great flood created by the Brothers filled many of the ancient tunnels and submerged all of Atlantis. Hopefully — and I believe this to be the case — the place we'll have to search for Mutuum in present time is not part of the ancient world that remained submerged after the flood waters receded. I'm hoping it is hidden somewhere in the tunnels carved deep beneath the ancient sands of Turkey, just as were the grimoires. However, we must prepare in advance for the possibility that Mutuum is hidden in a place that is now under water. We must memorize and practice certain spells before we leave."

"Oy vey, oy vey! Those are monumental problems, definitely," muttered Jager, his face and gestures reflecting his thoughts. "But Pumpkin, brilliant person that you are, I'd bet you know how to do all that. Correct?"

"Uhhhhh, not exactly. But Fianna and I found the grimoires in a room protected by magic, and I assume Mutuum is similarly sheltered from the ravages of time. I believe he is shielded by a means similar to the bubbles we use for protection when traveling the tube-chute. So I guess the first thing I need to do is ask you for the riddle you mentioned, Joli. The one from Dagmar. Judging from what you said, I suspect it will help us. But first, West, are you able to shed light on any of this?"

"Perhaps I can, child," replied the Mentor, "but you have

done a wonderful job so far. I would like you to think about it for a little longer, to see if you can come up with a solution on your own."

"Oh. Okay. I understand," said Celine, a bit disappointed. Since the day West had rescued her and Jager from Byrne's ice-cave prison, the girl had sensed the Mentor pulling away from her students. One evening, saddened and concerned by this, Celine had discussed it with Jager. He had confessed the same concerns. After some deliberation, the two had decided not to speak of it further. They believed West had her reasons, and assumed she would explain them if necessary.

Now the girl mulled over their present situation, and was rewarded with a brainstorm.

"Okay, I have an idea," she said eagerly. "I believe I know someone who can help us locate Mutuum. And, come to think of it, I bet this even answers the riddle Dagmar gave you, Joli. It's Mr. Koondahg — I believe he could be a great asset in all this."

"Excellent, my dear," said West. "I think that you are correct. Alden Koondahg is a preeminent authority on Mutuum, and also an expert on everything related to Prince Deet. Including his baton and grimoire."

"Those were my exact thoughts," said Celine, cheerily crossing her arms in triumph. "Mr. Koondahg left hints in his many books regarding a time-traveling spell, and, seeing as we are short on time to figure this all out, I believe my favorite author is just the person to come with us to find and collect Mutuum."

"That deserves another oy vey," Jager grinned. "I assume, then, that he's still alive, and you know where to find him."

"Ah...yes and no," replied Celine, with a momentary look of

exasperation. She was about to ask West if she knew where the elderly gentleman could be found, when Joli spoke up.

"Celine, I have some information you should know, concerning the spell you seek. You see, according to Teacher, Mr. Koondahg must be present with you when you cast the time-traveling spell. She cautioned me, though, that I must not tell you this; instead, the decision to invite him along on your mission must be yours and yours alone. And so it is! As you see, things are playing out just as they should. I find this reassuring."

"Thank you, Joli!" said Celine. "I, too, find it reassuring. And I can use all the reassurance I can get." The others voiced their hearty agreement. All but West, who gave only a quiet, knowing nod.

"There is more," said Joli. "Teacher also informed me that, in order for the spell to be successfully performed, there must be one more being present."

"Another?!" asked Celine, shoulders sagging. The task before her seemed to be becoming more complex every minute.

"Yes. But only one other. "Teacher stressed that to release Mutuum from his bindings, you must also have the assistance of a Nibiru Dragon, *born upon Earth*. And that, I think you will see, would be me! So I, too, must accompany you on that portion of your quest."

"What?!" exclaimed Ahimoth. "I will not allow it! You will do no such thing without me at your side. And there shall be no argument."

Joli smiled warmly. She had expected just such an objection from her mate.

"Oh, my!" Celine groaned, shoulders sagging once again.

This complicated things even further. She submerged into thought; the others waited patiently. The young girl spun out several possible scenarios and solutions in her mind, concerned now with the added responsibility of the two Dragons traveling with them — *as Human avatars.* And returning them safely! Clearly stressed, she finally stood, but still did not speak. Instead, she surprised her friends by circling the refectory a few times at a fast trot; then she abruptly stopped to address them.

"Okay, I think I have something," she said. Settling at the large tree table where West and Jager sat, she continued. "Here's what I think: Mutuum was appropriately named, for the word 'mutuum' has a powerful meaning. It's a contract for the loan of commodities from one party to another. 'Commodities' meaning physical objects that are meant to be consumed. Such a loan is to be repaid with something else, of equivalent amount and value."

"Oh, I like that," grinned Jager. "Not only does it have a good ring to it, it has a cool meaning. Mutuum, Mutuum, Muuuutuuuuummm. I do like it."

Celine gave him an appreciative smile. He was always trying to keep things positive. It was like a physical energy boost for her, and she always appreciated it. And right at this moment, she surely needed it. She smiled at West too. The Mentor nodded to let her know she was doing a good job, and to prompt her to continue.

Jager could see Celine was still affected by what Joli had said, so he took another shot at lightening the mood. "This is all a little grim, I'd say." He smiled wide and rubbed his hands together. "It presents a troublesome and difficult future. We'll deal with that as it comes, I'm sure. But let's take one thing at a time, eh? That means sending our comm stone to Nibiru. We can go on to the next step from there. What do you think, Pumpkin?"

Celine sighed, but then her smile broadened. "Good thinking. That way we can check off each thing we accomplish as we move down our rather long list. Just checking things off will feel good — on top of the satisfaction of each accomplishment. It will all add up to more attention and energy to bring to bear on the ultimate goal: retrieving Mutuum. I know I, for one, will feel less scattered. More focused. So, thanks, Jager!"

"Yes, good suggestion, Jager," spoke up Ahimoth. He glanced at Joli to reassure himself she was still doing all right. "Not to stray from the subject at hand too severely," he continued, "I still have much attention on our prophetic cave paintings. From the many interesting images we have recently seen in Vin's cave-home, it has become obvious to me that we all are intimately involved in profound events to come. Even Alika and our other unexpected young travelers."

"Those are my exact thoughts," said Jager. "There's another thing about those paintings. It seemed to me that there were *missing* paintings. As if pages had been torn from a book. Did anyone else get that idea?"

"Ah, you took notice too, dear friend," answered Vin. "When I was still a fledgling, I spent many a night listening to the elders tell the stories shown in our cave paintings. Every story mentioned that the magic that protects the paintings also controls which ones are visible at any given time. This feature was meant as a protection for our prophecies and legends. Disaster could result from incorrect or untimely interpretation, or if the images should happen to be discovered by our enemies."

"Now, that is extremely clever!" exclaimed Jager. "But, at

the same time, it leaves us with some glaring problems."

"Yes, truly it does," sighed Vin. "It will be difficult to figure out the missing information, especially since we are not presently on Nibiru to watch for newly revealed paintings. They seem to appear daily, of late. We will just have to rely on Orgon or some other to visit the cave-homes regularly, and somehow send us updates. Could he perhaps do that using your comm stone — the one we are about to send?"

"That's a great idea, Vin," exclaimed Celine. "I'll add that message to the stone before we send it through the chute. I'll also set it up so that the stone will be receptive to Orgon's report. Oh! And West, are there more comm stones we could send, so Orgon can send more than one update?"

"Your idea is a fine one, Vin," said the Mentor. "And yes, Celine; I will have East bring you several more crystals before we travel to Loch Ness. Now I must leave you briefly. I will rejoin you in a few minutes; then we can proceed to the transbeam room together."

The group returned to their dialogue on Mutuum and their other pressing concerns. After a minute, Fallon and her friends slipped into the room. They were noticed, but not sent away, for it is the custom of Dragons to encourage their young to sit and listen whenever elders converse: a proven method of education. But as Fallon sat and listened, she soon grew restless. To everyone's surprise, she approached Celine and the others.

"My apologies, Prince," she said, bowing to Ahimoth. All felt the tension; Dragons, no matter their race, considered interruption — especially of royalty — the height of disrespect. Even more severe if perpetrated by a youngster.

Fallon raised her azure head from its deep bow. "I do not

mean disrespect, Your Highness, but I could not help but overhear your discussion of paintings. We of Remini also have legends and prophecies depicted in such a manner."

Ahimoth grumbled loudly and stood to chastise the youngster. She must be made aware of just how far she had overstepped. But all he managed to do was open and close his mouth a few times, without a word. Then he fanned out his ebony wings with considerable force. The room tensed, expecting a furious tirade. But instead, he withdrew his wings, grunted, and nodded to Fallon. The young Dragon studied him, uncertain. He tilted his head slightly, inviting her to continue with what she had to say. The others' high tension deflated at once.

"Thank you, Prince Ahimoth, for your blessing and for permission to speak." The young Dragon bowed, first to Fianna and then to Ahimoth. "It is because of our great paintings that I knew of you Fianna, and you, Ahimoth." The youngster bowed again to reiterate her deep respect, then cleared her throat and continued. "I knew of you because you both are depicted in several of the most revered of our paintings, in the cavern-halls of our beloved Pagan Mountain. This I tell you all. She swung a wing to include the gathered Dragons and their Human friends.

"Hmmm," huffed Ahimoth. "The mysteries of the universe do indeed increase."

"It seems so," spoke up Jager. "You Dragons never cease to amaze me with your brilliance. What an ingenious method you chose, to conceal and preserve your treasured knowledge."

"My! It certainly is ingenious," added Celine. "So, I'm thinking that after we send the comm stone to Nibiru, and before we do anything else, we should go to Remini to view the Pagan Mountain paintings and see what they have to tell us. There may be something that can help us on our way, or warn us away from danger."

"Yes, I believe that makes sense," Jager concurred. "It would seem logical, since some of the images in Vin's cave clearly depicted Fallon. What I mean is, the paintings are clearly connected in some way. I'd bet the paintings Fallon is talking about hold many of the answers we've been trying to piece together. The missing pages of the book, so to speak. Any knowledge we gain could complement our understanding of all we've just learned on Nibiru. We might even find something crucial to finding Mutuum faster, and Prince Deet's incant-baton and grimoire, too."

Fianna had been sitting quietly by, listening and watching. She did not want to speak, for her mind's eye pulsed so hard it had begun to hurt dreadfully. It took a great deal of her concentration to endure the pain, and to conceal it — and her desperation — from her perceptive Companion and mate. She gave her head a stiff shake, back and forth, to relieve some of the pressure. The motion raised eyebrows, but she spoke at once to divert attention. "I do not understand this," she said, "but I know it is what we must do. And at once!"

Though Fallon was still very young, Fianna understood the significance of the connection between the two planets. She put herself in the youngster's position, then responded to Fallon as she herself would want to be addressed: as a worthy contributor in solving the difficulties they all faced. "Fallon, what do you think of our suggestion?"

The juvenile Dragon stretched taller and beamed. "Thank you, Princess. What Companion Jager said does make sense. The legends of my people say the caves of Pagan Mountain hold many answers to the mysteries of the universe. As fledglings, we were required to study the most prominent ones. I can take you there, if we can somehow make it to Remini."

"That is certainly good, Fallon," said Fianna, still managing to keep the pain and despair at bay. "Celine, would you let West know of our plans, and ask if she could transport us to Remini as soon as the new shielding will permit it? I mean no disrespect, but it occurs to me that we could visit Pagan Mountain concurrent with our trip to restore your father."

"Consider it done," replied a smiling Celine, proud that her friend was more a leader with each passing day — but still unaware of Fianna's present difficulties. "I'll ask West during our flight to Loch Ness. It would be so helpful if some of us could examine the paintings of which Fallon speaks. Great idea, Fianna. Seeing as Fallon and her father appear in paintings on Nibiru, it only makes sense the Remini paintings would include depictions of Nibiru Dragons."

"Sounds like a good plan to me," grinned Jager. He reached over and squeezed Celine's hand.

"Joli, are you up to the trip?" asked Fianna.

"Even if I were not, you would have to tie me to one of the beams above to prevent me from coming with you." Everyone laughed, for although Joli was the smallest and youngest of the adult Dragons, she sometimes appeared the largest, her heart was so great.

They had all just confirmed their acceptance of the scheme when West arrived to pilot them to Earth. Before they embarked, though, Celine quickly filled her in on what had been determined about the paintings.

"Ah, the prophecies are indeed coming to fruition," the

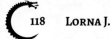

Mentor said.

"It appears so," said Celine. "West, what time does Major Hadgkiss usually arrive at the outpost?"

"Close to our late morning."

"Excellent," replied Celine, grinning at Fianna and the others. "No disrespect intended, but I believe there is time for Jager and I to join you on your next little adventure."

"Undeniably," laughed Ahimoth. "And truly, I sense no disrespect."

"West," smiled Celine, "we've made a slight addition to our plans. If the major arrives at late morning, we should have time to visit the cave paintings at Pagan Mountain. We want to see them because we believe they may provide some needed answers."

"Ah, how clever," replied West, her aura brightening to indicate a smile. The sight comforted Celine. Lately she'd been worried about the Mentor; she had not often seen the aura shift that she assumed indicated happiness.

"I believe you are correct in your assumptions," continued West, "and agree with your plan."

West was pleased with Celine's insights, and willingness to act upon them. The Mentor smiled her inward smile; once again, her young student had surprised her. And in light of her own surpassing skills and knowledge, her surprise meant remarkable, unexpected skill and intuition had been demonstrated. It also gave her a great sense of relief. For one day she would no longer be available to guide the young girl.

West turned to address the Dragons. "Dear friends, I do not think you should remain long at Pagan Mountain. The Humans of Remini have lost none of their animosity toward Dragons, and they would not hesitate to attack, should they detect your presence."

"I agree," said Jager. "We need to do this rat-a-tat-tat."

"Rat-a-tat-what?" asked Ahimoth, a look of confusion crossing his dark face.

"Oh! Sorry," laughed Jager. "In and out, I mean; do it quickly. Ha! West, how long is the shield penetrable?"

"For no more than one hour," replied the Mentor. "You must not dally; it is dangerous for the Dragons, as I have warned."

"We can learn what we need in less than an hour's time, if we know where to find the paintings we seek," spoke up Ahimoth. "I am able to record what I see, and to store it in a safe place in my mind. I can call up such mental images to review and closely examine whenever I wish. I need only to see the paintings briefly; then I can return and describe them to you in every detail."

"Wow!" laughed Jager. "I guess I need not bother taking any image captures, then?"

"Very well," said West. "I shall ask North to take you to Remini early tomorrow, so you may examine the paintings. If Major Hadgkiss contacts me while you are away, I will give him the good news that you will soon join him at the outpost."

"Excellent," said Celine and Jager together. They joined hands and followed in step behind the Dragons, heading toward the transbeam room. West held back, though, and mented to Fianna, asking that she remain behind for a brief time. Fianna acknowledged, told the others she would join them shortly, and returned to where the Mentor stood.

Celine sent the Dragon a questioning ment — no words, simply the concept of wondering.

West perceived the girl's concern. "It will be all right, Celine," she said. "Fianna and I will be right behind you."

"Okay," replied Celine, though still somewhat concerned. She let Jager pull her on toward the transbeam room.

Fianna looked down at West. At once she felt a wave of comfort and love. She sighed deeply, relieved at the strong sense that West was aware of what troubled her. She sighed again, then closed her eyes to lessen the throbbing pain in her head.

Without a word, West approached the Dragon, raised her slim hands and held them close to Fianna's shimmering white foreleg. The Mentor began to chant softly; she continued for several long moments until, suddenly, Fianna raised her head in surprise. "It has gone!" she cried. "The pain is gone! Oh, West! Thank you ever so much."

"That is what friends are for, or so I have heard," smiled the Mentor.

"Ha-ha!" laughed Fianna, remembering Celine using the same phrase on several occasions. "I suppose Celine could have done the same for me, but I did not want her to worry, or to ask about what troubles me."

"Yes, I know," said West.

"Oh! I assume, then, that you know all that torments my mind."

"Yes, I do, and I am sorry that you must endure it."

"Thank you. I continually review it all in my thoughts, searching for a better solution. My searching has been in vain so far, but I pray to the Ancients and still have hope that things will end differently for our dear Celine. Differently than it appears they must."

"I know, dear Fianna. My hope is the same. It is a matter I work hard upon every day. You are a wonderful friend to our girl; she is blessed to have you at her side. Do not fret though, brave one, for there are many sentient beings all around us, working together to alter the course of the future — to shift it from what has been portrayed as inevitable. We all want to save our dear Celine and Jager. I am well aware you protect her from many hurts and dangers, and I thank you for doing so. And I hold strong hope that she will surprise us all when the time comes. There is a strength which yet lies within her; a potent strength of which she is not yet aware.

"So, please, continue to love and cherish her. I believe we may yet save her in the end."

CHAPTER 10

Consequences

S oon the little group of friends stood elbow to elbow at the
Mentor craft's cargo bay threshold, hovering high above
Loch Ness.

"Fianna and the others can fly down from here," explained
West, "and the rest of us can 'beam down, including Alika."

In minutes, the party had assembled on the pebbled
shore. Nessie arrived, and the traditional greetings and introductions proceeded with enthusiasm. The silvery moon,
nearing the height of its climb, seemed mystical in a sky
strewn with wispy cloud. The magical mood was intensified
by the quiet background chanting now underway just off-
shore; Nessie's Water Dragon clan had arrived and launched
into their role in the vortex-calling rite.

"I thank you and your good people for aiding us yet again,
Nessie," said Fianna, bowing. "Your efforts will not be forgotten. Neither by our little group here, nor by my people.

Our legends shall see to that, and our paintings as well."

"Just as my own people's legends shall record your deeds, Princess," Nessie replied, "and those of your wonderful family and friends."

As the time drew near to hurl the comm stones into the vortex, Celine handed the case that contained them to Ahimoth. Just weeks before, she had entrusted a similar stone to the black Dragon. A stone he had cast into the vortex, conveying a crucial message to Nibiru and preventing the demise of their precious eggs — and so their very race.

As the rite rolled onward, Ahimoth watched and waited for his cue. The first signs of the vortex's arrival appeared. "The time is almost upon us," he said. The scent of wormwood and sage wafted up from close by — potent elements of the magical ceremony.

Now the vortex made its always-dazzling appearance; at first what seemed to be a space-black hole, widening in the moon-enchanted sky, expanding and filling with swirling, mesmerizing light and color.

The Water Dragons and their Nibiru cousins chanted on, with the young Reminis, the Humans and even the Mentors joining in, caught up in the wonder of it.

"Can it be that it's more beautiful every time it appears?" Celine wondered aloud.

"It is!" agreed Jager. And then, in a whisper for her ears alone, "Just as you are more beautiful to me with every new day." He leaned in to place a delicate kiss on her ever-so-slightly blushing cheek.

Celine's skin tingled as his lips brushed her face. Before responding, she gazed into his eyes for a long, wonderful

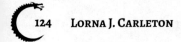

moment. No words were really needed here, neither voiced nor mentally relayed. They had grown so close over the recent weeks that their thoughts were almost as one. They maintained a tacit agreement, though, to converse aloud as often as they could, reserving their expanding extrasensory abilities for difficult times. Wonderful though it was, there was yet something unnerving about the process. They hoped for a chance to discuss it with West — soon.

"It is time!" Fianna shouted. "Are you prepared, Ahimoth?"

"Yes, dear sister."

The chanting swelled in intensity. With not hint of hesitation, Ahimoth stood forth, just below the open vortex. He reared back, then with all his strength cast the case of precious comm stones into the swirling, scintillating portal.

For a moment, the vortex's fantastic display intensified; then, just as swiftly as it had appeared, it vanished with a sharp crack, like the ice on a frozen lake exploding to greet the springtime. Nessie and her Water Dragon clan would continue their chant throughout the night, to ensure the tube-chute would remain open and convey the little case of stones safely to its destination.

AFTER FOND GOODBYES WERE EXCHANGED, West and the other Mentors transbeamed up to their ship, leaving their charges behind. At first, West and her sisters were reluctant to leave Celine and the others on Earth, out of concern that the Volac Forces might be monitoring Loch Ness and tube-chute usage. Nessie convinced them, however, that it was safe to allow the little party to stay. She explained that she had been doing some monitoring of her own, and had not found anything suspicious over the past while. She'd also placed additional spells around the already well protected area, to confuse anyone checking on local activity. And so West's concerns were alleviated. Nessie did accept the Mentor's offer to reinforce the shielding she had in place.

West's concerns, and her wish for extra security, were aroused when Fianna and the others decided to spend the night at Loch Ness, to get in some flying exercise in the safety of the shielded area. More importantly, they had decided to stay because Ahimoth wanted to add some normalcy to the younger Dragons' days. He reasoned that a bit of flying and fishing would do just that.

"I also believe," he commented, "that it will help to mitigate the mounting stress we all feel. I fear our own strong emotions as adults may be affecting the little ones."

So, after a pleasant but brief visit with Nessie, the exhausted troop selected a spot a short distance inland to bed down for the night. They were too spent to help with the chanting, and Nessie assured them no one would hold it against them if they left the work to her and her friends.

"It is my gift to you for all that you have done, and are yet to do," stated Nessie. "We will see each other tomorrow, so rest now. You deserve it."

Once the campsite was readied, the group sat round a cheerful fire to chat for a bit before calling it a night; everyone except Celine. With the comm stones safely on their way to Nibiru, the girl grabbed the opportunity for some crucial study. She carefully withdrew the ancient Atlantean grimoires from Fianna's saddlebags and sat down to search for the spell she must soon use, when they had recovered Mutuum. She worked quietly for a while, then felt someone's eyes upon her. She looked up to see Jager grinning at her from across the flicking flames.

"Don't study too long," he said softly, then gave a cavern-ous yawn.

She blew him a kiss. "I won't." He grabbed at the air as though catching her kiss, and put it into a pocket of his uniform. He returned the kiss, then turned back to re-join a conversation with Ahimoth and Joli. Later, he waved good-night to Celine and curled up between Vin's forelegs.

Celine longed to lie down and sleep as well, but wouldn't yield to the desire just yet. Instead, she gave her head a little shake, stood, stretched, and sat again to peer over the spell books. Eventually, satisfied with the work she'd done — and too tired to concentrate any longer — she wrapped the old volumes with tender care and placed them safe in the folds of her bodypack. Making her way to where Fianna slept, she curled up against the Dragon's warm underbelly and joined her friend in dreamland.

As the others slept, Ahimoth remained alert, determined to keep watch over Joli. Nessie and the Mentors had assured him more than once that the protective barrier surrounding the area was impenetrable, but still he watched. He knew he *should* rest, but concern and his troubled thoughts kept sleep away.

He decided to make use of the sleepless time to think about the many prophetic cave-wall paintings he'd so recently studied back on Nibiru, particularly those in Vin's cave-home. He knew the ways of the universe were in some measure predictable, yet always enigmatic. He had, as many Dragons do, a photographic memory. He used it to call up the wall-images he'd studied.

In his mind's eye, he scanned images of Dragons from other worlds, such as Remini and Kerr; images that told of centuries of Dragons living blissful lives, working happily together and with their Human friends and Companions.

He recalled a particular painting that had always intrigued him — the same one that had deeply disturbed Celine. It showed Kerr Dragons massacring a band of Humans; decapitating some, burning others at the stake. Ahimoth pondered the image, wondering why in some depictions Humans were clearly admired, even adored, while in others they were reviled, tortured and killed. He mused that perhaps it had something to do with the Dragon-hating Humans of Remini; he was unsure.

The Nibiruan prince continued his study — calculating, making assumptions, drawing conclusions, all so he could share his thoughts with the others. For the most part he was fascinated at what he saw. In some cases, he was horrified, but studied on.

One of the most expansive of the images, found in the depths of Vin's cave, depicted a young man and woman, their backs pressed together, incant-batons held firmly before them. They faced shadowy flying figures that flashed fire toward them from all angles. Beside the beleaguered couple flickered a campfire, and in its light lay three open volumes; grimoires, he guessed.

Another depicted the same two Humans casting a spell — presumably from the same grimoires shown earlier — their incant-batons pointed high at a ring of circling Kerr Dragons. A few Nibiru Dragons flew among the larger Kerrs. It appeared the Nibiruans were none other than Joli, Fianna, Vin and himself.

Ahimoth wondered whether the painting indicated a triumph, or perhaps cooperation between the two Dragon clans, because an adjacent image showed the Kerrs bowed down before the Humans. Also showing their deep respect were Gibneys, Repts, Pleiadeans, Dragons of different folds, and other races. All was as it should be, he had assumed; but then the most disturbing image of all had revealed itself, just before he'd had leave on this present journey.

Ahimoth took great care to conceal this final, frightful image from Fianna and Vin. It clearly showed the boy and girl being *slain* by a masked creature. The proud prince studied this last memory-image into the wee hours, trying to reason out who or what the masked creature might be, or represent. Most important, he pondered how he could prevent the presumably prophetic image from becoming a reality.

He had been greatly disturbed when he first came upon the painting — fearful beyond words — for the ancient depictions most often came true. He knew Celine and Jager had also seen the painting, but neither of them had mentioned it. He therefore assumed they wished to keep the image secret from Fianna and Vin, and so kept his concerns to himself.

Ahimoth scanned the image over and over, until he nearly dozed. Then, suddenly, his weary face lit up. He'd been struck with a chilling realization.

He finally knew! He sighed so loudly that he feared he might waken someone. He held his breath and glanced rapidly around; he was relieved to discover he hadn't disturbed his friends. He slowly let out his breath, barely able to rein in his excitement. At last, he understood how he could save Celine and Jager from the awful fate to which the image seemed to doom them. The Brother of Death — he himself — would indeed be savior to them all.

The conundrum had haunted him for days. Thankful the puzzle had been resolved, it took no effort to close his mind's eye to the images. He nuzzled in next to Joli and fell almost instantly asleep.

He'd slept only moments, however, when he was startled to semi-wakefulness by his voice-friend. At first his every muscle stiffened, but soon Dagmar's words of comfort soothed him back to sleep, assuring him that his loved ones would be safe until morning; she would watch over them.

As Ahimoth dreamt, he saw things he had no desire to see. He struggled toward wakefulness, but Dagmar's voice came again. She insisted this was a dream he must visit, but promised to guide him through the confusing, unpleasant images. Her words remained strong in his mind when eventually he woke, the dream completed:

"Dear Ahimoth: Strange as it may seem, your enemies may prove to be just the people you need. So do not hold to such anger towards them. Be ever mindful that those who act against you, no matter how great or small, may yet become your friends, even your salvation. The solution is not to kill everyone who opposes you, or what you represent or strive for. The solution is to assist your enemies to kill the demons that haunt them. For once they have overcome such hauntings, they will be free. Free to choose right from wrong, good from evil; free to be your friend, to support you, even in your most difficult times.

"Battles, young Ahimoth, are won by a combination of two elements: intelligence and force. The trick is to learn how to use and mold this powerful pair. But first, strong one, you must also make them your friends. For if you do not, they may well become your worst enemies, bring you to ruin, and destroy those you love and cherish; even our beautiful Joli."

"But...but..." Ahimoth said, still in the dream, "but force is something I understand. I know its every nuance, how to guide and wield it. It helps me to protect those I love. It has saved me many times, and will do so again and again. As it will my loved ones."

"Yes, you are correct, Ahimoth, my gallant warrior. Use of superior force may bring a victory. But remember, always remember, such a triumph is often only for the short term. The infinitely short term. So, if you must use force, ensure it is applied so thoroughly as to completely obliterate your enemy. And know that long-term victory only arises from perfect balance between intelligence and force. So, study your enemies well. Know what forces they command, and whether they understand them and how to manipulate them. Only then will you know how to defeat them utterly. If an enemy shows any imbalance, no matter what it may be, no matter how small, turn it against them. Always. Failure to do so opens you to failure. It will bring destruction and death to those you love most. And hear me: Joli will be the first."

"No! NO! NO!" shouted Ahimoth. "I will not permit any harm to befall my loved ones, especially my Joli."

"Shhhhh, dear Ahimoth. Do not worry so, for I have taught Joli to be strong. It is your job now to expose her to the ups and downs in life. Her reactions to them, whether good or bad, will strengthen her. She needs you as much as you need her, brave one, but please know there is another, unknown player in all of this. You must find him. He does not go by any name, but if you find and befriend him, he will be of great benefit to you, your friends and your cause. If you do not, beware, he will bring you to your doom. You, and all you hold dear."

"NO!" cried Ahimoth, in his dream. "I will not permit it. No harm must come to Joli or my sister, or any of the others!"

"I have no control over your enemies, my dear Ahimoth; only you do. So, mighty prince, please remember that ignorance itself is often used to entrap. The knowledge that I have imparted to you can save you all; so never forget it. Remember also that the most vicious of enemies are actually those who sow and nurture guilt to destroy all that is good. Do not allow such evil-doers to win. They would destroy us all — and even themselves. This is how such parasites have existed throughout the millennia. As we speak, they are destroying many good worlds, merely by falsely crying foul. They have no strength of their own; they can only reflect the strength of good people, such as we, back upon ourselves, in ways that lead to our destruction."

"I will remember, Teacher," murmured the sleeping prince.

"Also, my dear Ahimoth, do not forsake the prophecies, for it is believing and understanding them that will save you when all else may fail. Study the Dragon lore well; study it long and hard. Vital in this study are the paintings you rightly find fascinating. Evaluate what appears important. Discard the insignificant. You must continually question each step you or your friends and family make. One wrong move, no matter how small, could lead to the demise of all good that exists in the universe — forever.

"Without fail, brave prince, ask Joli to create a barrier around you and the others. Tell her to make it exactly like the one which surrounds her old home. She will understand. Tell her never to let the barrier waver. Especially when you follow Celine and Jager to the tunnels of the Ancients. For it is in those tunnels that the present war is most at risk of loss."

Ahimoth groaned loudly. His eyes flashed open.

CHAPTER 11

Quade

"Fallon! *Noooo!!!*" cried Quade, rushing forward to stop his young daughter. Too late — she and her two young friends were gone, vanished into the vortex. The Remini king couldn't believe what his eyes had seen; his heart hung heavy. He spun round to face the mighty King of Nibiru. Remini Dragons are significantly larger than their Nibiru kin, but the Nibiru king did not need size to emanate greatness; his power and wisdom were crystal clear to Quade, looking down into Neal's intense chartreuse eyes.

"King Neal, how can this have happened? Why would my daughter enter the vortex? Can you retrieve her? Please, I beg you: bring her back! Return her safely to me!"

Neal did not respond at once; he stood silent beside his queen, their eyes and minds scanning the mystified, confused gathering of Dragons spread all about the ceremonial space and out into the adjoining fields.

Finally, the gold-hued sovereign spoke, his head shaking in disbelief. "I cannot explain it, Quade. I have not the slightest idea what may have possessed the young ones to do as we have seen. And most unfortunately, my dear new friend, I know of no way to recover them. Not immediately. They must survive the passage through the tube-chute, all the way to its terminus on Earth. Neither we nor they have the power to reverse the process.

"No! NO! NO!" cried Quade. "You *must* bring my Fallon back. She is too young to survive such a passage. Oh, what are we to do?!"

"We must hold our magic sound and strong," spoke Queen Dini, stepping forward. "We must insist that every Dragon who is able, Nibiruan and Reminian alike, continues to chant the chute-sustaining spell of protection. Only then can we hope to see the moon rise at next nightfall, to signify our efforts were pure and good, and our loved ones delivered to their journey's end.

"Come, join us now, dear Quade. Let us take part ourselves in the chant. It is what we can do, here and now. And in addition to all we Dragons do here, I know my children, Ahimoth and Fianna, together with their Dragon mates and potent Human Companions, will do everything in their power to ensure Fallon's safety. Have faith, cherished friend."

The Remini king nodded agreement, knowing Dini spoke wisely. He moved closer to where the vortex had appeared and joined his strong voice to the rest, all led by Orgon and his wife, Tamar. They chanted on and on for hours, until at last the sun rose. As the day began, the exhausted crowd left for their homes to rest, praying to the Ancients that the moon would rise again that night.

But the moon did not rise.

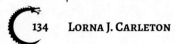

134   LORNA J. CARLETON

For some reason they could not fathom, their magic had failed to keep the tube-chute intact. And that meant that the precious travelers it bore had not arrived safely at their destination.

King Quade stood weeping in the moonless dark; he peered in desperate hope at the spot where the silvery sphere should have appeared. The crowd that had gathered within and all around Dragon Hall's courtyard joined him in silent tears.

For hours the mournful throng peered anxiously toward the sombre heavens, praying that somehow the errant moon would appear. But appear it did not. Finally, near exhaustion, all sadly abandoned the vigil and returned to their homes to mourn in private.

The brutal shock of new loss — following so soon on the heels of the last — overwhelmed Queen Dini; she grew rapidly, gravely ill. Orgon and Tamar spent hours tending to her, using all they knew of both herbs and magic. But to no avail. In fact, she worsened. Word of her suffering spread; one and all feared — most especially King Neal — that she would succumb to her grief. So great is the love of a Dragon for her children.

The following evening, scores of Dragons gathered again to join their kings, Neal and Quade, in solemn vigil. All shared the fervent hope that their prayers to the Ancients would be answered. All the Dragon elders were present, save Dini; the queen remained deathly ill. Though her condition no longer deteriorated, she was still at death's door.

In the final minutes before midnight, and much to everyone's excited relief, a hopeful sign appeared. The trickle of water down the sheer wall behind the Cynth Pedestal suddenly vanished. Instantly, every Dragon fell silent; every breath was stilled. Then, one and all perceived a whirring vibration, infinitely slight at first, but growing second by second — the sign that the vortex would shortly reveal itself. Then, as if one entity, the Dragons let out their breaths. With a resounding pop, the vortex appeared in its familiar but fantastic swirl of color and liquid light.

In that instant, hopes soared. Would their loved ones emerge?

And then, just as quickly as it had arisen, hope turned to surprise. For instead of Dragons, what emerged from the vortex was a small, bright-yellow case. It bounced across the Hall's smooth, rocky floor and rolled to a stop.

Many of those present had seen such a case leap from the vortex's mouth before, and not long ago. Orgon the Wise had received that case; now it was King Neal who approached it. He raised a golden wing for silence, then bent down to inspect the object more closely. He sniffed it. He sniffed it again.

"Ahimoth!" he shouted, rising up and fanning his wings. "My son! It has the scent of our dear Ahimoth!"

"Brother, this is wonderful news," whispered Orgon, standing a wing's length from the king. "And I know what to do with this gift from the vortex."

"Thank you, Orgon," said Neal. He stepped aside to let his brother pass.

Orgon gently lifted the case, carried it to the Cynth Pedestal and opened it to reveal, nestled in velvety fabric, several small, oval-shaped crystalline stones. Each was beautifully polished and seemed to glow with an inner light.

He plucked the center crystal, purple in hue, from its place and set it atop the smooth surface of the pedestal. In a moment, the stone connected with the pedestal's energy links and glowed purple-bright. Everyone gasped. From the stone there came, loud, clear and resonant, Fianna's firm and gentle voice.

Orgon smiled at the memory of just such a stone as this, sent by Fianna and Companion Celine to stay the decline of Nibiru's precious eggs.

The stone delivered its message, and the crowd responded with a roar of joy and relief. The Hall and the ledges all around and above were filled with dancing, shouting Dragons, Remini and Nibiru alike. King Quade danced and shouted right along with the happy mob.

Suddenly, the celebration ceased; the stone had begun to speak again, with another message of comfort, hope and reassurance. And just as before, when the message ended, the revelry resumed. None cheered louder than King Quade.

King Neal mented his queen with the happy news. Within minutes, as if by a miracle, she felt so thoroughly restored that she joined the crowd in Dragon Hall. She was not yet up to dancing, but she cheered with the best of them.

The night's celebration lasted until mid-morning; Quade was the last to head for home. He slept better than he had in quite some time, and dreamed of future days spent with young Fallon, watching her grow and mature.

CHAPTER 12

Back on Remini

"This food is terrible," growled Mia. She slammed down her utensil and shoved away her plate. "It's a good thing I'm not actually hungry."

Remi looked across the table at her daughter. She was about to chastise the girl, but noticed the flushed face and smiled instead.

"Mia," she said softly, "you're pregnant."

Over the past few weeks, Mia had begun to change. She'd become more pleasant, more accepting of others and their actions and beliefs. Of late, though, she'd reverted to her old behavior. Once again, her response to any communication she found the least bit disagreeable was an automatic bark-back. Now she reflexively began such a response, but stopped cold when she registered what Remi had just said. Her reflexive look of annoyance shifted to one of horror: mouth wide open, speechless. She pressed her arms against her newly tender breasts, reconfirming worried thoughts she'd been shoving away. She burst into hysterics.

"OH, NO!" she screamed, jumping up. "I *can't* be! How terrible! Not *now!* This is *not* a good time. *Not* in this hideous bunker. Not before I'm married!" The girl plumped back down, hid her face in her arms and sobbed.

Remi smiled at Major Hadgkiss, seated at the other end of the table. "Never a dull moment in the life of the Zulaks," she laughed. She gathered Mia up and guided the girl, still crying, back toward her cabin and her waiting fiancé.

"Oh, Mother," sobbed Mia as they walked, "what ever am I to do?"

"What any new mother would do, blessed with a child," replied Remi, knowing the temperamental girl would most likely slam her words back at her. It was a good thing Mia's attitude had generally improved these past few weeks, she thought; otherwise, her reaction to this new news would have been much worse.

"How could you, Mother?" wailed the girl. She ran up the cabin's front steps and burst through the door.

Remi remained outside and watched Hyatt take her daughter into his arms. He glanced desperately at Remi through the half-open door, but she just smiled, waved, did a quick about-face and walked back toward the mess hall, hoping to chat with Dino some more. She was glad to find the major still at the table. She stopped to collect two strong cups of teala, then sat down next to him, hoping to finish an earlier conversation.

"As we discussed last night, Dino, we can't wait any longer to go fetch Celine. I need my daughter home with me. It is time."

"I agree completely," he smiled. "How about you come

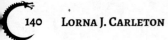

with me on my daily trip to meet with the Mentors? Besides, I have a confession. Ah...I haven't mentioned this before, but...well, let me explain before you get angry." Remi stiffened. "You see," Dino continued, "we know where Celine is, and I expect her back any day now."

"What?!" growled Remi. She stood, hands planted on her hips. "What are you talking about? And why haven't you said anything? Unacceptable! Totally, any way you look at it, Major. Sometimes you make me *so* angry!"

"I know, Remi," he replied, chuckling to himself at the similarities between Remi and Mia. He was glad Remi's outbursts were normally brief, and less hysterical. "I'm sorry, but I felt it was the right thing to do until the kids arrived back safe. That should be soon, maybe even today. But look, go get ready and I'll meet you at the transbeam platform. *Spitfire* is waiting for us." He glanced at his timepiece. "Say, twenty minutes?"

"All right," Remi half-growled, glaring. She remained thoroughly annoyed, especially at Dino's seeming indifference to her chastisement. But the prospect of seeing Celine alive and well, or at least talking to her, quieted the anger that seemed always to lurk near the surface these days.

Remi knew she'd been overly protective of the girls since Raff's death. She felt well justified, though, considering everything she and her family had been through over the past couple of years. Besides, it was one of the few things that helped keep in check her deep grief, oddly alternating with rage.

She glared at Dino once more, huffed, then hurried off to her cabin to grab a few things and prepare for the trip.

On the way, she scolded herself, annoyed that she was so

often angry. She was mad at many things, but mostly at herself for not protecting her family better. She blamed herself for Rafael's death, sure he'd only made the foolish decision to 'beam down to Scobee — straight into a trap — because she had made things so difficult for him that he was desperate not to disappoint her.

If only she'd been less obstinate and more understanding! More understanding of all he was up against as a Fleet officer. Then he would have followed protocol, and he'd still be alive. She knew the only reason he'd been so careless was because he was trying to appease her and meet her unreasoning demands.

And then Remi realized that just now, with Dino, she had behaved just as she had with her husband. She hated herself for it. She chastised herself again, with some not-too-nice language. Thankfully, she had little time to stew over her failures right now: Dino was waiting. She quickly donned a clean outfit and rushed to the transbeam platform.

CHAPTER 13

Playtime

Celine stood waist deep in a creek, water dripping from her cupped hands. She splashed her face with the icy-cold water, then called to Fianna. "How about we go for a flight up the Loch Ness valley before you and the others catch your morning meal? The protective shield Nessie has in place will prevent any locals from seeing us."

"What a superb idea!" exclaimed Fianna, stretching and fanning the sleep out of her wings. "How wonderful it will feel to fly the currents; we have been cramped inside so much these days! I do not believe Dragons were made to be indoor people."

"I agree," came Vin's eager response; he too flapped his wings. "I overheard you just now, and would love to join in. Jager, are you coming?"

"I wouldn't miss it for anything!" laughed Jager. Celine dried off, and she and Jager leapt into their saddles. Soon the friends were reveling in the pure joy of flight, Fianna and

Vin skimming above the water. They all had a good laugh when several local birds joined in the fun.

"Joli, you go join them if you like," said Ahimoth, "and take Fallon and the others with you." He smiled lovingly at his mate. "I will stay here with Alika."

"You are always such a prince. So thoughtful," said Joli, returning a smile just as big as his. "Thank you, my dear, but I am not yet myself after yesterday's adventure. I believe it best that I just watch, and tend to Alika. You go ahead. That way, I can admire your remarkable flying skills."

"Ha!" laughed Ahimoth. "Flattery will get you everywhere, my friend. Just so you know, though, I would not leave your side, were it not for Nessie's protective shield surrounding us all." With that he gave her a quick bow and departed. Soon he circled high above, playing aerial tag with Fianna and the others.

Celine's heart soared as the wind rushed through her hair. It was still somewhat short, since she had recently hacked much of it off as part of the rite to reverse the hex on the Nibiru eggs. But it still felt wonderful. She lifted her arms straight out at her sides and laughed some more, with the wind whipping by.

For a brief time, her face radiated pure joy and love. She wrapped herself in a mental bubble, corralling her thoughts and feelings securely in the present. A present with no war, no evil Lords, no Scabbage — nothing bad, nothing threatening. Just herself and her dear friends, spending a wonderous time together.

Jager, Fianna and Vin sensed Celine's rapture. They too enwrapped themselves in exultant mental states. At least for the present moment. All still knew that great evil was all too likely to find them soon, and much death. Very soon.

Celine could not remember a more wonderful time. The

bond between her and Fianna had evolved into a superior force. Anyone would feel exhilarated and blessed to be so united. The two had had little time, of late, to think or even talk about such things. And the same sort of bond had now formed between the four of them — Fianna, Celine, Jager and Vin — as a group, and as couples. They were amazed at the increased speed of their thoughts and reactions, and the power of their mental communications. But each was most surprised to perceive and understand what the others sensed and felt, as if those sensations and emotions were their own.

As they flew, Celine felt it safe to relax somewhat—thanks to the lulling aura of security all around her. Almost casually, she lowered the blocks and barriers she had erected around her mind and soul. But then, in a flash, she was wrenched violently down to her darkest, innermost places. She tensed up at once, the old anxiety gripping tight round her throat.

She wrestled with the powerful inward shadows, managing to haul herself back to the present by concentrating on her precious bond with Fianna. It gave her a respite, but only a brief one. Unable to hold back the darkness for long, the overpowering gloom sucked her back down, enveloping her all over again. It was as if someone else controlled her.

In recent days, Celine had found herself concentrated more and more on the future. Would those she loved survive the war? Would she herself survive? If they lost the war, how would life change? And if they prevailed over the wicked Volac Forces opposing them, what then? These were concerns almost too weighty for even someone old and wise to ponder. They were nearly beyond the capacity of most any young person. She quailed at a sudden wave of overwhelm, and nearly succumbed to despair. She shook her head as before, this time harder. It didn't help. Panic rose in her throat. And then, another possibility struck her. Another way to win the struggle with terror. She closed her eyes, gripped tight the horn of Fianna's saddle, and watched the passing scene through the Dragon's eyes.

It worked. She was back in the present moment, free of the darkness. She opened her eyes, hugged her Dragon friend and took in all she could see around her. And relished it.

Sensing the change, Jager gave her a mental hug; she relaxed further, reassured. "Pumpkin, things will be all right," he said.

"Yes, Little One," said Fianna. "We are here. You need not worry."

Celine thanked them both and smiled, feeling humbled and blessed to have such friends. Dragons! And a boyfriend from another world. Life is indeed full of mystery, she thought.

"Jager," she mented, "close your eyes." She need not have said anything; he'd already sensed her thought. He closed his eyes, and at once found himself amazed and enthralled at the utterly new experience: he was perceiving the beauty of Earth through Vin's crystalline vision. Vin acknowledged the connection; both marveled at the unparalleled joy of it. They decided to use it to show off a bit — and hopefully lift Celine's spirits. They launched into a couple of difficult maneuvers, to delighted cheers from one and all, Celine included. The girl was all smiles and cheers.

"Yeah, Jager!" she cheered, as he and Vin came in for a picture-perfect landing. "My hero! You've got this. You're going to be a better flying Companion than I am! In no time!"

"Ha! I doubt that," he laughed, taking a dramatic bow from the saddle. "But there's so much fun in the practice, I'll keep at it. No question of that!"

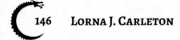

The friends continued their play and practice. The strategy worked: all their darker thoughts, worries and pains were held at bay for the rest of the morning.

"I have truly missed this too," said Fianna, eager to do her part to help Celine. "I too hope all the present troubles are over soon, so we may just be ourselves and live normal lives once more. There is a tremendous amount of good and beauty in life; let us try to keep that fact always in our thoughts. And remember too, my dear friend, that positive thoughts are ever superior. For they will keep our strength high and our vision clear."

"An excellent suggestion," replied Celine, patting Fianna's glistening white neck. "You couldn't be more correct. Wallowing in negatives is exactly what our enemies would want. Thanks for your words, Fianna. It certainly is a wondrous morning, and wondrous to be able to share it with you."

"You are most welcome," replied the princess. "A good friend of mine once said, 'That is what friends are for.'"

The two laughed and went back to their fabulous fun, doing dips and turns and showing off to the others. Their hundreds of hours of practice under Orgon's tutelage were clearly in evidence, comparing their skill to that of Vin and Jager, who'd logged little flying time together.

After an hour of fun, the Humans asked to be dropped off. They'd become quite distracted by their growling stomachs. Soon they were happily stuffing themselves while the others fished nearby. After the Dragons had eaten their fill, Ahimoth brought plenty ashore so Joli and Alika could enjoy a bit of gluttony, too.

Expecting North to arrive soon to transport them to Remini, Jager made sure the fire was out. Celine sat down beside the doused firepit, and soon fell to brooding again, despite her earlier efforts.

Even though she was a witch, Celine was a thoroughly scientific person. She sought to logically compartmentalize the newest feelings and abilities she and Jager had forged between themselves. The new sensations were extremely intense. One of the most tantalizing was the ability to "hear" each other's thoughts nanoseconds before they "vocalized" them as ments. At first the phenomenon unnerved them both, but they soon welcomed it. It made them feel more complete, more a couple, to be communing as though they were a single person — as though they'd healed an old wound.

After they'd analyzed this new mode of communication and practiced it a few times, it ceased to seem odd or unnerving. Instead, they looked forward to the wonderful sensation of one-ness it invoked. They read each other's thoughts as if both were seeing the same reality, in precisely the same moment. The phenomenon sharpened to the point that, if either so chose, their menting resulted in their arrival in the other's space, experiencing all the other's perceptions. Almost at once this seemed so natural that neither questioned it. Having been telepathic friends for so long, it seemed the logical and natural next step.

These same abilities had also arisen in their connections with Fianna and Vin. This intrigued Celine, for she recognized the phenomenon had been foretold by the images on the Dragons' cave-home walls, and linked to events soon to take place. Events, she unhappily recognized, that could change life as it was known far beyond just Earth and Nibiru.

The girl realized that the four of them had, to some degree, ignored this new intimacy. But with the growing darkness, she understood they could ignore it no longer. Indeed, the time had come to embrace it. All of it. Especially in light of their quest for Mutuum, and what the paintings in Vin's cave had revealed about the future.

Celine forced her thoughts to more mundane and immediate matters. The perilous journey to ancient times they would soon undertake frightened her — and fascinated her at the same time. But for the moment she must calm herself and prepare.

CHAPTER 14
Alika in Trouble — Again

Celine and Jager sat together on a shore-side rock, munching brattles. The Dragons chatted among themselves as they finished their breakfast fish.

"Good morning, Celine, Jager," called West's mental voice.

"Good morning," the two replied. "We're ready to be picked up," said Celine. "Thank you so much for arranging for us to stay the night. It's been most beneficial to all of us."

"You are most welcome, my dear," replied the Mentor. "Moments of normalcy and pleasure are important, especially in such trying times. I am sorry to end your pleasant stay, but glad you are ready; North will arrive shortly."

Celine relayed the update to the others, who confirmed they were ready to go.

Fallon moved to stand before Ahimoth, Alika at her heels.

"Dear Prince," said the young Dragon, bowing, "may I

speak with you?"

"Yes, Fallon, you may," replied Ahimoth. "I am listening." The others listened, too, intrigued to hear what Fallon had to say.

"Thank you." Fallon again bowed. "Dear Prince, I must tell you that the entrance to Pagan Mountain is magically protected. Once we land, we can be safe inside our sanctuary within seconds. Then my friends and I can quickly show you the paintings."

"Fallon, thank you for this information," said Ahimoth. "We shall leave your friends and young Alika with the Mentors, though, until we return. I will not endanger any of your lives. I am only permitting you to come because you can guide us quickly to the paintings in question."

Fallon sighed and lowered her head. "Yes, Your Highness."

"Also," said Ahimoth, "while we are on this mission, you must adhere to my every command, without fail. Is this understood?"

"Yes, Prince," replied Fallon and Alika at the same time.

"No, Alika," said Ahimoth sharply. "You will remain with the Mentors. Your presence is not necessary to this task, and, as I just stated, I will not needlessly put your life at risk."

"But..."

"No, Alika. No 'buts,'" interrupted the prince. He puffed out his chest. "You remain with the Mentors. It is settled."

Alika's heart sank as low as his bowed head; he remained silent as they waited for North. When she arrived, he continued his sulk, eyes downcast.

He looked up only when Ahimoth, Celine and Jager stepped up onto the transbeam platform. Then, suddenly,

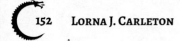

the little Dragon rushed to the platform's edge and pleaded. "Dear, Prince, may I at least fly along in the ship with Vin and Joli and Fianna, to be closer to you? It would comfort me a great deal."

"Hmph," snorted Ahimoth. He stomped and grumbled some more. He caught Celine smiling at his consternation; he rolled his eyes at her, then turned to Alika once more.

"All right, young one," he said. "You must, however, stay out of the way and *follow my every order.*"

"Yes, Prince! Thank you! Thank you!" shouted Alika. He scampered up onto the platform.

Moments later, the group stood in the orbiting ship's hold. Alika stood near Fallon, who winked down at him. Everyone quickly secured for flight, and within moments, the ship moved into a parking orbit behind one of Remini's small orange moons.

North watched as the girl helped the Dragons free of their restraints. "Please, Celine, make this quick," said the Mentor, "and call me when you are ready to leave — or if you encounter any difficulties. I shall remain nearby; do not hesitate to contact me."

"Thank you, North," replied Celine, with a look to Jager as she spoke. "Please don't worry, North. We'll be safe. This shouldn't take too long, because Fallon knows where to find the paintings we need to see. We'll be sure we are ready to leave in an hour."

The ship's large door began to slide open. Celine joined Fianna and made herself comfortable in the saddle, as did Jager with Vin. Moments later, the door now fully open, Fianna, Vin and the others stepped to the threshold and sprang straight outward and away from the ship, wings tight to their bodies. They plunged downward for several seconds; Fianna was the first to spread her wings wide and catch the air, then bank into a tight, steep spiral toward the mountainside ledge below.

Alika watched in silence from beside North, exactly where Ahimoth had ordered him to stand. But suddenly the baby darted for the closing hatchway and jumped through, just seconds before it slammed shut. At once he began to screech, flapping frantically, tumbling downward like a wounded bird. He'd never flown before. The others, hearing his screams and North's urgent ments, braked heavily to halt their descents.

Ahimoth, who had been the last to leap from the ship, looked up to see the struggling baby plummeting downward. He beat his great wings to maneuver alongside the youngster, and after some effort, managed to catch and firmly but gently grasp the terrified little golden Dragon. The baby was safe from crashing to his death.

"Spread your wings, Alika!" yelled Ahimoth, beating his wings to hover despite the baby's weight. "Good. Good. Spread them some more. Good. Now, tuck in your feet. Tighter now. That is the way, but tuck them some more. Tight as you can. Good. Now, I am going to let go of you, and you are going to fly on your own."

"*NOOOO!* No, I cannot!!" screamed Alika. He began to flail about. "Nooooo! I will fall! I am afraid! No, NO, NO! I am too young to fly."

"You will be fine," said Ahimoth sternly, and he began to loosen his grip. "I will be right here. You will do well, I am certain. You are strong and smart. And besides, you must learn how to fly someday; it might as well be now. Especially since you have gotten yourself into a bit of a predicament.

You are most of the way to solo flight now anyway. You should be excited, not afraid."

Alika shivered and for a moment considered protesting some more. But he wanted so much to please his prince, he resolved to do as he was instructed. "All right," he conceded.

"Very good. Let us try this again. Please spread your wings and tuck up your feet."

The terrified fledgling made several attempts, but each time he flinched and withdrew his wings before he'd fully spread them.

"Good, good! You'll get it," coached Ahimoth, though the baby still floundered. "You are doing well; easy, easy. Do not worry, I will stay with you. I will help you land."

"I cannot land!" cried Alika, tensing again, then struggling. Ahimoth re-tightened his grip on the youngster to prevent a fall.

"I will crash!"

"Do as I say, and you should be fine."

"Yes, Prince. I am sorry, Prince. I do not know what happened. I do not know why I jumped from the ship. I am so sorry."

"We will discuss that later; no more talk of it for now. Just do as I say, and we will get you safely to the ground. We shall make something positive of this unfortunate incident."

The others, now safe on the ledge below, watched and listened as Ahimoth released Alika, then guided him down toward them. The little Dragon did well, but it was obvious the sight of the rocky surface coming up to meet him frighted the little Dragon terribly. He began to falter once more.

Still Ahimoth coached and reassured. The fledgling tried

to obey, but he spiraled too widely, over-compensated and gained speed rather than slowing. Celine, Jager and even Joli could have cast a spell to ensure a safe landing, but all three realized it was more important for the young Dragon, and Ahimoth as well, that the process be concluded without the use of magic. Celine had drawn her incant-baton and had it poised, just in case, but she slowly slipped it back into her tunic.

"Alika, use your wings! Thrust harder!" ordered Ahimoth, descending alongside the floundering fledgling. "Yes, that is correct. Flap with more force. Good! There. You are doing fine again."

Everyone cringed as the baby hit the ground a bit too fast, and much too hard. He tumbled for several meters, pebbles and dust flying up all around him. He came to rest against a large boulder, looking like a spider squashed on a wall. The little Dragon moaned, then slowly stood up and shook himself. A worried Ahimoth rushed to his side, but the prince saw that the worst bruise the youngster had suffered was to his pride. His concern vanished; he began to berate the youngster for his foolhardy leap from the ship.

"Wait, brother," interrupted Fianna, drawing close. "It appears the mysteries of the universe have once again imposed their intentions upon us. I say this because I do believe young Alika's claim that he was not in control. I believe some outside force brought about his hasty exit from the Mentor's ship."

"Hmph," snorted Ahimoth, but his stance and stern glare softened. "All right, dear sister. Perhaps your words are true." He turned back to the frightened fledgling. "Alika," he said firmly, "remain by my side until I say otherwise. Do you understand?"

"Yes, Prince." The trembling fledgling bowed. Ahimoth strode toward the others, with Alika scurrying to keep up.

CHAPTER 15

Pagan Mountain

After Celine assured North of Alika's safety, the Mentor said her goodbyes and the ship vanished from orbit, bound for its base.

The travelers gathered behind Fallon, who stood before a massive, sheer rock crag. She settled herself and began a low, quiet chant, which grew gradually more intense. Narrow seams appeared in the featureless wall. They widened slightly to form the edges of a stone portal, tall and wide. The great door swung slowly inward to reveal a dark passageway. Fallon led the way into the mountain, wall-mounted light-orbs lighting at her approach. The door swung silently back into place when the last of the little band had passed safely through.

The others had to trot to keep up with Fallon as she led them down the long tunnel. As they went, the light-orbs flicked on one by one, illuminating their passage, then going out a short while after the party had passed.

Before long the passage came to an end, opening upon a vast cavity within the mountain. Pagan Mountain was apparently an extinct volcano. A roughly circular opening to the skies high, high above admitted some light. The natural sunlight was supplemented by the powerful rays of a huge, orange-hued light-orb, hung high on the walls above, close to the summit's opening.

"By the Ancients!" exclaimed Fianna, taking in the scene that spread below them, kilometers across at its lowest levels. "Such a beautiful place, Fallon. It is indeed a tragedy that you and your people had to leave a world graced with such beauty as this. I do hope that we of Nibiru can provide you all with a measure of comfort in your new home, to soften your loss."

"Thank you, Princess Fianna," replied the young Dragon. "Our paintings foretold our departure, though. They showed that someday we would have no choice but to leave Remini. So, although we were greatly saddened when the day finally arrived, at the same time we were not entirely unprepared.

"But come, the caves where our prophecies are displayed lie on the far side of this cavern." Without waiting for a reply, she leapt skyward and soared high over the valley below. Despite their surprise at her precipitous departure, the others followed fairly quickly. All but Ahimoth and Alika.

Alika hadn't yet learned how to take off, so Ahimoth remained behind to assist him. The little Dragon caught on quickly, and soon the pair were airborne, following the rest of the party — though slowly, and in Alika's case, somewhat clumsily.

Reaching the far side of the cavern, Fallon landed on a

large outcrop high up the wall, almost directly opposite the spot where they had entered the mountain. She paused for a few moments to survey the scene below. Her people's former home was unquestionably a place of great beauty. Foliage was plentiful, supported both by the light from the opening to the sky and the radiance of the great light-orb. Verdant growth could be seen everywhere; it was especially lush along the banks of the small river that wound across and along one side of the cavern floor, but some could be seen reaching as high as the sky-opening far above. Birds were plentiful, nesting in the trees and on the rocky walls. The river and several spring-fed pools teemed with fish.

Fallon's reverie ended with the others' arrival — all but Ahimoth and Alika, still nearly a minute behind. With nothing more than a nod to acknowledge their arrival, she turned, walked toward an oddly shaped boulder, and abruptly disappeared.

The others rushed forward to find the young Dragon had entered an enormous opening, hidden in the shadows of the sizeable rock. They stopped at the entrance, waiting for Ahimoth and Alika to catch up. At last, the pair arrived, and the whole group hurried to follow Fallon. Celine and Jager remained in their saddles, for the Dragons were now moving faster than their Human legs could have carried them.

The group had gone several hundred meters when they encountered Fallon; she had stopped to wait at a fork in the tunnel, to ensure the others would choose the correct path.

"We shall go this way," she said, indicating the tunnel to the right. "As you see, we have now reached the first of the paintings. The specific murals we seek are still quite a distance in, but if one or more of you wish to inspect these first images — which I am certain you would find instructive

— you are welcome to do so and catch up with the rest of us later. There are no further forks, so there is no danger of your becoming lost.

"Most interesting," Ahimoth replied, scanning quickly over the nearby paintings. "I can see these would indeed be quite useful. I shall stay behind for a short while so that at least one of us will have the knowledge they offer. Then I shall follow you."

"And, of course, I will stay too," said Joli, stepping closer to her mate.

"And we will keep Alika with us," added Ahimoth.

"Very well. A wise decision, I think," said Fallon, and she led the rest of the troop on down the tunnel at a brisk pace.

Ahimoth and Joli scanned the enormous, colored walls. The expansive images were indeed beautiful; many, to the prince's surprise, were quite similar to those he'd studied back on Nibiru.

Fianna and the others followed Fallon farther and farther down the tunnel. All of a sudden, she stopped to look up at a gigantic mural. "Of all our paintings," she said, gesturing at the colorful depiction, "I think this may perhaps be the most important for you to see. All my people are required to study it." Her friends scanned it with rapt attention.

"My, Fallon," said Celine, "This is simply amazing. As are all those I've seen here. I see more and more how they fit into the story told — and foretold — by those we've seen back on Nibiru." The girl shined her light-orb up high for a better look, and to make sure she and her companions would miss nothing.

"Fallon," said Fianna, after examining the mural for a while, "thank you for guiding us to this particular painting.

It holds answers to questions I have pondered for quite some time."

"Yes, yes," said Vin, tilting his head from side to side, not wanting to miss any detail or nuance.

"Agreed," interjected Jager. "What we've seen today has resolved several confusions I've had. I wonder what we'll see next!" When her guests had finished their study, Fallon led them yet farther into the mountain. Vin's mind's eye recorded everything he saw as the group passed painting after painting.

"Celine!" said Jager in an excited whisper. "Look!"

Celine, still atop Fianna, stretched up to get a better view of what Jager had pointed out. She gasped and cried out. A stunning rendition of her father shone out, high up the tunnel wall. The man wore a huge grin as he walked Mia down a flowery white, yellow and purple wedding aisle. The young woman's long gown flowed past the feet of many guests. Now Celine whispered too, not in excitement like Jager, but because she was at a loss for words. Adding to her surprise were renditions of Jager and herself, with Fianna and Vin. Every figure depicted was all smiles — clearly this was a joyous occasion.

"Well," Jager said at last, "if I hadn't already thought of using Lazarus, I'd think this was the first painting I'd seen that didn't foretell the true future. But it must be true, Celine. I will bring your father back to life!"

Celine was silent, tears flowing. The two climbed down from their saddles and embraced until the girl's tears were replaced with a bright face. The Dragons waited patiently by as the young Humans walked arm-in-arm in silence, scanning other nearby paintings. Celine stopped to point and shout. "Look! Look! Another that explains what we are to do!"

Jager and the others gathered around her, looking where she pointed. Despite their great age, the colors were vibrant; they shone as though created with iridescent paint, in stark contrast to the gray Pagan Mountain walls. Jager saw at once what Celine referred to: an image of himself, bent over an open stasis unit that held what was clearly Commander Zulak's body.

"Lazarus," whispered Jager, he clenched his fists high and did a little jig of victory. "This confirms it!" He snatched Celine's hand and spun her around, back toward the tunnel entrance. "We must get to the under-world — fast. We've got to get to your father at once."

The girl nodded, but planted her feet. "I agree, but we should see the rest of the murals first. They may hold other information we can't afford to miss. For one thing, we haven't yet seen any that show Mr. Koondahg, or tell us anything about Mutuum."

"Ha!" laughed Jager. "You are so right, Pumpkin. Sorry, I got a little ahead of myself — again. I've felt so guilty since I realized I could have helped your father weeks ago. I'm just eager to get to him. So yes, Pumpkin the Wise, we should take the opportunity to see all we can here. We may not get another chance." The Dragons smiled at the exchange, and agreed they should all continue on. And so they made their way on down the tunnel, examining paintings as they went.

A short while later, Jager piped up again. "Well, Wise One," he said with a bow, "it seems you are right again. It's clear the paintings we saw on Nibiru have sister paintings coming to life right here in front of us. They're filling in information we didn't have back there. I assume the same would be true of the paintings Joli mentioned, in caves near her home back in Germany."

"Likely so," smiled Celine, thankful as usual for Jager's lightheartedness. "It's as though we've found missing pieces to a puzzle. Or maybe they've found us!"

"I have an idea," said Fianna. "With the limited time left to us, perhaps we should split up to cover more ground."

The others agreed, and Fianna mented Ahimoth about their plans. Jager and Vin moved along one side of the tunnel, while Fianna and Celine moved down the other with Fallon.

Ahimoth and Joli continued their studies farther up the tunnel, always with an eye out for their impulsive young charge. "Alika," reminded Ahimoth, regarding the baby somberly, "stay close. Do not wander." Alika nodded and stuck fast by the prince, as young ones do with their parents. Joli also remained close to her mate's side as they moved along, meticulously inspecting each painting.

"Fascinating!" said Ahimoth, "These are different from ours back home, yet similar. I would be interested to know who painted them. Clearly the work was not done solely by Dragons. Yet the Humans on this planet are not kindly toward our race. So who could have created these? Perhaps in earlier days all the peoples of Remini were friends."

"Hmm, yes — that could be so," said Joli. "And look over there!" she exclaimed, pointing. "I recognize those images! They are very like the ones Teacher showed me, back on Earth." She hurried to the wall she had indicated, Ahimoth and Alika close behind.

"That was a strange day," Joli mused. "The day she showed me the paintings, that is. They appeared to us on a well-hidden rock face near our home. So beautiful. Teacher explained that the Ancients had painted them, which added to their intrigue for me. I loved to sit and gaze at them, dreaming about the Dragons who must have stood on that very ground, helping their Human friends paint. Being young and naïve, I fantasized about meeting those Dragons someday." She turned to Ahimoth. "It made me feel closer to home — to you. To all of you."

Ahimoth smiled; no words were needed. In his captivity he'd spent years dreaming of seeing Joli again. The pair returned to their studies. Then, suddenly, Ahimoth shouted. "The Ancients! Of course!"

"What is it?" Joli queried.

"I believe I have just solved a mystery of one of the things Dagmar spoke of: your personal insight! Your ability to perceive unspoken thoughts from others to whom you are not linked. With your help, I think we can connect these paintings with those on Nibiru and on Earth."

Joli, somewhat startled, could only look at her mate, confusion plain on her beautiful face.

"I'll explain," said Ahimoth. "Are you able to visualize the paintings you saw on Earth?" Joli nodded slowly. "Good. Now, can you share with me what you saw? May I link with you to do so?" She nodded again. They made the link, she visualized the ancient paintings, and Ahimoth gasped in surprise. The images were similar to those on the cave walls before them, in almost every detail.

"They were painted by the same people!" Ahimoth exclaimed. "This is fascinating, my dear." He gently hugged her, careful not to squeeze too tightly; he was still concerned about the previous day's scare. "Joli, it's clear now. You, me, the others — we are most definitely the Dragons told of in our Nibiru prophecies. And those of Remini and Earth as well. This is wonderful!"

Seeing that Joli was struggling to understand, Ahimoth went on. "I am sorry, my dear. I will try to explain. These paintings are clearing up much of the confusion I have carried all my life. I have always felt like an outcast, never a true member of our society — even though I was a prince. Yet these murals depict a different story." He swept his wings wide, indicating the paintings. "I matter. You matter. We all matter. Everyone matters, for every living sentient being contributes to the continuation of existence. We all have a part to contribute, and that part is valuable.

"We live during interesting times," he continued. "And we truly are instruments of our ancestors. We must explain what we have learned to my uncle Orgon and our elders, and as soon as possible." Joli smiled and nodded agreement, even though she was still somewhat fuzzy on what had Ahimoth so excited.

The Nibiru prince returned his attention to the painted walls. He was silent for a long while, scrutinizing them. A newer painting, stretching high up a wall and part-way across the ceiling, grabbed his attention; he stood for several minutes, forefeet against the wall and neck craned back as far as it would reach, taking in every speck of color. Joli studied the image as well, turning her attention to Ahimoth from time to time, to gauge his reactions to what he saw.

At last, Ahimoth turned to ensure Alika was still with him and all right — only to discover the youngster was nowhere to be seen. He called out to the baby, and he and Joli retraced their earlier steps, all the way back to the entrance. But they encountered neither sight nor sound of the fledgling.

Ahimoth didn't alert Fianna and the others right away; he

saw no need to alarm them, figuring that Alika would not, possibly could not, fly off by himself. The prince was also extremely surprised that the youngster would directly disobey him, considering all that had transpired earlier.

The black Dragon could only maintain his calm for a short while, though. Becoming more and more frantic, he searched up and down the tunnel, Joli doing her best to keep up with him. They scoured the area near the tunnel entrance, too, calling for the baby and checking in every niche and behind every boulder, no matter their size. The pair even flew out over the chasm, scanning the spaces below. But still there was no sign of the youngster.

The Nibiru prince finally called his sister.

"What unfortunate news, brother," Fianna replied. "We have finished our study and are on our way back towards the entrance. Perhaps young Alika missed our company and wandered this way. We will let you know if we meet up with him." Fianna told the others what had happened, and urged them to pick up their pace. A few short minutes later, the two groups came face to face.

"Where could he be?" growled Ahimoth, stomping back and forth on the ledge outside the tunnel entrance. "When I get my talons on him, he will surely know what it means to disobey me."

"Brother," said Fianna, sighing and ruffling herself in a fashion similar to a Human experiencing chills down the spine. "I sense mysterious entities are once again at work here. For some reason, our Alika is connected to the spirits of the universe. He appears to be an integral part of all that is occurring. You must remember, dear brother, he appeared in one of the paintings we viewed, back in Vin's cave. And again just now, we have seen him in several of the paintings deep inside Pagan Mountain.

"And further, dear Ahimoth, remember that little Alika was our great warrior Haggis just weeks ago — before he took on his new little body. Deep in the tunnel, we just viewed paintings depicting dear old Haggis; paintings adjacent to others which depicted Alika. This leads me to believe our little comrade is perhaps a bigger player in the future of our universe than we now understand. Remember that, like your name and mine, his name comes from an ancient people of Earth. In their tongue, the name meant protector; guardian of the people. That in itself could explain a great deal. It may explain why old Haggis chose the name to use in his new life. There is one more mystery to consider, too: Alika was the name of Celine's brother, who gave up his life to protect her."

Ahimoth thanked Fianna for her wise remarks and welcome comfort.

"My dear friend, I feel as Fianna does," spoke up Vin. "I too sense the mysteries of our universe at work here. Perhaps the same forces that induced young Alika, Fallon and the others to leap into the vortex have again taken hold of the young one. Perhaps it is also the reason he joined us here on Remini in the first place."

"Hmmm," replied Ahimoth, relaxing somewhat. "You each present good theories which could explain why Alika wandered off, but we still do not know where he has gone. I need to find him."

The Nibiru prince resumed calling and menting for Alika. He searched up and down the tunnel, but found no trace of the baby. The others searched too, inside the cavern and out.

A while later, Celine mented privately to Fianna. "I'm

afraid it is time to head back to the mountain entrance. We are unable to contact North while under the mountain's protection, so we must leave these walls. If we do not call her soon, she will think something has gone wrong. Indeed, dear friend, something terrible *has* happened, but we have no choice. Can you talk with Ahimoth and get his agreement to come with us?"

Fianna did not answer right away; she wanted to re-think everything before she spoke to Ahimoth. After a few moments she replied. "Yes, dear Companion, I can, although I am afraid it will be difficult."

Fianna let her brother know the situation and received his anger, full-force.

"We cannot just leave him!" he growled as he stomped, huffed and fanned his wings. He even let loose a small, controlled breath of fire, but directed it away from his sister and the ledge where they all stood.

"I know how you feel, dearest brother," said Fianna, in as soft and calm a voice as she could, "but we cannot remain here much longer. Please remember how unsafe West said Remini is for Dragons. The native Humans moved to destroy this mountain settlement just a few days ago, and I believe that only the forces which have been manifesting themselves to us of late have kept this cavern intact up to now. We must return to the entrance above, so North can safely transbeam us back to her ship."

"Well," barked back the prince, "the rest of you can go, but I am staying here. I will not leave without Alika! He is just a baby. I failed to protect him, and will not abandon him. Now or ever! He should not suffer for my failure."

"I'll stay with you," said Joli softly, giving him a gentle pat

with a green wingtip. "We will find him. I feel it in my bones. And, as you know, Dragon bones are never wrong. Most especially mine." Joli's words and demeanor calmed the great Dragon enough to agree.

Joli addressed the others while Ahimoth headed off to search some more. "I know we can only stay for a short time, but hopefully we will find young Alika. If we do not, I will make sure Ahimoth returns to the mountain entrance. He will not want to endanger me, so he will go when I ask him to."

The others agreed, and flew back across the chasm towards the mountain entrance while Joli and Ahimoth continued their search. A few minutes later, though, the party returned to the chasm's edge so Fianna could call the prince.

"Brother!" she called excitedly. "North has news of Alika! Come! He is no longer on Remini."

"What?! How is that possible?"

"All will be explained once we are safe at the outpost again," replied Fianna. "Hurry. We must leave Remini quickly, for we have been detected by the native Humans."

Ahimoth ruffled himself in frustration, but soared back across the valley, Joli steadfast at his side. Before long, everyone was safe at the Mentor outpost. All but the missing Alika.

West greeted the travelers on their arrival. "Come," she said, "let us gather in the refectory. We may speak freely there."

CHAPTER 16

Matters of Life and Death

Weeks earlier, on the day West had rescued Celine and Jager from Byrne's ice-planet prison, the Brothers and High Chancellor Scabbage had been put to flight by a mysterious, powerful being, perceptible only as a blinding point of purest white light. Although the evil gang had managed to escape to safety aboard their stolen warship *Queen Morrighan*, they remained sorely perplexed by the mystery and power of the light-being. They were unaware that it was the newly ascended West who had confronted them.

"What the hells was that light all about?" growled Lancaster, as he and Dodd stumbled off the transbeam platform. They slumped against the nearest wall, gasping for breath and clutching at their pain-wracked chests. Recovering slightly, they glared back at Scabbage, still slouched over in his hover-chair in the middle of the 'beam platform. Lancaster pointed an unsteady claw. "We were almost killed because of you, you blundering idiot! That was your final chance. I'd be very worried if I were you."

"My exact thoughts, brother," coughed Dodd, arms still clutched across his chest. "What should we do with him? Torture? Byrne demanded the incompetent rodent be punished, so that is exactly what we should do, eh?"

"Yes. It is exactly what we *will* do," snarled Lancaster. "Guards! Escort this idiot to his quarters and keep him there. He's not to leave his room, no matter what."

Scabbage wanted to protest, but 'beaming — always a struggle for him — had triggered a fresh coughing fit. So all he could do was sit and hack while his hover-chair was shoved out of the transbeam chamber and down the corridor. By the time his fit ended, he'd been locked in his quarters. Dazed and confused, he could only stare at the locked door and mumble to himself. "How could Kurucz and Bsrn have known I ordered Soader to take Jager to the Dulce compound?"

The exhausted Rept gripped the hover-chair's arms, too weak to do much else. When Byrne's minions had shown up back on the ice planet, he'd wanted to explain that Soader had acted alone. But before he could utter a word, that damn light had appeared — whatever the hells it was — and nearly disintegrated the lot of them. Scabbage wiped a sleeve across his face, pulled a flask from his robes, and managed to down a drink without triggering a new coughing fit. After another couple of swigs, he began to relax, normal color slowly returning to his half-reptilian face.

"Har!" he chortled, feeling more alert and recovering some self-assurance. "Those Brothers are fools. I know the truth about them. And they don't know that I do. They'll be gloating at my suffering, but let them. Their little amusement will be short-lived. Oh, yes."

The High Chancellor recognized the look of impending death. Indeed, he recognized it well — for it was the look he'd faced each morning of late, in his own mirror. He laughed at the thought of the Brothers' looming demise, but quickly turned his attention to more pressing matters, prime among them his own dire need of a new body. But, working at the computer console he'd been provided, his concentration soon strayed back to that furious light, bearing down upon him in the ice-prison concourse. Just the thought of it shocked and confused him anew. The thing had torn apart the concourse with ease. So why hadn't it sliced him and the others to pieces? It had clearly had the power and ample time to do so.

The more important question, though, was how to get that power for himself. All of it.

"I *must* have it," he mumbled. But how, he mused. He pulled a kerchief from his robe and hacked and hacked.

Glancing at the sodden kerchief, he winced. Too much blood there. Far too much. He raised his head to gaze at a garish, oversized painting of the Brothers hanging on the wall above his bed. It was the same image that hung in all *Morrighan's* living quarters. He threw the soiled cloth at the painting, and coughed out a laugh at the bloody smear it left on the face of one of the twins.

How he hated the Barbdews. He hated their wealth, their confidence, and most definitely their abiding contempt for him. Bloody hells, he just hated everything about them. He knew they'd locked him in his room to scare him, but their effort had failed. He didn't fear them. Not anymore. They were even closer to death's grim door than he. He managed a wry grin.

True, Byrne had ordered the Brothers to punish him, but

he knew he needn't concern himself with the threat. In days gone past he would have worried, but not now. He pulled a clean kerchief from his pocket, spat into it, then threw it at the painting to smear the other brother's face. He laughed as it hit its target, dead on. He was confident time had run out for Lancaster and Dodd.

"Har!" he laughed as he climbed into bed. Before he drifted off, another sneer crossed his face. "I believe the morning will bring the promise of a better future." And surprisingly, he was so right. For at that very moment the Brothers were on their way to see Villa the Witch.

WHEN MORNING CAME, LOUD VOICES outside his room woke Scabbage.

"What the bloody hells is all that gods-damned noise?" he yelled into his comm pickup. Within seconds a servant rushed in.

"I said, what's all the bloody ruckus about? Well?! What is it?!" roared Scabbage.

"It's the...the Brothers, sir," stammered the Grey. "They... they're dead. Down below. On the planet. Yeske. They burned up. They didn't transfer into new bodies. The crew is...er... The crew doesn't know what to do, sir."

"Harrr!" Scabbage laughed; but his celebration was derailed by a new fit of hacking and coughing. When the fit subsided, he knew things were serious. Blood filled his hastily grabbed kerchief, but that wasn't all. Blood still spewed from his nostrils and welled in his throat, threatening to choke him. He had to get some scouts out looking for that damned Jager kid, before he joined the unlucky Barbdews in death.

"Get me my medicine!" he ordered, stifling a gag and coughing more blood into his already saturated kerchief. "Then get me my breakfast! Then take me to the control room!" He paused, considering the new circumstances. "The control room of MY ship!" He hurled the blood-sodden cloth at the wall.

The Grey scurried off, leaving Deebee chuckling. Despite the urgency of obtaining a new body, he still had time and avarice enough to rejoice in his new status.

"My ship! My ship! *MYYYYY SHIP!* Har-har!" He shouted it again, and cackled long and hard. Until yet another fit racked his dying body. When he'd regained his composure, he laughed again, in spite of his physical miseries. Things are finally falling into place, he thought. In a matter of hours, he'd gone from being the Brothers' pawn to freedom and command of their ship. The only ship with universal jump-shift capabilities! Among all the people of this, the Phoenix Universe, he alone had the means to enter and exploit the Serpens Universe. Life was surely looking grand.

His enjoyment ended abruptly as another fit racked his frail body. When it ended, he remained motionless and quiet, dabbing his lips. Servants stood by, stunned at the grim reality that *this* was the new top boss. The Barbdews had been horrible to work for, but Scabbage was famously thirty times worse. Nervous, they stood off as far from him as they dared. Scabbage turned on them: "Where's my damn *breakfast?!*"

They turned and rushed away.

Scabbage ended his little personal victory celebration. He knew very well that he must stop negating the harsh reality of the problems confronting him. Events back on the ice planet meant the Volac Forces no longer had the boy — or the blasted girl! So he no longer had access to the optimum body for his all-important transfer. Neither did he have the two people he needed to steal the Nibiru treasure, and Soader's treasure trove too.

He scowled and shook his head. He *had* to shake off the images that haunted him, of Dragons and their magnificent riches. He *must* focus all his time, attention and resources on finding a temporary Human body, preferably an Earther, and making the transfer. If he failed, joining the Brothers in oblivion was inevitable!

He slapped his chair arm in disbelief at having the best opportunity in his life — landing ownership of *Queen Morrighan* — threatened almost at once with loss. "Gods damn it," he rasped aloud. "Soader, this is all your fault! I wish you were here so I could kill you, you bloody useless peon!"

The High Chancellor sat, seething, until he found the strength to rise, dress, take his medicine and eat.

AN HOUR LATER, HIS BREAKFAST FINISHED, Scabbage returned to his most immediate problem: finding a temporary body. He hit upon a plan. Although another jump-shift would punish his failing body nearly to the point of death, the only viable option he could see was to jump *Morrighan* to Planet 444 — Earth — pick up an Earther body directly, then take it to the soul-transfer station on Earth's moon to effect the transfer. That would at least buy him time to track down the boy Jager, and claim *his* body at last.

He bellowed at his crew to make the jump and take up an orbit above Soader's Dulce compound. He knew Soader had many Earther prisoners, and figured he was owed a favor or two.

Within minutes, a shuttlecraft set down outside the Dulce gates and the chancellor and his entourage disembarked to face two hulking guards, whose hungry-looking beasties tugged at rather short leashes. Recognizing the high chancellor, the guards allowed him to pass. Approaching the compound's gates, another jolt of searing pain struck the dying Rept. He clutched his chest tighter and focused on his goal: a fresh, new body. Above the gate flashed a yellow sign: "Report at once to the Commanding Officer – T.C. Soader." Despite his suffering, Scabbage managed a scowl of annoyance. Pretentious worm, he thought.

His pain subsiding slightly, Scabbage activated his comm pickup and barked for Soader. His demands went unanswered. "Where *is* that scoundrel?" he growled. About to let fly a hail of obscenities, he cut himself short. It occurred to him he'd recently heard something about Soader. Perhaps it was true — maybe Soader *had* been sent to RPF113. Maybe the scum wasn't even here.

"Gods damn it," muttered Scabbage as the realization hit him. Frustrated at his ailing mind and memory, Scabbage cursed some more, furious at the fact he hadn't made the connection — if Soader was in prison, that meant the scum wouldn't be here to do his bidding. Even more infuriating was the fact that he'd no longer be able to enjoy killing the wretch himself. He barked at the nearest guard: "Who's in charge of this bloody place?"

"Orme, sir," responded the trembling Rept, reaching for the button to release the gate.

"Well, get your ass in gear and find the moron. Tell him to arrange for a body transfer for me right away," snapped Scabbage.

The shaking guard reached for his radio, but forgot that

his other hand hovered over the alarm button. He'd reached for it instinctively at Scabbage's sudden appearance; now he accidentally followed through and activated the alarm.

Within seconds, several aggressive guards rushed in, blast weapons leveled at Scabbage. The chancellor growled at this new insult. The guards promptly recognized who he was and lowered their weapons, just as Orme, head of the Dulce complex in Soader's absence, entered.

"Well! High Chancellor Scabbage!" said Orme, saluting clumsily. "I'm Orme, currently in charge of this establishment. To what do we owe the honor of your presence on this fine day?"

Scabbage remained silent for several seconds, wondering what sort of character this Orme might be, and whether the bloke was aware of Soader's demise. "Soader. Where the hells is he?" He punctuated his demand by spitting blood at Orme's feet.

"Don't know, sir," answered Orme, as politely as he was able. In fact, he was thoroughly annoyed at Scabbage's interruption of his plans for the day. "He's been gone for about a week. Last we heard, he ran off to hunt for some blasted girl and her pet Dragon. We've heard nothing since."

"Hmmm," replied Deebee. Although extremely interested in any information about Celine and the Dragons, Scabbage knew he was short on time. "I'll look into it later," he coughed, fighting back the beginnings of a new fit. "Take me to Soader's office."

Orme led the strange little group through the massive entrance, across the entry concourse to a lift, down to the uppermost of the underground levels, and finally to the double doors of Soader's office. A servant pushed open one of the doors, revealing the lavish but disarrayed office inside.

"Open the other blasted door too!" Scabbage bellowed. "Can't you see my chair won't fit through?" The servant nervously complied.

Once inside, Scabbage, cursing, ordered the Grey to remove the large chair from behind the desk. The creature took too long for the chancellor's liking. He battered him with his stick. *"MOVE!* Can't you see you're holding me up here? Hurry the hells up and get that chair out of there, you useless rodent!" The Grey ducked to avoid any more blows and dragged away the cumbersome chair as fast as his skinny frame would allow.

"Inept moron," grumbled Scabbage, guiding his hover-chair into place behind the desk. He ordered the blaster-wielding guards to stand outside and barked at Orme to sit down.

Orme glowered, but obliged. The desk was an utter disaster area of papers, manuals, magazines, eating and drinking ware, and just about everything else one could imagine ending up on a desk. And a few that one couldn't imagine. No actual work could possibly have occurred there. And from somewhere in the heap, the stench of something none-too-recently alive arose to assault their nostrils. Neither Scabbage nor Orme mentioned the stink, not wanting the other to think him weak.

The chancellor stared at Orme, then loudly cleared his throat and spat into a kerchief. "You know, Orme," he began slyly, tapping his claws on his protruding chins, "I like you. I do, you know? I've had my eye on you for quite some time." Orme sat straighter and began to smile in the devious manner common to petty criminals.

"Yes, you have reason to smile, my friend," grinned Deebee. "I need a replacement for my louse of a cousin, your boss Soader. As you surely have experienced, he's not good at all at his job." He waved an arm at the shambles all about them. "What a bloody mess. And he's nowhere to be found. Over the years I've received several reports that you do most of the work around here anyway."

Orme's sneer broadened. He was already sitting steel-rod straight, but made an effort to appear even more alert, attentive and thoroughly efficient.

"Soader," continued Scabbage, "has done nothing but disappoint me of late. So I think it's time I *did* something about it. Do you know what I'm talking about?"

"Yes, sir, I believe I do," replied Orme. "I agree, High Chancellor, that Soader has been a problem for a long time. What this installation needs is someone who thinks and acts more as you do, sir. Someone more qualified to administer the whole operation, and especially to oversee its vital experimental programs. Several of which have reached crucial points, I might add."

"Harrr," snorted Deebee. He chortled and tapped his lower lip with a claw. "I think you're more like a cousin to me than Soader, you know? You think more as I do. So, Orme, my dear fellow…"

The chancellor paused. As though in deepest thought, he gazed at the ceiling. Abruptly he spoke again. "Yes. Yes. I'll do it." He paused again to stare meaningfully at Orme. "Yes. I shall make you warden of this base. What do you say to that?"

Orme rose officiously to his height of nearly two meters; his 150-kilo bulk was imposing. He saluted the dying Rept.

"I am honored, sir. I shall not disappoint you."

"I know you won't," sneered Scabbage. "That's why I've chosen you." Orme completely missed the chancellor's true intentions; he was too excited at the prospect of total control of the base, at long last. He'd been trying to oust Soader for years, using every criminal scheme and schoolyard bully tactic he could. And now, after he'd done nothing at all, his dream had crystalized. He let his guard down completely, in the presence of someone he knew to be a criminal of the worst sort. He sat down again, wearing a ridiculous grin.

"Good. Good, Orme," said Scabbage. "Glad to see this makes you happy. It makes me happy too." He extended a hand; Orme took it and shook it gratefully. With a bit too much vigor, though — the action triggered a fresh fit of coughing and hacking, the most violent Orme had witnessed yet. The spectacle confused Orme; having no idea what to do, he just watched, trying to look sympathetic. He was greatly relieved when, in a brief lull, Scabbage regained control just long enough to buzz for his servants, who burst through the door and rushed to their master's side.

As the Greys attended to Scabbage, Orme speculated. *This scum looks as though he could keel over at any time,* he thought. *If he does, maybe I can take control of his ship, too — not just the base. More power than I've ever dreamed of. More than old Soader ever had. Harrrr!*

It took a considerable effort for the brute to keep from laughing out loud. He sat quiet, waiting for Scabbage to regain composure. Orme glowed and chuckled in disbelief; his life had changed so greatly for the better, and with no effort of his own.

"As I said, Orme, my dear fellow," said Deebee, wiping droplets from his chin after downing a flask of medicine a

Grey had handed him. "I'm glad to see my offer pleases you."

"Yes, it pleases me a great deal, sir. Thanks for the opportunity to serve you." Orme figured it would be a good idea to be extra pleasant until the old cur died. *Best way to ensure my hold on the boss's title and position,* he thought.

"Warden," Scabbage continued, "first thing I'll need you to do is bring me a male Earther for a transfer, as quickly as possible. One suitable as a temporary, until the permanent one I've chosen is available."

"Uh...," stammered Orme, thrilled at being called 'warden,' but aghast at Scabbage's demand. He decided that in this case, the truth was his best option. "Uh...sir, males are not housed at this facility."

"What the hells?!"

Orme stiffened and put on his best charm. "Sorry, sir. I know it's doesn't make sense, but...Soader's orders, you know. The idiot was afraid that having too many males around — even as prisoners — would threaten his control of the complex. Besides, most experiments are conducted on females. No worries, though, sir. I'll send someone off-compound right away, to capture a suitable Earther for you. Any other preference, aside from male?"

"Hmmm," mumbled Scabbage, chin in hand. He went silent, letting the tension build for his new minion. "Well, no. No other preferences. It'll just be a temporary. A strong, young, handsome one would be nice, though."

Deebee chuckled; Orme was clearly a simpleton. The perfect replacement for Soader. The lout would have no idea what was in store for him. Easy to slit his throat when the time came. Scabbage licked his lips, proud of his newest scheme. It would bring him one step closer to being Supreme Ruler of the Serpens Universe. And, more immediately important, closer to the treasures of Nibiru.

He continued to muse, saddened somewhat that he hadn't been the one to snuff out Soader's miserable life. But then the thought of claiming Jager's body as his own banished all his regrets. Once the body was his, he would target Byrne and the other Lords, and any of their minions who wouldn't yield to his rule. He dreamed of what life would be like as ruler of the Phoenix Universe. And then there would be the thrill and satisfaction of destroying it — and every pathetic fool in it — once he'd escaped to the Serpens Universe with an unthinkably huge haul of stolen treasures.

He laughed aloud at the puzzled look Orme gave him. He didn't care what the fool thought. Once he owned the Jager kid's body, no one — not Orme, not anyone in all the Volac Forces or anywhere else — would dare harm him. The Earther's body was that valuable. And the perfect ticket out.

"Har!" he laughed again. "I'll be invincible! Safe forever!!" He chuckled on and on. The others in the room glanced at each other, shrugging. Who knew what this depraved lunatic found so funny?

Orme was a bit concerned at the chancellor's maniacal behavior, but shrugged it off, requested permission to leave, and headed off to arrange for a male Earther to be nabbed and brought in. He also sent word to Montgomery, at the soul transfer station on Earth's moon, to prepare for an immediate transfer.

CHAPTER 17

TS 428

As Deebee watched Orme exit, another fit began. The convulsing invalid asked to be taken to a room to lie down; he didn't dare 'beam back to *Morrighan*. He tossed and turned, eventually drifting off to tortured nightmares. Many hours later he awoke to a comm-link screech. "What the bloody hells?!" he barked, struggling to sit up. He was startled by the noise, but pleased to discover he was still alive. He glanced around the room, looking for where the comm link could be.

"Chancellor Scabbage! Chancellor Scabbage, sir! He's on RPF113," squealed the voice from the link. "Soader. It's Soader! He's on RPF113!"

"So? I already know that, idiot!" He struggled to get out of bed. "Some help you are. I've known for days. Clean up your act or you'll be joining him. And soon!"

Scabbage switched off the comm link and slowly made his

way to the facilities. Suddenly, the hairs on his neck started to prickle. "If Soader is on RPF113, I could be next," he said aloud. "Byrne has a short fuse. Damn, I shouldn't have told Soader to take the boy off *Morrighan*. That's what must have angered Byrne so much. He must be the one who sent Soader. I've got to know."

He finished his business and returned to the comm link. Feverishly he fiddled with the communicator to get the squeaky voice back. Several minutes passed before he managed to reach the informant.

"Soader. Tell me about Soader. Who did it? Tell me! Who the bloody hells sent him to RPF113?"

"The boy!" came the eager response. "That Earther kid; the scrawny runt captured Soader and had Zulak's ship despatch him."

Deebee gasped, confused at the unexpected news. He switched off the comm link without thanking his informant, and sat staring into space. He never suspected anyone but Byrne or the Brothers would dare send Soader to the dreaded prison planet.

Scabbage barked at his servants for a meal. He chewed on large chunks of the raw meat they delivered, deliberating. He dreaded the upcoming transfer, to a body he didn't intend to keep. He hated the idea of having to transfer twice, but it was now almost certain his present body would die before he could commandeer Jager's. Soader had foolishly thought *he* was going to take over the Serpens Universe, but Scabbage had slyly manipulated him into doing all the hardest work needed to fulfill his own secret dreams. For the moment, the only thing more important than grabbing the vast treasures of Nibiru was Jager's body. Once he had it, everything else would fall into place. Without it, all the treasure and power he sought, everything he'd worked so hard to obtain, would be beyond reach.

Annoyed that Orme hadn't returned yet, Scabbage ordered a Grey to pull down the painting of the despised Brothers that hung above the bed. He was surprised Soader hadn't had a painting of himself up there; the half-Rept had been known for his continuous primping.

Once the painting was gone, Deebee tried to focus again on his future plans. He failed, and fell instead into a fitful sleep. Late the next morning, he was once again startled awake by the blare of the comm pickup. He swiped away a smear of drool across his chin and reached for the pickup at his lapel. "What is it?" he grumbled.

"Sir," replied one of the Grey staff, "Orme is here to see you."

"Gimme a minute," he replied. Still in a sleepy fog, he moved his chair towards a mirror. He didn't much like what the mirror showed, but he made himself as presentable as he could. He slapped at his pickup. "Okay, send him in."

Orme waltzed in, smiling. A scrawny Earther trailed behind, shackled to an unnecessarily thick chain. "Here's the body you ordered, sir."

"IDIOT!" bellowed Scabbage. "You can't possibly expect me to occupy THAT disgusting thing!"

Orme jerked back, his face a confused contortion. It was just an act, though; he knew precisely what he was doing. It was plain Scabbage was running out of time, fast. He calculated that if he brought the wretch a debilitated Earther, death for the chancellor was more than just a probability. Orme was smart in his own way. Not smart enough, though. Scabbage was smarter still. The dying chancellor took another look at the pathetic Earther and knew what had to occur.

"You *are* an idiot, Orme! But you leave me no choice. Ready the transbeam. Alert the transfer station I'm about to arrive."

"Yes, sir," smirked Orme. He glanced around the room, realizing it would soon be his — along with the whole installation. Hells, he thought, when this ass goes to transfer — and perishes in the process, thanks to an unfortunate "malfunction," he'll be out of my way forever. All this will be mine. And much more! Har-har!!

Orme had ever felt such exhilaration. Not even when he'd beaten several Greys to death with one hand tied behind his back and blindfolded — just to see if he could. Just one of the many fun activities he'd indulged in, to pass the boring days at Dulce. Soon, he'd be free to do anything he might dream up. Free to come and go from the place, too, since Scabbage's ship would be his. Life ahead looked grand indeed.

"Yes, sir," repeated Orme, yanking himself out of his momentary reverie. "Right away, sir." The Rept bellowed orders into his comm pickup, then turned again to Scabbage. "Please follow me, sir. I'll escort you to the platform."

Orme found it hard to conceal his excitement as he led the dying chancellor to Level 7 and the transbeam platform. Scabbage was fighting to conceal something too, but his limbs quivered with the completely opposite emotion.

As the lift descended, Scabbage snuck several sidelong glances at Orme's impressive physique. Despite the impending onset of a fit, the chancellor managed a grin, and reviewed his latest strategy.

Soon the elevator doors opened, and the group, in a rush,

stepped into a long, dim tunnel to wait for the chancellor's fit to subside. Orme smiled at the spectacle and stepped off to the side to call Monty, the transfer technician at the transfer station high above.

At last, Scabbage's fit subsided, and the odd group of characters resumed their trip down the long tunnel to the transbeam platform. A host of girls and women watched them pass, from their dimly lit, shabby cells lining the corridor. A few of the newer prisoners gasped when they recognized Scabbage, but most long-time inmates gave the visitors little more than a passing glance. Little did they know that within a few days, they would all be rescued by Celine, Jager and their team — liberated from their chains and years of torment, never again to be exploited by creeps like Soader and Orme.

Deebee gave the prisoners a cursory glance, annoyed that his wife, Shellee, was no longer among them. She'd been freed by that scum, Zulak, along with his own wife and daughter. He made a mental note to send out a crew to track down and kill Shellee. Once he was in his new body, of course.

It was not long before the motley crew clambered up onto the 'beam platform. Scabbage grinned, eying Orme as they took their positions. Yes, Orme was a fine specimen of a Rept, he thought, sneering. Orme caught the look and smiled back, mistaking Scabbage's sneer for happy relief that he would soon have a new, healthier body. Orme's own smile was in part due to his certainty that the high chancellor was about to meet his end.

Moments after the group arrived at TS 428, a small, humpbacked half-breed greeted them. The creature bowed again and again, his oversized head almost touching the ground with each bend of his twisted, tattooed body. The multiple eyes and tentacles of a colorful, body-length tattoo — a monstrous beast native to Monty's home planet — shone brightly through holes in his torn coveralls.

"Is the transfer table ready?" growled Orme, in the manner he thought appropriate for a warden. Monty nodded.

Orme, excited about his first official act as warden of Dulce, almost smiled, but caught himself before anyone noticed. Instead, he growled again. "Take us to the transfer facility. This instant."

Monty wanted to ask where Soader was, but refrained; instead, he bowed some more, backed up and turned to lead the way out of the bay and down a long, rickety, creaking catwalk that appeared older than the moon itself. Before long, the strange ensemble arrived at the far side of the complex, peering at a dilapidated sign that read "Platform 5." It was an old facility which had been assigned for use in Rept transfers.

Orme grinned. Scabbage grinned wider.

The nearest official Rept transfer station, light-years away, was out of commission. It had been for years, but G.O.D., though usually at odds with the Repts, had agreed to let them use this station even though Planet 444, Earth, was not a Rept planet. G.O.D. figured the gesture strengthened relationships. The Repts figured it brought them closer to taking over G.O.D.

Once inside the facility, Orme led the terrified Earther to a large vat of bubbling liquid. "Hook this thing up," he snarled at Monty, and flung the poor Earther's chain-leash at the humpback. "Be quick about it." He sneered, intending to impress everyone with his brutish manner. He dusted off his hands, imagining the gesture as something Soader would have done, then crossed his arms and scowled. A great performance, sure to enhance his tough-warden image, he thought.

Monty bowed as usual, then obliged Orme. First, he gave the Earther an injection to quiet his frequent terrified outbursts and babbling fits. Then he lifted the now quiet and more compliant man up onto a transfer table beside the vat, strapped him down and connected the various tubes and electrodes necessary to the transfer process. Despite the drugs, the Earther put up some resistance, but Monty overcame it; being half-Rept, he was quite strong despite his short stature.

"Get a muzzle on him," barked Orme, annoyed at the Earther's renewed protests. Monty quickly obliged, then finished checking the various connections. Orme glared and paced all the while, glancing every so often at the chancellor for approval. But Scabbage was too preoccupied with hacking, coughing and trying to breathe. His servants offered fresh kerchiefs and a breathing mask, when they could get close enough to the flailing chancellor without being batted away.

Suddenly, with no warning whatever, a violent explosion rocked the building. The doors blew inward, but air and smoke rushing in, not out, meant the installation's thick outer walls had not been pierced. Everyone present, except the poor Earther, strapped to the transfer table, was thrown violently to the floor. As the blast's last rumblings subsided, Scabbage lay sprawled face-down in front of his hover-chair, motionless, blood pooling around his head.

CHAPTER 18

Lazarus

Moments after Celine and the others had settled down to eat and converse with West, North entered to inform them that Major Hadgkiss had arrived, and that he and his guest were on their way to join them.

"Guest?" asked West.

"Yes, Celine's mother. South is bringing them directly here."

"Perfect timing, I should say," replied West.

"Fantastic!" laughed Jager. "Great timing indeed!"

Celine stiffened at the mention of her mother. She would eventually have to confront Remi about having been away so long, so she might as well do it now. There was no time to be emotional over small things, so the girl calmed herself and quelled the impulse to be defensive when her mother stepped through the entrance, two steps ahead of Dino.

"Celine!" cried Remi. She rushed to embrace her daughter, then held her at arm's length to look her over. "I'm *so* angry with you, Celine, for leaving without my permission. Or even telling me where you were going and why. But because I'm so happy to see you, I will save my anger for later. I'm just happy you're all right." She glanced at Jager and smiled. "That you're both all right." Jager returned her smile.

"Mom, it's great to see you. And you too, Major."

"Good to see you too, Cadet. And you, Ensign," said Dino, wrapping his "nephew" in his bionic arms. Then, wanting to avoid any difficulties Remi might bring up, he went quickly on: "How did things go on Nibiru?"

"Great," grinned Jager. "We have so much to tell you! But first, we have some wonderful news, which makes it necessary to get back to Zulak City immediately. I don't mean to be rude, sir, but I'll have to discuss the details with you later. We must leave at once!" The young man started for the entrance.

"Oh?" replied the officer, proud of the young man's direct, dynamic manner.

"Uh...," said Celine, seeing her mother's eyes widen at the sight of the Dragons. "Jager," said Celine, "not to be disrespectful, honey, but, uh, perhaps we should first introduce our friends."

"Oh, yeah. Sorry, Pumpkin," said Jager, moving back to stand beside her.

Celine was about to begin the introductions when, to her surprise, Remi approached Fallon and began a conversation with the young Dragon. Celine's surprise intensified upon hearing what her mother had to say.

"Greetings, Fallon. It's nice to see you again. I learned

from Major Hadgkiss that he assisted you in saving your people. I was so happy to hear that."

"Yes," replied Fallon. "Thanks to you, we were able to help my entire fold escape the Humans. You will be forever remembered in our legends for what you did to assist us." To everyone's surprise, Fallon gave Remi a formal bow — in a form normally reserved for royalty. More than one of those present suddenly had tears in their eyes, knowing the significance of the gesture.

"Wow!" said Celine. "I guess I'm not the only one in our family who's full of surprises." Everyone laughed, and Celine gave her mother a hug.

Once the introductions were complete, Jager couldn't contain his excitement any longer. "Major!" he blurted. "Take us back to the under-world. I can revive Commander Zulak! I can bring back Celine's father!"

"What!?" exclaimed both Dino and Remi. They spun around to face the young man.

"No time to explain," replied Jager. "It was in some paintings. It's so clear to me now, I don't know why I didn't see it before." He shook his head, annoyed at himself, but his self-chastisement ended when Celine gripped his hand tighter. He gripped hers back, then pulled her toward the exit, bound for the transbeam room. The rest of the Humans and their Dragon friends followed close behind.

"See you later, West," said Celine, glancing back and waving at the Mentors.

West sensed uncertainty and hesitation in Celine, and mented the girl. "It is all right, dear. There is sufficient time for you and Jager to go assist your father. Our thoughts will be with you on this momentous occasion. However, I ask that you return as soon as you are able. As you know, we need assistance with pressing matters; assistance only you and Jager can provide."

"Thank you, West," she mented back. "We'll return very soon." She gripped Jager's hand tighter as they rushed down the corridor.

Everyone was caught up in the excitement that followed, though most were unclear as to what was truly happening — Remi among them. She grew more and more excited though, and quickened her pace. Jager's words echoed in her mind; revive Commander Zulak! Dino understood better than she, and he didn't hesitate a bit. His bionic legs had him quickly in the lead, on the way to the transbeam room.

"Celine..." said a worried Remi, arriving at the foot of the transbeam platform. Her daughter just smiled and patted her arm.

"Please, Mom," she said. "You go ahead to the ship with the major. I'll join you on board shortly. I need to talk to my friends before I go." Remi frowned, but obliged. Celine turned to Fianna and the others.

"We'll be back soon, Fianna. I know this is rude, considering Alika is still missing, but West can help you. I promise I'll be back as soon as I can."

"It is fine, Little One," replied Fianna. "What you and Jager are about to do is most important. Yes, it is important to find our Alika too, but we Dragons also need to put attention elsewhere, and have pressing matters to discuss. So, you see, no time will be lost if you are away for a short while. Besides, you have done so much for me and for my people that I am sure the others, including Alika, will understand. I feel most certain that we will have our little friend back with us soon."

"Thanks," said Celine, and she kissed her friend's snout. "I love you with all my heart."

"I love you deeply too, my friend," replied Fianna. "My life is forever complete, with you in it."

Celine gave Fianna's neck a quick squeeze and departed for the transbeam room, tears of love gracing her cheeks. North transbeamed her up to join Jager, Dino and her mother, who waited in orbit aboard the tiny *Spitfire*.

Short minutes later, the ship jumped them safely to Remini. Jager was out of his flight couch and on his way to the ship's small transbeam platform before the others had even released their restraints. He suddenly realized he was being disrespectful, though, and stopped to wait until the others could join him.

"Thanks, Jager," said Dino with a smile. One by one they transbeamed down to the planet, to find themselves looking out over the beautiful fields surrounding Zulak City.

"All righty," said the major. "Let's first have a little meeting in that big tent over there, so Jager can brief all of us on exactly what he's got planned. I'm particularly interested in hearing more about this idea of 'bringing Rafael back.' Does that mean what I think it does, Jager?"

Jager nodded. "I'll explain, don't worry!" The group headed for the tent and soon gathered inside the spacious shelter.

"So, yes, Dino!" said Jager, responding to his "uncle's" question. He addressed the whole group. "I've done this before. I might have thought of it weeks ago, but I only just recently learned that Commander Zulak's body has been in a stasis tube since minutes after he passed."

"Oh my!" gasped Remi, trembling. She steadied herself

against a bench. "We need to get Mia."

Celine ran off to find Mia. Dino pressed his comm pickup to call his senior officers to join them. A short while later Celine arrived back with a very white-faced Mia. Hyatt supported the young woman, his arms wrapped tightly around her. A large gathering of base personnel now stood with Jager and the others. Somehow, they had sensed something of great importance was about to occur here, and had come to learn more.

"Okay, everyone," said Hadgkiss. The tent grew instantly silent. "Jager here, unknown to most of you, is a skilled sorcerer." Dino winked at Jager, then looked back to the crowd. "I'll cut to the chase. He has a skill that he's used successfully in the past to bring recently deceased people back to life."

Numerous gasps could be heard, the loudest from Mia. "What?" she barked. She swung around to glare at her sister. "Why are you playing such a wicked joke on us? Is this your doing, Celine? I should have known you hadn't changed. You've been nothing but trouble since you were brought to our home years ago. Always trying to be the center of attention." She turned to stomp out of the tent, but stopped abruptly at a shout from Major Hadgkiss.

"*Cadet Zulak!* About-face!"

She stopped, then slowly turned around, eyes staring at her feet.

"Now that I have your attention, Mia," said Hadgkiss sternly, "I won't ask you to apologize for your outburst. I know you've been through difficult times recently. Also, I know you are not feeling well at the moment. However, I do ask you to grant Ensign Jager here the courtesy of listening to what he has to say."

Mia gave a sheepish nod, then glared at Celine again before slinking back to stand beside Hyatt.

"Thank you," said the major, now in a normal tone.

Jager thanked Dino, then explained that the effects of the stasis unit would preserve Commander Rafael's body, making it possible to do what he proposed. The young man went into greater detail about what he would do. Excitement in the tent grew, but Remi remained silent, scowling. Before she could voice her concerns, though, she was caught in the press of bodies heading out of the tent and on down the valley towards a secluded field. A lone chamber stood at its center, in the shade of a large canopy oak.

The chamber had been specifically built to hold the stasis tube housing the body of Commander Rafael Ramon Zulak, killed by the scoundrel Soader during the commander's attempted rescue of his younger daughter, Celine.

"I don't know what to say, Jager," said Dino. "This is incredible. If you can really do this, I...wow! What fantastic news. Well, let's get this done!" He laughed, eager to see his best friend alive again. He'd missed the man more than he thought possible. He'd thought the death of his own wife and young son had numbed him to the subject of death and all it entailed, but he'd been wrong. He smiled in anticipation of Rafael's return.

More cheers and grins erupted; it was the happiest many of them had been in weeks.

Soon others, caught up in the excitement, joined the procession toward the chamber. Dino turned to Jager and slapped him heartily on the back, forgetting for the moment the power of his bionics. "You never cease to amaze me, young man." The slap made Jager stumble, but he quickly regained his balance and followed his "uncle" towards the small tomb.

The two men, however, began to walk slower and slower until they tailed the large crowd. Each slowed his pace for a different reason. By the time they reached the shiny walls of the chamber, the crowd was spread around the clearing, waiting eagerly for their arrival. Celine rushed towards Jager, with Remi and Mia close behind — their blond heads in sharp contrast with Celine's chestnut tresses.

"I don't understand what is going on, Dino," grumbled Remi, hands to her hips. "I'm not taking another step until someone tells me exactly what is happening."

"It will be all right, Remi," soothed Dino, giving her arm a gentle squeeze.

"Don't patronize me, Dino," she barked, pulling away. "I'm not a child. Nothing is making sense to me. People cannot be *raised* from the dead. Dead is dead! That's what it is. *Dead!!* What the hells is going on?"

Dino turned to Jager, who stood quietly a few meters away, nodding to indicate the young man should respond. Jager returned the nod, then waited until Remi had calmed a bit.

"Ma...ma'am," stuttered Jager, unsure of what to say at such a moment. "I...I know what you have heard is hard to believe, but it is true. I have perfected a special skill and technique for reviving people who have very recently departed their bodies. Mind you, the person cannot have been dead for a long period. Normally just minutes. But that essentially is the case with your husband. His body was placed in a stasis tube moments after his death." Jager paused and looked toward the major, who nodded for him to continue.

"Yes, I know that," growled Remi, adding a snort of disapproval.

"Yes, yes, of course you do. My apologies," Jager replied, chastising himself in silence for saying such a stupid thing. "Sorry. I should explain further. Ma'am, what this means is — ahhh… Let's see. What's the best way to explain this?" He remained silent for several long seconds, thinking.

"Ma'am," he continued. "Your husband's body has been in, well, a different time dimension, for want of a better choice of words. Which means his body has not yet begun to deteriorate. Thus, if I can locate him in the spirit world, I can almost surely bring him back to his body."

Remi glared at the young man, but now with less intensity. She sighed and swallowed a couple of times; her tears continued to fall. She gestured for him to continue.

"I have done this successfully before, Mrs. Zulak. More than once," said Jager, in barely more than a whisper. "If I can find Commander Zulak's spirit, I can bring him here. Then, together, he and I will revive his body. He will be back with us, in life."

Remi crumpled; Dino rushed forward to catch her before she hit the ground.

CHAPTER 19

Happiness

J ager quickly knelt to assist Dino with Remi. He flicked his
incant-baton, chanted a few words, and the woman slowly
opened her eyes. Dino assisted her to sit up. Her cheeks were
soon wet with tears again. Unable to speak, she grabbed
Jager and hugged the young man hard. He returned the embrace, understanding her silence.

"Ma'am, is it all right with you if I do what I've proposed?"
he asked softly. Remi gave two small nods.

Dino helped Remi stand and guided her to the side of the
stasis unit, within the memorial chamber. Jager entered the
chamber with Celine at his side. A reluctant Mia followed,
still supported by Hyatt.

Celine could not stop grinning as she helped Jager prepare. She smiled at her mother, who now stood beside the
stasis unit, one trembling hand atop its transparent cover.
Remi spoke silently to her Rafael; when she had no more to

say, she lifted her head, nodded to Jager and stepped away from the unit to join Mia, who was now quiet and seemingly calm. Still, Remi's tears continued.

Celine hugged Jager, then turned to look upon her father's body, at rest in the stasis unit. How peaceful he looked — as though he was just taking one of his infamous afternoon naps on their sofa back home. She said a silent prayer, though she didn't believe in a deity. It just seemed like the right thing to do in this moment. Tears welled, but she brought them quickly under control.

Mia stepped up to one end of the stasis unit, but remained silent and looked away whenever she noticed Celine glancing her way. Celine finally caught her eye, smiled, and gestured for her to come join her, sitting beside their mother. Mia hesitated at first, but followed Celine to the seats that had been set up for them.

Minute by minute the crowd outside the chamber grew. Dino scanned the faces and motioned for certain senior officers to come forward and enter. He asked that they stand along the back, behind the now-seated Zulaks. It was a small chamber, but some of the crowd outside couldn't contain their excitement and tried to make their way in. As more arrived, they pushed themselves into a large cluster, until Dino asked for everyone but family to leave, excepting only the handful of senior officers he'd named, Madda and Doc Deggers included.

He gestured for those who remained to form a circle around the stasis tube so each in turn could give Rafael one last look and word of love. Respectfully, everyone stepped away to sit in chairs now arranged a couple of meters back from the tube, or to stand behind the chairs.

Jager was the only one left beside the tube. He winked

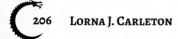

at Celine and then stood calmly beside Rafael, closed his eyes and began to chant in a muffled voice. This seemed to calm and reassure those watching. Soon his chanting was the only sound in the chamber, growing loud enough to drown out the noise from the excited crowd outside. After a minute, Jager swirled his incant-baton in a slow motion, up and down and over the stasis unit in a continuous wave. After a few passes he stopped, opened his eyes and looked at Dino with a look of embarrassment.

"Major!" he said, urgently. "I need your help." Dino gently separated his hand from Remi's vice-like grip and made his way to Jager.

"Sir," whispered the young man, "there's a problem. I cannot find him! I need to leave Remini to search — not physically, but mentally and spiritually. But the protective barrier around the bunker is blocking me. I'm sorry I didn't think of this earlier, but I cannot continue unless I am able to search off world for Commander Zulak."

"Oh, this *is* a problem," replied Dino, wide-eyed. "I don't want to let the barrier down while you and Celine are here, but if this is going to work, I guess it's the only way." The Major reached for his lapel pickup as he hurried from the tent. "Ensign Peggers," he called.

"Aye, aye, sir."

"I know this will not make sense, but I need you to lower the shield. Use the recorder the Mentors gave me, as I've shown you."

"Uh, right away, sir." Peggers ran across the compound to the control room to carry out his task. The crowd inside the chamber grew restless. Shortly, the major's comm pickup spoke: "Major, the shield has been lowered, sir."

"Good," replied Dino. "The moment you hear back from me, raise it at once. But if you deem it necessary for any reason, you may raise it without orders."

"Aye, sir."

Dino re-entered the chamber and gave Jager a thumbs up.

Jager grinned, pleased that the major had remembered the Earther gesture he'd taught him. He winked at Celine again, and blew her a kiss. Her heart swelled with love for him.

The ensign made himself comfortable and resumed the incantation. Within moments, a thin layer of mist began to swirl about his feet and the legs of the platform that bore the stasis unit. It continued to thicken, hanging like a thick, early spring morning fog. The more he chanted, the thicker the mist grew. Remi gasped at the sight. Then, except for Jager's soft voice, the room was silent. Soon he and the tube were no longer visible; only the fog could be seen. His quiet words from within the fog were the only indication he'd ever been there.

The entire room remained quiet, except for a stray cough — a chilling background for Jager's soft words. The watchers sat rigid, as though Jager's words had forced them to do so. They remained utterly still, even when his voice tone changed to an intense eeriness, floating out from within the covering fog.

Gradually his voice faded, and the mist began to dissipate — though the platform and stasis tube were still completely obscured. Then, there was a barely perceptible disturbance in the circle of fog, just in front of where Remi, Mia, Celine and Dino sat watching. They rose from their seats, not sure what was occurring or what to expect.

A piercing scream shattered the silence. Remi.

She screamed again, followed by the same shrill sound from Mia. They both clapped their hands to their faces, gasped, and screamed again. Celine, however, laughed. As did Dino, Madda and Doc Eggers. For out of the fog stepped a tall form: Rafael, as if he were simply returning from a morning stroll.

After a moment of frozen shock, Dino slapped at his comm pickup and called Peggers to raise the shield.

At first, Remi too was paralyzed with wonder, but then rushed into Rafael's arms and burst into tears. Mia was soon at his side too. He was as surprised to see everyone as they were to see him. He wasn't quite sure what all the fuss was about, but he welcomed any happiness.

Celine stood to the side while her father comforted her mother and sister. She moved toward Jager, who was clearly drained, both physically and spiritually. He sat cross-legged on the floor, leaning against a leg of the platform that held the empty stasis unit. The two hugged and kissed, then Celine rested her head on his shoulder, and together they watched the incredible reunion before them.

Remi found it hard to release her grip on her husband. She clung fast, afraid that if she let go, he would disappear. With wet cheeks and much reluctance, she dropped her arms to release Rafael as Celine and Jager approached. Slowly, half-heartedly, she stepped back to give her husband room to hug Mia, then Celine. He hugged Celine especially long and hard; the last thing he could remember was that she had been missing, and all his efforts to find her had been frustratingly fruitless. When he was finished greeting his daughters, he took Remi in his arms once more.

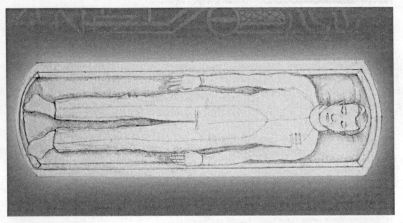

Turning to examine his surroundings, Rafael noticed the stasis tube, and guessed why everyone was staring at him, awestruck, as if they'd seen a ghost. For a moment, he was awestruck himself. He hadn't seen a ghost, though. He'd realized he *was* the ghost! The painful memory of what had happened on Scobee slammed into his consciousness. Scobee...and Soader! Soader and his goons had *shot* him. Shot him dead? he wondered. No, that was impossible, because here he was. Alive. At least he seemed to be! He could recall nothing else, though. Memory simply ended with the blast-rifle shots. Then it resumed just moments ago, in that cloud.

"Was I in a coma?" he asked Remi. She leaned in and answered quietly.

He stood back from her and scanned the crowd around him "Really? This is no joke?" he asked loudly. Remi leaned in again and spoke softly.

"What?" he asked, incredulous. "No! But...really?! How? Who?"

Remi pointed at Jager. The entire room grew silent. Rafael motioned for Jager to approach. The young man stepped forward, grinning widely. Celine came with him, her hand still gripped in his. When the boy came within reach, Rafael grabbed him, pulled him in, and gave him an enormous bear-hug. Then he hugged Celine just as hard.

Later, when everyone in the chamber had had a chance to personally welcome the commander, Doc Deggers ordered Rafael to Medical, insisting he have a clean bill of health before any further merrymaking.

Remi remained at Rafael's side for the visit to the nearby medical facility, and during his examination. The walk to the medical tent was another moment that Rafael would never forget. After he stepped out of the memorial chamber, the cheering crowd quieted down and formed a reception line all along the route, standing at attention and saluting until he, Remi and the others reached their destination.

To Doc's amazement, the commander was in perfect health. More surprisingly, in better health than before his deadly encounter with Soader. And so the doctor released his patient.

The crowd outside had departed, to gather in one of the compound's larger mess halls to wait for him. Rafael felt he should go to them; Remi agreed, but suggested he change into fresh clothes first. He had to agree, since the uniform he wore was badly blood stained, burnt and torn.

Before long, the happy couple rejoined the loud and boisterous crowd. Rafael was particularly thirsty and famished, eager for some of whatever it was that smelled so damn good. The mess staff were quick to oblige him, and he dug heartily into the large tray of food they brought — and the several different types of beverages they'd lined up round his plate. There were fresh Dortes, too, for his dessert.

Although happy to celebrate his return, Rafael also silently celebrated something different. He thanked the Ancients that Celine was home, for in his reality, he'd never died. It was his daughter who had been gone.

Later, however, Rafael found yet another cause for celebration. He jumped and cheered and slapped Jager heartily on the back when he learned that the young man had removed Soader from his Rept-hybrid body and sent him to RPF113, where the vile creature would spend the rest of his existence.

"Jager, I can never repay you for all you have done for me and my family."

"Sir," replied Jager, grinning widely, "there's no need to even think about any sort of repayment. Besides, it appears episodes like this are just everyday events when one is close to your younger daughter. So I figure it's all good practice for what the future holds."

Everyone laughed, none harder than Rafael, for he surely knew what Jager meant.

The mess hall now overflowed with enthusiastic celebrants. More tables were set up outside, and these rapidly filled as well. The rejoicing was especially exuberant since most had been through many hardships in recent times, and needed little excuse to revel in happy moments. And seeing as Rafael had literally returned from the dead, the partying continued for days. Many had never seen anything even remotely like such a miracle, for magic had been banned in the Pleiades years before. Banned by High Chancellor Scabbage, who feared his own ineptitude in the ways of magic.

Thus, Jager's skills were magical indeed.

The only thing to dampen the festivities occurred when Rafael learned that several of his crew had been injured while trying to rescue him, back on Scobee. At first, he thought he might be able to walk that news off, but when he heard Sreach had died in the assault, he had to take a moment off by himself. He took the tragedy personally, adding her death to the mental list of personal failures he used for self-punishment. If he'd only followed protocol and listened to Major Hadgkiss, he never would have gone down to the planet's surface, and neither would Sreach. She would still be alive. Rafael would berate himself every night for the rest of his life, for causing her death through his stupidity and selfishness.

Noticing the troubled look on the commander's face, Dino dragged his friend back to the party and got him chatting about silly things. In next to no time, Rafael was again laughing and joking with others, often with one arm around his wife and another around one of his daughters.

Later, he sat with Remi close by his side as they listened to Mia describe the lavish wedding she wanted. He grinned non-stop when she told him the news that he was to be a grandfather, and hugged her tight. Seeing that her father was so happy about the coming birth, Mia began feeling more amenable to the idea of her own motherhood. She even came up with a couple of names she liked: Kai for a boy, and Rita for a girl. Everyone loved the names, Hyatt included.

Jager, exhausted after performing the Lazarus spell, excused himself to go take a nap, leaving Celine with her parents. She couldn't remember a better time spent with her family. Jager rejoined the festivities at dinnertime, making it an evening of memories Celine would always hold dear. She sat back, glowing with pride as her father, Dino and Jager chatted together. But she sat up and leaned in when they began to discuss what Jager had learned about universal jump-shifting.

"It's absolutely amazing!" explained Jager. "When inside Soader's mind, all his knowledge 'downloaded' into my own memory. It's incredible, really, and most fortunate; all his memories are now mine. All of them!" He looked at Rafael and nodded in respect, knowing the commander must be thinking of the memories that included himself. Images that most likely tormented the senior officer.

"Yes, there are some I wish I didn't have or don't need," Jager continued, nodding again to Rafael to reaffirm his understanding of what the commander was thinking and feeling. "But I will soon figure out how to get rid of those. Others are right there for me to grab whenever I desire." Jager pointed to his head and laughed as he stood up. "I'm smarter than I think. Ha!"

"Well, that itself is quite a feat, I'd say!" laughed Dino. Jager, Rafael and others laughed along.

Celine sat back again, to watch in silence as the happy crowd celebrated. How she wished life would forever be as it was at this moment. And that the war were over, so she could go back to just being the daughter of Rafael and Remi Zulak. And Mia's annoying sister. She chuckled, thinking of the years of fun she'd had, pestering the obnoxious Mia. However, when her eyes rested on Jager, she ended her daydreaming with a deep sigh, knowing that come morning, reality would return.

Celine sighed again and reminded herself that facing reality was for the best. Especially because of what would soon be asked of her and of Jager. Her self-assurance didn't lift her spirits much; she sighed some more. Jager looked her way and smiled. He understood; he felt the same apprehensions intensifying, despite his celebrating.

"Let's live in the moment, Pumpkin, shall we?" he mented.

"Okay, let's," replied Celine, and she moved to stand near her parents.

Throughout the evening, Remi never left Rafael's side. Their arms often interlinked. Celine smiled, never having seen her mother happier, or her parents happier as a couple. She desperately hoped it was a sign of the future to come, for more than just her family's inner relationships.

She heard Jager's mental voice. "I feel the same, sweetie,"

he said. "I wish life could always be like this. Come, let's continue to enjoy tonight for what it is, and forget about everything happening outside this place. We deserve that. You especially, for all you've been through the past couple of years."

"You are right — as always," giggled Celine. He swooped in and dragged her up to dance.

The hours rolled by, and at last it was time to call it a night. Most were reluctant to, truly grateful for the miracle they'd experienced together. All knew that a few more such miracles were desperately needed if they were to win the war. As good-nights were said, Rafael gave Jager another bear hug. Just as though he were already family. Remi hugged the boy tight too, and kissed him hard on his reddening cheek. Then the couple walked to their cabin, arms around each other.

"Major Hadgkiss," said Celine, happily watching her parents head away, "Jager and I need to speak with you before you turn in."

After Dino had watched everyone else head to their sleeping quarters, he sat before Celine and Jager on the opposite side of a cluttered picnic table. "I know what you are going to ask, and yes, I'll take you back to the Mentors' outpost first thing in the morning."

"Thanks, Dino," smiled Celine. "Jager and I figure you can fill my father in on events and keep him and my mother calm when they discover I've left again. I hate to leave you to deal with them, especially my father, but I don't see any other way. Jager and I still have lots that we must do to prepare for coming events. Besides, I think my father has changed."

"Yes, my dear," replied Dino, "your father has indeed changed. He appears more in control of his emotions and more willing to let the universe do what it must. I don't think you'll have his usual pushback. Actually, I think you might be surprised at him, for I believe he'll be doing the opposite."

"Thanks, Dino," said Celine. "I needed to hear that."

"Also, you two," said the Major, "I should congratulate you again on your successful trip to Nibiru. That was quite the feat, to my understanding of what had to occur to get the protective shielding up. West mentioned that we need to keep the Dragons safe, so it appears you've made an incredible stride toward doing that. And on your own, without the need of a great force like Fleet. I'm so proud of the both of you."

"You're the best godfather I could ever have hoped for," smiled Celine. She came around the table to hug him. "Now, Major, as you are probably aware, we will need to leave before everyone else wakes up. It's important we get back to help Fianna and the others search for little Alika. He recently went missing, and we must help to find him if he hasn't yet been located."

"I knew you would be asking this of me," replied Dino. "I'll get filled in on what's needed once we're at the Mentor outpost. Then I'll come back here and explain things to your parents."

The pair smiled and followed Dino to their cabins. They both slept soundly until the major woke them, just before dawn. An hour later they sat in West's office discussing the search for Alika, and some additional steps required to ensure Fianna and the other Dragons would be safe in the coming weeks and years.

CHAPTER 20

Nibiru

B ack on Nibiru, after another long day of waiting with no sign of Fallon or the others, King Quade huffed and snorted, then stomped from the courtyard before taking flight.

He was not the only one feeling anxious and annoyed.

Dragons from both folds regularly visited the Cynth Pedestal. Including the Nibiru king, minus his queen. She was once again ill and distraught beyond words that her children had not yet returned or sent word that they were still safe at the Mentor outpost.

A few minutes after Quade left, King Neal followed, his frustration also plain to see. He had the same burning question in mind: Why does the vortex remain closed? It had been days since the purple comm stone had arrived.

"I cannot take much more of this waiting," groaned

Quade. Neal had caught up to him and they now sat on an outcrop overlooking the neighboring valley. "I think it is time we went looking for our loved ones."

"I must admit," said Neal, "that is a thought I have mulled over. But we should only embark upon such an undertaking after taking counsel with our inner circles."

"Ah, more wise words," said Quade. "Your great nation is fortunate to have you as its king. I am sorry for being selfish, unwise and emotional. You are correct. Perhaps tomorrow, just after the morning meal, we could proceed with a meeting with both the Remini and Nibiru councils."

"Now you are the one who speaks wisely," smiled Neal. "That is an event I can arrange."

Some of his frustrations alleviated, Quade bid Neal good-bye and soared off after others of his fold, whom he had seen heading down the valley to the new homes the Nibiru Dragons had so generously provided.

Neal made his way to Orgon and Tamar's cave-home. Orgon greeted him, and the two conversed as they walked along the nearby river, the day's light waning. It was a custom they had come to love, now that Neal was back on Nibiru. Orgon teased that their walks were typical of Dragons such as they, late in their lives. Neal laughingly agreed. Their discussion, however, touched on more serious topics.

"Yes, dear brother," said Orgon. "I concur. Once again, we must visit the cave paintings of our people. I recently did just that, but the images could have changed in the past few days. It should be clear, from what we shall see, whether we are meant to seek out your children. The prophecies of eons past are being revealed here in our time, and we must adhere closely to all that is presented upon our mountains' walls. That is what is expected of us. Come, let us do so now, so that we may be well prepared for the council gathering on the morrow."

"Wise words." Neal drew up to follow Orgon, and the great Dragons traveled down the light-orb-lined walls of Vin's kilometers-long cave-home to where they hoped to find guidance on how to move forward. As they walked, they resumed their earlier conversation.

"Seeing these paintings again," said Neal, "I cannot help but think that you and I will be creating a new cavern of depictions, to tell future generations all that has transpired in our lifetimes — despite having followed our prophecies."

"And why is that?"

"I am aware of no painting that foretold the capture of Dini and me, or our decades-long captivity on Earth. Or that our son and Vin would be held captive there, too. We still have so much to learn about the ways and magic of the great spirits of the universe."

"Yes. I too have been considering such things," said Orgon as they ambled along. "I did not foresee many of the new images that have appeared over the years, and still understand very little of all this. Still, more than just small fragments of the prophecies have indeed come to pass."

"Yes, you are correct," voiced Neal.

Orgon suddenly stopped to peer upwards. "This is interesting," he said. "I looked at these very walls just days ago. Now new paintings have come forward. We will need to study them, once we have found and considered the specific painting we now seek."

The two walked on in silence, stopping roughly 950 meters from the tunnel's mouth — just steps from where Celine and

Jager had discovered significant paintings days earlier.

"There," shouted Orgon. "Up there, near the ceiling. Do you see it?"

"Yes, brother, yes, I see it, but I do not believe my eyes."

"Nor do I. Nor do I."

"What can this mean?" asked Neal. "It does not make sense. Yet it must, as our paintings never depict an untruth."

"I can only guess at its meaning. Perhaps if we travel a bit farther into the cave, other images may help us understand what we see here. Come."

Neal followed until they stood before the paintings Orgon sought.

"There," said Orgon, "up near the ceiling and all the way across." Orgon's great wing spread high like an arching green wave.

The two elderly Dragons stood in silence, stretching their long necks high to catch every aspect of the colossal paintings. The images covered the entire ceiling and continued down both sides of the upper walls. The vibrant colors were spectacular, but the messages were another matter. The two tried observing from different angles and searched for nuances they had missed, hoping the message would be different from the one they'd seen just earlier. To their dismay, it was not.

"I cannot believe what we see," gasped Orgon, his head shaking side to side. "I have never seen such paintings, nor imagined such things existed. These images greatly confuse me."

"My dear brother, I am perplexed as well. But it is painted, and therefore it must be true. And what it tells us to do must be done. I do not think we can wait until the morning to tell the others."

"Agreed," replied Orgon, still shaking his head. "And, hopefully, someone among our wise council, or that of the Reminis, will have a logical explanation for all we now see."

"Indeed. Come, let us call a gathering. Whether or not we follow what has been shown us here, we still must send word to Fianna and the others. Lack of this knowledge might cause their deaths."

"My exact thoughts," replied Orgon. "We must send them one of the comm stones Fianna sent us. Tonight."

Orgon sighed, feeling older than he ever had. He straightened his tired body and followed Neal back up the tunnel. Once at the entrance, he mented Tamar. A short while later, Neal and Orgon touched down at Dragon Hall, where the noble councils of both folds had gathered. The council members were surprised to see the elder Dragons looking so confused and concerned. The feeling of foreboding was nearly overwhelming.

The brothers briefed the council on what they had learned. Hours of deliberation followed. Occasional breaks were called, so the attendees could rest briefly and enjoy the food and drink Tamar had prepared for the occasion. But the breaks were more to rest weary minds than to satisfy bodily needs.

At midnight, and at the direction of the councils, a comm stone was sent through the vortex to Ahimoth and Fianna. All agreed, however, that they could not wait for a response before taking action. The two days that followed were filled with a bustle of activity. Even the youngest fledglings were put to work, anywhere they could be of help. Soon many glistening suits of Dragon-armor were arrayed around the perimeter of Dragon Hall's ceremonial plaza.

As midnight drew near, two nights after the comm stone had been sent, the Dragons — Nibiru and Remini folds alike — filled the hall before the Cynth Pedestal, shoulder to shoulder, their kings Neal and Quade at the fore. Neal looked out over the large crowd; his heart swelled with immense pride to see so many of both folds ready to do battle, together, though they were from different worlds. The universe was full of surprises, and he hoped the prophecies would ring true in the outcome the newest paintings portrayed.

The crowd, about to begin the vortex-opening ceremony, stopped abruptly. The vortex was already opening. Someone was coming through!

"Perhaps it is our precious Fianna and Ahimoth," exclaimed an eager Queen Dini. She sat close by, feeling much better now that her husband and others were to search for her children.

The crowd gasped when a luminescent, yellow-hued object popped through the vortex and bounded across the hall — just as a case containing a comm stone had done not long before. And, just as he did at that earlier time, King Neal approached the object and sniffed it carefully. Ahimoth! Once again, the king detected his son's unmistakable scent. He raised a wing to silence the crowd.

The king picked up the case, took it to the Cynth Pedestal, opened it, extracted the crystal it contained — a purple stone, warm to the touch — and carefully set it on the pedestal's polished surface. The stone linked at once with the pedestal's vibrational energies, and Ahimoth's clear baritone voice rang out loud and strong.

"Father, Mother, people of Nibiru, and people of Remini: please do not fear. It is I, Shakoor Ahimoth Uwatti, Prince of Nibiru. My sister, Fianna, and my fellow travelers, are still safe and well, as am I. We shall return home to you all soon; very soon, so please do not attempt to follow. We are not lost, in serious peril, or in need of rescue. Again, please do not follow us, even though the ancient paintings seem to indicate that you must.

"In fact, dear friends, what is needed at this time is that you *not* follow what the images appear to direct, but instead to listen to my words. I realize that what I ask goes against our peoples' most revered traditions, but I must implore you to follow what I say. There are powerful forces at work in our universe. Not all of them look kindly upon us — some even seek our destruction. Such forces have infiltrated *false* paintings into our treasured archives, with wicked intent.

"So now, dear people, great warriors of Nibiru and Remini, I entreat you to remain safe on Nibiru, to protect our treasured young and yourselves as well. I, Fianna, and the others shall return to you soon, ready to proceed with the glorious weddings you have planned for us, and to live out our lives in love and harmony.

"We love you all dearly and miss you deeply. We will see you soon."

The stone went as silent as the crowd.

CHAPTER 21

Redemption

"Celine!" shouted Fianna to her Companion, who stood on the transbeam platform with Jager and Dino.

As one, the pair let out immense sighs — then looked at each other and laughed aloud. More and more, they felt and thought as though they were a single person. They hugged happily, then trotted down the ramp. As would be expected, being deprived of their links with Fianna and Vin during their travels had drained them, both mentally and spiritually. But the stress of separation had also caused them physical aches and pains. This was a problem they tacitly agreed to push as far back in their minds as possible, because the only apparent solution was not something they could face at the present moment.

Their greetings complete, the group made their way to West's office, where she and her sisters had their heads together over a couple of consoles. Before anyone could even say hello, West's silken voice rang out, her graceful form seeming to glow from within. "I have great news, everyone! We have located Alika! He is safe and uninjured. We'll trans-beam him back here very soon, but first we would like him to assist us with something, if that is all right with you."

"Fantastic!" trumpeted Ahimoth, following with several loud hoorahs.

"Oh, what wonderful news!" cheered Fianna. Celine gave the Dragon's neck a quick hug.

"Great news, indeed," said the girl. "Again, I am sorry that Jager and I had to leave as we did, but I am thankful that Alika is now found."

"Yes, indeed," said Ahimoth. "And yes, if the youngster is willing to be of assistance to you, West, I think it would make a fine start to the amends he should make for causing such trouble and worry."

"All right," said the Mentor, "My communication with him shall be open to you all, so that everyone may hear our dis-cussion with the wayward little traveler."

IT HAD BEEN TWO DAYS since Alika had last seen Prince Ahimoth and the rest of his friends. He folded his wings tight round himself and stared at the walls, his eyes wet with recent tears. All his efforts to learn anything of his where-abouts had revealed nothing. And he had no idea how he had ended up wherever this was. All the young Dragon could think about was how angry Prince Ahimoth would be that he had disobeyed, and strayed from the noble Dragon's side.

The youngster plopped down on the stony floor and began again to cry. He did not know how his friends would ever find him. Exhausted from all his worry, sadness and efforts to learn more, and terribly thirsty too, Alika made himself as comfortable as possible and fell into a restless slumber.

Hours later, something woke him. Having forgotten his circumstances for the moment and eager for a nice walk, he stood and started forward. And then his enthusiasm deflated in a gush. He remembered he was still in his fusty prison. There would be no nice walk. The heaviness he'd experienced earlier returned and he hunkered down on the floor once more.

A few moments later, to his dismayed surprise, he sensed a presence close by. Frightened, he held his breath, afraid to move or even breathe. When nothing happened, he told himself to act as Ahimoth would, and grew calm. Almost at once, the baby felt a soothing comfort envelop him. He smiled, proud of his smart choice and successful effort. And then he heard a gentle voice inside his mind, whispering his name in a sing-song fashion.

"I am here!" Alika shouted, leaping up again and dancing about. His golden wings flapped so hard he was lifted off the ground, more than once. "I am here!"

"Ah, that you are, my little one," said the kind, soothing voice. "It is going to be all right, Alika. You do not need to shout; in fact, you can just think a thought and I will hear it. Do you understand?"

"Yes, yes," said Alika. "Oh, it is so good to hear someone. I have been so afraid. I do not know where I am or how I got here. I am stuck in a dark, cold place and I am all alone. I miss my friends terribly."

"Yes, I know, my dear," said the mental voice. "That is why I have come to help you get back to Prince Ahimoth and the others. But you must work with me, so I can make this happen."

"Yes! Yes! I will do whatever you ask," said the fledgling. "I will not be so hot-headed as to think I know everything. I will follow all orders given to me, especially those from Prince Ahimoth."

Back in West's Mentor outpost office, where everyone had gathered to hear the Mentor's conversation with Alika, all glanced at the smiling Ahimoth. It was the first smile they'd seen from him since the baby had disappeared.

"That's the smart little Dragon," said West. "You will make a great leader someday. Now, let's get you out of the mess you are in."

"Oh! Please!"

"First," said the Mentor, "I am going to break the spell that surrounds your location. You must hold your wings very tight about you, and cover yourself as best you can — especially your head. You must also crouch down and face towards a wall. All right?"

The little Dragon hunkered down, faced the closest wall and folded his golden wings, stretching them taut around himself. "Okay, I am now covered as you asked."

"Good. You can chant along with me if you like." Alika recognized some of the words, so he repeated the ones he knew over and over, along with the Mentor's voice. As the chanting went on, he learned more and more of the words until he was able to intone it in its entirety. Suddenly, a massive crackling erupted around him. The young Dragon perceived an almost painfully brilliant flash, even though his eyes were closed and his wings covered his head.

"Eiiiiieeee!!!!" he screamed, holding himself tighter. The sound and bright light, however, disappeared just as quickly

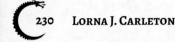

as they had appeared.

"It is all right, my dear," soothed the voice. "I am still with you. It is now safe to uncover yourself, so slowly open your eyes and look around. Please tell me what you see."

Bit by bit, Alika unfurled his trembling wings. Once his eyes adjusted, a gasp escaped his lips. He was not in a small cave, as he had assumed, but in an alcove off a huge cavern that appeared to go on forever. Numerous light-orbs lined the walls farther than he could see. And all around him the walls shone bright with light reflecting off the most incredible luminescent paintings he had ever seen.

"I am in the most beautiful place," gushed the young Dragon. "Although I will admit I have seen few cave-homes in my short life, this one is the most amazing. There are paintings on the walls and ceiling, like the tunnel in Pagan Mountain, but...but they are even more magnificent."

"Ah, good," said the voice. "Now there is something else that I need you to do."

"All right," said the eager youngster. "Whatever you need, I am glad to help."

"Thank you, Alika," replied the voice. "My name is West. I am a friend of Celine and Prince Ahimoth and the others; the one who rescued you when the tube-chute broke. Do you remember?"

"Yes, yes," Alika replied. He wiggled in anticipation, as most young creatures and children do when keen to please.

"Good," said West. "Here is what I would like you to do next. But first I must know if you trust me. Do you trust me, Alika?"

"Oh, yes," replied the baby, still wiggling from head to tail tip.

"Good. Good. You are being very brave. Ahimoth and your friends will be so proud of you. What you are about to do will help them, and everyone on Nibiru."

"Oh, that is wonderful," exclaimed the fledgling. "I have been such a burden! I want to do something to help. I want Prince Ahimoth to be proud of me, not always angry with me." Everyone smiled at Ahimoth again. "What do you need me to do?" asked the youngster.

"My request is a little out of the ordinary. I need for you to allow me to see through your eyes, for I would like to examine the images on the walls before you. Would this be something you would permit me to do?"

"Yes. Yes, of course! You may use my eyes. It is an honor to assist you, Celine's friend. But, oh, will it hurt?"

"No, it will not hurt, Alika. Not in the least. And thank you! It is very brave of you to agree to this. It will not take long. Is it okay to do it right now?"

"Yes. I am ready."

West performed a short spell and was soon looking at the beautiful images with Alika. They were indeed spectacular. The Mentor had Alika walk up and down the tunnels for quite some time, while she made mental records of each painting. When she had finished, she thanked the fledgling warmly for his assistance.

"Now, my brave little one," said West, "how would you like it if we got you out of that place, and brought you back to your friends?"

"Oh, yes, please do."

Everyone headed to the transbeam room, where West asked North to enter Alika's location into the transbeam console. In moments, the young Dragon stood on the platform, a look of surprise on his face. Looking about, he realized whose company he'd suddenly joined — and took a flying leap off the platform and straight into Ahimoth. The little one hugged one of the big Dragon's forelegs and cooed with pleasure at the reunion. Ahimoth folded a wing about the baby, happy to see the little guy alive, despite the troubles he had caused.

"Prince Ahimoth," cried Alika. "I am so sorry for everything. I deserve any punishment you give me, and I will not complain about it. Not one bit."

Ahimoth grunted, intending to leave it at that. But, noticing that all eyes were upon him, he thought better of it and replied. "I am glad you are back safe and sound, Alika. To my understanding it was not your fault that you disappeared, so I am not angry with you. You proved that youngsters can achieve great things. Ah, um...it must have been a scary experience."

The young golden Dragon's head bobbed, and he wiggled in excitement.

"West mentioned that the paintings you helped her see on the walls of your prison will be most beneficial in our battles to come," continued Ahimoth. "So, for that I thank you, and consider it amends for your bad behavior of the past. You are welcomed back into the group."

Everyone cheered and chatted happily, making their way to the refectory so the very hungry and thirsty Alika could get his fill. All wore large grins, happy the baby had been rescued and that he was uninjured.

After a time, Dino excused himself, saying he had urgent business to attend to. He said his goodbyes and soon met with Rafael. The two had much to discuss regarding G.O.D.

and Fleet's latest ventures and exploits. Rafael was especially eager to right some wrongs; he felt obliged to, now that his family and friends were safe.

CHAPTER 22

Key, Paper, Crystal

Two days later, Dino looked out over the *Asherah* crew
members he'd called together. Rafael sat nearby. "Okay,
now that we are all here, I'll address the many questions I
know you must have. "Yes, I am very happy to confirm that
Commander Zulak is back — as you can see right here — and
will resume command. He and I have discussed at length
how we will move forward to ensure your safety and..."

Dino tried to continue but was drowned out by a flood of
cheers, whistling and applause. He let the jollity go on for
a bit, for he knew that at the back of everyone's minds was
the realization that the future could be worse than anything
thus far. When the cheers started to die, he cleared his throat
and raised his hands; the room at once grew silent.

Rafael stood, saluted the major, then turned to salute
the crowd. Everyone rose and silently returned his salute.
The commander took his seat again, and, after a respectful

pause, the crowd sat too.

"I believe most of you trust Commander Rafael and me in any decisions as to how we are to move forward," continued the Major. "So, I will tell you this: We feel too much corruption has infiltrated Fleet and G.O.D. And so, we will continue to operate as we have over the past few weeks — without Fleet sanction."

A couple "yahoos" slipped out at the back of the crowd, followed by smothered chuckles.

"I'm glad my announcement makes some of you happy," grinned Dino. "I assume this means you agree with our new operating policy." More "yahoos" and "yups" could be heard. "Good. We will put all our support behind the Aadya Coalition in their efforts to end this war. Those of you who are with me, please remain. Those opposed, thank you for your service, but please leave. Immediate transportation will be provided for your return to Erra, with no hard feelings harbored. However, know that we will fight against you if the need should ever arise — although we will be saddened to have to do so."

With arms crossed, Dino paced the platform and surveyed the crowd. A huge smile lit his face as everyone remained seated.

"Good. I now ask you to please be silent for your commanding officer..." He didn't get to finish; the cheering drowned him out.

Rafael stood and accepted the raucous welcome. After a minute, he gently waved for silence. The happy group quieted and settled down to listen. "Thanks to you all," said the commander. "I know some of you might still think this is all a dream — I know I do, much of the time — but the reality of what is happening outside this outpost has reminded me of why I became a Fleet officer in the first place."

He paused to look some in the front rows straight in the eyes. A few fidgeted under his gaze.

"As many of you know," he continued, "as we sit here safe under our shielding, a task force of freighters with Fleet escort, including some ships commanded by Repts, is on its way to Transfer Station 428, on Earth's moon. I'm sad to say that some time ago, G.O.D. directed a harvesting station be erected there for a mass harvest of most of Earth's spiritually-oriented humans, for use in soul transfers. Many G.O.D. officials are in urgent need of new bodies, including our own sector's High Chancellor Scabbage. In the past, few Earthers were taken at any one time. But the present plan is to harvest millions upon millions, and to continue to do so for years to come.

"I know this is how some cultures choose to continue their existence, but I cannot condone such atrocities. I believe it deeply immoral. And I believe it should cease. An alternate form of perpetuating our races should be found and practiced, instead of the barbarism being deemed acceptable, on the excuse that Earthers are far behind us in terms of their technological advancement and their understanding of the universe. We are supposed to be accepting of all cultures, but when one blatantly harms another in the name of its own beliefs — reproductive, religious or otherwise — I consider it utterly wrong. I will not support such activities. And I will make it one of my life's missions to stop it, wherever it occurs.

"Ensign Jager here is from Earth, and to think that someone in G.O.D. would want to take his body from him is something I find appalling. To do what I propose, however

— excuse me, what Major Hadgkiss and I propose — requires some help. We hope some of you will be willing to assist us."

Almost the entire room stood and raised their hands, hoping to be found worthy to be among Zulak's primary flight crew.

"Thank you," came Rafael's baritone, scanning the forest of raised hands and the willing, eager, earnest faces. "You have always made me very proud to call myself your commander." He bowed to the silent assembly. "Later today, I will convene a formal meeting with my senior officers, for the purpose of setting our new objectives in motion. I ask you all to prepare yourselves and your families for our next moves. Thank you. This meeting is adjourned, though I ask senior officers to remain behind briefly for instructions."

The senior officers remained seated as everyone else filed silently out.

"Okay, team," said Rafael to his officers, "we will meet back here in an hour. Bring the names of the personnel for your teams, along with your ideas — your best ideas. We have much work to do. And quickly. Dismissed!"

Dino remained behind. He approached the commander, carrying a hot mug of teala an orderly had just handed him. He offered it to his friend. "You know, Raff, we didn't talk about it much, but if we prevent G.O.D. and the Repts from getting the Earther bodies they need, they're likely to get mighty desperate and start doing irrational and very stupid things."

"Yeah, I realize that, Dino. And I've been racking my brain, trying to figure out how we can react in a well controlled manner. As you know, I'm still annoyed at you for helping my daughter leave this outpost while I slept the other day, but I realize the universe has set certain things in motion, of which Celine is an essential element. I know I cannot control or stop such things, but on the other hand, I expect I'll be annoyed with you for some time."

"I expected it Raff."

"Okay, good. So, seeing as Celine and Jager have a part in all this, and since it appears their Dragon friends do too, we should work our own plans around their next steps. You mentioned the kids will soon head out to retrieve a weapon capable of leveling the entire TS 428 complex, yes?"

"Yes, Raff. Celine and Jager filled me in on what they have worked out with the Mentors. Today they will begin their search for the weapon, which they believe is hidden on Earth. But first they have some logistics to iron out."

"That's what I thought," replied Rafael, in an uncomfortable tone. "Earth will be a safe zone for a short time. Once Celine and Jager have retrieved whatever it is they're after, we should confer with them and with the Mentors — before they execute their plan to destroy the transfer station."

"Oh? Okay," replied the major, "but, why?"

"Because we need to make sure they only destroy the station, not the entire moon. It would be disastrous otherwise, since the moon has to be there to exert its strong gravitational pull on the planet. For one thing, it keeps the moon's own rotation speed in check. I'd bet the kids and the Mentors thought of this, but I have to check anyway, to be certain. If that moon rotates too fast or not at all, Earth's rotation will speed up and its days will grow shorter and shorter. That in turn will cause a substantial drop in the planet's surface temperature, since there will be less and less time for the sun to heat the planet's surface each day. This would have a major impact on food production, for one thing. And other catastrophes would occur as well. There would be a rapid climate change."

"Oh, good thinking," said Dino.

"Thanks," said Rafael. "Another plus is that once the transfer station is destroyed, G.O.D. and the Repts won't be capturing any more Earthers. I'm positive about that; they would have to transport any they captured to another transfer station. There are none nearby, and their transports aren't jump-shift capable. They don't have the capacity to carry a worthwhile cargo of captives plus the necessary food, water and facilities on a long voyage. So the Earthers will be safe from capture for the moment. That's good for them, but it also means the next species G.O.D. plans to harvest for transfer bodies is going to be in danger sooner."

"Good point," replied Dino. "Destroying that station is a great idea, but we'll need to be ready for whatever G.O.D. and the Repts do next. I suspect they'll pull something despicable and idiotic, once they have no access to Earther bodies. They'll be in real trouble, with so many G.O.D. and Rept people in desperate need of transfers. At this point, I don't know what to do; I hate to cause so many deaths."

"Yeah, that's a tough one," said Rafael. "But war is war, my friend. And remaining true to one's ethics and morals is the correct thing to do."

"True. And supporting that is the fact that death is a part of life. Many races have been cheating death for a long time. We're just helping life realign itself."

"Indeed."

"I guess we'll need these," said Dino, dumping the contents

of a well-worn envelope in front of Rafael.

"Really?" gasped Rafael, picking up one of the items. "You still have these? I'd forgotten about them completely. What are they for, anyway? I asked you once, but didn't get an answer. Do you even know? You never had a chance to tell me. I've racked my brain, wondering why Admiral Stock ever gave them to me."

Dino grinned. "Fortunately or not, I do know, Raff. I've already used the location noted on this slip of paper—he pointed to a folded note. That's how I found this under-world."

Dino picked up the paper with his free hand, then set it down again. He noticed Rafael's enquiring look. "All these things are from the Mentors, who gave them to Admiral Stock. And he passed them on to you. The third item here..." Dino held up and twirled the key, mulling for a moment over what to say next. "Well, I'm thinking it will soon be time to use this little item as well.

"Believe it or not, Raff, this key will be an enormous help. It unlocks a magically sealed room on Rinder."

Rafael cleared his throat and frowned at his friend.

"I know, I know, Raff. You're not much into magic and all, but it does have its place. I've found it very useful at times. I don't practice it myself, but I've witnessed Celine and Jager doing things that are frankly incredible. I'm a true believer in the power of magic, and its importance in society today. Just so you know, I believe without a doubt that we will not win this war without it. Without a doubt."

Rafael took a deep breath, then nodded. He remained pensive for several moments, then spoke. "I agree." Dino raised his eyebrows.

"Don't look so surprised, Major. I wouldn't have agreed a

year or two ago. Absolutely wouldn't have. But I've seen and heard too much recently to think like that anymore. Hells, I was just raised from the dead! So carry on, Dino. Have you already figured out our next step?"

The two men talked for hours. When they finally called it a night, Dino left for his cabin. Rafael told Remi he needed a bit of time alone, and moved out to the porch. What he didn't tell her was why he needed to be alone.

After he had said goodbye to Dino, Rafael's head had suddenly felt like it was going to burst. In a brilliant flash, all the memories that had been clouded since his revival had burst back to consciousness. He'd known at once there was no way he could possibly sleep. He lay in the porch hammock for quite some time, enjoying the gentle breeze. Trying to keep his mind and attention on good things, he watched some small animals collecting night crawlers.

He was only able to maintain his efforts a short while. He raised his hands to his forehead, hoping to ease some of the discomfort. But he knew it was useless. He lay that way for a long while, trying to think. He began to sweat.

For several hours after being brought back to life, Rafael had had almost no recollection of what had happened on Scobee, or where his mind and soul had been since that traumatic encounter. He had just gone along with everyone's assurances that everything was fine now that he was back with them, alive. He didn't want to worry anyone — especially Remi, because of all she'd endured in the intervening weeks.

The first morning after returning to consciousness, his memory had begun returning in short bursts. It was as though he'd been a sponge, immersed in one small puddle after another, soaking up a burst of memories each time. The latest memory surge had conflicted his new spiritual awareness; the resulting dissonance had created a migraine. He'd gained a lot of knowledge while bodiless, traveling the universe. However, the evil and devastation he'd encountered on the journey were almost too much for a good and well-intentioned person to confront. He knew he *must* confront them, though, so he lay still, contemplated the experience, and sought to quiet the spiritual pain and the horrible dread that came with it.

Rafael had his reasons for not mentioning what he'd experienced during his "death time." Not even to Dino or Remi. Especially not Remi, for he needed to protect her from what was sure to come. Protect her, and their daughter Mia, too. He was well aware he had no power over Celine, but he prayed to the Ancients that she would survive the next few months. He knew they would be difficult in the extreme. And that was putting it mildly.

Before Dino had left for his quarters, Rafael had told his old friend all he felt he could. He hoped that some day soon he could fill the major in on what was truly troubling him. The weight of the knowledge recently forced upon him was increasingly difficult to bear — and he knew the knowledge and the responsibilities that came with it would soon be too much to bear alone.

At last Rafael rose, stretched, descended the cabin steps and headed for the nearby tent that housed his new office. He had a lot to prepare. He entered the tent, flicked on the computer, then made himself a strong cup of teala before plopping down at the console to get to work. Soon he was immersed in new plans and calculations that not even Dino would be seeing.

CHAPTER 23

The Transfer

Scabbage groaned and gingerly touched his pounding head. His face hurt, too. Hells, he hurt all over. As the lingering smoke from the explosion gradually dissipated, he tried to lift himself off the floor, but failed — his face smacked back down on the grimy metal. With considerable effort, he finally managed to roll onto his side and screeched for his servants. Two stumbled over, righted his hover-chair and helped him into it.

Nearby, the still-unconscious Orme lay sprawled amid spatters of blood. He moaned and twitched a couple of times, then sat up and cradled his head as if it were a large Dragon's egg.

As Scabbage and Orme sat nursing their injuries, Monty slipped through the side door and perused his unwanted guests. Seeing they were not seriously hurt — in his estimation at least — he turned his attention to the heavy emergency door to the transfer facility, which had suffered some damage in the blast. Fortunately, the damage was only superficial, and the mechanism still functioned. He was able to close and quickly lock it as a secondary precaution.

"Everyone must stay here. You must keep quiet," he whispered. "There's been a malfunction. Huge malfunction. Some equipment exploded." He grumbled something unintelligible at Scabbage, then scuttled away out the side door, locking it behind him before anyone could object.

For the next few hours, Monty scurried about the complex, cleaning up minor messes caused by the blast and tending to essential daily duties. He still didn't know what the blast was all about, but it hadn't done so much damage that he couldn't proceed pretty much as usual. As he worked, he grumbled about having been kept at this damned station far too long.

A normal day for Monty meant that when the transfer station glow lights flickered, he threw a red switch that controlled a massive tower set in the middle of the compound. Activated, the tower's gigantic light shone bright: The legendary "white light" of many Human cultural death stories. Next, he switched on a UV-wavelength beam to draw dying Earthers out of their bodies and toward the light. As they arrived at the station, Monty activated a few more mechanisms, and within seconds the bodiless souls' memories were erased and they were sent back to Earth, to take up blank, soulless newborn Earther bodies.

Recently, Monty had been busier than usual, and he'd occasionally gotten careless and missed the memory-erasure step on a soul or two. This meant an Earther would remember the life it had just left. Monty hated making this mistake; it always resulted in a lengthy lecture from his boss, and more time added onto his sentence on this godsforsaken moon. When he finally made it back to his bunk on such nights, he drank himself to sleep.

Another important aspect of his job involved preventing bad souls from entering Earther bodies. For some reason, these troublesome entities predominantly entered babies of royal bloodlines, high-society families or government officials. G.O.D. was adamant that Monty prevent these dangerous beings from tainting such important bodies. Richter, his boss, had emphasized that these wicked souls would ruin G.O.D.'s harvest plans, which in turn would ruin his own plans (and others', including Monty's) for getting reassigned to another station.

For years, freighters tasked with transporting criminals and other undesirable spirits to faraway places such as RPF113 had short-cut their assignments and deposited the riffraff on Earth. It was a hell of a lot cheaper than traveling to legal dump sites halfway across the sector. The practice ended in disaster more often than not — such garbage souls had contributed greatly to many of the atrocities that had occurred throughout Earth's history.

Thus, Monty was required to keep a close watch on souls being sent through the depository tubes to new bodies, catch any undesirables that had gotten into the system, and store them in soul-containment vessels until they could be disposed of properly. It amazed him how often such frantic spirits tried to sneak into Earther bodies, but he had realized that being stuck without a body was prison itself. Regrettably, such demented spirits feverishly sought to seize any body they could. And too often, they succeeded.

Even if a wicked spirit moving through the transfer system had its memories wiped clean, it could still wreak havoc in its new lifetime as an Earther. An evil being is an evil being, memory or no memory; a fact of which many were aware.

Soader, on the other hand, had loved it when evil souls reached Earth. They contributed greatly to his devious experiments. After his capture and exile to RPF113, it was discovered he had been being paid handsomely by the freighter captains who dumped their loads of evil souls near Transfer Station 428.

Thousands of years in the past, when G.O.D. built the station on Earth's moon, they did it as part of their program to monitor the thousand or so Pleiadeans they had stranded on Planet 444 — their designation for Earth. The station ensured G.O.D would be able to guide the Pleiadean souls back to Pleiadean bodies. It was then that they had introduced the myth of the "white light of heaven" to help ensure souls would head for the transfer station after leaving their bodies in death. Sometimes, if a spirit was particularly strong, it bypassed the station, roaming free to wherever it wished and taking whatever new baby body it desired. Child prodigies are typically such free spirits, as are great soothsayers and creators.

These days, life at TS 428 was hard for Monty. But when a Human girl and some Dragons had arrived a few weeks before, he had begun looking seriously for an opportunity to escape. He thought about it constantly.

Now, with Scabbage ordering him about, he knew he *must* leave, or die trying.

Returning to the entrance to Platform 5, Monty stared unhappily at the sleeping bodies. He released the emergency door, which rattled and rumbled as it returned to its open position. The noise woke the snoring Scabbage, who began yelling at no one in particular, even before he was fully awake.

"Get that bloody Earther ready so I can transfer! *Now!*"

"Yes, yes," replied Monty, bowing obsequiously. He rushed to the transfer vat, no longer out of fear, but because he was eager to get the uninvited guests out of his life. He looked down at the Human floating peacefully in its life-support vat and began his pre-transfer check — then stopped abruptly. "Uh, sir, I..." he stuttered, "uh, the Earther...the Earther is... he's dead, sir."

"What the bloody hells?!" yelled the pale-faced Deebee, panic gripping his throat. He took several deep breaths, calming down enough to remember the idea that had been brewing at the back of his mind ever since he'd met Orme. He reviewed the notion and calmed even further. He grinned, but only to himself — a skill he'd learned years ago. No one must suspect what he was plotting, so he pretended to have a fit. When it ended, he wiped some spittle from his chin and asked Orme to move closer and assist him.

The brute hesitated; the chancellor's servants were just steps away, so why should *he* help? On second thought, he figured it could do no harm. The idiot would soon be dead anyway.

Moments later, Orme's face told a different story when Scabbage jabbed a huge needle into the brute's thigh. The chancellor's flowing robes hid his arms well, so Orme had not seen him pull the syringe from a pouch on the inside of his hover-chair. Orme clutched his leg and gurgled, but could form no words. He slumped hard to the floor.

Deebee cackled, then yelled at Monty, pointing to Orme's inert form. "Get me into this body at once!"

"Sir, ah...but sir," said Monty, "the body needs to be

prepped first. Yes, it needs time to be readied, that's what it needs."

"I don't have time for that useless crap," bellowed Scabbage. "Get me into that bloody body right now!"

"But, sir," said Monty, swaying and bobbing, "must prep, you see? It's vital. Yes, vital. Otherwise, it will die. Yup, will die. Not know when, but your transfer will fail. Yes, it will fail."

"Well, make it as bloody quick as you can!" screamed Scabbage, spittle dribbling down his many chins. "Do only what is absolutely necessary to make the transfer a success, then get me into that damned body!"

Monty and the guards and servants exchanged looks, shrugged and shook their heads. The humpback reached for a grapple and used it to lift Orme's bulk up onto a nearby gurney. The guards helped move the gurney and its load to the transfer room at the back of the facility; Scabbage and his servants followed. "Now we're getting somewhere," he mumbled.

Monty led the way to the nearest table, centered beneath a large bank of equipment — the transfer mechanism that would extract Scabbage's soul and transfer it into Orme's body — just as Monty had transferred Soader into Jager's body not long before.

Monty used a hoist to position Orme's limp form on the transfer table, then secured it using more straps than usual. He didn't want a disaster if the powerful brute awoke mid-transfer. He maneuvered another device to tableside and positioned it over Orme's head. It would capture the Rept's soul. Seeing as they would not be placing Orme's soul into the Universal Soul Containment Unit, the procedure would be quicker and simpler than usual. Scabbage had ordered Orme to RPF113.

Monty directed Scabbage to a similar table, a few meters from the first. Scabbage made his way to the table and, with help from two servants, managed to mount it and lie on his side. Without a word of thanks, he ordered the pair to wait by the transfer room door.

"Sir," said Monty, "please put your..."

"I know what the hells I'm doing, imbecile!" interrupted Deebee, between hacks and coughs. He hated the whole transfer process, and hated even more being forced to make a move without careful planning and replanning, but now he had no choice. He would have to make the best of it. Nothing to worry about, he reassured himself, he'd find Jager soon enough, transfer into his body, and be back on track.

He rolled carefully onto his back and lowered his head onto the cushion at the table's end. Exhausted, he soon fell asleep.

Monty hurriedly prepared Orme's body for the transfer, limiting himself to only those steps that were absolutely necessary. Then he woke the chancellor — who promptly berated the poor wretch for letting him sleep so long, even though it had only been mere minutes.

Scabbage was deathly afraid, and looked it. It had been more than a day since their arrival at TS 428, and he knew he wouldn't be leaving here unless it was in another body, or via one of the transfer tubes that would send him down to some Earther-baby body — after an unfortunate memory wipe. The very idea of such a fate was appalling. He made an effort to raise an arm, but only succeeded in touching off another long fit of coughing. The fit passed, but he knew his body had only a few breaths remaining. He spoke in a raspy whisper. "Is the body ready?"

Monty responded with his usual head bobbing, followed by a stuttering ramble. "Y... yes, yes, good, good enough. It will do for a *short-term* transfer, yes."

Scabbage tried to respond, but passed out.

Monty fumbled about with the transfer equipment. If the idiot had had half a brain, he'd have realized he should just let the monster on the table die. But, unfortunately for everyone everywhere, the thought never crossed his simple mind. Instead, he hastily secured the High Chancellor's body to the transfer table, did one final check of the equipment and the two silent bodies, then activated the transfer mechanism.

Instantly Orme's body flopped like a fish on a hook. Black-red energy particles — the physical manifestation of Orme's soul — pulsed outward from the back of his massive head and floated up a transparent tube toward the temporary soul-containment chambers. Now, following orders Scabbage had given him before the procedure began, Monty lifted a small cover and pushed the red button beneath. Instantly Orme's departing soul was diverted up and away to a special containment vessel, reserved for souls condemned to RPF113.

Normally, being Dulce compound staff, Orme's fate would have been insertion into one of the hybrid babies born at Dulce. But unfortunately for him, karma had come full circle.

Monty continued to fidget with the now-uninhabited body. Once satisfied, he again busied himself with the transfer mechanism. He fiddled and fussed, adjusting the settings on the big, flashing console behind the transfer tables. It was important that the equipment be tuned to the correct and very specific characteristic wavelengths of the soul being transferred. At last, everything was ready.

Monty began pulling hard on knobs and pounding buttons. He came to a huge red switch, hesitated, then slammed home its contacts. A sizzling flash of electric fire erupted around the two tables, then settled down into a glowing field, like a yellowish-orange electric cloud. Scabbage's body screamed and arched violently, up, down, up, down, before falling lifeless. Monty watched as the creature's onyx-black soul inched its way up the transfer tube, then down into the body that had been home to Orme.

Monty flicked a switch; a low whirring began, grew to nearly a roar, then slowly subsided. The process was complete. Orme's body gave a single, brief twitch, went limp for a moment, then gulped convulsively for air. After several deep gasps, it struggled hard against the restraints that bound it. Fiercely it jerked and struggled; then, with a vicious scream and a mighty strain, it burst the restraints and leapt from the table.

Terrified, Monty tried to scurry away, but he was too slow. Reveling in the power of his new body, Scabbage caught the creature by the neck. He laughed uproariously, beating Monty mercilessly until, tossed to the floor, he lay near death amid a pool of his own blood.

The Greys shrank back in terror as Scabbage stood tall, stretching the body to its full height. He laughed long and hard, loving the deep sound of his new voice. He kicked Monty's pulverized body another time or two, just for fun, then rushed to the far wall to gaze at a cracked, dirty mirror that hung there. The brute remained silent, staring and leering at the reflection that stared and leered back. What a glorious day!

The deep brown skin and eyes were more beautiful than Scabbage had hoped for; and to be so tall and strong was perfect. The chancellor would have preferred to be in Jager's young body, but only for the powers the boy possessed. On a sheer physical level, he would enjoy this body much more. Thinking of Jager, he remembered he'd recently figured out how to usurp and use the powers of both the boy and the girl, Celine.

"Where the Xenu is my shuttlecraft?" he barked at the closest Grey. The minion scurried off to find out.

Scabbage spotted the hover-chair, his prison, so to speak, for far too long. He grinned wide as he snatched it up, raised it overhead and heaved it up and over his frightened, cowering servants. The chair flew across the room to smash against a wall; he laughed uproariously.

"Take me to my shuttlecraft, this instant," he hollered at the nearest Grey, "or you'll be the next thing to hit the wall!" Still grinning, he watched the servants scamper out the door, heading for the shuttle port. He followed with a laugh and a bounce in his step, loving the fact that he could walk on his own again.

Life was wonderful indeed!

CHAPTER 24

The Solution

His stomach full, the exhausted Alika gave a loud burp and an even louder yawn. Ahimoth chuckled, then ordered all the youngsters to follow him as he escorted the fledgling to bed. Fianna and the others looked on, smiling.

"Okay, everyone," said Celine, eager to make certain arrangements for what was sure to come. She opened her hand computer; her fingers flashed across its panel. "When Ahimoth returns, we need to plan out our next few moves."

"I agree," said Jager, moving to sit beside her. "Our future looks more complex and confusing each day, so we should try to formulate as solid a strategy as possible, and act on it. Especially considering that things could escalate without notice. So far, we've had to be reactive in most of our movements. I, for one, am tired of being so subject to random forces and events in my environment. I want and need more definite control of my life, my surroundings and each step I take."

"I feel the same, dear friend," said Vin, as he too moved closer to Celine. The friends continued to chat until Ahimoth reappeared.

"Ah, brother," said Fianna, "we waited for your brilliant mind before beginning our discussion in earnest. I, for one, need your help to determine our immediate future plans."

"Indeed, sister," smiled Ahimoth, honored at Fianna's respectful tone. "You do flatter me. I agree, it is time." The prince made himself comfortable next to Joli, gave her a gentle nudge of affection and then smiled at the others to begin.

"All right, everyone," said Celine, as she passed her hand computer to Jager. "I've created a list of actions I believe we need to take. I may not have thought of everything, and I'm not certain they're correctly prioritized. So don't hesitate to speak up if you think there's anything to be added or changed. Jager, would you please read this out?"

"With pleasure, Oh Wise Pumpkin." He stood up, gave Celine one of his best smiles, then held the computer at arm's length, cleared his throat and made the sort of gestures old-time public orators affected before speaking.

"One: List and discuss all pertinent paintings, in order of proposed implementation. Two: Decipher the riddle Dagmar gave Joli, for use in locating Prince Deet's spell book. Three: Go to Kerr to recruit Narco, Choy and the Dragons of Kerr, because they appear in numerous paintings — indicating they have important roles in future efforts. Four: Find Alden Koondahg and enlist his help in performing the incantation that will take us back in time to find Mutuum. Five: Destroy the transfer station on Earth's moon."

Jager continued on down the rest of the items. "Wow!" he exclaimed. "I think you've captured all that needs to be done, Pumpkin. Great job!"

"Thanks," smiled Celine.

"Oh!" exclaimed Jager. "I just thought of something not yet mentioned. Something we should put near the top of the list."

"Oh? What's that?" asked Celine.

"It's Piccolo; we need to find out all we can about this character, and how he fits into all that's gone on."

"Piccolo?"

"Yeah, I need to ask the Major about him. I'll explain. Sorry, but to do that I need to mention what happened to your father."

Celine pursed her lips and nodded to indicate it was all right, seeing as her father was back among them. Jager gave her a smile.

"When Soader killed Commander Zulak," said Jager, "A crewmember named Piccolo 'beamed off *Asherah* seconds behind the commander. I found that extremely curious, especially since this guy hasn't been seen since."

"I've never heard of him," said Celine, "but his actions sound suspicious, so I agree. We should add him to the list. Was he someone of importance?"

"Yes, in a manner of speaking," replied Jager. "He's a cousin to Soader, which makes him a cousin — or second cousin, actually — to Scabbage."

"What?!" exclaimed Celine. "Wow! That *is* extremely curious."

"Without a doubt," replied Jager. "It took a lot of research in several databases to discover some of the information, but my having been linked with Soader's memories helped to solve the puzzle. I learned that this character Piccolo was born as Tate Hobbs, a cousin to Soader who helped him pull off some heists when they were teenagers. During their last heist together, Soader killed several security guards before he and Hobbs made off with a big haul of diamonds, emeralds, sapphires, and other jewels — none of which were ever recovered. The boys weren't caught, either. But more important, Tate was never seen again. Soader beat him close to death and left him on an asteroid to die. Unknown to Soader, but fortunate for Hobbs, a junk collector came upon the barely breathing boy and rescued him."

"How interesting," said Celine. "But how did Piccolo end up aboard *Asherah*? I'm confused."

"That confused me too," replied Jager. "But it turns out Hobbs was so badly beaten he required full facial reconstruction. During his recovery, he apparently came up with a plan to get revenge for what Soader had done to him. Hobbs's vocal apparatus was also damaged in the beating; though it was repaired, his voice was significantly altered. So it was easy for him to create an entire new identity. And with that identity he decided the best way to get back at Soader was to help his enemies. So he enlisted in the fleet as Piccolo, and worked his way into a posting aboard *Asherah*. He chose that ship after learning of the enmity between her captain — Commander Zulak — and Soader. He figured if there was anyone in Fleet who might lead him to Soader, it would be the commander."

"Okay, that makes sense, but it doesn't explain why he 'beamed down to Scobee and helped Soader kill my father."

"I agree it doesn't make sense, but Piccolo *didn't* help

Soader. There is no memory in Soader's mind to suggest he even knew Piccolo was there on Scobee. My guess is that Piccolo planned to confront his cousin, but was caught off guard by the attack on your father and missed his opportunity. Now that Soader is dead, I believe Piccolo will come back to take some of Soader's treasure, believing he's entitled to it for all that Soader put him through. So, we should be ready for him. I also think there's more to his story.

"You see, I believe Piccolo has information that could be very useful to us. I can't quite put my finger on why I feel this, but something is not adding up, and it feels right to follow this guy's trail."

"A remarkable story, truly," said Vin. "And your proposal should most definitely be added to the list Celine has compiled. I should add my thanks to you, Celine, for creating the list. It is good to define what we need to accomplish. And we must begin to address these issues. I feel as Jager does — I am tired of merely reacting to events and circumstances. It is time to take a more causative stance.

"Too much of my life was wasted in Soader's compound. Because of that, I too want to take better control over my actions and what happens around me, so I can better protect those I love."

Vin caught Fianna's eye, held it for a moment and went on. "Jager, could you please repeat the first item on the list? I am anxious to get started, and the first item seemed to be in an area of my own expertise."

"You bet, Vin," said Jager. He scrolled back on the hand-held. "One: List and discuss all pertinent paintings, in order of proposed implementation. You're right Vin, I believe this is something we can get started on right away."

"I agree," said Vin. "As we all know, the paintings comprise the Dragons' record of our past, present and foretold future existence. Unfortunately, it appears the present turmoil in this universe revolves around our little group right here, for we are depicted in numerous paintings. Even some that clearly show events on different planets.

"I believe the paintings depicting the future are the ones we must focus upon. The ones we must truly understand, especially those recently viewed by West through Alika's eyes. We can apply the magic they depict to effect the outcome the images foretell. I believe I speak for us all when I say that I want the current unrest and craziness to end, so that we may return to our homes and live more harmonious lives."

Again he smiled lovingly at Fianna. "In several paintings, we have seen eggs at our own feet. I want those eggs to appear! I want brave little Vins and beautiful young Fiannas running about the fields of Nibiru and learning to fly its skies." Fianna blushed.

"Well said, Vin," said Ahimoth, with an unabashed grin at Joli. "I wish the same. And I agree that understanding the paintings is key to resolving the situations we face."

He paused and stood taller. "Everyone, if I may be so bold, I would like to be first to offer my opinion on all we have discussed so far. I have much to say regarding the paintings we have viewed, and especially those recently shared with us by West."

The small group all nodded consent, so the prince cleared his throat and began. "Every night, before I sleep, I study in my mind's eye all the paintings we have come across. So I possess a good knowledge of how they fit into the path we must follow — a path that aligns with our prophecies." Joli smiled at him and leaned gently into his side; he reciprocated, then continued his discourse.

The friends planned into the wee hours. Each of them believed — without voicing their belief — that their proposed actions were the last hope for the survival of the Dragon races. Though all the Dragon Worlds were now surrounded by protective shielding, danger still lurked a transbeam transmission away. They knew that if they did not succeed in their next missions, it would not be long before someone penetrated the planetary shielding, with malicious intent.

Jager stretched. "It's late, everyone. We've done a good job. I think we should call it a night soon, but I would like to try to get through the list first, if we can." Everyone agreed. "Okay, good. We're all in accord on how to move forward regarding the paintings. Let's move on to the next two points." There were no objections, so he continued. "Point two of Celine's list says, 'Decipher the riddle Dagmar gave Joli, for use in locating Prince Deet's spell book.'" He looked at Celine, who responded right away.

"I can get to work on that first thing tomorrow."

"Awesome," smiled Jager. 'Three: Go to Kerr to recruit Narco, Choy and the Dragons of Kerr, because they appear in numerous paintings — indicating they have important roles in future efforts.'"

"Oh," smiled Celine. "I guess we should do *that* first thing tomorrow. I can work on the riddle afterwards."

"Yeah, that makes sense," replied Jager, typing into the hand computer. The friends renewed their dialogue until they had arrived at what seemed a sensible timeline for all the list's actions. Although all were tired, they were happy to have a firm, agreed-upon idea of how to proceed in the coming days.

Jager spent some time in Celine's room before retiring to his own. During their small talk, the topic of their newest skills and abilities came up. Their discussion and speculation were interrupted by a faint knock at the door. Jager opened it to find West.

"May I join you?" she asked.

"Yes, please come in." He stepped back and gestured for the Mentor to enter.

"I'm so glad you are here, West," spoke up Celine.

"It is good to see you as well, child," replied West. "I have not had time for either of you of late, and wanted to say hello and hear your plans for tomorrow."

"Oh, that's nice. And I'll gladly share our plans," said Celine, picking up the hand-held. "This works out well, for we had some questions we planned to ask you in the morning. But if you have time right now, we'd love to discuss them with you."

"Yes, right now works well."

Jager looked at Celine to see if she wished to speak about their newest concerns and questions. A couple of weeks earlier, both had discovered they'd acquired a new, enhanced telepathic ability which linked them to extensive chains of memories that did not belong to either of them, but were from five different people in different periods of time and from different worlds. The memories did not actually come from the conscious minds of these people, but were hidden within the unconscious of each. And, for some unexplainable reason, Celine and Jager had a direct telepathic connection with these same individuals, in their present lives.

At first, both found the phenomenon both mind-blowing and confusing, so they erected barriers to form impenetrable mental walls around the memories. The two agreed to keep the memories locked away until they could discuss the matter with West. With all the recent unexpected activities, they'd forgotten about the situation, only to be reminded of it upon seeing West, on their return from Nibiru.

"What does all this mean, West?" asked Celine. "I know it's related to the injections you gave us as infants, but you explained to me years ago that those injections were to facilitate retrieval of recessed ancient memories. So presently I'm conflicted — it seems you told me an untruth."

"You are correct, Celine," West replied, after some hesitation. "On both counts. I did tell you an untruth, I'm sorry to say, but I will explain. During that period, my sisters and I felt it was the logical and proper thing to do, considering your age and what we knew the future held for you and for Jager. I hope you both can forgive me."

"I have no difficulty forgiving you, West, and I believe Jager feels the same. I just want to know if our thoughts on this are correct. And if not, could you please fill in the details?"

"Absolutely, my child."

"Good," continued Celine. She grabbed one of Jager's hands and pulled him to sit down with her on the sofa. "Jager and I understand what you've explained about needing both of us for your weaponry, and that we're to be linked spiritually in a special unification. But we now feel that somehow Fianna and the others are also required for this linking. Is that correct?"

West nodded affirmation.

"Okay. So we deduce, then, that these other people we're somehow mentally connected with — their energy is needed as well."

"Correct, my dear," replied West. "And once again, we did not tell you about all this as we felt it safest for everyone involved to wait until you had immediate need of the knowledge. We Mentors believed it was important to teach you to believe in your own strength and abilities first. Then, after exposure to the many sides of life, good and bad, you both would naturally be ready for whatever new elements surfaced."

"We understand, West," said Jager, "and trust your guidance in all aspects of our lives. I believe I speak for both of us in saying that your choice of methods was correct. Celine and I barriered off those memories, but what exactly are we to do with them in the future? Who are these people? Are they aware of us? I'm a tad confused."

"Ah, and rightfully so, Jager," replied West. "Those are all good questions. And it is commendable that you both set up barriers around the memories. I recommend you keep those barriers intact until it is time for you to link with these people."

Celine and Jager exchanged confused looks, so West continued. "I'll give you an example, so you can better understand. Think of what happens when you ignite a fire. When the source of heat connects to a fuel source, in the presence of oxygen, that is the moment when an incredible power is unleashed. This is the same with your new abilities. Although magnificent, your power needs to be controlled, or it may cause irreversible damage. It will need to be controlled on every level, as will the powers possessed by the people you are to connect with. Those five people are the weak links in the equation."

"Ohhhh," said the young couple.

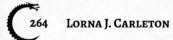

West nodded. "Good. You are understanding me, so I will continue. These other individuals are like wood that is to be burnt in a fire; it must be prepared and ready for what will come." The Mentor took a sip of the water Celine had brought to her. "Over the years, we have tried to protect the owners of the memories you now perceive. But it has been difficult, for their suffering has contaminated much of what they have experienced. My sisters and I developed a formula and special incantation to ensure the contamination is addressed before it is necessary for you to link with them.

"I know this is a lot to comprehend, and I apologize once again for my dishonesty in not telling you everything, and for using you as I have. But please believe me when I say that we could not think of any other way to ensure we would defeat Byrne and the other Lords."

"Again, no apologies necessary, West," responded Jager and Celine without hesitation.

There was a knock at the door. It was North, so West politely excused herself. "I am sorry to leave you with your minds whirling so, but I must leave. I will answer any more questions you have, the next time I see you. Goodbye for now."

"Bye," said Celine and Jager, returning to their seats on the sofa.

"All of this is sure to keep me from sleep. All over again!" laughed Celine, "I'm still exhausted, though. It was quite the day!"

"Me too. See you in the morning."

The two hugged and kissed, then Jager quickly made his way to his room. Both were asleep within minutes.

CHAPTER 25

Second Chances

With his arms flexed and his stomach taut, High Chancellor Scabbage looked like a pin-up fashion model as he assumed one pose after another and maneuvered down an imaginary catwalk. He almost stumbled, trying to gaze at himself in the wall mirror as he strutted. He grinned and waved, moving closer to the mirror to drool some more at his new reflection.

"Wow! I'm gorgeous!" he exclaimed. His bronze arm muscles gleamed as he felt their hardness. He stroked and patted them as he spoke. "It's too bad I must abandon you, sweet thing, but I must. I need to take over the blasted piddly Earther body of that annoying Jager kid, but it will only be for a short time. I promise, sweet thing. I promise that I'll come back to gorgeous you."

Scabbage threw back his head and continued to posture and admire himself; by the second, his adoration grew for what he ogled and stroked. He hadn't realized how restricted life had been in his old, fat, former shell. The extent of his esteem for his new stature surprised him somewhat. But he brushed off the reaction; this new body made him feel alive. It was as though he hadn't been living before.

The chancellor watched admiringly as he flexed his arms some more, amazed at the sheer power. Power that was *all* his. He especially enjoyed how easy he was sure it would be to crush the neck of any servant unfortunate enough to walk too close, when he felt the urge to kill.

After a few more poses, Deebee grew tired of the mirror and made his way to an overstuffed divan surrounded by other items of furniture, lavish but tastelessly ugly. He smiled as he looked around his new room, pleased with the results of the recent renovations.

He picked up a grotesque tankard to slurp his favorite drink, then sat daydreaming about his new ship, *Queen Morrighan*. He'd ordered the Brothers' rooms there completely stripped and refurbished, then conjoined into one large chamber, similar to what he'd had back home in his luxurious palace on Erra. He'd also 'beamed all of his favorite possessions to the ship and had revered trophies arranged about his special new room. So many treasures, so many treasured moments.

His *most* prized possession, though, sat right at his bedside, here in his Dulce compound quarters: an intricate, exquisitely detailed white crystal sculpture of a Nibiru Dragon and Companion. The crystalline stone seemed to glow with an inner light that he couldn't resist. He kept it close always, to fondle and admire.

"Now we're talking," he laughed as he refreshed his tankard with the last of the Earther elixir and downed it in a single gulp. He hollered for a servant to bring him two more jugs, then reached toward a table piled high with assorted meaty delectables. Before long, the bloody contents of several more tankards had made their way down his gullet. From time to time, he laughed and postured some more before the mirror, amazed at how his life appeared to be following a golden path. Not only was he High Chancellor of a vast section of the Pleiades, but he now had control of everything the Brothers had operated, plus a superb new body.

Life was indeed grand.

Scabbage toasted his reflection and celebrated on into the wee hours, until at last he passed out, draped across the divan. The next morning, he awoke to the prodding of a stick held at arm's length by Mullins, one of Soader's unfortunate servants. He swatted at the Grey, but by pure luck the creature managed to dodge in time. The poor thing had the shakes for most of the day afterwards, for he'd seen blows from Orme prove fatal.

"What are you morons staring at?" yelled Deebee. "Bring me my breakfast before I make one of you the main course!" The Greys needed no further prompting. They scampered out the door, praying they'd soon find the treasure Piccolo was after. The three of them had marveled at their luck when Piccolo had contacted them in secret and asked for their help in his search, promising a generous reward.

Scabbage went about his morning rituals, then grumbled as he made his way to his desk. "Time to get some serious strategies into play before Byrnzee discovers those blasted Barbdews are dead."

Deebee fired up the computer, and soon pages of freshly written gibberish stared back at him. He read it all aloud, several times. He knew Byrne would not want Lancaster and

Dodd's sector to fall into the wrong hands, so his proposal needed to be perfect. So perfect that Byrne would not hesitate to choose him. Whether Byrne gave him the domain or not, Scabbage planned to rule it anyway. It would just be easier if Byrne were to grant him the posting. If not, Byrne would soon join the Barbdews in death. Along with everyone else in the Phoenix Universe, according to Scabbage's plan.

"Har har," he laughed, envisioning himself detonating the unthinkably powerful explosives he'd heard were soon to be put up for bid on the galactic black market. "Life is indeed grand." He laughed, downed another gulp of elixir and turned back to the computer.

The wretch plunked away at the console for hours, writing more drivel and doing research. Along the way, he learned some surprising things about the Brothers. He selected the most appropriate and scandalous files to include in the proposal he planned to present to Lord Byrne later that day — before the scoundrel heard about the Barbdews' death. The job was as good as his, he assumed, because few talented thugs were still alive; he'd seen to that.

"Gawd, this is so much fun," he laughed. "Criminals don't seem to have the right motivations and skills anymore. Except for me, that is. Good thing I was smart enough to kill off most of the competition. Now Ol' Byrnzee *has* to give me this job. Har har har!"

Scabbage laughed loudly for nearly a minute, remembering his latest bloody streak of kills, easy to pull off with the Brothers gone. He had only had to use the Brothers' comm link, contact anyone recently employed by the Barbdews, and dispatch his own assassins to terminate the targets. Quick and efficient. Within hours, dozens of his supposed allies were dust.

"Commissioner Scabbage," he laughed. "I do love the sound of that. Har har! But Lord Deebee...Lord Deebee Scabbage. Now, that sounds even better. Har har har."

After several more guffaws, he turned back to the console, talking to himself all the while. "I can see that my first priority will be to gain full control of Byrne's bloody minions — Kurucz and Bsrn — and whomever those two have manipulated over the years. Gawd! Look at all these bloody files! I don't think many of these wretched lumps are worth keeping. I've got my own corps of snitches who've proven loyal and most useful over the years."

The chancellor combed through more files until he came across one labelled "Pratt."

"Har har," he laughed, recalling the look on the late High Chancellor's paralyzed face. "Thank gawd that scoundrel no longer poses a problem." The Rept's smile quickly turned to a frown when he came across the largest file yet. The name flashed across the screen in bold, bright letters: Witch Villa.

"Oh, damn!" he growled. "Gods damn her. That witch will be a huge problem if I don't immediately find and vaporize her. Now that the Brothers are toast, she'll be out for revenge and won't give up until someone pays for what they did to her. Or what I did to her, for that matter. And damn, she also knows I had something to do with her imprisonment on Yeske!"

Scabbage started to throw things around the room and barked for his servants to bring him more elixir.

"Damn it all!" he growled again. "I'm not safe until that witch is disposed of. And come to think of it, there are a couple of other rats I hadn't thought about — vermin who hate me as much as she, and she knows them, too! She won't try to come after me alone. She'll recruit some of those others. Bloody hells, this is going to take some serious planning."

Deebee worked himself into a huge tizzy, but after a few more swigs of elixir he calmed down enough to sit again at the console. In his demented mind, Z equaled Z equaled Z — everything equaled everything else. Villa would be after him, so others would be after him, and therefore *everyone* would be after him. Not logical, but that was how he "thought." And right now it made the wretch more paranoid than he'd ever been.

Meanwhile, as old Deebee chomped, slurped, and contemplated his next move, Villa, back on Yeske, relished her new freedom. The Brothers' demise had broken the spell they'd used to hold her captive! She celebrated for three days straight, amazed at the stupidity of the Barbdews. They'd fallen victim to their own foolishness.

On the fourth day of her freedom, Villa looked up at a huge black ship that hovered high above. She'd already given her animals and home to a local family. Now she sat on her favorite garden bench with two scruffy bags at her feet, holding all her meager belongings. She grinned wider as a transbeam field appeared and intensified about her. She picked up her bags and clutched them tight, then closed her eyes. She had no desire for a last look at the hated little hut that had been her prison.

Arriving aboard ship, she reveled in joyful, long-awaited greetings with Yetta and her other sisters. They had thought they would never see each other again, yet here they were.

Settled back on her home world of Katlele V, Villa quickly got reacquainted with her family, then went to work on the first of many moves she'd planned. Her sisters helped her search for information on the various nasty schemes

Lancaster and Dodd had been working. She knew they'd had grandiose plans, for she'd heard them brag about them many a time. Now she wanted to take advantage of anything they'd already set in motion, to garner some of their immense power and vast riches for herself. She felt much of their power was rightfully hers, since she'd helped them amass a great deal of it. She also had plans for revenge against Scabbage, for his unforgivable actions against her.

At the end of the first day's work, though, Villa pushed all thoughts of Scabbage and the Brothers from her mind. She was simply overjoyed to be back home and eager to re-establish all her old contacts. One never knew when good cronies might be of service. Especially her five powerful sisters, standing with her now before a glowing fire in their family mansion: Uli, Winta, Xylia, Yetta and Zaza. And, rounding out the little family party, her half-brother Bill.

CHAPTER 26

Piccolo

A cloud of dust billowed up as Piccolo's spacecraft thudded to rest in the narrow canyon, situated not far from Soader's Dulce compound. The force of the landing caused the Rept to lurch hard against the console. "Gods damn it!" he grumbled loudly, standing to stare blank-faced out a viewport. He remained like that for several minutes, rubbing his bruises. He was more frustrated at having allowed himself to become so agitated than at having hurt himself.

Still frustrated, Piccolo turned from the port. "What's happening to me?" he growled. He gave the wall a vicious punch, which only added to his injuries and anger. "Why can't I focus on anything?" Then, as he had done numerous times during the past few weeks, he shook his head and whacked it repeatedly, as if emptying a piggy bank.

"I must be too tired. That's all it is. It can't be anything else. There's *nothing* wrong with me. Nothing! Nothing whatsoever."

He spat and swore, hitting his head yet again — and then several times more. Then, with a dazed stare at nothing, he stopped, fell to his knees in a quiet slump, and stayed that way for a long minute. He dragged himself to his feet, rubbed at his eyes, and made his painful way out the main hatch, grumbling non-sequiturs.

Once on solid ground, Piccolo scooped up a handful of dirt, brought it up to his snout, took several long, deep sniffs at it, then tossed it aside. Watching the dust he'd kicked up settle calmed him somewhat. A weak smirk appeared on his flushed and dirty face.

The smirk grew to a smile, which spread wider as he made his way down a well-worn path. It wound from the landing spot into a sickly-looking wood of stunted trees, dotted here and there with oddly multi-colored stones and boulders. Sparse patches of feather grass grew at the bases of some of the bigger rocks. The farther he went on, the more his mood improved. Soon there was a bit of a spring to his step. He even looked up and smiled at several birds flying overhead; their melodious songs seemed to lend him life, and invigorate the foliage scattered about.

It had been a long week, and Piccolo had come up empty handed yet again. He'd searched for days and days, but hadn't found the slightest sign of Soader's hidden treasure, nor any clue to its whereabouts. The thought of it soured his mood again; he growled and kicked at a lump of dirt.

After he'd gone a few more meters, he stopped abruptly and, with a heavy sigh, stared off into the distance. After some time, a couple of orange-breasted buntings caught his attention, and a faint smile again lit his reptilian features. The birds appeared to be building a nest in a thorny thicket at the edge of the woodland. Piccolo loved birds. He envied their freedom to come and go, whenever and wherever they chose. But as he watched the buntings go about their birdly business, the fog crept over his mind again, and his gaze turned to a blank stare. His eyes began to glaze over, control of his body rapidly slipping away. His knees shook and began to buckle — but the threat of falling yanked him back to alertness. He straightened, shook his head, cursed, and gave his forehead a few more healthy whacks.

"How am I going to find that damned loot?" he snorted. His frustration back in full force, he picked up a stone and whipped it at a fat marmot, sunning itself on a rock.

For hours Piccolo had fitfully examined and re-examined maps of the Dulce compound's myriad tunnels. But it was no use. The maps yielded not a single clue as to where Soader's tainted treasure lay. In the end, Piccolo had just given up and began digging at random, relying on luck, hoping for any clue, any spark of intuition. He dug and dug, leaving messes everywhere.

After the shoot-out on Scobee, he had managed to stay under the radar, concealing his identity well enough to reach Earth and hire on as a Dulce guard. Before working his first shift, he hacked into the compound database and set it up so that he had no assigned post or duties, and no one to report to — but his identification badge would still allow him access to the entire facility.

If someone were to notice and challenge him while he sleuthed about, he planned to respond by saying that he was following Soader's strict orders to locate something he had misplaced.

By the time news of Soader's exile to RPF113 reached Dulce, Piccolo had been around long enough to be considered a normal fixture, so no one bothered him about his continuing search.

Piccolo threw another stone at the marmot, but his foul mood had returned, and he abandoned that diversion. Hoping to regain some composure, he focused on his newest plans for spending the treasure. That seemed to do the trick; soon he was singing to himself as he strutted through the stunted forest. He even pulled out a ciggy and lit up. Between puffs, he chuckled over the news of Soader's demise. But that was the wrong thing to think about. Just like that, his foul mood returned.

"Soul imprisonment on RPF113 is too kind for such a wretch as you, dear cousin," he growled. "I would have tortured you for weeks! At least then I would have gotten the location of our loot from you. Even in your death you torture me!"

He shook his head again, hard, for part of him knew that he didn't have time for such rants. He knew that Soader would be a distant memory once he had the treasure and embarked on his new life as a member of the uber-wealthy elite on some far-away planet.

Beneath all his insanity, Piccolo was still professional enough to know he'd better get hold of himself. He managed to do so by concentrating on something Soader himself had said when they were growing up: "You know, Hobbs, you'll never be as smart as me."

"Har, har, cousin," Piccolo laughed, "Yes, you were smart, but not smart enough! Har har har!!"

Feeling better, Piccolo returned to daydreaming about his future. This time he thought about the planet Rinder, where he hoped to build a luxurious palace where he could swim in his hordes of jewels and precious treasures, hidden in a secret room. He quickened his pace towards the complex, now visible in the far distance. He pushed away thoughts of his parents and home planet — thoughts that often haunted him. He truly wanted to visit them, especially his mother, but was afraid to do so.

Years earlier, Piccolo had convinced himself that it would be best to remain hidden, to increase his chances of destroying Soader. At the time he hadn't anticipated the task would take decades. Now, with so many years gone by, he felt it was too late even to let his family know he was alive. He'd come up with a tale of amnesia to tell them, to explain his long absence — so he knew deep down that he truly wanted to return home. He couldn't get himself to go, though. Which he knew meant something else must lie beneath his fear.

The Rept grumbled and stooped to pick up a stone. He flung it as hard as he could, pleased when it smashed a window in the building he'd aimed for. He kicked at a rock in his path, which brought on a bigger smile.

Of all his life's misdeeds, his greatest regret was disappointing his parents. He told himself Soader had been the cause of that. "That scum took away the only people that loved me," he mumbled, believing that if his parents still loved him, he might have a chance at redemption and a normal life.

Piccolo had never been implicated in the biggest heist he and Soader had pulled — the one in which several guards had been killed. Soader made sure he was given sole credit for the robbery. He alone took all the glory, and zoomed to the top of the trans-sector most-wanted list. Not long after the incident, Soader had been approached by the Brothers to help with their dirty work; Scabbage had offered to hire him too, soon after. Piccolo had been left out of everything.

Over the years Piccolo realized he'd started down the wrong path in his youth. But his guilt was not sincere enough to keep him on the road to good citizenship. His desire for Soader's ill-gotten treasure was too strong for that. And so he found himself in this present conundrum.

Hearing some squawks above, Piccolo looked up at some small rose-bellied buntings, harrying a large black bird that had approached their nests too closely. And that's when it finally came to him.

"I've got it!" he shouted, so loudly that all the nearby birds burst into the air, frightening off the bigger black one. "What a fool I've been! Har! Har!" he laughed. "Of course. How stupid of me. The treasure is in one of the Dragon chambers. Har har har!"

Piccolo approached a dilapidated gray warehouse and entered through a faded green door that hung by one bent hinge. Windows along the length of the building gave him ample light to make his way around the assorted old equipment strewn about the place. Halfway through the large building, he climbed a long flight of stairs that rose from the room's center. Reaching the top, he raced down a corridor that led to the adjacent building. Soon he stood in a windowless, rundown factory room. He moved to the back of the dimly lit space, and entered a small room that held a cot, table and small kitchen cook station. He settled down and enjoyed a few drinks, then fell into a deep sleep, dreaming his usual dream of swimming in treasure.

Hours later, Piccolo woke, ate, and returned to the compound at Dulce for another round of digging. He'd lost track of how many days he'd been at this, but with his new realization about where the loot must be, he felt revived. Even the annoyance of having to do all the work himself seemed less.

Once inside Narco and Choy's chamber, Piccolo cased the immense space and decided that, knowing his cousin, the treasure was probably hidden in the least likely place. So that was where Piccolo began the day's digging.

He dug and dug. Soon there were dozens of holes, from one end of the vast cavern to the other. The Rept felt he was free to dig anywhere he chose, since Soader's pets no longer inhabited the dungeon-caverns. But after a few days of failures, he realized it was time to get help. Otherwise, he'd be digging holes for years. The next morning, the Grey guards Max, Vic and Mullins, persuaded with significant bribes, joined the project and began digging as eagerly as Piccolo. The three Greys didn't know precisely what Piccolo was looking for, but they had a good idea, and knew it must be extremely valuable in any case. They agreed among themselves that if they discovered anything of value, they would remain silent.

On the Greys' third day as part of Piccolo's prospecting expedition, Mullins found what the Rept was after. It wasn't in a hole in the dirt, but in an opening in one of the rocky walls of Narco and Choy's cavern. The day before, Mullins had noticed a shiny spot on the wall and had worked his way toward it while digging his exploratory holes. When close enough to take a good look without drawing Piccolo's suspicious attention, he examined the spot. It was a coin. A silver coin, resting on a tiny ledge atop the opening of a small crevice. He examined more closely. From a slight variation in the rock wall's texture, and some straight lines where there shouldn't be any, he realized he was looking at a false façade — and knew at once that it must contain what Piccolo hunted.

That night, while most of the compound slept, Mullins,

Max and Vic made their way back to the Dragon cavern, pulled back the façade and hauled out crate after crate of jewels and other beautiful valuables. They loaded everything into several bins they'd brought along, and used an anti-grav levitator to haul it all back to a secure hiding place they'd prepared on Level 7 of the main compound. The three Greys chuckled among themselves as they made their way back to their quarters, envisioning their escape and new life ahead.

"Perfect, Max," said Mullins, rubbing his hands. "Great idea. We'll use the train and take the entire haul to Soader's shuttle at Salt Lake City. Once the shuttle's loaded we can go anywhere we wish. Finally, we'll be free of this stinking place."

The next morning, before their shift started and the new warden, Orme, was out and about, the three Greys moved the fortune to the very same train car they'd used to transport Celine, and then later Jager. Their plan was to take the train to Salt Lake after their shift was over, and cache their treasure safely on board Soader's shuttle craft.

"Ha!" laughed Max, "I wish Soader were here to see this!" The Greys had a good laugh.

They went about their daily business, eagerly anticipating their evening escape with the treasure. Before making the trip, though, they wanted to gather one additional item, vital to living out their dreams.

CHAPTER 27

Kerr

A few weeks earlier, Celine and the others had openly welcomed the two-headed red Kerr Dragon, Narco and Choy, to the Mentor's outpost. They had done so despite the pair's past violent acts, understanding how Soader had subverted them; they were convinced of the red Dragons' sincere reform since their release from slavery to the wicked Rept.

The Kerr brothers, like Fianna and the others, had been injured during the battle with Soader in Germany's Vogelsberg Mountains. Narco and Choy could scarcely believe their good fortune — they'd been freed from horrible bondage, forgiven by those they'd sought to harm, transported to a Mentor facility and given the best possible care for their battle wounds. In deep gratitude, they vowed to do nothing but good toward others from that moment on, wishing to pay forward the kindness bestowed upon them.

Once the brothers were on the mend, the Mentors

arranged passage for them back to their home planet, Kerr. They weren't quite ready to face their parents and others of their home fold, so they asked to be transported instead to the isolated island they'd lived on before Soader tricked them into slavery. But before the pair left the Mentor base, Celine gave them a long-range comm stone, asking that they call her if they should ever need assistance of any sort.

Tears rolled down the Kerrs' scaled faces as they lumbered onto the transbeam platform. They were sad to leave their new friends, and more than a little touched by all the kindness shown them. They waved goodbye to all who'd gathered, still amazed and astonished that they had been treated with such compassion and generosity.

Once back on Kerr, with thoughts of their forgiving new friends, the twins worked together, building up the courage to visit their family. They so wanted to be back home, to ask forgiveness for their past misdeeds, and, hopefully, to be loved and to love.

After several weeks, Narco and Choy were almost ready to fly to the mainland to see their parents, after many decades of separation. The painful sadness in their heart lessened with each day's growing anticipation of their return home. Then, the day before their planned departure, the comm stone Celine had given them rang out loud and clear.

"Narco, Choy, it is I, Ahimoth. Are you able to hear me?"

At first the brothers were stunned to hear another's voice, for they'd been alone on the island for weeks; both feared their isolation had caused them to lose their minds. Narco then remembered the comm stone and rushed to stand before it, cradled on a small ledge inside their cave.

"Uh, uh...uh," stuttered Narco as he touched the small

stone with his snout to activate it. "Uh, uh," he repeated. "Ah...yes, yes. I hear you. We hear you."

"That is good. It is nice to hear you. This is Ahimoth and Vin," the voice spoke gruffly. "How are you both doing?"

"Uh, good, good," replied Narco, his eyes wide. He was pleased to hear the stone speak, yet deeply concerned. Even though the Nibiru Dragons had not displayed any antagonism towards him or his brother while the Mentors were tending their injuries, in the backs of their minds the Kerrs harbored a great fear that Ahimoth and Vin might still want revenge.

Both brothers realized the Nibiru Dragons had more than ample reason to be vengeful. For years the Kerrs had taken part in Soader's hateful acts, inflicting much pain and suffering upon the Nibirus and their loved ones. Perhaps Ahimoth and the others had only acted nicely towards them because of the Mentor's presence.

"That is good to hear, dear friend," said Vin. "I guess that you and Choy are wondering why we have called. Do not fear, we do not wish to harm you. Instead, we have news that you and your fold should know. We would like to visit you, if that is all right."

"Uh, yes," said Narco, sharing a quizzical look with Choy. "Yes, uh, please, come visit. We...uh...we would really like that."

"That is good," replied Ahimoth. "We will arrive shortly. Is that all right?"

"Uhhhh, yes," said an incredulous Narco. "Yes, indeed. Uh, please, yes, please come." Both Narco and Choy's worried grins wouldn't relax as they waited for their new friends to appear. Deep down, the two knew the visit would most likely be friendly, but living under Soader's brutal reign had been like being in a cult. The many years he'd brutalized them had fostered a strongly suspicious attitude in each, from which it would take years to fully recover.

"I wonder what they have to say," said Choy. He was apprehensive, but excited at the same time, having grown bored with only Narco for company. "It must be important, for them to travel all this way."

"Yes, brother, it must indeed be important. I am still amazed at how kind Prince Ahimoth and the others were toward us, considering all the harm we caused them and their loved ones. Hells, we even tried to kill them several times, yet they are kindly toward us. Nibiru Dragons are as remarkable as our legends say. I do believe they do not come to do us harm, but as true friends. Though I must admit I am a tad worried."

"I believe the same, Narco," said Choy with a nervous grin. "And I too am somewhat worried. However, they truly are extraordinary Dragons and I believe Prince Ahimoth's words to be truthful." Choy was about to say more when he stopped, surprised to see several winged figures spiraling down from above.

"Greetings, friends," said Ahimoth, as he and the others came in to land with a *whoosh*, close to the still-tense Narco and Choy.

"We are honored to have you visit our humble island, Prince Ahimoth," said Narco. The pair bowed their long necks in respect and welcome.

"Thank you for having us, and for the generous welcome," said Ahimoth, as he and the others gathered round. After greetings and chit-chat, the Nibiru prince explained to the

Kerrs the reason for the sudden visit.

The twins were delighted to hear that their new friends had come to them for help. They were eager to make amends for their past abhorrent behavior. Soon Ahimoth and the others trailed behind the fast-flying Kerrs as they headed toward the mainland. The closer the brothers drew to their parent's home, though, the slower their wings pumped. When, after a couple of hours, they reached their destination, the apprehensive Narco and Choy just circled round and round, high above the lush valley of their home, dotted with what seemed, from this altitude, to be red specks — Dragons all, in fact.

"It will be all right, friends," said Ahimoth. "Have faith in yourselves."

The Kerrs sighed, nodded, and reluctantly began their decent, Fianna and the others close behind. A short time later, they all huddled in a close-knit group at the edge of a beautiful meadow, lush with blue and magenta grasses.

Not long after touching down, Celine and the others regretted having come to Kerr. Dozens of enormous red Dragons circled the meadow, screeching and blasting flame-hot breath at the small group. Within minutes, dozens more arrived and barricaded them in; row upon row of fiery eyes glared, enormous teeth gnashed, and huge blasts of fire-breath flashed so close that Vin and Ahimoth, at the front of the group, were nearly singed as they tried their best to protect their loved ones.

Celine gulped. "I know Narco said we would not be attacked," she mented, clinging tighter to Fianna. "But I'm not so sure he was correct." Fianna and Jager responded with the same considerations.

All four Nibirus, with Jager and Celine gripping hard in their saddles, stood straight as flag poles behind Narco and Choy, who themselves appeared surprised at the hostile reception. Perceiving their surprise and fear, Fianna and the others squeezed tighter together behind the twins, glad Narco and Choy were considerably larger than they.

"I don't know how long huddling here is going to help," mumbled Jager, "and I'm not sure whether being atop Vin is a good or bad thing at the moment."

"My exact thoughts and feelings," replied Celine as she clung tighter to the saddle, crouching as low as she could.

The Nibiru Dragons, however, held their ground, despite being uneasy and doubtful. They believed in the prophetic paintings they'd seen back home and on Remini, and felt sure of their decision to trust the brothers. But it was hard to hold fast to their faith, in the face of the flashing teeth and fire-breath blasts.

Perhaps the two-headed oddity had an ulterior motive for bringing them to stand before so many hostile Dragons, thought Celine.

The surrounding crowd closed in tighter and grew in numbers. And then, precipitously, there came a thunderous roar from the edge of the clearing. The encircling crowd stood aside to allow an enormous, war-scarred Dragon to stomp through. Narco and Choy cowered as the rugged Dragon strode straight up to them and roared again in anger.

"Why have you two ruffians returned?" bellowed the Dragon, Wiese. "What do you want? Do you know your mother and I are extremely disappointed in you?"

"Yes, Father," replied Narco, raising his head, only to bow low once again. "Choy and I would be disappointed in you, sir, if you were not angry with us." His head still down, Narco continued to address his father. "With the help of our new friends here, we have come to realize how our earlier, utterly unacceptable behavior violated Kerr traditions. Severely so."

Narco motioned with a wingtip and looked back over a shoulder to indicate Ahimoth, Vin and the others, hoping to appease the huge Kerr. "Father, we wish to ask for your forgiveness, and for that of our dear mother."

Narco and Choy were much larger than Fianna; Wiese towered over his sons. The imposing patriarch growled, reared up, and fanned his gigantic wings. The force of the draft and the growing restlessness of the crowd made Fianna and the others stumble backward.

The twins bowed once more, and Narco spoke again. "Dear Father, Choy and I realize we do not deserve your clemency. You are, however, a great warrior, and all great warriors have compassion for fools who've strayed from the morals and ethics of their groups, but repented and asked for absolution. We humbly ask, sir, that you be merciful with us."

The twins remained stooped, hoping for a favorable response.

"Hmph!" snorted Wiese. He rolled his eyes and huffed. "Just like that? You expect me and your mother to forgive you just like that?"

"Uh...y...yes, s...sir," replied Narco, his breath kicking up puffs of dust. His head was now so close to the ground, he could lick it. "We know we have been a great disappointment, sir. And we fear we can never make it up to you, or to Mother or our many brothers and sisters. But we are willing to make whatever amends you deem appropriate, so that we may once again be in your good graces."

Fianna and the others took several additional steps backwards to find themselves backed up into a wall of rocks.

"Hmph!" snorted Wiese, pawing the ground. He again paced back and forth before his sons, who pivoted on the spot, heads still lowered, trying to continue facing their angry parent. "Hmph. I will have to converse with your mother. If she is willing to accept you two disappointments, I suppose I shall as well. Although I probably should not."

With another snort, Wiese turned and approached a matriarchal Dragon who stood close by. The two exchanged a few words, and then Wiese noisily shuffled back to tower over Narco and Choy again. He raised himself as tall as he could manage and rumbled loudly. "You two sorry-looking creatures are lucky to have the wonderful mother that you do. She has decided to consider your request. So shall I, though not without dire reservations.

"Of course, considerable amends will be required before you are fully and unequivocally accepted. But, providing you perform well and faithfully, family and fold shall forgive and accept you."

Relieved but hesitant, Narco and Choy cautiously raised their heads and surveyed the large gathering. They were pleased to see all their siblings had joined their parents, as had many other members of the fold. Kerrs are not typically as warm, loving and forgiving as Nibiruans, so what Narco and Choy were experiencing was better than they had hoped for. Both smiled earnestly at the gathered group, and were nearly taken aback when smiles were returned.

Celine and the others also heaved sighs of relief, for in truth, they'd been unsure whether their new friends had led them into a trap.

"I'm glad that's over," Jager mented to Celine with a sigh. "Now for the harder part of this mission — convincing the Kerrs to join us in battle against the Lords and the Volac Forces. Perhaps once they hear Kerr is one of many planets Byrne has in line for implosion, it will be easier."

"Exactly what I've been thinking," replied Celine, relaxing her grip on the saddle horn.

"Father, thank you," said Narco and Choy, bowing to their parents and to the crowd. In no time at all, a celebration was underway, to rejoice in the troubled twins' homecoming. It wasn't as boisterous as most Dragon-kind celebrations; there was still the matter of amends, and clear evidence of reform. But for the Kerrs, it was quite unexpected. All were clearly glad that two among the increasing number of troubled youth, disillusioned with Kerr beliefs and culture, had recanted and returned. The same rebellious tendency could be found in the youth of many worlds. It seemed, unfortunately, almost a necessity, for no culture is perfect. And so change is required for any race to move forward ethically, in all times and on all worlds.

Much good often arises out of troubled times. And, fortunate for Narco and Choy, their new friends had guided them to numerous life-changing realizations — including a new-found appreciation of their homeworld, and the real possibility of a good and happy life there. They truly knew that their circumstances could be worse. Much worse, as life under Soader had proved, many times over.

After making their rounds to greet the family and friends in attendance, Narco and Choy returned to speak with Ahimoth and the others.

"See?" Narco laughed, a bit nervously, "We told you Kerr Dragons are not as bad as rumor might make you think."

"It depends on your definition of 'bad,'" chuckled Vin.

"Narco, Choy," called Wiese from across the courtyard. "Please, it is time you introduced your friends."

"Yes, Father," replied Choy. He gestured for Ahimoth and the others to follow, leading them up onto a slightly raised ledge. The grinning brothers addressed the crowd.

"Family, friends," began Choy, "We would like to introduce to you our friends from Nibiru. Princess Fianna, her brave mate Prince Vin, Fianna's brother, the great Prince Ahimoth, and his lovely mate Joli. And, accompanying Fianna and Vin, their Human Companions, Celine and Jager."

"Why have you come home?" asked a surly Dragon standing next to Wiese.

"Uncle Cleeve!" shouted Narco happily. The gruff Dragon didn't return the cheery greeting. "It is grand to see you," continued Narco. And, because he was still worried that he and Choy would be punished, he answered the elder Dragon's question. "Such a straightforward question deserves a straightforward answer, Uncle. We are here because our new friends helped us to see what is truly important in life — family, friends, and our precious home and community."

A few wry comments could be heard from among the crowd — "It's about time," "Finally!" and the like — but their tone was more positive than disparaging.

Narco heard the comments and acknowledged them, then resumed his address. "Yes, Choy and I led a disgruntled youth, as do many young people of our world. But in our case perhaps especially so, because of our unusual disfigurement. For many of the years of our absence from Kerr, we were held captive and in the hypnotic thrall of an evil Rept-hybrid. His unrelenting cruelty, twisted views and demented ways affected us badly. Since our rescue from that foul captivity, we have become aware of our own shameful failings. Some so terrible that we feared we could never forgive ourselves, let alone hope for forgiveness from anyone else."

Narco paused. His remorse was clearly visible, as was Choy's.

Narco let out a puff of air, stood taller and scanned the crowd before continuing. "In our shame, we wanted to hide; to keep far away from Kerr. Such was our fear that we had not only shamed you, but that we might relapse into reprehensible, even criminal ways."

The two then turned to Ahimoth and the others.

"Our new friends here," said Narco, raising a wing toward them and bowing, "helped us see many of our crimes were not willingly committed. They were forced upon us by our captor, through his hypnotic powers. We truly desire to live, from this time forward, as accepted and contributing members of Kerr society."

There were a few quiet cheers of approval.

"We want to live *with purpose*. We want to do good deeds. We want to be here to support and help our family and friends, especially as our enemies draw near. All just as any true Kerr would and should.

"Out across the universe, we have seen many terrible things. We do not want such things to come here, to our beautiful planet. We desire to be beside our dear family and friends; to stand with you, to defend and protect our home. We want to ensure your lives and those of future generations are free from the many evils that wicked ones in this universe seek to inflict upon any who will not bend to their evil desires.

"We now understand that when life's elements are misaligned, harmony among races suffers. It is quite clear to us that life is a true gift, and that we must make the most of the brief time we have. Planets exist for billions of years; we are only here for a speck of time. We should live our time to the fullest. That can only truly be done righteously, ethically, helping those we love and hold dear, and all our fellows. Life is precious; we should not waste the great gift we have been given, so my brother and I intend to live good lives from here on out, doing everything we can to help our family, friends and fold."

Narco stopped to smile at Ahimoth and Vin, then resumed.

"Our friends standing here beside us are willing to help defend our home, but first they need us to help them." A few growls could be heard; Narco paused, swallowed, and continued.

"We all grew up aware of our ancient paintings. The Nibiru Dragons you see before you are depicted in those paintings. If you look closely, you will see that what I say is true. You will also see that their Companions are the Humans the same murals portray. They have been working tirelessly to end the evil contagion spreading across our worlds. And with our help they will succeed."

An elegant Dragon who had been watching from the back of the gathering glided forward. As she passed, everyone bowed, then moved aside without a sound. Narco and Choy froze in place. It was Empress Pinpin Pula who approached. With exquisite grace she climbed the steps to the ledge. She stopped a meter or so from the brothers. In their excitement, they had neglected to address their royalty in a respectful manner.

"Oh, no! Your Highness," blurted Narco as he and Choy bowed repeatedly, up, down, up, down. "Oh, please, Your Highness, please excuse us. In our exuberance we forgot ourselves, and failed to pay you proper respect. Before beginning, we did not request your permission to address your people."

"You need not bow to me, Narco and Choy," said the empress. "Please, I welcome your boldness and your honest desire to help your new friends. Besides, you appeal for help in ensuring the safety and well being of Kerr. This is refreshing. You have my blessing. Please, let us know how the noble people of Kerr may help."

Ahimoth and the others helped Narco and Choy explain the assistance they hoped of them. The discussion was much shorter than the visitors had expected, for the willingness and desire to help shown by Empress Pinpin and her people was surprisingly strong.

"Prince Ahimoth, you must celebrate with us before you leave," said Pinpin. "We shall rejoice in Narco and Choy's return, and in our fortuitous encounter with all of you." And before they knew it, Celine and the others were wrapped up in the Kerrs' festivities. It wasn't long, though, before the visitors retired to one side and waited for Narco and Choy to notice and join them.

"Narco, Choy," said Ahimoth when the brothers approached. "We are sorry that we must leave in the middle of a grand celebration, especially one in your honor, but present circumstances confront us with much to address. We will depart shortly, but within a few days' time we will once again use the comm stone to inform you of the day and hour of our return. When we have rejoined you here, we wish to meet with your leaders to lay out and finalize our strategies and plans for the unfortunate but inevitable war that approaches. We do yet have hope no battle involving your people will be necessary. If that proves to be the case, we will inform you so in a comm-stone message. That is the message we would greatly prefer to send, and I pray to the Ancients it will be so."

"We do not know how ever to thank all of you," said Choy. "Not only have you helped my brother and me when we did not deserve it, but you came here to help our people as well. You are truly remarkable beings. Both Narco and I will do everything we can to ensure that every last Kerr is ready to assist when you return. Fly safe, stay strong."

Fianna and the other Dragons bowed to the twins, as did Celine and Jager from their saddles. Final goodbyes were said, and Narco and Choy watched their new friends speed skyward.

CHAPTER 28

Satchels

The morning after their trip to Kerr, Jager joined Celine in her room to find her hunkered over *The Book of Atlantis*. He'd just made himself comfortable next to her when she jumped up.

"We need to go back to Mu," she gasped. In a rush, she darted about the room gathering items and stuffing them into her bodypack. "And right away, too!" she exclaimed, stopping to fix Jager with an anxious look. "I know we have other plans for this morning, but I'm afraid we need to see Father Greer. Before we do anything else, we've got to get ahold of whatever it is he has in the satchels he gathered on our last trip to see him. I just know it."

"Hmmm. Okay. This is unexpected," laughed Jager. "What's happening?"

Celine explained the difficulties she was having with the time-travel spell they'd soon need to use, and he agreed it sounded like the satchels probably held the solution. He grinned, his love for her growing by the second as she stood there with her hands on her hips and her lips pressed tight.

"Ha ha!" he laughed.

"What are you laughing at?" she asked, frowning.

"Oh, sorry, Pumpkin. I was just admiring your brains and determination, that's all. Sorry if I came across judgemental. I just think you are amazing!"

"Oh," said Celine, a blush rising in her cheeks. "Sorry I was rude. I think my sister has rubbed off on me more than I realized."

"No worries," laughed Jager. He gave her a quick hug. "By what I just read, you are spot on, sweetie. Heading to see Father Greer is reasonable, even though it will affect our timeline. West is not expected back for another day, but I'm sure North will help us again."

"I'm sure she will," said Celine. Smiling, she pulled on her bodypack. Jager went to his room, grabbed his own pack, threw in a few items, and rejoined Celine to race off to the transbeam room. Before long, they found themselves on Mu, standing before Father Greer. The old man chuckled, as though he'd been expecting them.

"Come," gestured the priest. He led them through the crevice which led to his home within the mountainside; the opening disappeared without a sound once the three had passed through. The youngsters grinned at each other, memories of their last visit here coming to the fore. They followed the elderly man to his humble home, stepping into his chamber just as steam began to spiral upward from a whistling kettle. The aroma of a batch of fresh biscuits teased them from a plate in the middle of Father Greer's small table.

Celine laughed as even more shared memories surfaced between her and Jager — as though their thoughts arose from a single entity.

The two sat down and dug into the priest's famous and delicious teala and biscuits.

"Yes," said Jager in between chews, "you are correct, Father, we've come for some things we believe are in the satchels we gathered while on Pax. Recently we saw a cave-wall painting on Nibiru that depicted Celine and I poring over documents and a grimoire. Right beside us — in the painting, that is — was an open satchel, just like the ones you collected. And earlier today, when we were trying to decipher a spell from *The Book of Atlantis*, we realized we could not proceed without the items portrayed in the painting."

"I expected as much," replied the priest, "and that is why I rummaged through all the satchels and gathered the specific items and documents you would need. And, I should add, the riddles you'll need to find Prince Deet's grimoire."

Celine and Jager laughed. "Of course you did," chuckled Celine. The cleric joined them in a good laugh.

Seeing as Father Greer had saved them considerable time, they took the opportunity to relax, if but a little. They enjoyed a pleasant conversation with the priest, sipping teala and munching biscuits. It was a welcome moment of normalcy.

"Father," said Jager, after polishing off another cup of teala, "is it all right to enquire about your relationship with Jaecar?"

"Yes, of course," replied the man. "That must have been quite a shock, discovering you had a brother. And a twin, at that. And mentored by *me*, of all people!" He grinned, his eyes alight with their mischievous twinkle.

"Yes, it was a bit of a surprise, to say the least."

"As I believe you know," continued Greer, "I have been a Mentor to Jaecar for quite some time, much as West has been to you."

"Yes, I figured that to be the case. Are you able to ment with him regularly, as we are with West?"

"Yes and no. Since you and Celine conducted the unification ceremony, the protective barrier between Nibiru and Pax prevents me from reaching him."

"I was afraid that would happen," said Jager, "and that's why I asked. Is there any way of getting through the barrier? I know the one that surrounded just Nibiru was not penetrable, but I was hoping this new barrier was somewhat different, especially since I was able to get through after it was first created."

"Yes, it is a different form of magic," replied Greer. "And, yes, there is a spell that can penetrate the barrier. That is another reason we collected the satchels. The spell, which only you or Celine can cast, will enable you to get through to Jaecar. It's right here." The priest gestured toward a nearby table covered with old books and some scattered papers, held down by colorful dragon figurines of polished stone. "Come, see what I refer to."

The young couple stepped up to the table and were quickly immersed in the ancient parchments and grimoires spread before them. The craftmanship and beauty of the relics was awe-inspiring. Father Greer prepared more teala, which they sipped while discussing which items and information they'd need to locate Mutuum, and to help them if unexpected circumstances arose along the way. Soon both their bodypacks were stuffed full of grimoires, parchments and artifacts — as well as a couple of bundles of delicious biscuits.

"Oh, one more thing," said the Mentor-priest. He pulled a small grimoire from within his robes, followed by an incant-baton. "I figured time was of the essence, so I took the liberty of tracking down Prince Deet's grimoire and incant-baton for you, too. And here they are!"

"Ha-ha!" laughed Celine and Jager together.

"Of course you did," said Celine. "I thought we were going to need Alden Koondahg's assistance to find these. You are so full of surprises, Father." She rushed to give the old man a warm hug. As she pulled away, she caught Jager's thought. "Yes, you are correct, Jager." She turned to address the priest. "Although we've enjoyed the visit immensely, Father, we should get back. Time is slipping by." The couple said their goodbyes and were soon back in the Mentor outpost's refectory, talking with Vin and the others about their trip and all the treasures they'd brought back — Prince Deet's incant-baton and grimoire foremost among them.

Celine felt humbled as she lovingly took up the well-worn grimoire Prince Deet himself had once used. She sat down, and with gentle fingers, loosed the leather thong tied tight around it. She opened the book and began tenderly turning its pages. She was impressed with the simple beauty of the book's design, and the adornments each page bore. To her surprise, the spell book even had a pleasant scent to it. There was none of the musty odor one expected from such an ancient object. The others sat nearby in silence, watching and waiting for the girl to speak.

"I found it," she laughed, after a few minutes had passed. "I can't believe how easy that was. Finding a spell in *The Book of Atlantis* typically took days, yet I found this one just like that."

"Wonderful," said Fianna. "This is a good sign."

"Indeed," said Vin. "A very good sign, and a blessing."

"Good job, Pumpkin," said Jager, holding Prince Deet's personal incant-baton. As soon as the boy had picked up the ancient implement, he'd felt its warmth. He was intrigued by the sense of strength and certainty it seemed to impart. And, oddly, it felt as though the wand were a part of him. As if it had always been his.

Celine sensed what Jager was experiencing. "Feels good, does it?" she asked.

"Surprisingly so," he replied, looking down at the cherrywood baton cradled in both his hands. "I'm not going to want to give this up when all this is over."

"Maybe you won't have to," smiled Celine. The young man smiled back. "I guess there is no time like the present to get to work and learn the spell for finding Mutuum," she said, and returned to emptying her bodypack and arraying its contents on the table.

"I'll assist, if you like," offered Jager. She nodded, and he rose to help organize the items, placing each one just so.

"Fianna, my dear," said Vin. "I have a suggestion. I believe this is a good opportunity for us to spend some quality time with Fallon and the others."

"That is a great idea!" said Ahimoth. "Oh, my," he exclaimed. "I cannot believe it! I just interrupted you! Celine is rubbing off on me." He and the others laughed, but for Celine — who stood with her hands to her hips, scowling. Everyone, Celine included, knew the comment and laughter were just in fun. The Dragons headed off, and Celine and Jager were alone.

Working as a team, they soon had everything in order. "Okay!" said Celine. "Let's begin." With a firm grasp on Prince Deet's incant-baton, she made several attempts at performing the incantation, but to no effect. "I don't understand," she grumbled. She stood up, stretched, then bent down again over the ancient book. "I did exactly what the spell states, but it just doesn't work. I don't think I'm doing it incorrectly; it's as though something is missing, or a part of the spell isn't here."

Jager gave the spell a couple of tries. "Hm. I'm confused, too," he said. "What should we do? We need to figure this out, but fast."

"Hmmm," said Celine. "West or one of the other Mentors could probably help, but for some reason I'm sensing we should be looking to someone else entirely." She picked up her bodypack and dug deep into it to pull out a dog-eared yellow book. She pointed to the cover and beamed. "Alden Koondahg!"

"Oh! And who is he again?"

"You remember! My favorite author! I used to talk about him *all* the time as a kid. *Alden Koondahg!* I'm certain he can help locate Mutuum. Joli has told us he must also be present when we cast the spell, but perhaps there is more to that — and to why the spell isn't working for us now. Maybe he is meant to teach us how to properly render the spells from Prince Deet's grimoire.

"I've read all his books on magic. Several times. They're magnificent. He hid riddles in the text, with resourceful answers to many of society's problems. Quite ingenious, really. I used to cross-read his books and piece together powerful spells. It was some of those that helped keep me alive when my mother, Mia and I were kidnapped."

"Well, I'm very grateful for that," said Jager. "He sounds perfect, then."

"Yes, I believe he is. I learned a great deal from him about many interesting and wonderful things, including ancient and black magic."

"Interesting," said Jager, paging through the small, well-worn book. "Where do we find him?"

"Good question. I believe I'll find the answer in his books, though. Give me a couple of minutes." Jager handed the book back and Celine went to work, flipping back and forth through its pages. Occasionally she paused to make notes in her hand computer, mumbling to herself. She came to the end of the first book, set it carefully aside, pulled another from her bodypack and repeated the process. Meanwhile Jager sat at the computer console, researching spacecraft.

Half an hour after she began, Celine raised her hand-held high and shouted, "I know where he is! And he's not too far from here. We could use one of the shuttles and be back in no time."

"Sounds like a plan," smiled Jager, and they headed down the corridor toward the transbeam room, menting North as they went. Celine explained what they intended, and North agreed at once to send them to Koondahg's location in a shuttle with jump-shift capabilities. "Thanks, North," said Jager. "We definitely owe you for all your tremendous support."

The Mentor acknowledged the young man, saying, "It is I and my fellow Mentors who should be thanking you. Now, please take this long-range comm stone with you, in case you need to leave the shuttle and are not otherwise able to reach me or my sisters."

"Thanks."

A few minutes later the Humans clambered into the small craft and guided it into orbit above the Mentor outpost, still within the cloaking barrier. Jager, at the controls, grinned at Celine as she secured her restraints. He programed in their destination and engaged the jump-shift drive. The ship hummed and vibrated, and in seconds they found themselves uncounted light-years away, orbiting a tiny, green-blue planet. From space, it looked like a tri-colored marble, thanks to abundant patches of bright white cloud cover. Celine, a much more experienced shuttle pilot, took the controls and brought the craft to ground beside a small lake — the spot where she'd deduced they would find Mr. Koondahg. The pair exited the craft and were pleased to find the air fresh and the temperature pleasant. They gazed across the water towards a small cabin, smoke rising almost straight up from its crooked chimney.

"How beautiful," exclaimed Celine, bending down to pick an orange-colored flower. She took several whiffs of its deep fragrance, a pleasant, heady scent.

"Yes indeed," replied Jager. "Such a place would be a dream vacation spot for many an Earther. Look over there — that man fishing from the end of the pier just landed a fish."

The man looked up, directly at Jager, and smiled as if he'd been waiting for their arrival to show off his fishing skills. He gestured for the pair to join him, so they made their way through the tall grass surrounding the lake and met up with the man at the foot of his cabin's porch stairs.

"What a pleasant surprise," laughed the man. "I've had few visitors in recent years."

"Hello, sir," said Celine, offering her hand. The elderly

gentleman gripped it with both of his and shook with great vigor, the sleeves of his ostentatiously multi-colored robe flapping about.

"Once I decided to find you, sir, it wasn't really difficult at all," she said with a smile.

"No?" laughed the man. "I suppose I didn't make it *too* difficult, but I had hoped more would come seek me out. Magic must not be appreciated much these days. Because of ol' Scabbage, I reckon. After he banned magic, I figured this would be the case. Please, though, tell me: How are things on Erra?"

"Well, uh, sir," replied Celine, "we do not have much time to socialize, but I would gladly explain anything you want to know, and more, if you would come with us. I promise we'll return you home as soon as we are able, but we first need your assistance with a couple of old spells."

"Oh? How completely unorthodox, young lady." The wizard scratched at his untamed beard. "But most interesting," he continued. "I've always loved a good mystery. And unorthodoxy even more! So, I guess I'm going on an adventure today. Just this morning I was telling myself how bored I've been of late. And lo and behold, you two arrive."

The man rubbed his dry old hands together like a child anticipating a birthday surprise. "This should be fun. Where did you say we were going?"

"I didn't say," answered Celine, "but I would like you to come with us to a Mentor outpost. Jager and I must travel to Planet 444 — Earth, you know — and we need your assistance in casting a spell from some ancient grimoires once we get there. You see, we found you depicted in an ancient cave-wall painting on Remini. On the walls of Pagan Mountain, to be exact. So, we believe you are connected with our quest, and that you're the one person who can assist us with the spell in question. Our belief has been reinforced by information from a wise and powerful being known as Dagmar, relayed to us by one of our company, whom Dagmar mentored and trained in the magical arts."

"Hmm!" said the colorful wizard, and he rubbed his hands together some more.

Celine continued. "I guess it's important to mention that the Mentors have said that Jager and I are needed to protect the Dragon races, and the knowledge the paintings hold bears directly on how we're to proceed."

"Well, that is most unorthodox indeed," said Koondahg. "To protect the Dragons of the universe, you say. Hm!" Celine and Jager nodded. The sagacious old man raised a hand to his beard and began to stroke it — and bobbed his head, much as Dragons do when deep in thought. Celine and Jager recognized the mannerism at once, and shared a look of surprise. The wizard continued to bob in silence, eyes closed and hands now clasped at his bearded chin. His young visitors knew not to interrupt.

After a pause, the man stopped bobbing and opened his eyes. "I need to go inside and gather some things," he said, and quickly turned to go. Celine and Jager moved to a rickety bench at one corner of the porch, but didn't get to rest for long. The wizard soon reappeared and stepped down from the porch into the sunlight, a large leather bag in one hand and a peculiar-looking, purple-hued, raven-like bird perched on his left shoulder. The bird cawed loudly at Celine and Jager.

"Yes, you are quite correct, Leopold," chuckled the wizard. "I couldn't have stated it better. And yes, these two are most powerful in the ways of magic."

The pair shared a smile, and were about to lead the tall man back to the shuttle when he whisked his incant-baton back and forth a few times and began to mutter. Seconds later, a whirling funnel of wind spun around them at tremendous speed. Celine gasped and grabbed Jager's arm. Moments later they were swept up into the air and whisked away, the wizard and Leopold right beside them and looking utterly unconcerned. Moments later the four were deposited beside the waiting shuttle in a spew of flying debris.

Alden chuckled at his young friends and stepped up to the little craft's hatch to await their permission to board her.

"Please," said Celine, with a grin to Jager and a "go ahead" gesture to the wizard. "Do make yourself comfortable." Jager winked at Celine and the two followed the old man. Before long they were safely back at the outpost, where North greeted them at the transbeam platform. She was delighted to be introduced to the wizard and called for South, who quickly arrived.

"Please, kindly follow me," said South. The trio followed her lead as she showed the colorful man and his even more colorful bird to their accommodations.

"We must leave you now," said Jager, "but we'll be back in a few minutes to collect you, sir."

"I'll be ready," replied the wizard. "But please, call me Alden. Yes, Alden. I'd like that. For few have ever called me by my name. Besides, 'Mr. Koondahg' sounds much too formal. Yes, much too formal."

Alden strode into the room he'd been shown and placed his bag on a table. Leopold leapt off his shoulder and sat on the bag. "So, Leopold, what do you think of this lovely room?"

The bird replied with a long string of gurgling croaks and one long, raucous caw.

"I quite agree, my friend," replied Alden. "It will be a nice change, that's for sure. I do believe I am enjoying this adventure. And I believe it is the sort of thing we should perhaps do more often."

A few minutes later, the little party met with Fianna and the others in the refectory. Alden was beyond charmed to meet the Dragons. And amazed, after a quick briefing on what the Dragons and their Human friends had accomplished in recent weeks. The briefing completed, the Dragons excused themselves so the young Humans and their new guest could get to work, untangling and perfecting the spell from the prized grimoires.

It soon became apparent how imperative it was to cast the spells without error. The three decided to practice in an empty corner of the room, where less damage would be caused if an error were made in the spell-casting. Nonetheless, before long, they had destroyed several chairs, two tables, a vase of pretty pink flowers and four ceiling panels.

After several hours it became obvious that the only sensible solution was for Alden to be present when the spell was cast. So he must also accompany the two youngsters to the Atlantean tunnels. The idea was discussed with West, who agreed wholeheartedly. The wizard, she reasoned, was proficient in casting intricate and ancient incantations, similar to those they were dealing with; his presence would be invaluable. The Dragons also felt better knowing he'd be along — an additional power to protect everyone involved. This was no ill reflection on Celine or Jager's abilities. Rather, it appeared that Alden was *meant* to be present at the casting — even though the images in some of the paintings appeared to indicate otherwise. It also helped explain why Alden was represented in a key painting on Remini.

Failure to correctly cast the traveling spell could mean death, so everyone wanted to ensure only success with their hazardous travels back into time.

After the midday meal, Alden said he required a nap, so Celine and Jager escorted him to his room, then headed back to the refectory. Although the wizard would join them for their time travel to the ancient tunnels, the Humans continued to practice for hours, until they were competent at casting the time-traveling spell on their own — now that Alden had taught them the elements they'd been missing. They figured this was vital in the event that their plans went sideways. They knew Dagmar had insisted Alden must be present when the incantation was performed, but thought it best to be prepared for anything. When finally satisfied with their abilities, they began to pack things and clean up the considerable mess that had grown over their hours of practice. When they'd nearly finished the job, Fianna and Vin arrived.

"It's in case the unexpected happens," said Celine to Fianna, explaining why they had practiced the spell so long and hard, even though Alden was to be on hand.

"Most wise, dear friend," replied Fianna, only somewhat comforted by Celine's words. She kept her premonitions to herself; she was deeply concerned over her increasing distress. It filled her mind's eye with darkness.

Despite Fianna's apprehensions, the friends enjoyed a fun evening, with Alden joining them for a fine meal, then for a gaming session. Ahimoth didn't let anyone down with his "Who can do ___ better than I?" challenges. Everyone was determined to keep their attention focused in the present, throughout the evening. For the most part, they managed to bar wandering thoughts until the hour was late.

"Sleep well," said Fianna to Celine and Jager. "May your dreams be pleasant."

"Thanks, Fianna. Good night," they replied, to Fianna and to the others as well. They raced each other to their rooms, where they gathered what they'd need for the next morning's dangerous journey. They set everything out near the transbeam platform, then went to West's office to bid her good night. They were surprised to find her chatting with the wizard, and even more surprised to discover that the two were old friends.

"Ha ha," laughed Celine. "West, I should have known that my favorite author of magic books would be a friend of yours." Everyone had a good laugh before the young Humans said their good-nights and headed to their beds.

As had become too usual, both Celine and Jager had a difficult time falling asleep. Each tossed and turned, struggling with dire scenarios of what might transpire in the morning. Both feared what their failure might mean to those they loved, and to the entire planet of Earth.

It had been announced earlier in the day that the harvesting station at TS 428 was near completion, so both young Humans knew time was not on their side.

In order to fall asleep, Celine decided to divert her attention onto other things. She began reminiscing over her wonderful relationship with Fianna, but that didn't help. She tossed and turned some more, begging for sleep to come. Realizing at last that sleep was unattainable, she called softly to Fianna, to see if her friend was still awake. Sure enough, Fianna was having similar troubling thoughts, and unable to sleep. That was all the excuse Celine needed; soon she stood at the entrance to Fianna's cave, laughing. For there was Jager, already curled up between Vin's forelegs. Celine smiled when he raised his head to grin at her. She hugged Fianna, settled down against the Dragon's warm underbelly, and quickly fell asleep.

CHAPTER 29

Surprise Assistance

Jager, although curled up next to Vin, still had his usual
difficulties getting a good night's rest. First, a particularly
bad dream dragged him awake. He sat up to rub his throbbing temples, using circular motions that brought sighs of
relief.

In the dreamworld the past few nights, he'd perceived and
analyzed vibrations that originated from sentient beings.
Now, as he rubbed his temples, the answer to a problem that
had troubled him for weeks suddenly became clear. He sat
straight up, mouth agape, then mented Celine, forgetting it
was still the middle of the night.

"Huh?" asked a groggy Celine. "Jager, is everything all
right?"

"Oh. Sorry, Pumpkin. I was so excited I didn't realize the
time. Go back to sleep and I'll tell you in the morning."

In more normal circumstances, Celine would insist that

Jager fill her in immediately. But because of the poor sleep she'd been getting for weeks now, she was more than happy to do as he asked. Jager, delighted with his realization, lay happily back down and soon fell into a restful slumber.

The next morning at breakfast, Jager explained to Celine and the others what he'd surmised during the night. "I am *so* embarrassed," he groaned, "and don't know why I didn't think of this before. As we discussed a few days ago, we were going to use Soader's body, stored at TS 428, to lure Scabbage out. Dummy me, not thinking of this at the time, but we also might be able to use it to trap Piccolo."

"What a great idea!" exclaimed Celine. "Although I'm not eager for you to be inside that repulsive person's body, I see the brilliance in your suggestion. Perhaps it's something we should do sooner, rather than later."

"I believe you're right," replied Jager. "You and I ought to head to TS 428 right away and retrieve the body. If we do this correctly, we could draw Piccolo out of hiding, maybe even today. By now he's most likely heard Soader was sent to RPF113, so I figure hearing from his cousin will surprise and confuse him. Knock him off balance, so to speak. I think it'll be easy to find him; all my research has convinced me that he's almost surely searching for Soader's loot right this minute.

"Also, my studies indicate Piccolo is every bit as tenacious as Soader. I'd bet he's already at Dulce, searching up a storm. He's going to be surprised and shaken when I show up in Soader's body."

"Good point, Jager," said Celine. "And I know you've told me before that being in Soader's body isn't dangerous, but are you absolutely sure? I really don't like the sound of this." A shiver ran down her spine; Jager put an arm around her.

"I understand, sweetie," he replied. "Truth be told, I don't relish the idea, but do you remember that painting where you appear to be holding Soader's hand?"

"Yes. Yes, I do, and I hated it. I hated it the first moment I saw it, and I always will. I believe the Dragon prophecies, though, and that's the only reason I'd let you go through with this."

Jager grinned at her and squeezed her tight. "It will be fine, Pumpkin."

"Celine, is correct, Jager," spoke up Vin. "There is still time to do what you propose before we search for Mutuum. Your plan has merit, but I too have misgivings about your entering that vile body. I do not fully understand what role this Piccolo character plays, but I feel it is somehow crucial that we find him. We Dragons have a saying that applies to such situations as this. It bids us to follow our hearts and minds. It emphasizes the importance of acting upon our assumptions and premonitions, even though one may tend to prefer facts and solid evidence before taking important steps."

"Well said, friend," said Ahimoth. "The proposal has my vote." He chuckled at having used one of Jager's favorite sayings. "Besides," said the Dragon, "I look forward to watching what you've suggested you'll do with Soader's body once our mission is complete. Soader won't be animating the body, but I will enjoy the proceedings nevertheless. It is something I dreamt of doing more than once, during those many years he tortured me."

"I too will enjoy the event, Ahimoth," added Vin, pacing. "I know that we, as caring and compassionate people, should not feel this way, or look forward to such a thing, but I believe it will greatly assist the healing process. Besides, the act will also do the entire universe a great deal of good."

"True, very true," said Ahimoth. "And there is also this bonus: If Soader were to learn how much he had helped the universe, he would probably suffer some spiritual ailment and die on the spot."

"Ha ha!" laughed Vin. "That is a comforting thought." The Dragon paused, then turned to Jager. "Jager, you are sure this will not damage you in any way, yes?"

"That's correct, my friend. I will not come to harm. I'll be very sure to exit Soader's body before it's destroyed. So, no worries. I'll be safe. You must wait, though, until we lure Scabbage out after we've captured Piccolo. The High Chancellor is the ultimate prize."

Jager patted Vin on a foreleg, then continued. "I believe the easiest and best way to get word out regarding Soader, and to proceed with our plans, is to drum up some fake 'news' and cycle it through the channels across several sectors. We could say he was seen blowing up an academy, killing thousands of cadets, as revenge for what I did to him. We need to make sure to use some obscure, distant planet to make it sound plausible. In the same report, we can say he destroyed two Fleet police vessels that had chased him across several parsecs before he escaped, and that a major manhunt has been launched, with a juicy reward for information leading to his capture."

"Oh, this is fun," giggled Celine. "I've never been one for this sort of thing, but we haven't been having much fun these days. I must be lowering my standards to see any pleasure in this, but I surely do!" She giggled some more. "Years ago, my mother warned this would happen if I didn't stop my pursuit of magic. Perhaps she was correct." She and the others burst out laughing when Jager did a pretty good imitation of Remi —hand to his hip, wagging a finger at Celine.

"Okay, Jager," laughed Celine. "You win the prize for being the funniest." Everyone laughed some more; a good thing, for strength is drawn from laughter. It felt especially good after all the talk about the hated Soader and Scabbage.

"We need to do this right away," said Celine, matter-of-factly. "Before we blow up the transfer station. It won't be easy, but I think we can get some help from the fellow I met there. From what you've said, it sounds like he's the same guy who helped Soader transfer into your body."

"Good idea, Celine," replied Jager. "Just the two of us should do this, though. A group could draw unwanted attention, especially if it included a couple of Dragons." To their Dragon friends, he added, "No offense intended."

"None taken, my friend," laughed Vin. "I do not want you and Celine to do this on your own, but you are correct. And I know you will be careful. I also know I will not be the only one worrying every single minute until you return. Return unharmed, I must add."

Fianna was visibly upset at the imminent parting, so Celine took a moment to soothe her. Then the group joined North, waiting for them at the transbeam chamber. Before she stepped up to the platform, Celine, looking pensive, addressed her friends. "With each passing day I am more amazed at what I see and experience. I look back to when Jager and I were younger, learning new skills under West's tutelage. Back then, I could never have envisioned my life as it is now. I cannot imagine what it will be like in the near future. Even the present is nearly unbelievable. But I thank all of you from the bottom of my heart for all your tremendous love and support. You all make what we are doing more than worthwhile. I love you all dearly."

Jager gave Celine a tight hug. All remained silent, deep in

their own thoughts on life and living. Celine and Jager stood tall while North, with one graceful move, 'beamed the three travelers — Celine, Jager and herself — to the waiting ship above. The Dragons sadly left the transbeam chamber. They met up with East and South, who assisted them in getting the word out regarding Soader's latest alleged exploits.

North soon deposited the pair at Transfer Station 428, 'beaming them from her ship to the same platform Celine, Fianna and Ahimoth had arrived upon not long before, by way of the Chalice Well. As the 'beam field dissipated, they were surprised to see that the little-used transbeam bay was not empty. There was Monty — the very fellow Celine had met last time she arrived on the platform — walking away from them toward the entrance.

Jager, seeing Monty's back, instantly cast an invisibility spell. So, when the little transfer technician turned to see who had arrived in the transbeam, he was befuddled to see the platform empty.

"Gods-damned equipment," growled Monty. He spat on the floor. "It's all falling apart. Everywhere!" He continued to growl and grumble as he exited the bay and ambled toward the other side of the complex.

Since G.O.D. had arrived to set up the harvest equipment, the creature had found the place too damned loud and too damned overcrowded — things he complained about non-stop. To alleviate some of his annoyance, he often hid in his favorite place to enjoy a nap. Transfers from Earth had been reduced, so he had more time on his hands — time he used to disappear for his little snooze breaks. The last of the recently installed equipment had been assembled incorrectly, requiring extensive correction. And those in charge were at odds over what really needed correction, and how any correction was to be done. So it was easy for Monty to vanish while the bigwigs bickered and shouted amongst themselves.

The new automatic mechanisms would increase station capacity by twenty times. That meant twenty times as many Earther souls popped into Universal Soul Containment chambers than what Monty could manage manually. Once the faulty installation had been corrected, the new machinery had mysteriously broken *again*. Monty heard his boss Richter arguing with several G.O.D. officials, adamant that it must be sabotage. Monty made a mental note to be more careful in the future.

As he sauntered off, Celine and Jager — still invisible — slipped from the platform and followed Monty until the three of them were the only people around. Jager was about to reverse the invisibility spell, but held back when Monty stopped in front of a partially open roll-up door, looked cautiously around to be sure no one was watching, and ducked through the opening. The pair crouched down and followed him. Once inside what appeared to be a long-unused storage space, Jager flicked his wrist and their invisibility cloaking lifted.

Jager cleared his throat and Monty, startled, spun around — thinking his boss had somehow caught him. He was more than surprised to see Jager and Celine, both of whom he recognized at once. "Oh! It's...it's you," he stammered, worried eyes darting here and there for any sign of the Dragons. "Uh...uh, surprise, yes, yes, what a surprise. Indeed. What a surprise. But then again, perhaps not."

Jager held his incant-baton high and flicked it toward a light fixture in the ceiling above. The light shattered violently. "Okay, mister," he said. "As you've just seen, I'm deadly with this thing. So you'd better do as we ask."

The trembling creature nodded his cooperation.

"Take us to Soader's body. He won't be needing it anymore."

"I heard, yup. Yup, I heard. I heard what you did to that wretched monster, and I am pleased. Yup, I am," said Monty, bowing over and over. "Come. Come this way." He led the two out the way they'd just entered.

"We need to be discreet," whispered Jager.

"Yup, yup indeed. That is what I assumed," replied Monty, stopping to look Jager up and down again. "Come, this way is safe." The creature did not wait for a reply, but headed on down the corridor toward another facility.

A minute later, Celine and Jager were looking down at Soader's body, floating in a vat of preservative fluid. They cringed at the sight. It looked as though the Rept was just sleeping; it was hard to believe that the body was now soulless, inanimate. To Celine, it still had a sinister presence about it. She shivered in disgust.

"I took care of it, yup, that's what I did," said Monty, his strange, twangy voice seeming to hang in the air even after he'd spoken. "Don't know why, no, don't know why, 'cause he was evil. An evil one, he was. I thought it important, though. Yup, so I did. It's good. The body is good. I took care of it."

"I am glad you did," said Jager. "Thanks."

"Good, good," said Monty, his eyebrows raised, pleased and surprised at the courtesy Jager had shown him. "Body is good. It is ready. You want me to transfer you into it, right?"

"That is correct," replied Jager, giving one of Celine's hands a gentle squeeze.

"I still don't like this," mented Celine, "but you are right. It will help a great deal to get us into Dulce, and perhaps even to get aboard *Morrighan.*"

"How long is it going to take you to get everything ready?" asked Jager with a glare, pointing his incant-baton toward Monty with a steady arm. He wanted Monty to know that, courtesy aside, he still meant business.

"Right sir, uhhhh, thirty minutes, sir." With that, the little fellow got to work.

Jager and Celine exchanged a look, then peered down at the body once again, silent in their own thoughts of the Rept-hybrid's horrendous acts, and how those acts had changed their lives forever.

Jager clasped Celine's hand and pulled her close. They stood that way for several moments, sheltered from bad thoughts in their own private space. They drew apart and shared warm smiles, then settled at a workstation at one side of the room. Celine carefully drew Prince Deet's grimoire from her bodypack so they could study the crucial incantation some more. They sat with knees touching, silently rehearsing the spell. Before they knew it, Monty returned and urged them to come forward.

Celine gave Fianna a quick mental call to let her know they were fine, and then joined Jager at the side of the hated body, now strapped to a transfer table.

"As I said, I really don't like this," repeated Celine, "but I know it is a necessity. Jager, please, make it quick."

"I will, Pumpkin. I love you." They embraced and kissed. Then Jager lay where Monty indicated, on the adjacent table.

CHAPTER 30

"Soader" Comes Alive

Celine didn't want to watch, but the technology fascinated her, so she stepped back and observed from a few meters away. First, she saw Monty attach tubes and leads to the Rept body, then to Jager. She wanted to tell the man to stop more than once, but managed to keep silent — even when a sling-and-hoist mechanism lowered Jager's body into the same preservation tank that had held Soader's not an hour before.

The transfer process was completed, with the usual dramatic flashings and noises. And when it was over, Soader's body sat up, swung around, and dangled its legs over the table's edge. Jager found it strange to see the humpback through Soader's eyes. And stranger still, to use the Rept's body to nod. He looked down at the hands and feet he now controlled. Very strange indeed, he thought. And *very* uncomfortable.

"Do not talk," said Monty, fiddling at a nearby control console. "You must not talk. No, not yet. Come, carefully get down and step over here into the cleansing unit. It will clean off the preservative fluids, and dry you off nicely, too."

"Are you okay?" Celine mented at once, not wanting Jager to answer using the body, against Monty's warning. And besides, she did not want to hear Soader's voice, even if it were Jager behind the words and thoughts.

"Yes, Pumpkin, I'm good," he mented in reply. "Just getting used to how this body feels and moves. It's so much larger than mine. I'll need a few minutes at least, to figure out how to master these huge limbs before we head to Earth. Please thank Monty for me, and tell him we'll be back soon, so he shouldn't stray far."

She relayed Jager's message, and Monty nodded, bobbed and bowed. "But remember, do not talk," he grunted. "Not yet. In thirty minutes, it will be okay then. This body will be okay. Not like the one Scabbage has."

"What?!" asked both Celine and Jager — though Jager's query was mental only.

"What are you talking about?" she asked, at the same time receiving a flurry of questions from Jager: "What body? When? Is he sure it was Scabbage?" She relayed his questions.

"A few days ago," replied Monty. "Yes, him I know, that Scabbage. He is an evil one; evil like Soader, but worse. Almost dead his old body was. Took the body of a big guard chief, he did. Soader's number-one guard. Scabbage's old body died in the transfer. The big mean fellow's body, that's what he's got now. Orme, they called him. I saw him before, so him I know."

"Wow!" exclaimed Jager to Celine. "I didn't see this coming.

I knew Scabbage was dying, but I didn't expect him to end up on Earth. And in the body of one of Soader's people. This helps us a lot, do you see that?"

"Ah...yes. Yes, I think I see. It's indeed a surprise," mented back Celine. "I need to think a bit on this." She paused, then went on. "Okay, I can see it will change our plans for snagging Piccolo. It might make things easier. It will definitely make it more dangerous though, as both Scabbage and Piccolo appear to be at Dulce. You know, Jager, you don't have to do this. We can come up with a different plan. Besides, Piccolo might not be that important after all."

"It's okay, sweetie," said Jager. He tried his best to give her an encouraging smile, although he could see right away she was having difficulty interpreting his look, since it was coming from Soader's face.

"I can do this, and I'll be okay," he said. "We should get going though. Shall we?" He offered his arm, and Celine grudgingly took it. They made their way back to the trans-beam platform and were soon back aboard North's ship.

A short time later, with Jager fully in control of the body, he and Celine found themselves peering from around a large rock near the main entrance to the Dulce compound. Though Celine had cloaked them in invisibility, both were at maximum alert, supremely cautious.

Jager flexed his unfamiliar vocal apparatus several times, then whispered to Celine. "You know, Pumpkin, there was a bounty on this body. And now there's probably a heftier one, since we've spread all those fabricated tales of Soader's latest exploits. So you'd better keep that incant-baton at the ready, in case someone decides to try to cash in. Besides, when Piccolo sees me, he's going to want to do the same thing. Or, more likely, just kill me on the spot. I read that his entire adult life has been about taking revenge on Soader, so he could be the one to slice this very thick neck."

"I *still* don't like this, Jager. I don't want to leave you alone here. Not for one moment. And I won't. Especially now that Scabbage is probably here at the compound, too. There's no telling what he might do. Back on Erra, Scabbage is infamous for being devious in the extreme. I'm staying right with you, invisible, no matter what. I'm going to protect you whether you like it or not."

"Yes, ma'am," he mented, with a quick salute. He loved how protective she became at times like this. "I think it's a great idea. Really, I do, Capitan Zulak."

Celine giggled in spite of herself. "But, 'capitan?' Sounds like 'captain,' but not quite.

"It is 'captain,'" Jager explained, "but in another Earth language called Spanish. Just a little joke, that's all!"

She laughed again, then lifted the spell from around Jager. Now visible, he stepped from behind the boulder and strutted toward the compound gates. The guards' eyes widened with his every approaching step. Their huge guard-beasties, familiar with Soader and so not aware of anything unusual, showed no sign of concern.

"Whatcha staring at?" barked Jager at the nearest guard. Jager, intimately familiar with Soader's memories, knew exactly how to behave toward his minions. "Open the gods-damned gates, you useless pieces of dirt."

The confused guards gaped at Soader, then at each other and back to the big Rept. They shared a look again, shrugged, and released the security barriers. Jager strode past them, scowling. Celine was right beside him, but went undetected by the guards and security sensors. Even the beasties didn't sense her, thanks to an extra tweak she'd given the spell.

In moments, Jager realized he had a problem. During the time he'd been in close contact with Soader's mind and memories, he hadn't paid attention to the more mundane details of the Rept's day-to-day life. So now he found himself unsure as to where Soader's office or quarters were. Nor was he clear on the details of the Dulce complex's layout.

Thinking fast, he spun round to bark at the guards again. "So, what are you idiots waiting for? Get one of my servants out here to carry this bag for me! Or do I need to come over there and make *you* carry it?"

"N...no sir, no sir," replied a trembling Rept. He spoke briefly into his comm pickup, then announced, "Someone will be right here, sir."

Jager knew the real Soader would never thank a mere guard, so he just growled, spat on the ground, and paced, his hands clenched behind his back. Celine couldn't help but smile at the performance.

Five minutes later, Max arrived, his face beyond surprised. The entire complex had celebrated for days after hearing the great news of Soader's demise. The celebration had only ended when Scabbage had returned as Orme.

"Uh, sir," said Max, "Uh, you see, we weren't expecting you, sir. Um, there is a slight problem, sir. Uh, it's just that..."

"Out with it, you idiot," barked Jager. "Don't you know how to talk anymore?"

"Yes, sir. Okay, sir. Ah...there is someone in your quarters, sir. Um, should we, uh...what should we do, sir?"

"What in all blazes?" growled Jager, even though he'd expected Scabbage to have made himself at home. "What do you mean, 'What should we do?' Kick the bloody idiot out of my room, whoever it is! Then clean it, but good. Make sure you disinfect it. I don't want any pesty critters left behind. Get it ready for me, exactly as it always was.

"And take me to my office while I wait — assuming you haven't let someone steal that, too. This place is unbelievable. I'm away for a couple of weeks and it falls to crap."

"Uh...um, well, sir," said Max, "You see, sir, your office actually is being used as well, sir."

"What in all bloody hells is going on?" demanded Jager. "Out with it, you blundering idiot! What's going on?" Jager wanted the Grey to say what he himself assumed to be the case. And Max did just that, even down to useless details.

"What the bloody hells?!" screamed Jager. "You tell Scabbage, or Orme, or whatever the gods-damned jerk calls himself these days, to get the hells out of my office right this minute. Then disinfect that, too. I don't care that he's a high chancellor. I'm warden of this bloody complex, and everyone here answers to me. Got that?"

"Y...yes, yes sir," stammered Max, taking several shaky steps backwards.

"And get me some brand-new furniture. I don't want any of the stinking crap that's been sitting around this place. Have it ready for me in an hour, or you'll wish you had. I'm going to go see if my Dragons have returned. And when I'm back, my office had better be ready. And my quarters too! Do I make myself perfectly clear?" The Grey nodded and scampered away to do his bidding.

Jager figured mentioning the Dragons would add credence to his masquerade. Celine agreed.

"Ha ha ha," mented Jager to Celine. "That was fun! Now, on to the next task at hand: finding Piccolo. If I were he, I'd look for Soader's treasure in the Dragon caverns. No one would want to fight a fire-breathing Dragon, let alone two, so I figure Narco and Choy's chamber is the best place to look for Piccolo."

"Brilliant," laughed Celine. "I came to the same conclusion. After you, sir." Celine bowed and made an elaborate gesture, just as she'd seen Jager do on several occasions. She told him what she was doing, and they shared a good laugh. Jager was about to lead off, but Celine changed her mind, insisting that she go first. After all, she was invisible and had her incant-baton ready for action. Jager had his wand concealed under his tunic, only to be used if he had no other choice. He complimented her reasoning, and off they went.

Their first objective was to find Mullins. Fortunately, he was nearby; Jager accosted him and demanded the Grey take him down in the lift to the lower levels. "You sure you're okay, going back down there, Pumpkin?" mented Jager. "I can do this on my own, you know."

"I'll have none of that," replied Celine, even though the thought of being anywhere near the cell that had held her, her mother and sister made her skin crawl. "I'm okay. Just keep walking so no one thinks you've lost your senses, standing there laughing to yourself."

They reached the lower levels, and Jager ordered Mullins to take him to Narco and Choy's cavern. Soader would have known the way very well, and Jager knew it. So he covered the oddity of the order by adding that Mullins was to open the cavern and sweep it for any danger before he ventured inside himself. The nervous Grey led the way, often glancing furtively back at his Rept boss, hoping for a reprieve from his awful assignment — and from the high probability that "Soader" would discover his treasure excavation project. He abandoned all hope when they arrived before a massive steel door.

"Open it up!" bellowed Jager. "What's taking you so bloody long? I want to see if my blasted Dragons have returned."

Mullins hesitated and looked up and down the corridor, hoping for a diversion. Any diversion. He knew the last two crates of recovered treasure lay just behind that door. The Rept couldn't miss them. And if Orme hadn't locked the door behind him when he went in, Soader would know something was up for sure. Mullins froze.

"What the bloody hells is keeping you?" shouted Jager. "Open the gods-damned door!"

Mullins' hands shook as he worked the massive door's electronic lock. "I...I do not think your Dragons are back, sir," he said, "but...but I will gladly check the cavern for you. You must be tired after your long trip. It would be a waste of your time to look for the Dragons right now. I'm certain they aren't in there. But if you insist, perhaps you should put on your fire-resistant armor first, just in case they have returned after all. I mean, the red Dragon with the two heads seemed very angry with you, last time you were here. And Dragons don't forget such things, as I know you know."

At once both Jager and Celine were suspicious. Celine remembered this Mullins character from when she was Soader's prisoner here. And she knew he and a couple of his friends were often up to no good, when they didn't think anyone was watching. She passed that information to Jager right away. He had already figured Soader would be suspicious of these Greys, and Celine's information added weight to his hunch.

"What in blazes is going on?" he growled. "Why are you

trying to keep me out of this chamber? Are you hiding something in there? What are you up to, you scoundrel? Did you steal something of mine? That's it, isn't it? You stole something, didn't you?"

"Uh...ah, no sir," stuttered Mullins, his eyes flitting everywhere but at his furious boss.

"Then do as I ordered!" roared Jager. "Open this bloody door before I blast you into outer space!"

The trembling Grey fumblingly released the last of the lock mechanisms, opened the door and stepped back. Jager stomped through, with Celine right behind him. Mullins followed, certain his life was about to end. Horribly.

All three were more than a bit surprised to see Scabbage (wearing Orme's former body) emerge from behind a boulder only a few meters away, carrying a crate and moving at a leisurely pace. Suddenly noticing he was not alone in the cavern — and seeing (apparently) Soader before him — Scabbage dropped the crate, leapt at Jager and clamped his throat in a death grip. As he snarled and squeezed, Celine flicked her incant-baton; the big Rept gave a howl of pain, released Jager and grabbed at his own arm, which seemed to him to have caught fire.

Scabbage's yellow-red eyes frantically flashed left and right, searching for the source of the mysterious injury. For a brief moment, Celine feared he'd sensed her, a mere arm's length away, baton ready. Fortunately, the large Rept saw nothing, and returned to nursing his arm. The severe burning sensation had passed, replaced by a painful cramping. A look of fear crossed his face; he released his injured arm, grabbed at his lapel comm pickup and barked for the *Morrighan* to 'beam him up. He bent down, snatched up the crate and was gone in a swirl of colors. Arriving aboard his newly acquired ship, he hailed the bridge, barked a quick order, and *Queen Morrighan* made the shift to the Serpens Universe.

Celine lowered her incant-baton, her face a mask of horror and surprise.

Jager rubbed his throat, shook his head, and thanked Celine for her quick action. "Yeow. That could have been unfortunate. Thanks, Pumpkin. You were right to insist on coming along. Remind me to give you a raise when we get back to the outpost." She stuck out her tongue at him. Though he couldn't see her, the intention came across loud and clear. They laughed.

"But Jager," said Celine, "it wasn't me. I only gave him a zap. It would burn for a moment and ache a little, but it wasn't anything serious. Just meant to get him off you. But he acted like he sensed something much worse was going on. As if some serious danger lurked close by."

"Wow!" he replied. "That's interesting, and most unexpected. Could he have sensed that you were there? What the hells is going on?"

"I don't know," replied Celine, "but I'm worried more than ever. Maybe West will have an explanation."

"Perhaps, but it'll be all right. You'll see," said Jager. "Let's follow through with our plan to nab Piccolo. We can deal with what just happened once we're back with the others. If West doesn't have any explanation, perhaps someone else can shed light on why Scabbage reacted like that."

"You there!" shouted Jager to Mullins, who had been slowly retreating, and wishing he could disappear completely. "Don't move a muscle." Mullins froze again. Jager tapped his lapel comm link and called for guards and some servants to get to his location, fast. A while later, two burly Repts arrived, along with Max and Vic. Jager ordered the guards to lock Mullins up. Grinning, they jumped to comply. They'd never liked the conniving Grey.

As the guards led Mullins away, Jager ordered Max and Vic to lead him into Narco and Choy's old home. Jager knew from Soader's memories that the three servants hung around together, so he figured that whatever Mullins had been up to, Max and Vic were involved, and just as guilty. Between Celine's earlier advice, and Max and Vic's looks of horror at seeing their pal hauled away, he was sure of it.

As Celine and Jager followed the two nervous Greys into the cavern, they heard a horrendous howl, like an animal caught in a trap, perhaps two hundred meters away. "Sounds like it came from over there, by the cavern wall," said Jager. "Follow me." He quickened his pace, heading toward the sound, Celine keeping pace beside him. The Greys hesitated, but followed. Approaching the wall and rounding a tall pile of stones and boulders, they encountered a Rept: Piccolo. He stood with his back to them, facing a hole in the rocky wall and cursing like a spacer. He picked up a rock and hurled it at the empty hole, then another and another. "Gone!" he screamed. "All of it! Gone! STOLEN!!"

Remembering that Soader wouldn't recognize Piccolo as his own cousin Hobbs, Jager acted as though he was confronting a stranger. "What in all blazes are you doing here? And what are you doing in *my* cache?!" He drew his blast pistol and leveled it at the intruder. Piccolo, recognizing "Soader" at once, went for his own weapon.

Celine had been poised, incant-baton high. In an instant she saw that Piccolo intended to fire, and that Jager would be forced to defend himself by firing first. So before either could get off a shot, she mented "No!" to Jager and simultaneously froze Piccolo with a spell. Crisis averted. Hearing a noise behind her, she turned to see Max and Vic beating a hasty retreat toward the cavern entrance. So she froze them, too.

"Well, well, well," said Jager, well aware that Piccolo and the Greys, although frozen stiff, could hear his every word. "Looks like some nasty characters have been busy while I was away. Who wants to be the first to explain, so they can watch the others die?"

Looking back and forth between Piccolo and the frozen Greys, Jager and Celine were startled to hear North's mental voice, with an urgent message. Now they too stood frozen. But only for a moment. They left the three immobile miscreants behind and rushed out of the chamber, sealing the massive door behind them.

Soon the three — North, Jager and Celine — were back at the Mentor outpost's transbeam platform, where they were greeted by Fianna and the others.

CHAPTER 31

West

Despite the fact that she was floating a foot off the floor, West felt heavier than she ever had. She continued slowly toward her sleeping chamber. She had no idea when she'd last slept well; she hoped tonight she'd have the chance. The Mentor dared not let anyone know the harsh side effects of her recent transformation and hoped no one would see her before she reached her room. This too shall pass, she told herself. Though it was wonderous to advance spiritually, she'd paid a huge price. One always must, for such things.

Still, knowing what she knew, and despite her recent trials, West would willingly sacrifice herself for the salvation of those she loved. She was the first All of All in centuries to reach the stage of Grand Marshal. Although she and her sisters were proud of her accomplishment, the personal ramifications were too swift and weighty for her to deal with adequately. She bore the burden alone, and in extreme pain.

Each day brought new revelations of precious knowledge and skills which both thrilled and astounded her. They were invaluable resources that would greatly assist in defeating Byrne and dismantling the Volac Forces. And so, she told herself, the pain and suffering were well worthwhile.

And, as the pain intensified each day, she found herself repeating that assertion more and more often.

Although thrilled with her progress, West was deeply saddened by her fading ability to take on Human form. Soon she would depart completely from the realm of bodies as she moved through to the next stage of her spiritual enlightenment. She did not want to dwell on the price she was willingly paying for the transformation, especially as new insights confirmed her conclusion that she must hurry through to the other side.

She would desperately miss her sisters, but she would miss young Celine and Jager so much more. The Dragons, too. She cut off such thoughts, though, for she knew once her viewpoint changed, the actions to follow would be fixed, unalterable by anyone — in the present time or otherwise.

Finally, she was able to lay her weary body down. She pulled up the covers, but then chastised herself, believing she was exhibiting weakness. Then, a few moments later, she laughed — her thoughts and actions were echoing Celine's! How she loved the girl.

"I do hope I prepared you well, child," whispered West. "I believe I did. I know you will always remember first to establish your anchor points before you take action. And to evaluate what is important and what is not, give scant regard to random, frivolous significances, and continue your self-examination and self-questioning.

"I hope you realize how loved you are by so many, and pray you will let their love support you when the days are dark and you feel trapped within the sphere. Yes, I have taught you well, but — perhaps unfortunately — you are so perceptive that you clearly recognize the many, often harsh imbalances of existence, and ache at the suffering and discord they breed.

"I do hope Jager forgives me for what must come to pass. Your ignorance of it is itself unfortunate, and ignorance is a mechanism of entrapment. But the event to come is necessary to save us all. I do hope you realize, in time, that if you alter the manner in which you perceive the universe around you — perceive physically, mentally and spiritually — that your actions thereafter will be altered as well. And so will the thoughts, perceptions and actions of others. Such is the magnitude of the power of those who, though they may not be the purest at heart, yet display the greatest ability to love.

"I have never known anyone so young as you to understand love so well, or to love others so truly, despite their flaws and no matter their size or race. You and Jager deserve each other more than you will ever know. I am sorry for the eons of separation and sadness I have caused you both. I hope my efforts in the present will balance all that between us, and that you will survive what I have doomed you to experience. I love you, dear, sweet child."

As West continued to muse, her uncertainties increased. Her breath came in wheezes, and grew more and more labored. She felt blind to what lay ahead, and wrestled with her thoughts into the wee hours. She wished she might see tomorrow, so she could continue to protect her dearest students — but knew her wish was in vain. For a moment, guilt hung heavy upon her. But gradually, gradually, a soothing warmth washed over her, and she settled into a wonderous sleep, deep and sound. Her first in months.

Hours later, East knocked at West's chamber door. No answer came, so she silently, gently opened the door. The room was empty, as was West's bed. The only trace of the Mentor was her silken gown, empty but still faintly warm, nestled beneath the bed covers.

CELINE'S TEARS HAD RUN DRY, but she kept her head on Jager's shoulder. Her disgust for the body he wore had been numbed by the news of West's departure. Her own exhaustion after all the recent tough weeks seemed to have caught up with her at last. She couldn't imagine life without West. What were they to do, she thought. How could they carry on through all the terrible events that seemed inevitable, without the help of her beloved Mentor?

The girl wanted to cry some more, but she was spent. Jager, Fianna and the others sensed and shared her grief; they were not faring much better. Their loss was great, but Celine's searing anguish was unnerving to perceive.

"We haven't really lost her," said North. "She still exists; she has simply departed our immediate realm. She did not wish to leave, but the need for her elsewhere was greater and for the greater good. She knew the choice she made was the only righteous one. I know that does not ease your grief at this time; nor may it make much sense. But please know, my dear Celine, that she will be with us, aiding us in the battles to come. She has not abandoned us; she never would. Our West will return; I know this to be true. In a different form and manner, perhaps, but she shall ever be our West. I hope you are able to understand this, and forgive her choice."

The room filled with silence until Celine eventually spoke.

"Yes," she replied with a sniffle. "I do understand. And I do not need to forgive her, for there is nothing to forgive. She is merely doing what she must. Nothing more, nothing less. I do not mean to demean you, North. I do not doubt your power or abilities — nor those of any of the other Mentors. I just find it painful and hard to lose such a loved one so unexpectedly." She paused for a moment in thought. "Can West communicate to us, like Dagmar does?"

"That is a very good question, my dear," replied North, "and the answer is yes. West, at times, will visit you as an inner voice, just as Dagmar has done with some of your Dragon friends. But, like Dagmar, West will no longer appear to you in physical form — in a body.

I must tell you, she visited me in the inner-voice manner not long ago — less than an hour past, in fact. She wished you to know she is sorry to have left you so suddenly, and before she could facilitate the remainder of your training, and Jager's. She sends her love, and assures you she will be there in days to come, when you need her most. For now, circumstances far from here made her immediate departure imperative — for the sake of many peoples and their worlds.

"West intends to contact my sisters and me regularly, to ensure we have what we need to assist the Aadya Coalition. She retains a vital and integral role in our efforts. The only change is that she now holds a different 'command position,' for lack of a better choice of words. She wanted to explain before she left, but it appears that was not what the universe had in mind. Come child, she left some items in her room, for you and Jager."

North led the pair to West's room, where they found various objects and books. Celine recognized several as having belonged to her brother, Alika. She sat down and handled a few, turning them in her hands and stroking their beautiful covers. She opened one — and gasped at the inscription inside.

Jager read it too, and echoed her gasp. "Wow!" he exclaimed. "This is most interesting. Makes it even more urgent that we go retrieve Mutuum as quickly as possible. First, we've got to carry out our plan here, while I'm still seemingly Soader."

"Yes, you are correct as usual," said Celine, trying to sound positive. "I guess we'll have to push thoughts of West away, just like I had to do with my father."

"Yes, my princess, that's what we'll have to do. And do it well we shall." The two hugged, gathered up the things West had left, and headed to Celine's room. They stowed the Mentor's gifts and headed to the transbeam room.

"North," said Jager, "could you please take us back to Earth so we can finish with that Piccolo character? I have a feeling we need to get there right away."

Jager was so right. As the two approached Narco and Choy's cavern, out came Max and Vic, arguing over the quickest way to reach the shuttle train station. Celine instantly threw up her cloaking spell; the pair would only see "Soader" approaching. Odd, thought Celine, something must have broken the spells we left them under. And the door spell too. Or maybe they just wore off.

Before the Greys could get away, Soader grabbed them, took them back into the cavern, slammed the entry shut, flung them to the ground and restrained them with the cuffs they carried on their own duty belts. He put both under a well practiced truth spell.

First, he asked where Piccolo was; the Rept had been under the same spell as they, so presumably he was free now, too. They explained that when they had awakened from their restraining spell, Piccolo was still there, and still under. They had quickly tied him up so he couldn't follow them if he woke. Satisfied with that, Jager next extracted their story of collaborating with Piccolo to locate Soader's treasure, then stealing it all from right under his nose and hiding it aboard Soader's Salt Lake shuttle train.

Jager called for guards to come and take Max and Vic away. "Lock them up with that rodent, Mullins," he ordered, "and don't let any of them out — for any reason — until I order it." The guards acknowledged and hauled off the dejected would-be thieves.

After rounding up the still-spell-frozen Piccolo and tightening the Grey's hasty tie-up job, Jager called to North and requested she transport him, Celine and their prisoner to the orbiting ship. He had her 'beam Celine and Piccolo first, while he stayed behind long enough to round up the last of Soader's treasure. Then North 'beamed him up too, recovered loot and all. Only one task remained before returning to the Mentor outpost. Celine and Jager transbeamed to the Dulce compound's shuttle train platform, located the treasure the conniving Greys had hidden aboard it, and returned to North's ship with all of it. Fortunately, the ship had just enough cargo capacity to handle it all.

"Wow! What a load!" exclaimed Jager. "Enough to buy a planet or two."

"Yes, it certainly would," laughed Celine. "Now to find the rightful owners of as much of it as possible. Soader's been gathering it for decades, so there's no way we'll be able to return all of it. But what's left over can go to people in need.

Like some of the victims of Soader's many other crimes!"

"Perfect idea," said Jager.

"Thank you! Now, let's get you out of that horrendous body."

"You know," said Jager, "I'm kind of getting used to this thing. I think I might just keep it for a while. It's much stronger than my own piddly thing. Besides, I kind of like the power that goes with it, just because of the former owner's reputation."

"Yes, but you'll do nothing of the kind!" barked Celine playfully. "You'll never get another kiss out of me until you're back in your own body."

"Well, when you put it that way..." laughed Jager.

Within hours, the two had paid another visit to Monty's transfer station and Jager was back in his own body. Much to his own relief, and Celine's delight.

"Gawd!" gushed Jager, hugging himself. "Truthfully, I can't believe how good it feels to be back inside my own body. I sure as hells hope I don't have to use that vile thing again. Maybe we can come up with a different plan to catch our little ol' friend Scabbage. Still, if there's no better way, I'd be willing to sacrifice my own comfort one more time. Definitely a noble and worthy cause."

"Ha ha," laughed Celine. "I hope you don't ever have to use that disgusting thing either. Welcome back." She threw her arms around him, and they kissed and hugged long and hard. At last, the nervous Monty cleared his throat to remind them he was standing there. They both blushed, but thanked him for all his help and told him to expect another visit in the near future. And, to his surprise, they asked if there was anything they could do for him.

"Uh...uh," he replied, caught completely off guard and unable to think. "Not...not at the moment, but I, uh...maybe soon, maybe soon. When you return. I'll ask then." The creature's face was still full of wonder as he watched the two Humans disappear. He hadn't known kindness for years.

CHAPTER 32

Unexpected Winds

Safe at the Mentor outpost once again, the two Humans stepped from the platform.

"I guess we should deal with Piccolo tomorrow," said Celine, "and make finding Mutuum first priority. Do you agree?"

"Absolutely, my princess. Piccolo's not going anywhere, so whatever information he has can wait until we return. I'm not clear as to what he could have, but since he's Soader's cousin, and therefore related to Scabbage too, he might have some insights that could be useful in days to come. Especially when it's time to capture Scabbage."

"Good thinking," smiled Celine. "Shall we?" She motioned towards the refectory.

"Yes, we shall," he said. They locked elbows and he pulled her along. "We need to celebrate," he laughed, "even if it's just for a few minutes. I'm *so* relieved to be back in my own body. What an experience! Come on, double tealas for us both."

"Augh, you're impossible," she groaned, but silently gave thanks once again, for his bringing sunshine to her troubled days. He laughed louder and she couldn't help but join in.

They called the Dragons, who quickly joined them in the refectory. All were delighted to see them — and surprised too, to see Dino was also there, seated at a table across from Jager and Celine. They learned he'd just arrived for a short visit.

After all the welcomings were complete, Celine briefed the major on West's departure. His deep solemnity at the news was as they all had expected. They remained quiet, giving him time with his feelings. His quiet manner hid his truest concerns; there had been secrets between himself and the Mentor, and her absence meant he now had a greater part to play in coming events. As he mused, he took a snap-seal pouch from a pocket in his tunic, opened it and drew out two objects: a small pink crystal and old mechanical key. He fingered them absently as he sat, eyes downcast. After a minute or two he looked up to see Jager watching him with a comforting smile.

He returned the smile. In truth, he was overjoyed to see Jager and the others. Setting aside thoughts of West, he engaged with his friends again. In part to alleviate their concerns for him, but even more to take his mind off his new fears.

The group shared stories of events old and new, and Dino, cheering up, pitched in with a couple of his own. His mood grew even lighter when Jager told the story of Piccolo's capture and the recovered treasure.

Although everyone did their best to remain positive, lulls in the conversation often found more than one of them pushing back and walling off unspoken concerns brought on by West's absence. Particularly Jager and Celine.

Granted, West was not actually dead, nor lost to them forever. But she was no longer just a ment away, and they realized how much they had come to rely on her swift, decisive responses and aid. Sure, the other Mentors would be quick to respond at need, and were supremely wise and capable. But West had been like family, and her unexpected departure had left an immense void; a reverberant emptiness they sought to avoid by turning their attention elsewhere. Anywhere but to thoughts of her.

Both Celine and Jager had numerous unanswered questions. Questions they'd thought only West could have answered. These "unanswereds" weighed heavily upon them. Fortunately, both were stronger than even they themselves were fully aware — for the near future held some difficult surprises. They were soon to discover and come to comprehend the immense power of the ways of the universe. Unfortunately, they were also soon to realize that West's departure would not be their last or most painful loss. And yet they would have to accept what came.

After a quick meal, the friends accompanied the major to the transbeam room, to say goodbye as he headed back to Remini. Celine asked Dino to assure her parents she was fine, and that she'd be home soon. He promised to relay her message, but knew in his heart it was unlikely to work out so simply. He was all too aware that the search for Mutuum would be fraught with peril, but he tried to ignore such thoughts.

Once her godfather had gone, Celine turned again to

Fianna and the others. Once again, she felt obliged to express how much she cherished them. "Well, everyone," she said, collecting her thoughts, "Ummm...before we begin our search for Mutuum, I must thank you all, from the bottom of my heart. Um...words cannot express how grateful I am for everything you have done for me and for our cause. And for all I know you are ready and willing to do in the days to come. We are about to embark on perhaps the most dangerous venture we've attempted to date, and your love and bravery touch me deeply. I am truly thankful you are here with me, for with you all by my side, I know we will succeed."

Everyone murmured acknowledgements and love; then Celine and Jager climbed into their saddles, and reached down to hug their Fianna and Vin. Without hesitation, the Dragons moved to the middle of the transbeam platform; Alden stepped up to stand close beside them. "We will be back soon, dear brother," said Fianna.

"I'm afraid I will worry until I see you again, dear sister," said Ahimoth, heaving a huge sigh. It had been decided that because of the extreme dangers inherent in the trip, one of the royals should stay behind. He thoroughly understood the reasoning, but Ahimoth was furious nonetheless, adamant that he should be by Fianna's side. Fianna was just as adamant that he remain behind. And she had the concerted agreement of all the rest, the Mentors included — regardless of what the paintings had seemed to indicate, and what Dagmar had said.

"Do not worry, dear Ahimoth," said Koondahg. "I will take good care of my charges." He nodded to North, and in a swirl of raw energy, he and the others vanished, to reappear almost at once on a tall hill overlooking Derinkuyu: the Turkish city that lay above the ancient tunnels and caverns where Fianna and Celine had found the Atlantean grimoires.

Upon arrival, the little group took a moment to look over the picturesque countryside and get their bearings. They were about to be on their way when, to their amazement and consternation, Ahimoth and Joli materialized a few meters away.

"Brother! Why are you here?" gasped Fianna. "This was not what we all decided. You agreed to stay behind."

"We are here because of me," said Joli. "Dagmar spoke to me this very morning. She insisted I accompany you in this endeavor, no matter what. I consulted with North, who agreed I must do as Dagmar bid me. That is why she has sent us. I did not dispute the group's decision earlier; I felt it would be more prudent to act in this way, despite the upset it was sure to cause."

"I received similar messages," spoke up Ahimoth, eager to support and defend Joli. "Fianna, my sister, do you remember how beneficial it has been, more than once, to heed my little inner voice?"

Fianna nodded, thoughtful, her alarm and anger cooling.

"Besides, we can only be of help on such a treacherous quest," he grinned.

"Indeed," laughed Vin. "I suppose I could have saved us some trouble if I had spoken up myself. For I received the same message — but doubted it, and kept silent. So! What do we do now?"

"It is time to collect Mutuum," laughed Alden.

"I agree," said Celine. "As we all know, we desperately need Mutuum. And we know it can only be located by traveling back through time. The riddles that point to its whereabouts were never recorded in writing. They were spoken only, in the tunnels of the Ancients beneath the Earth, near this place. Those words can only be heard — indeed, they *were* only heard — by persons at the precise location and time of their voicing. So it is to that precise place — and time — that we must now travel.

"Unfortunately, traveling back to that precise moment is no simple task. Yet it is a difficulty we must overcome.

"According to history, Mutuum remains hidden somewhere in the tunnels below us, which Fianna and I visited not long ago. It is a uniquely powerful incant-baton; in our hands, it will be instrumental in destroying the G.O.D. soul-harvest stations. As I understand it, from what West has told me, it will also be a vital weapon in our crusade against Lord Byrne and his allies."

"Yes, you are correct, child," said the wizard. "Come, I know where we must begin our journey." The group followed the elderly man, who set off eastward at a determined pace. They had just come to an opening at the base of a nearby bluff when loud, blustering winds sprung up, sweeping up clouds of dust and debris. To escape the sudden storm, they dashed through the opening and into a small cavern beyond. There they found themselves looking up at a simple, almost crude chapel. Carved angels and crosses adorned the walls, which angled inward toward an altar, set at the rear of the chamber and considerably more elaborate in design and workmanship than the rest of the little room.

"As perfect a place as any for a little time travel, I guess," laughed Jager. He helped Celine and Alden make the necessary preparations for the rite.

With everything in readiness, Jager called for attention. The others went silent, and the young man began to voice the spell. He had not uttered more than the first phrase, though, when the little party was battered by a blast of wind — *inside* the cavern — more brutal than what they'd just experienced outside.

All were severely startled, alarmed and confused. Even more so when Celine screamed in sudden terror. And then, in an instant, their world went black as deepest space.

CHAPTER 33

Time

"What's *happening?!*" wailed Celine, the brutal winds intensifying by the second.

"I don't know!" yelled Jager; he groped for her hand in the darkness, found it and grasped it tight. "Hang on!"

The gale growing stronger still, Vin and Fianna wrapped their wings tightly about themselves and their Companions. Ahimoth and Joli did the same, enfolding Alden and Leopold the bird as well. There was a momentary lull in the gale, though the darkness was still complete. Then, before they could even begin to feel relief, there came a new burst of screaming, whirling wind. They felt themselves being sucked downward, in what seemed like a tornado's funnel, black as black and without end.

"This is worse than the tube-chute!" mented Celine.

"Much!" replied Jager. "You screamed. Are you hurt?" There was no reply. "Celine! Are you okay?" Still no response.

"CELINE!!" he screamed aloud, as she was wrenched from his grasp. He called out again and again. Utter black and the wind's roar were the only replies.

FIANNA LANDED WITH A THUD — alert, unharmed, her own heartbeat sounding in her ears. She leapt up at once, muscles tensed and wings ready for quick departure. She was truly frightened, for she couldn't sense Celine. She swung her head in every direction, again and again, searching. To her right she spotted the motionless bodies of Ahimoth and Joli; there was no sign of anyone else. Then she saw her saddle — empty, lying a few meters away. She panicked.

"Celine! Vin! Jager!" she shouted repeatedly. Her shouts stirred Ahimoth and Joli. Good, she thought. They live. "Celine!" she yelled and mented again, stomping about. "Vin!" She couldn't perceive any sign of either her Companion or her mate. She didn't want to think what that might mean. She continued to call, but still there was no response.

Although she no longer sensed imminent danger, Fianna stood rigid, ready to tear with her razor teeth and talons at any enemy who might appear. The lack of the soothing warmth of Celine's presence, physical or mental, triggered the awful memory of her Companion's capture by Byrne and imprisonment on his ice planet, RTC237.

Ahimoth moaned. "Brother, are you hurt?" Fianna called.

"No, I believe I am fine," he said groggily, rising. "I think I only have a few bruises." Then, in sudden panic, he swung his head around, searching. He calmed at once when his eyes rested upon Joli; she shook her lovely head and gathered herself together to rise.

"I too am unharmed," said Fianna, disappointed in

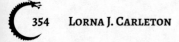

herself for giving attention to Ahimoth and Joli, dear though they were. Her only thoughts should be of Celine and Vin! "I just had the wind knocked out of me," she said. "I am deeply worried, though. I cannot sense my Celine, nor dear Vin, nor Jager."

"That is bad news," replied Ahimoth, scanning their surroundings. "Perhaps they are nearby, just out of our sight down a passage or some such." He stretched to his full height and tested his wings to confirm he was indeed uninjured, able to fight off any attacker. He approached Joli and nuzzled her. "My dear, are you uninjured?"

"Yes, my friend. I am fine," she softly replied. The two touched noses, then Ahimoth tenderly watched her rise to her feet, gingerly but with no sign of pain. Joli assessed herself, and announced she'd only suffered a few bumps and bruises. But only after she had checked herself one time more was the prince convinced.

"Does anyone know where we are?" he asked.

"No, not yet," replied Fianna. "We need to ensure we are indeed safe, then find the others. I do not sense any of them. This is terrible. I hope they are unharmed."

"Yes, it certainly is terrible," replied Joli. "But do not fear, Fianna, for the story our prophecies tell is not one of death and destruction for our loved ones. I feel it in my bones: Everyone will be all right, and we will see each other soon."

"Thank you, Joli," sighed Fianna, "I appreciate your kind words and comfort." She began a survey of the massive cavern around them, looking for any threat, but more concerned about locating the missing members of their party. Her careful survey yielded no sign of them, but at least revealed no apparent danger.

"I believe we are in some sort of religious courtyard," she said. "That appears to be a temple over there." She pointed to a looming structure several hundred meters up an incline. "I see numerous statues and paintings lining the walls along the stairway that serves it. They are not those of any familiar culture, nor do they seem to be mentioned in any of our teachings back home. And so I do not know where 'here' is. What is most disturbing, however, is that I believe we are no longer on Earth."

"That is odd, certainly," said Ahimoth. "And...oh my! I had forgotten the third Human in our party. Where is Mr. Koondahg? I do hope he is with our missing friends, and that they are all safe."

The three distraught Dragons searched a bit further, but in vain. Fianna's heart and hope sank further. She wished she had listened to her premonitions, or at least mentioned them to Celine. If she had, she thought, the girl would not have let Jager attempt the time-traveling spell.

"Sister, this is not your fault," said Ahimoth, interrupting Fianna's self-admonishment. "For weeks now, it has been evident that very powerful entities are controlling events. West herself hinted at this. And you voiced the same when Alika went missing. I truly believe our friends will be back with us soon. Have faith, dear sister."

CELINE TOUCHED HER THROBBING HEAD. To her relief, she felt no telltale stickiness of blood. Only an oversized lump that caused her to yelp in pain when she pressed it. The girl lay quietly for a bit, letting the pain subside. She lifted her head a few inches...and didn't black out, or trigger any new jolt of pain. Good. Even the dim light coming from high above hurt, though. She squinted as she dizzily surveyed her situation.

Her eyes told her what her heart already knew: Fianna and Jager were not with her. Nor were the others.

"Jager! Fianna!" she cried and mented, but her calls went unanswered. "What happened?" she mumbled to herself, half hoping someone would hear. The last thing she remembered was being snapped up by an intense, coal-black wind, just after they'd entered the cavern near Derinkuyu. That, and Jager beginning to recite the time-travel incantation. She knew he hadn't made an error that triggered this situation; he'd only chanted a few lines of the complex spell.

A fresh twinge of panic gripped her throat, but a few deep breaths calmed and cleared her mind enough to sit up and widen her examination of her surroundings. Useless emotion can only make things worse, she told herself.

She was surprised to discover she was in a sand-filled courtyard, at the base of a towering mountain that reached toward the bright blue sky. Broad, carved stone steps led upward from the courtyard to what appeared to be an immense church, with an imposing, barrel-vaulted entrance, set into the mountainside.

By now her pain and dizziness had subsided enough to take a chance; she rolled up onto her hands and knees, then stood up. A bit unsteady at first, she quickly regained her equilibrium and took a more detailed look around. Her courtyard was part of what she guessed was a monastic compound. Lovingly carved stone crosses, religious-themed statues, and simple, functional, but graceful architecture. If she'd ended up somewhere — somewhen? — back in time, it couldn't be Mutuum's time period, she reasoned. The art and architecture around her, and the magnificent structure on the mountainside above were too refined.

She reached out to the others once more, but was again

met with painful and throbbing silence.

A soft moan from behind startled her. She spun around to see the wizard, Alden. He was almost fully concealed behind a low stone wall, lying in a heap. The bird, Leopold, lay still beside him. The elderly gentleman stirred, but as she drew close, the jet-black ultra-intense wind burst upon her again — out of nowhere, just as before. The blast smacked her to the ground like an autumn-dry leaf and left her blind and oblivious.

JAGER LANDED HARD ON HIS FEET, but managed to maintain his balance, incant-baton high and ready, but head aching viciously. He stared hard, straining to pierce the darkness that surrounded him, filled with dread: He couldn't hear or see Celine or any of the others. He sensed a presence in the darkness — and suddenly realized he had a light-orb in his tunic pocket. He pulled it out and activated it; its rays revealed Vin's huge form, just meters to his left. The Dragon gave a low, weak moan. But before Jager could reach his friend's side, he stumbled, fell, grabbed his reeling head, and again blacked out.

In time, Jager woke. He had no idea how long he had lain unconscious, but through half-open eyes he could see Vin's breath rising in faint puffs in the chill, moist air. The boy held his aching head and tried to wish away the pain and intolerable ringing in his ears — positive he couldn't endure much more of the agony. But then, as if in answer to his wishes, the pain and piercing sound ceased. Greatly relieved, he rolled and pulled himself up to his hands and knees and gulped in deep, long breaths of the cool, crisp air.

"Vin. Vin!" he whispered. "Vin, can you hear me?"

"Yes," mented Vin. His eyes remained closed, but he was aware enough to sense Jager was close by. "I am awake. I do not think I am badly injured. Bruised, just bruised. Where are the others? I do not sense Fianna!"

Nearly frantic, the Dragon scanned the space the two occupied — as much of it as he could see by the limited light of Jager's orb. They appeared to be in an underground living space, carved from some sort of friable volcanic rock. There were a number of nooks and crannies carved into the walls. There was also a crude table and benches, apparently carved from the same soft stone.

"Where do you suppose we are?" Vin asked. He tried to unfurl his wings, but the little space was too restrictive. At least he could tell the muscles still functioned, and there was no evidence of a fracture or serious wound. "What happened? Where are Fianna and the others?"

"I do not know, my friend," replied Jager, flexing his arms and legs to ensure he hadn't been injured. "But I most definitely intend to find out. Just a moment ago, I caught a faint whiff of something we Earthers call incense. A sort of perfumed smoke. That means there are people in the near vicinity. Perhaps you should remain hidden while I take a look around. Dragons probably aren't part of the day-to-day scene here, my friend."

"A good suggestion," replied Vin, still reaching out for any sign of Fianna, mental or physical. "I shall stay here and continue to call for the others. Please do not stay away for long; and contact me often. If I do not hear from you, and you do not answer my calls, I shall begin a search."

Jager agreed. He slung his bodypack into place and headed in the direction from which he'd determined the odor of incense emanated. He picked his way carefully at first, not yet completely steady on his feet. It wasn't long before the shakiness passed; he picked up his pace. The faint odor became stronger, and he began to hear murmurings of speech, and, to his surprise, the sounds of musical instruments. Strange, he thought. *I don't think such instruments existed in the era we were supposed to visit. I guess it wasn't the spell that brought us here. And how could it have, anyway? I had only just begun the incantation when we were swept away. So how did we get here?* He continued his search.

Less than a minute later, he came to an anteroom. One of its large double doors was slightly ajar; the scent of incense was much stronger now, and the voices and music he'd been hearing were louder and more distinct. *They must be coming from in there,* he thought. Cautiously, he approached the open double doors and peered into the great room beyond. It was illuminated by what could only be an electric light. "What?" he exclaimed, aloud. "We're definitely in the wrong time period." He drew back from the doorway and turned to examine the dimly lit anteroom more closely — and his conclusion was confirmed. Here was a modern placard, describing the historical significance of the great room beyond — and the Hagia Sofia Grand Mosque.

"Hagia Sofia?!" gasped Jager. "What are we doing in Istanbul? *Modern* Istanbul! Something terrible has happened!" He tried again to reach Celine, to no avail. Deeply concerned, he reached out to North, but was met with the same silence.

"Vin!" called Jager, almost in a panic.

"I am here, dear friend," replied Vin. "Is everything all right?"

"Yes and no," said Jager as he headed back to the small room where he'd left Vin. "Something went wrong. I'm quite sure it wasn't the traveling spell that brought us here, and we have definitely been separated from the others. Even though we're still in our own time, I cannot reach Celine or North. I'll try the other Mentors to see if I can contact someone." Jager did just that; and this time, North responded. "Am I ever glad to hear you, North," Jager exclaimed.

Jager proceeded to explain the situation to the ethereal being. "Indeed, Jager," she replied. "Something has gone terribly wrong. I have no plausible explanation for it."

"Oh, this does not sound good!" exclaimed Jager. "I suppose Vin and I should come back to the outpost so we can all figure out what is to be done. I don't think it's safe to remain here, especially for Vin."

Within moments, Jager and Vin greeted North from the transbeam platform.

FIANNA TROTTED AROUND THE DESERTED courtyard, calling and menting Celine and Vin; there came no response.

"I am certain they are fine," said Ahimoth. "This is most strange, but I believe things happened as they did for a reason. Sister, are you sure that you are not injured?"

"Yes, brother," replied Fianna softly. "I am not hurt, just worried about our friends."

Ahimoth continued to talk, in an effort to keep Fianna's spirits up despite troubling thoughts of his own. His mind's eye flashed repeatedly over images of the many paintings he'd recently studied, hoping to spot any sort of clue to what was happening. Finding none, he addressed his sister again. "Joli and I are fine too, Fianna. I must admit to being rather disorientated, though, and worried for Vin and the others. That was a difficult trip."

"That it was," said Joli. "I am glad you two are not hurt. And Fianna, your concern is understandable, but as Ahimoth has said, it seems the universe has plans of which we are not aware. Come, let us see where we are, shall we?"

Fianna nodded, pleased at her friends' positivity and strength. They helped ease her anguish, but she maintained her vigil, religiously menting for Celine and Vin.

After a quick look around, followed by a whiff of the air and assessment of temperature, the three Dragons concluded they were in a desert area. They had spotted some smoke in the near distance, so they trotted toward it to investigate, Fianna with the saddle tucked tightly under a wing. Coming over a rise, they saw the source of the smoke: several low houses, each with a gently smoking chimney. The houses were situated on the sloping foot of a tall, steep hill or low mountain. Built into the hill's face was an ornate building, which struck them at once as religious in purpose.

"Oh my," said Joli. "I believe we are still in the area Earthers call Turkey — the region where we first landed. Teacher insisted I learn such things."

They all scanned the area for a few moments more, until Joli shouted: "Look, a motorized vehicle! Something has definitely gone wrong, to end up here. And it cannot have been the spell. Jager had only begun the chant when the black wind sprang up. I wonder if it carried off the others, too. I shall reach out to the Mentors to see if they can help — or if they have heard from the others. In the meantime, let us ensure we are not seen. Perhaps we should head for that building." She pointed to a low, stone structure, some fifty meters away, closer to the foot of the hill. "It appears to be abandoned."

Fianna and Ahimoth agreed, and they quickly made their

way to the building. To their relief, it was unoccupied. They slipped inside and settled down to rest and regroup. Joli was soon deep in conversation with North.

The Mentor was thankful to hear the three Dragons were safe, and gave Joli the good news that Jager and Vin were already safely back at the outpost.

"Yes, Joli," said North. "It is indeed strange that Vin and Fianna were unable to ment with each other."

"Celine!" shouted Fianna, "Is she there?"

"My dearest, Fianna," replied North, "I am sorry to say it, but Celine and the wizard are still missing. No one has been able to contact them."

North regretted relaying such disturbing news, and changed the subject at once. "Are you all ready to be transported?" They assured her they were, and soon they were reunited with Vin and Jager.

Everyone who was able to do so reached out to Celine and Alden, again and again. But without success.

CHAPTER 34

The Silver Crystal

Celine gulped for air, but instead of getting a healthy lungful, she gagged on water. Luckily, she had incredibly fast reflexes; she flicked her incant-baton in time to create a massive air bubble around herself, and the still-unconscious wizard and bird, too. The bubble floated them upwards. She halted their ascent just below the surface — she needed to decide what to do if there were hostiles waiting above. The failure of the time-travel spell suggested there was someone bent on doing them harm.

Although she worried the surface might not be safe, Celine was even more concerned they might drown if they were submerged too long. Weakened and losing her hold on the bubble spell, the young witch knew what she must do, no matter the danger. She released her hold on the bubble's ascent. It bobbed to the surface, near the shore of what proved to be an extensive underground lake, within a vast cavern. Sunlight shone down from a long, narrow opening high above, to illuminate the particular area they were in.

Celine held her baton ready as she scanned in every direction, but she could see no threat. Thankful, she guided the bubble toward the rocky shore. When it bumped against a shoreline rock, the unconscious wizard and bird awoke.

"Are you all right, sir?" asked Celine, still looking all around for any sign of hostiles.

The man coughed up some water, as did Leopold. Between coughs, Alden gave a strained reply. "Yes, it seems I'm fine. Just a bit of water down the wrong pipe, as it were. Leopold, are you all right?"

The bird answered that he was, but he was clearly distraught. He was far from a fan of swimming. The wizard comforted his friend, looking him over carefully to ensure he was indeed okay.

"Do you have any idea where we are?" Celine asked, not expecting the wizard would know.

Before Alden could reply, Celine was struck by a sudden memory — an experiment from her first year as a cadet. The incident had stuck with her through all these years because she'd dearly wanted to discover the answer to it. There simply hadn't been an opportunity to investigate. A professor had performed the experiment for her class, to demonstrate a fascinating phenomenon: If you use a sound wave to collapse an underwater bubble, a flash of light is generated. No one, then or now, as far as Celine knew, had ever satisfactorily explained it.

Celine knew intuitively that this information was somehow vital to her survival, but she also knew that it didn't apply to the present situation. She didn't know how or why, but she knew she needed to try the idea out soon — very soon.

She burst the bubble, and they all clambered up onto the rocks. Alden reassured her that he and Leopold were fine, then pointed to some twigs and sticks he'd spotted in some shoreside brush. "A fire," he explained. A few minutes later, they were warming and drying themselves beside a cheerful blaze. The bird perched close by, preening and re-settling his purple plumage.

Celine tried several times to reach Fianna and Jager, without success. She tried the Mentors, too, with the same disconcerting result. Thirsty, she reached for a water bottle in her bodypack. As she drew it out, she was surprised to hear a buzzing sound coming from the bottom of the pack. She dug around and found the source: the silver crystal she'd found many months before, in the river's shallows close to Fianna's cave-home. She pulled out the warm, shiny, and currently rather noisy stone and regarded it quizzically. Alden, watching all this, smiled knowingly.

A strange thought struck the girl, and she turned to question the wizard. At the same time, the stone began to vibrate harder and faster. She had to clasp her hands tightly together to keep from dropping it. This rapidly became more difficult, because it was also growing hotter and hotter. Then, suddenly, the stone cooled somewhat, and its buzzing faded to a low, soothing hum. Then something astonishing happened: Celine received a mental message...from the stone.

"Child," it mented, "follow your heart and mind and you will remain safe. I am with you. I will always be with you. You need only to use me to call, and help will come." And then the object cooled completely and lay still and silent in her hand.

"That was strange!" she said to Alden. "But you know, I think West is guiding us, through this stone. And my finding it was no accident." The wizard gave her a gentle smile, which she took as a knowing agreement.

She carefully returned the stone to her pack, this time securing it in a sealable pocket.

Once they were warmed up and dry again, they took stock of their surroundings. Beyond the brushy thicket that lined this part of the lakeshore was a broad stretch of grass. It extended some forty or fifty meters to an aged stone building, flanked by colonnades on either side and tastefully adorned with geometric patterns. At neat intervals there were also images — weathered and faded, but still discernable as depicting creatures Celine recognized as Earth-mythological, originating from the area Earthers called the middle east. From the architecture, the images and the building's apparent age, Celine concluded first that the building was a church or temple, and second that they were now in the time period they had intended to reach.

"Strange," she said, approaching the building and inspecting some of its stone columns. "Very strange." She was confused to see Pleiadean military symbols, painted or written at eye level on two columns. This was graffiti of some sort, as she and some friends had once marked on rock faces as children.

After one last look at the column markings, she spoke again to Alden. "I think we should go this way." She indicated a stone-paved pathway leading away from the building, toward an opening in the cavern wall about thirty meters away. Alden nodded; they headed down the path and into a tunnel. Once inside they could see that the tunnel was not particularly long, perhaps a hundred meters or so. They made their way down the gloomy passage, exiting at last onto a wide terrace that overlooked a beautiful chasm, several hundred meters across. They could see a similar terrace along the wall on the chasm's far side. Broad paths descended from both terraces, leading down to a lush valley below. High above, an enormous, circular volcanic opening framed the brilliant blue, cloudless sky above. Gazing upward in wonder at the beauty of the place, Celine let out a sudden gasp. High above the chasm floor were more than a dozen colorful Dragons, flying about in aerial maneuvers. She could see more Dragons speckling the fields and meadows below.

"Wow!" said Celine. "This was most unexpected."

"Yes, but wonderful!" exclaimed the wizard. "How delightful! How I do love Dragon folk. Look, some have seen us; they're heading our way."

"I sure hope they are friendly," said Celine. "I've had quite enough difficult situations for one day." She was fairly certain the Dragons would prove friendly, but drew and tightly gripped her incant-baton all the same. As they approached, she recognized the Dragons' coloring and features. "I believe these are Dragons from Nibiru," she said quietly.

"Yes, that was my thought as well," replied the grinning wizard. Leopold squawked his agreement.

It was not long before a wall of Dragons lined up to face the Humans along the edge of the terrace. Celine sensed no threat, so she took the initiative and bowed, before any Dragon did. She called out to the Dragon she guessed was their leader.

"Hello. I am Cadet Celine Zulak, Companion to Albho Fianna Uwatti, Princess of Nibiru, who is soon to be crowned Queen. This is my friend Alden Koondahg, and his avian friend Leopold." She bowed again for good measure, as did the wizard and the bird.

"Greetings," said the Dragon she'd addressed. "I am Princess Bobbess Linglu Uwatti; my friends call me Linglu. We are visiting here from Nibiru. Prince Deet told us to expect you, Companion Celine Zulak. Come, everything is ready for you."

Celine stood in silent astonishment, her mouth agape. The wizard grinned wider; Leopold gave the loudest squawk Celine had heard yet.

"CELINE!" CRIED JAGER, FIANNA AND THE OTHERS, over and over. The Mentors joined in the effort, calling repeatedly to the girl and wizard. Suddenly, Jager stopped. He had sensed West. She'd called to him briefly, her voice subtly different from the one he'd know all his life.

"Shush, everyone," he said. "I need to listen. It's West, she's trying to reach me." At once, everyone went silent. The boy listened hard — and there she was again, strong and clear this time.

"Oh, West! It's wonderful to hear you!" he cried. "We're all frantic with worry — we've lost all contact with Celine."

"Yes, I know, dear Jager," replied the Mentor — audibly, not mentally. Though she was not physically present, her voice reverberated through the refectory, loud enough for all to hear. "That is why I have come to you. Celine needs your help. You must follow her to where she has been taken. But first allow me to explain her disappearance. You see, a black magic counter-spell — a hex — was cast upon the time-travel incantation you began. It is unfortunate that we were unaware of the hex until it went into effect. It is quite fortunate, however, that Celine insisted Alden accompany her. Those who wrought the hex did not anticipate his presence.

As a result, the counter-spell did not kill you all, as was intended. For this we are eternally thankful.

"Alden is with our Celine right now; he will keep her safe. He is a most powerful wizard. So is his friend Leopold, though most would never suspect it. The two will regard our dear girl's life as above their own. Nonetheless, Celine needs you too, Jager. You, and your Nibiruan friends who have traveled to this place. Go to her, all of you. Go to her, for she cannot return here alone. She needs your strength. Above all she needs your love. Without it she will be lost to us forever."

Fianna and the rest gasped, none more anxiously than Jager. "This is terrible, West," he said, his eyes betraying his dread. "I understand we must go, but how can we, if the traveling spell is hexed? How can we save Celine?"

"Yes Jager, the situation is dire," replied the Mentor. "But you are quite capable of saving her, my dear boy. And saving Alden too. For you know the time-traveling spell and have practiced it well. It was not your fault that your first attempt to cast it was hexed. You still have Prince Deet's incant-baton and personal grimoire. I advise you to go to Nessie once again and request her help. She will keep you safe when you cast the spell. Black magic cannot reach you at her Loch Ness home, especially if my sisters also help bolster the protective barrier that surrounds it. All of us, working together, will make the spell work so that you may go to Celine. I ask you to trust me in this, Jager."

Jager heaved a heavy sigh. "Thank you, West," he whispered. "I believe you. I have never doubted you. Not once. I know your ways are wise, and that you never fail to perceive what is needed, what is best for our universe and its peoples."

"Thank you, dear lad. Now I must converse with my

sisters. And I am sorry to say it, but when I have finished with them, I must leave you once again. My departure does not mean you or Celine are unimportant to me. It is simply that I must be elsewhere at this crucial moment in time, to ensure your good efforts bear fruit. My sisters will keep you safe, just as well as I would if I were with you. Trust them as you would trust me, Jager. Follow their suggestions; they too know many ways to handle the sort of seemingly inexplicable events we have seen of late."

"Thank you, West," said Jager. "Thank you for everything."

Jager, his face a bit less ashen, waited patiently for North and her sisters to finish their private conversation with West. After a few minutes, the sisters approached the large tree table that had become the little group's official meeting place. Although no longer alive, the venerable wood seemed to offer comfort and understanding.

North gave Jager a gentle pat. "Hello everyone," she said. "We must hurry back to our waiting ship. Fianna, would you please contact Nessie to let her know we are coming?"

"Yes, right away," Fianna nodded.

"Excellent," replied North. "Also, please ask that she gather as many of her friends as she is able on such short notice, for we are in need of their assistance once again."

"Yes, I will," said Fianna over her shoulder, as she followed the others toward the transbeam room.

Soon the group was in the Mentor ship's hold, hovering above Loch Ness. Jager sat tight in the saddle as Vin prepared to leap out, with Fianna at his side. In minutes, the group — many Mentors included — had lined up along the pebbly shore, overlooking a small group of Water Dragons gathered close behind Nessie.

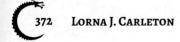

"Nessie," said North. "Thank you for again being so willing to assist us and our friends. We are forever in your debt."

Nessie bowed her elegant brindle neck. "As always, you are most welcome, dear friend. We are deeply proud of all our efforts to assist you; they will be remembered for generations to come, in the greatest of our stories. Our ancestors foretold that the Water Dragons of Earth would offer the universe staunch assistance when others were unable to do so. We feel blessed to be those very Dragons, and to fulfill the prophesies. We are truly honored to help each and every one of you.

"Come, we are ready to begin," continued Nessie. "Though the spell is ancient, and one we have never performed ourselves, we are all familiar with its every word and nuance. It is among the mandatory teachings given all our young, so that any Water Dragon, no matter where on the planet, may be ready and able if ever called upon. Do not worry, my friends. We will help you find your lost loved ones and bring them home safely. That we would someday do so has been foretold in our stories, and we know we will succeed."

Jager dismounted, stepped forward, and bowed long and deeply, with graceful flourishes. "Thank you, Nessie," he said upon rising. "I truly will be in your debt for as long as I live. You need only ask, and I will assist you in any way I can — always." He bowed again then climbed back up into the saddle.

"The honor and pleasure are mine, and my people's as well," replied Nessie, with another bow.

"It is time," announced North. "Let us begin. I have faith we will soon see Celine and Alden."

All assumed their places as the Mentors directed, and at

last the chant began. Fianna and the others stood close to the shore, encircled on one side by the Water Dragons, and by the Mentors on the other. As the chant progressed, a thick mist, silvery-white and pink, arose to swirl about the feet of the Niþiru Dragons. The mist thickened with each breath of the chanters, until nothing could be seen but the dense, pink-white cloud. No sound could be heard but the chant, and the soft rush of the swirling mist.

"Stand close, dear Fianna," said Vin. She moved closer, as did Joli to Ahimoth. Jager gripped the saddle tighter — and just in time, for Vin and the others were abruptly snatched airborne, spinning with the fog. Faster and faster they spun, the Dragons working their wings to stay in balance. Suddenly, with a sharp snap, everything went black. There was a brief sensation of falling, and the whole group hit the ground, jarred and startled but unhurt. The enchanted mist was gone, replaced by daylight and a billowing cloud of dust, kicked up by their impact.

As the dust settled, the Dragons scrambled to their feet. Jager, still clinging to his saddle, held his baton high, ready for action.

"Are you all right, Fianna?" asked Vin.

"Yes, I am unhurt," replied the princess. "My only hurts are bruises and bumps from earlier."

"That is the same with me, dear sister," spoke up Ahimoth. "My dear Joli, are you alright?"

"Yes, yes, my friend," she replied. "I am unhurt this time as well."

"Good to hear, all of you," said Jager, his baton still gripped tight. He peered around, surprised to see that they were on a broad ledge, looking down on a small but lush valley.

Beyond the valley a steep wall rose up to a mountain peak. "Interesting place!" he commented, "But we'd better get looking for Celine right away."

He was about to say more when they all heard muffled voices. They seemed to be coming from across the valley — from a cave or tunnel mouth, set in the mountainside at about the same height as their ledge. "Let's take cover," he said, his voice low but urgent. "There's no telling who we're hearing." They all looked around for some form of concealment, but there was none to be found. Their ledge was quite exposed, and quite flat and barren too.

"Huddle together everyone," said Jager softly. "I know an invisibility spell, but I'm not sure if I can make it work for such a large group. It's worth a try, though." He began to chant, and managed to succeed. And just in time: The voices from across the chasm were growing louder. The group expected the sources of those voices to emerge from the tunnel at any moment.

And emerge they did. To everyone's surprise and delight, out stepped Celine and Alden — followed by Leopold, with a squawk.

Jager tried at once to reverse the cloaking spell, but the group remained invisible. He spent no time wondering why, but began menting and shouting to Celine; the others joined in at once. They made quite a racket, both mental and vocal, but couldn't get through to her. In desperation, the Dragons began battering the invisible sheath with wings, teeth and claws. Jager struggled furiously to disperse it, or at least pierce it, with spells and his incant-baton.

Suddenly, Fianna pointed skyward and cried out: "Look!" The little group dropped their efforts at once and looked up.

"Nibiru Dragons!" cried Vin, astonished. "How intriguing."

"Yes, they are indeed from Nibiru," said Ahimoth. "Most interesting."

The group redoubled its efforts to escape the shield, still to no avail. At last they stopped, defeated. They watched in desperate silence as Celine and the wizard conversed with the new arrivals. Then the Nibiruans departed, and Celine and Alden disappeared back into the tunnel from which they'd come.

CHAPTER 35

Dragon's Blood

"It is an honor and pleasure to meet you, Princess Linglu," said Celine. She, Alden and Leopold bowed to the majestic Dragon, for the third time since her arrival.

"The pleasure is all mine," replied Linglu. "Prince Deet speaks highly of you."

"I am confused," said Celine. She glanced inquiringly at the wizard, who simply smiled in return. "But I guess that's the least of my problems right now. You're sure? Prince Deet? How is this at all possible?"

"The ways of magic are often the most mysterious of all," grinned the Dragon princess. "Come, we have set up a place where you can perform the spell you must. This is how it is to be. Just as Prince Deet said."

Celine looked again at Alden, wide-eyed. The wizard only grinned wider; Leopold, who couldn't grin, bobbed up and down instead. "Yes, quite the adventure, eh?" said the wizard. "Quite the adventure, indeed." Leopold squawked agreement.

Celine and Alden couldn't follow the Dragons in flight, and Alden didn't want to use his magic and so risk revealing himself to any hostile, prying eyes. So the trio made their way down a little-used path toward the luxuriant meadow that lay at the foot of the steep, rocky wall. As they descended, they could see the Nibiruans gathering and forming up into a circle. When Celine and Alden reached the meadow, the Dragons parted their circle to let them in; the Humans walked to the center of the group and greeted the handsome gathering with warm smiles. Celine half expected to see Schimpel step out from among the Dragons at any moment — so she was not surprised when he did exactly that. The man approached her and extended a hand in greeting.

"Hail, Celine," he said, "Companion to the granddaughter of my dear friend, Linglu. "What a pleasure to meet you at last. I am Shea Reginald Schimpel. My friends call me Reggie, as I hope you will."

"Um, uh..." muttered Celine, her mouth agape before she managed to collect herself; "Sir!" she said, accepting his hand and clasping it respectfully. "What a complete honor, sir."

Reggie shook her hand; his grin widened. "Reggie, please." He bowed briefly, released the hand, and turned to shake the wizard's, bowing again. He had to stifle a chuckle when Leopold held out a wing, but quickly assumed a look of respect and shook the wing as if it were a Human's hand, and bowed just as respectfully as he had to the others.

"Thanks for bringing her safely here," he said to Alden and Leopold, then turned back to the girl. "The honor is mine, Celine," he said, bowing again.

"Completely mine, my dear, for you have done great things, and will accomplish many more. I am thrilled at the opportunity to fulfill the legends of Atlantis, and assist you in saving the Dragons of Nibiru. And indeed, they must be protected, not only because it is the right thing to do, but also because of who and what the Dragons are — beautiful beings, crucial to the happiness of our universe and to upholding its morality — two objectives which wisdom tells us go hand in hand, inevitably. The Dragons will be our salvation. And you, dear Celine, are the only one who can make that possible. You, and you alone."

"Uh...well, yes. Okay," replied Celine, weakly. She didn't fully comprehend what this handsome and powerful person was saying, but felt she would, quite soon. Or at least she hoped so. "Um, meeting you, sir, ah...I mean Reggie...is such an honor, sir. Jager will be so envious!"

"Ha!" laughed Reggie. "I look forward to meeting him, too — and soon." Celine cringed a little, concerned. The man's comments reminded her that she still hadn't been able to contact Jager or Fianna. She pushed her worries aside for the moment, and brought herself fully back to the present.

"Oh, how extraordinary," gasped the wizard. "This is *truly* a wonderful adventure."

Celine couldn't help but smile at the elderly wizard before she addressed the princess. "Regarding your comments, Princess, I believe I understand what you are saying, but I am still a bit confused. Meeting you and Mr. Schimpel...I mean Reggie, or any interaction with Prince Deet — none of these events were depicted in any of the paintings we've seen on Nibiru or Remini. Nor have they appeared in my dreams."

"You are quite correct," said Linglu. "No, the present events comprise a new story. One that has not been painted anywhere. Events are as it proved necessary that they be. In fact, had this story been painted, or to attempt to paint it now, would bring about the end of your existence. You see, time — or, as we Dragons call it, the progression of events — does not permit such events as these. Time never favors or allows such circumstances, and never will. Odd though it may sound, if we were to fail to proceed as we are about to, here in what we all think of as 'the present,' then you never would have lived any of your previous lifetimes — those prior to this present time. In fact, you would not exist here and now. So you see, it is most important that we *do* proceed."

The Dragon looked at the worried girl. "Have no worries, my dear. You are most welcome and expected here. Expected by us, and by the Atlanteans. Even though we conduct our lives in different times. Your arrival has been anticipated this past season, and rightly so."

"Thank you, Princess," said Celine, though her expression betrayed lingering confusion. "I have faith in the truth of your words, though I may not show it well. But now, if I may ask, do you know anything of what has happened to Jager, Fianna and the others of our party? We have been separated."

"I am sorry, I do not," replied the Dragon. "Perhaps the prince will have the answer you seek."

"I hope so," said Celine, with a glance at the wizard. He responded with one of his warm smiles. "I suppose," continued the girl, "I should go speak with Prince Deet, since that is the reason I have come. And perhaps he will have some news of my friends."

"Yes," replied Linglu. "He has visited this place and our time on three occasions. He has mentioned you during each visit, and waits for you now."

"He's waiting for me?!" exclaimed Celine, nervous all over again at the prospect of meeting yet another famous and important person. At the same time, she was concerned her magic would not prove sufficient to carry her across time to where the prince waited. "Oh my," Celine said to Linglu. "I suspected this might be the case, but wasn't sure. It is difficult to believe it is truly happening."

"Yes, he waits for you in a different time—what we would think of as his own time," said Linglu. "And so we must help you prepare for your trip through time's wall."

Celine looked at the wizard. He just smiled on, as though everything happening here were normal and expected.

"Following your visit and your return to this present time," continued the princess, Prince Deet will leave this planet—in his own time—just as we Dragons must leave after you go to him. We will not be here when you return."

Celine's stomach began to knot.

"The prince," Linglu continued, "foresees difficult times for Nibiru. He sees the same for the people of Earth.

"But now to the business of sending you to meet him. First, he asked me to give you an item of great value and great importance. He said that without it, you will be unable to safely reach him."

Celine knew precisely the item Linglu referred to, and shuddered to think what obtaining it would require. "Let us begin," said Linglu. The beautiful Dragon held up a foreleg to Celine, as Alden, Leopold and Linglu's gathered friends began to chant. "There is no cause for concern, Companion Celine," said Linglu. "It will hurt me but little. And it is a small price to pay to save this world, as well as our own."

"Thank you," Celine said softly. She reached into her

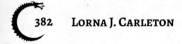

bodypack, knowing instinctively what she must do, and the magical elements she'd need. Efficiently but with great care, she worked with the items she'd selected — mixing herbs and arranging objects just so. She soon had a small fire burning; around it she sprinkled a circle of salt, and laid out several items, each in the precise position required. Satisfied all was in readiness, she unsheathed her dragon-handled knife and approached Linglu. The princess stood perfectly calm, waiting.

Celine thanked the Dragon again, kissed her knife, then made a small, swift cut across the Dragon's beautiful silver underbelly, beneath the upheld foreleg. She quickly set the knife aside, took up a small cauldron and held it just beneath the wound. A rivulet of bright red blood dripped into the cauldron; all eyes watched, fascinated. After a time, Celine handed the cauldron to the wizard, who carried it aside. The girl picked up a poultice she had prepared, pressed it firmly over Linglu's wound, and began to intone a spell of healing. Within minutes, the wound had nearly vanished.

The princess thanked Celine and stepped to the side, watching respectfully as the girl cleaned and wrapped her knife with a cloth pulled from a pocket, then returned it to her bodypack. Next, she made a new circle of salt, this time pink rather than white. She included the fire within the new ring, as well as the wizard and his bird companion. Alden held his baton in one hand, and the cauldron of precious blood in the other.

At a nod from Celine, Alden chanted a few words, then poured the cauldron's crimson contents into the fire in a thin, measured stream. In unison, Celine and Alden swirled their batons. The watchers gasped as bright crimson flames leapt ten meters upward — only to be replaced by a sheet of

white smoke. The smoke writhed and curled, wrapping itself around the two Humans and the violet bird until they were entirely engulfed. The fire flared once, bright orange, then died just as fast as it had flared; the swirling smoke dissipated, to reveal Celine, Alden and Leopold standing utterly still, staring into space.

As the watchers looked on, a tight, slightly pulsating cluster of blue-green points of light, about the size of an apple, drifted outward from the back of Celine's head. Similar "glows" appeared behind Alden and Leopold. All three of the energy glows drifted upward to a height of about three meters. A whirlwind of smoke and ash leapt from the fire, reaching upward to surround the glows. The whirlwind went from gray-white to deepest black, almost totally obscuring the spinning blue-green glows from view. And then, with a harsh snap, it vanished, taking the glows with it.

Celine began to panic. She was being pulled down some sort of tunnel, almost entirely in blackness — and black usually meant pain and separation. Her panic eased though, as the blackness was replaced by bright light and drifting patches of color. She was still troubled by the deathly silence of the place — if in fact it could be called a place — and a feeling of intense pressure all about her.

After what seemed several minutes in the strange tunnel, there was a sharp jolt, and Celine found herself looking at a large room; its rocky walls suggesting she was underground. She recognized at once that she was seeing through someone else's eyes. She looked down at callused hands, protruding from the sleeves of a simple garment. They moved when she willed them to, exactly as if they were her own.

She sensed Alden's presence and looked to her right; beside her was an elderly gentleman, much like Alden in appearance, dressed in a garment of the same color and fabric as hers. Just beyond the elder stood a slim, dark-haired young man, in much the same attire.

"Everything is as should be, my dear," came Alden's mental voice, steady and comforting. "We are borrowing these bodies for but a brief while."

The wizard cast a spell on the three bodies, putting their owners into a comfortable, oblivious sleep. "There," said Alden. "They rest now; they shall come to no harm. And when we have completed our task and departed, they will awaken, refreshed but with no thought or memory of what has transpired. Now come. We must go, and Leopold here will lead the way." He indicated the young man beside him. "He knows where we must go."

Leopold headed out a nearby exit, Alden and Celine close behind. They came to a lavishly appointed chamber, occupied by several people — all similarly dressed — busily packing beautiful lamps, serving pieces and other objects into wooden crates, carefully cushioning each piece as they went. Celine guessed they must be servants, and that the bodies she and her friends now animated must be servants as well. A strong, deep voice came from off to the side; the three turned to face the voice's source — a handsome, middle-aged man. From his regal bearing and air of kind command, Celine guessed at once that this must be Prince Deet.

"Hurry, we must all be aboard ships by nightfall," said the prince, addressing the busy servants.

"Yes, your majesty," they replied, their respect and affection for the man ringing clear in their voices.

The prince turned to Celine and smiled. "Ah, my dear," he said, face beaming and arms wide in greeting, "So lovely to meet you. As I'm sure you know by now, I have been expecting you."

"Yes, Your Highness," replied Celine, bowing. She was surprised that the prince knew it was she inside the servant's body, but more surprised at the deep voice her borrowed body produced.

"No need for that," said the prince, with a chuckle and a wave of his hand. "And hello to you, Mr. Koondahg, and Leopold too. Thank you for making sure this special young lady arrived safely." The pair bowed, grinning.

"It's been quite the adventure," laughed the wizard. "The best of my life. I wouldn't have missed it for worlds. Neither would my dear friend Leopold. We will talk of this for years to come. And to think, it's only just begun!"

The pleasantries complete, the prince led the three to a table at the back of the room. "Please, sit," he gestured. "We do have a moment, despite the late hour."

The prince, well known for coming quickly to the point, pulled Mutuum from within his robes. Celine gasped. The sheer beauty and riveting presence of this most famous of incant-batons was more than she'd expected.

"My dear," said Prince Deet, "I understand that you have been under the impression that in order to locate my lovely friend Mutuum in your own time, it would be necessary to travel back to *this* time and place, and hear me speak of its hiding place." Celine nodded. "And I can see your surprise at discovering that impression was incorrect." She nodded again.

"Very well," said the prince. "I should explain that that was a false idea, deliberately spread to throw off any person of ill will who might attempt to capture Mutuum.

This is why I contacted Linglu and Schimpel, in their time, to assist you. Anyone else searching for Mutuum would not have been able to travel from Princess Linglu's time to mine, for they would not know her assistance was needed. An extra but crucial safety precaution, you see."

"Brilliant," said the wizard, stroking his rather rotund body's beard.

"Celine, as you know from your studies of magic, matter's location in time is subject to manipulation. But surprisingly, the inter-relationship and interchangeable characteristics of matter, energy, space and time make the most powerful magic possible. This is why time exists. For if there is no movement of matter in space, there can be no time." Celine nodded her understanding, though her eyes were still wide with amazement.

"Thus," continued the prince, "matter appears to exist, and the concept known as space becomes measurable. This is the true nature of existence, and of what most regard as magic. It is a reality slightly different from that in which most people live and operate.

"Now, here is the secret of using Mutuum: He can reverse movement, or, as some call it, time. And he has power over all the elements. He is one of the most important artifacts in this universe. Indeed, in thousands of the known universes. He must never fall into the hands of Byrne, or others of that evil one's ilk.

"There exist only five beings who should ever hold Mutuum. You, Celine, of course. As well as Jager and I. There are two others, but it is not necessary for you to know of their identities at this time." Celine gasped.

The prince smiled at her. "It is unfortunate that solid

objects cannot be transmitted using the time-traveling spell you employ. Not without a living being to bear them. But if you follow my instructions, you will find Mutuum in your own time. Then you will wield his powers to save us all. But come now; it is time for you to visit Princess Linglu once again."

"Um, please, Your Highness," spoke up Celine. "May I ask a couple of questions first?"

"Yes," said the prince. "I expected you might wish to."

"Sir," continued the girl. "Do you wish for us to hide Mutuum in a particular place when he has completed his work?"

"Ah, that is a good question, deserving of a good answer. It would be expected that I would ask you to hide such a prized artifact here in our trusty tunnels, along with our other treasures such as the ancient grimoires. But I fear that Mutuum is not safe here, and would not be safe here in your time. That is why you must travel to the land where one named Amura abides, in your own time. There you may locate and collect Mutuum.

Amura knows how to contact the Snake of Peru — the Dragon of Machu Picchu. Mutuum is — or rather, will be, when you arrive — in his care. He is a great Dragon who has promised me to use his powerful magic to protect Mutuum through all the days of his life, holding the great baton ready for the day you come to his door and ask to retrieve it.

"The Dragon of Machu Picchu is able to travel the spiritual realms in a magical vessel, distinguished by its intense, orange, flickering lights. The lights ward off any who seek treasures in the Dragon's home. I left the craft in his care, in case the Brothers or others of wicked intent threatened this planet again.

"To safely enter Amura's home, you must travel first to the Land of the Stones, in the north. You know that land as Scotland. There you must locate the hidden portal which will take you to her. When you arrive and make your request, she will fetch the Dragon and bring him to you.

"Then you must bring Mutuum back through the portal to Scotland. It is there that he will be safe. Go now. Collect Mutuum. With you, he will fulfill his destiny. And when his work is complete, he will tell you where to return him — in your own time and place — so that he may remain safe. He knows where to await the coming of my descendant. He is the only being, other than I, who knows the proper location."

"Yes, Your Highness," replied Celine in a whisper.

"I will escort young Celine," said the wizard. "I will make it my life's greatest work to see your wishes fulfilled, dear prince." He bowed to the prince once again, as did Leopold.

"My friends, I was supremely confident you would undertake this task, and that you would perform it well and faithfully," replied Deet. "It is for that reason that you were chosen."

"And, my dear girl," he continued, "as to the second question you wish to pose, the answer is yes. You, Jager, Fianna, and the rest of your party are all safe. You will see them again soon; do not worry."

"Oh, thank you, sir," Celine gushed, feeling a great deal better.

When the prince had explained how to locate the portal in Scotland, goodbyes were exchanged. Alden gestured for Celine and Leopold to follow him, back the way they'd come. This time, though, the tunnel was deserted — all of Prince

Deet's people had already gone to his ship.

When the trio arrived back at the spot where they had first picked up their borrowed bodies, they placed the bodies just as they'd found them, and Celine cast the reverse spell. At once, she, Alden and Leopold were whisked up the colorful, pressurized tunnel that had brought them.

Moments later, the three were looking through their own eyes once again, their bodies just as they had left them. Still a bit disorientated and woozy after their remarkable experience, they stepped out into the sunshine.

"Yes, yes — I am having a truly great adventure, Leopold," laughed the wizard.

CHAPTER 36

Scotland

"Alden, were you able to hear what Prince Deet said to me?" asked Celine.

"Yes. And his words were strange indeed," said the wizard. "Yet at the same time, they made good sense."

"Quite sensible. Logical," she replied. "Mutuum to be found in Peru, not in the ancient tunnels. And only accessible via Scotland! That's a surprise. It makes sense though, in a way, seeing as that's where the vortex appears, for the tube-chute to Nibiru."

Celine began to say more, but gasped instead — she had spotted Linglu and Reggie, heading their way. They had not yet left! Perhaps they could have a further chat with the remarkable pair! And chat they did; not a long talk, but informative and thoroughly fascinating. When Linglu announced that it was time to depart, Celine and Alden thanked them warmly, wished them well, and watched as they flew up and up to the volcano's mouth, in the company of their Dragon friends.

Celine led the wizard back up toward the terrace where they had arrived. Along the way, it hit her: They couldn't head home! The time-travel spell required more magical power than the three of them could bring to bear. To make matters worse, she no longer had Prince Deet's personal incant-baton, which was instrumental in working the spell to carry them through time. Jager had been holding it, back when everything had gone wrong. He probably had it still, but that didn't matter — what did matter was that the baton was not here.

Celine shared her concerns with Alden; he opined that they were "surely in a pickle," and then explained to Celine what that meant. She laughed at the funny expression. "More of that Earther talk Jager uses," she laughed. She was about to head back down the small trail to where they had conducted the last spell, when she sensed something familiar and abruptly stopped. She thought she had heard Jager!

At first, she figured she must have imagined it. But she called out several times to Jager and Fianna all the same. There came no response. An odd thought struck her, so she spun around to look across the chasm, then upward. There! It was Linglu again. And Reggie upon her back — and the other Nibiru Dragons close behind, descending just as before. And then, also as before, they landed close by.

Celine turned her thoughts away from Jager and Fianna again, pleased to have another opportunity to speak with the legendary princess and her equally famous Companion. She was about to address them when she was struck dumb by a powerful light, blazing within her mind — so bright and intense that she was paralyzed. Impossibly, its intensity increased — and she experienced a desperation unlike anything she'd ever known. It was too much. She fell to her knees, silent and clutching her head, at Linglu's feet.

Celine had never been so frightened. In her mind, she pushed as hard as she could away from the burning light and dreadful desperation. With a burst of supreme effort, she broke its hold over her. She shook her head, trying to throw off lingering thoughts of the experience, then looked upward to see the Dragon princess peering down at her.

"Are you all right?" asked Linglu, as Reggie moved close to help the girl to her feet.

"Yes, Princess," she replied. "It is over now. I am most fortunate you returned. But, *why* did you return? Is everything all right?" She sat back down to steady herself. The awful desperation had begun to creep back. She did not want to face it again.

"Of that, I am not sure," said the Dragon. "I just had an overpowering premonition that you must not leave this place. Not yet. That you must remain here — but for what reason, I could not say."

"Oh, how extraordinary," gasped the wizard. "This is truly, truly an extraordinary adventure."

"I see, Your High...," the girl began; then a groan escaped her lips. She had heard them! Loud and clear had come several ments! She spun around to look across the chasm, toward the terrace on the opposite side. There they were! Fianna and Jager! Waving at her, but from behind some sort of transparent barrier. She had never felt such pure joy! And then the transparent wall shattered, the flying shards seeming to turn to vapor as they flew, then disappear. In an instant, the horrible desperation left her. In its place, a wave of love and warmth engulfed her in an indescribable embrace.

"Jager! Fianna!" she shouted again, and mented too, jumping up and down and waving with all her might.

Linglu, Reggie, the wizard, and the rest looked across to where the girl directed her shouts. To their surprise, there on the opposite terrace were four Nibiru Dragons, one with a Companion, waving and flapping just as joyously as Celine.

"Jager! Fianna!" Celine cried again. "It's you! It's YOU!!"

"Pumpkin!" shouted Jager. "Oh, Celine! Are you all right?"

"Yes, yes! And Mr. Koondahg and Leopold are fine, too," she replied through tears of joy.

Fianna leapt into flight at once, followed quickly by the others. Ever since Celine's terrifying disappearance, the Dragon had struggled to keep her churning emotions under control, and to push thoughts of loss — of never again seeing her Companion — back and down, down to the deepest depths of her mind. She hadn't been very successful, but now all the anguish was gone. Her Celine had returned, safe!

When the lovely white Dragon touched down, she couldn't even manage to get her wings pulled in before the girl had leapt to her and locked her in the tightest embrace she could ever remember. At last Fianna got her wings around her friend, and the two cried tears of joy and relief, hugging on and on.

"I am so thankful to see you," cried Fianna. "I was *so* worried." The Dragon was at a loss for any further words. The bond between them had become a *physical* phenomenon. Anything more than a brief separation sparked intense pain, mental and spiritual, even physical. Celine's return was like having her withered leg renewed all over again, the Dragon later explained. Yet the feelings were deeper, emotionally and spiritually.

"I was more worried than I can remember!" replied Celine, hugging even tighter. "I cannot believe this keeps happening to us. It has to stop!"

"I agree," said the Dragon, her embrace now even tighter. Neither wanted to let go, but Fianna sensed Celine was just as anxious for a comforting hug from Jager — so she reluctantly unfolded her wings. The two young people were in each other's arms almost at once. After a long minute, Celine pulled away to look at Jager, to satisfy herself that this was real, that he was back. Then she pulled him in again and held him feverishly as fresh tears fell. Their friends, watching, shed plentiful tears of their own.

"Oh, Celine," said Jager, brushing back her chestnut hair and caressing her cheeks. "I'm so grateful we found you."

"So am I," she laughed. "But how *did* you? For a while there I wasn't sure if I'd see you, any of you, ever again."

"West contacted me," explained Jager, "and said that someone adept in the black arts had hexed the traveling spell and caused us to be split up. None of us traveled through time, but we ended up in widely different places. We all managed to make it back to the Mentors' outpost, though. We've just come from there — from the outpost, and our own time. And we had to come by way of Loch Ness."

"Wow! That is so interesting," said Celine. "For Scotland is precisely where we need to go to begin our journey."

"What journey is that?" asked Jager.

"The journey to retrieve Mutuum, of course. So, first stop: present-day Scotland. *Our* present day, that is. Then we're off to Peru."

"It sounds like you know what you're talking about," said

Jager, "but how do you know all this?"

"Oh! I'm sorry. I haven't told you about that, have I?" said Celine, laughing and apologetic all at once. "After quite some dramatic adventures, we — Mr. Koondahg, Leopold and I — were able to travel back to Prince Deet's time, and to learn of Mutuum's location directly from the prince himself! We talked with him, Jager. In person! Can you imagine?"

"That is wonderful, Pumpkin. And just about unbelievable — but I *do* believe you, don't worry!" He embraced her again. "And look, just getting here, I've had about enough time travel to last me for more than a lifetime or two."

"Me too," chimed in Ahimoth. "But travel we must, to return to our own time. Which has me wondering, how are we to accomplish that, if the time-travel spell has been hexed?"

"I'm happy to say that West explained that to me as well," replied Jager. "Celine, we'll need to ask your new Dragon friends for help in making the trip, though."

"Well, do I have a surprise for you!" laughed Celine. She gently turned Jager to face Linglu and Reggie. "Jager, I am pleased to introduce you to Princess Bobbess Linglu Uwatti and her Companion, Shea Reginald Schimpel."

Jager stood speechless, regarding the pair with eyes wide. His watching friends grinned and chuckled. "Oh, what an honor, Princess Linglu," he said, bowing his deepest bow. "This meeting is one I shall treasure for all my lives."

"I thank you, Jager," replied Linglu. "But please, the pleasure is mine." She bowed as deeply as Jager had, and with incomparable grace.

"And you, Mr. Schimpel," said Jager, "I...I am just as honored to make your acquaintance, sir. As Earthers of my time and tribe would say, I'm a huge fan."

"Greetings, Jager," laughed Reggie. "Celine assured me you would be pleased to make my acquaintance. I must admit it pleases me greatly to make yours. Now please, call me Reggie, won't you? I do wish we had more time to talk, for I rarely have opportunity to talk with other Humans — let alone other Dragon Companions! A longer visit will have to wait, though; my friends and I must leave this planet soon. Great danger is near. You and your own friends must also return to your time and place as quickly as possible. Much depends upon the success of your present mission."

"I understand, sir," replied Jager, bowing once again. "It has been an honor. And I look forward to our next meeting."

Celine took a brief moment to greet Vin, Ahimoth and Joli before giving Fianna and Jager another fierce squeeze.

The Dragons exchanged formal greetings, as the Humans looked on. The formalities completed, Princess Linglu stressed the importance of concluding their business quickly, so that all could go their separate ways before the timeline shifted.

All nodded their understanding and agreement, and Jager began. "Please listen closely. I must brief you on what's needed to get back to our time, and to the proper place. And, as you know, time is terribly short."

CHAPTER 37

Machu Picchu

The small group clung together as loud popping sounds erupted like firecrackers all around.

"Wow!" exclaimed Jager, releasing his grip on the saddle horn. "That almost made the tube-chute seem like a kiddie ride. I definitely wasn't expecting that."

After ensuring everyone had come through, they all heartily agreed: they were glad that there would be no further time travel in their futures. And hopefully no more tube-chute ordeals, either!

"It appears as though the magic worked," said Fianna, "for I recognize where we are. We are at Loch Maree, near to Nessie's home. It is where Celine and I arrived the first time we took the tube-chute. Over there we bedded for the night."

"Yes, you are correct, Fianna," said Celine. "This is the place!"

"Excellent," said Ahimoth, surveying the area. "Now, does anyone know where we are to go from here, to locate the portal?"

"Yes," replied Celine. "Prince Deet explained it all to Mr. Koondahg and me. Come, we are to go to the top—she pointed to a snow-capped peak — up there. Soon the Dragons were airborne, heading towards the peak at a rapid clip.

Alden had assured everyone that even though he could not fly with one of the Dragons, he and Leopold would join them at the designated spot. He would employ a spell to transport the two of them, similar to the way a jump-shift drive transports a space vessel. The "jump-shift spell" was not sufficiently potent to shift the Dragons, too, or he would have quickened their trip as well.

Sure enough, when the Dragons spiraled down to the snowy crag, there were the wizard and bird, deep in conversation about the local avian population.

Jager climbed from his saddle and set off to join Celine in exploring the area. Just as he reached her side, the girl jumped in excitement and let out a joyful whoop.

"It's here!" she shouted, grabbing Jager's arm and squeezing it tight. "I can't believe how easy that was. Look! Right there — that rock that looks as if it were deliberately placed on top of that big boulder — it means the portal is behind the boulder!"

"Great!" said Jager. "Well done, Pumpkin. What now?"

"Mr. Koondahg," said Celine, "are you ready to send us on our next jaunt?"

"Yes, indeed," replied the wizard. "Leopold and I will remain here as Prince Deet explained we should."

"Augh!" groaned Ahimoth. "Not another chute!"

"Unfortunately, yes," said Celine. "I'm sorry this is how we must travel, but it should be over quickly."

"I will try to add something to the spell, to smooth the trip," said the wizard.

"That would be appreciated," said Ahimoth.

"All right, then," said the wizard. "Are you all ready? Remember, Leopold and I can reach out and bring you back, if you have not returned on your own by the appointed time — one hour from now, as we have agreed. Travel fast, and return in an hour. Remember, too, that if we must bring you back, the experience will be even worse than the one we've all just been through."

"Oh, that would be unfortunate indeed," groaned Ahimoth. "It does not sound encouraging at all, but I do have faith that Celine and Jager shall bring us back at the required time."

"As do I," said Vin. "Oh well, I suppose now is better than any other time. Let's do this." He and Jager grinned at each other, amused at Vin's use of another Earther saying.

"Yes, let's," said Jager.

"Very well, then!" said Alden, and he began the incantation. Soon the adventurers found themselves being sucked down a very powerful chute at a dizzying speed. Celine feared she would be yanked from the saddle; she was about to tell Fianna so, when they all splashed into a wide, deep pool of frigid water.

Fortunately for the Humans, they were perched on the backs of their Dragon friends and only received a light splashing. Had they been plunged directly into the frigid waters, they would have been at extreme risk. The Dragons had far better tolerance of cold than Humans; they found the pool refreshing. Even so, the four quickly found the nearest bank and climbed out.

As water dripped off the Dragons' scales, the four stared in wonder at the beautifully formed stalagmites and stalactites that lined the nearby shores of the deep, dark lake. More could be seen farther along the shoreline, and hanging from the cavern's ceiling high above.

To their right lay the cavern's enormous opening, framing the starry night sky beyond. The moon had just risen, full and bright. Its silvery light reflected off ripples on the lake's surface, and sparkled in the shiny veins of minerals that adorned the scaley cavity walls.

"Wow!" exclaimed Jager, "I'm quite sure I know right where we are. This has to be the Huagapo Cave, northeast of the city of Lima. Yes, that's exactly what it is. I recognize it from my studies, and from promotional tourist photos. Spectacular! We are definitely in Peru."

"Yes, I believe you are correct, Jager," said Ahimoth. "Long ago, these mountains and caves were also a favorite place for vacationing Nibiru Dragons. None have traveled here in quite some time, though. I feel honored to be here."

"Yes, it is indeed beautiful," said Fianna. She shook herself to shed a bit more water. "Where shall we go next, Celine?"

"This lake is home to Amura, a Water Dragon who can help us reach the Dragon of Machu Picchu," said Celine. "He is the one protecting Mutuum. Fianna, would you please see if Amura will respond to your call?"

Fianna mented to Amura, and no sooner had she done so, than a long, silver-colored neck broke the surface nearby, and a young Water Dragon raised her elegant head.

"Greetings," said the Water Dragon. "I am Amura. This is

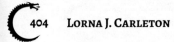

my home."

"Greetings, Amura," said Celine, bowing. "My name is Celine, and I am Companion to Albho Fianna Uwatti, Princess of Nibiru, in line for that world's throne." Fianna bowed.

Amura bowed her graceful neck. "It is a pleasure to meet you, Celine, and you, Princess Fianna. We Dragons of Huagapo have waited many years for your arrival. Rest, and I shall inform the Dragon of Machu Picchu of your presence." Without waiting for a reply, the Water Dragon slipped back beneath the surface, as gracefully as she had arrived. A gentle ripple was the only sign of her passage.

"Celine," said Jager, "I'm a little worried that we won't have enough time to wait for Amura. We are more than 400 kilometers from Machu Picchu, if I remember my geography correctly. That's too far for her to go and come back in the short time we've got."

"Sorry to interrupt," said Ahimoth, "But I can hear Amura menting. She has called to someone who has already answered, saying that they are now on their way. He said that he would be here in a matter of minutes. The Dragon of Machu Picchu must have some magic that enables him to travel in a fashion similar to that of the Mentors' spacecraft."

"Yes, brother," spoke up Fianna. "I heard the same ment. Amura will be back soon, and as you stated, the Dragon of Machu Picchu will be joining us in a few minutes." As Fianna finished speaking, Amura slipped above the water once again.

Fianna was the first to speak. "We did not mean to eavesdrop, but we heard your conversation with the Dragon of Machu Picchu. Thank you for you help."

"Do not worry, Princess," replied Amura. "I meant for you to hear my call. I wanted you to know that Pedro will arrive soon, for I realize that your time is limited."

"Thank you for your consideration," said Fianna. "People from my homeworld traveled to visit this area many years ago. Stories of your people's kindness are still told today."

"That is thoughtful of you to say," replied Amura. "Oh, Pedro is here." A rather small, coppery-colored Dragon materialized in a swirl of colors, only a few meters from where the friends stood.

"Greetings, Pedro," said Amura. "I would like to introduce you to Albho Fianna Uwatti, Princess of Nibiru, soon to be their queen, and to her brother Shakoor Ahimoth Uwatti, Prince of Nibiru. And these are their mates and Companions." Everyone bowed, as did Pedro, and further introductions and greetings were exchanged.

"It is a pleasure to meet each of you," said Pedro. He sat on his haunches, fidgeting and shifting position until he was comfortable, as though preparing for a long visit. "Yes, a pleasure, most definitely. I have waited for this day for quite some time. I would love to stay and enjoy your company, but I realize you must be on your way. I have faith in all of you, though, and know we will meet again under less strained circumstances."

The small Dragon paused, reached down, and lifted a scale on his underbelly. Carefully, using his talons, he extracted the precious incant-baton Celine and the others had come to collect.

"I believe this is what you have come for," said Pedro, presenting Mutuum to Celine. As soon as she took the baton in hand, it began to hum; the many tiny jewels adorning its

length shone brighter, as with inner light.

"Ah," said Pedro. "Mutuum is happy to see you again, Companion to Fianna. He will serve you well. I will miss him, of course, but I know he is destined for great things, and am proud to play a part in his adventure."

"It is an honor to meet you as well, Pedro," said Celine. "Thank you for taking such good care of Mutuum, and for making it possible for me to be here to collect him. You have kept your word to Prince Deet honorably, and I will keep my own word just as honorably, by ensuring Mutuum's safe-keeping for all future generations."

"You are most welcome; and thank you," said Pedro. "I would love to stay and chat, but I understand you have life-or-death business to attend to. Many lives and worlds depend upon you now, and upon your use of my dear friend, Mutuum."

More thanks and farewells were exchanged, and then the two Peruvian Dragons assisted Celine and Jager with the spell that would return them to Loch Maree. And return them it did — before long, the travelers emerged from behind the boulder, high above the loch's waters.

"Am I ever glad that is over," sighed Ahimoth. He huffed and ruffled, trying to shake off the ill effects of chute passage. "I do not look forward to doing that again any time soon. Not ever!"

Everyone laughed and assured the prince of their whole-hearted agreement. As they were enjoying the moment of humorous relief, up walked Alden, with Leopold perched jauntily upon his shoulder.

"Greetings," cheered Alden, with a glance at his time-piece. "I am so very glad you have returned safely! There is no time to spare, though. Come, we must return to your Mentor friends and the others, for there have been new developments."

"Oh, dear," said Celine. "That doesn't sound promising."

"No, it doesn't," said Jager. "I'll call North right now." Jager mented for North, but received no response. He tried the other Mentors, then North again. Still no reply. Celine and Alden tried as well, with no more success. "This does not seem good," spoke up Vin. "I wonder what has happened."

"I do not wish to think the worst," answered Ahimoth, "But it may be just that, nonetheless. What are we to do?"

"Good question, Ahimoth," replied Jager. "I think we should go see Nessie. I believe she can ensure our safety with her shielding — all the more important because of the precious item we now bear. Besides, it seems most likely the Mentors would look for us there with Nessie, rather than here."

"Good idea, Jager," said Celine. "It's only a short flight."

"I am ready," said Fianna. The rest agreed.

"And Leopold and I shall be there when you arrive," said Alden.

Less than half an hour later, the Dragons spotted the stretch of shoreline with the overhang that meant they were approaching Nessie's home. Upon landing, they were somewhat surprised that the wizard and bird were not there to greet them. Celine and Jager dismounted and searched the area, but the missing pair were nowhere to be seen.

"Oh dear," gasped Celine. "What could have happened to them? I hope they are all right. Maybe we should go back to Loch Maree and look for them."

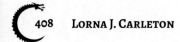

"I'm sure they're fine, Pumpkin," said Jager. "Maybe Alden had business to attend to before coming here. I'd bet they'll be along soon."

"I hope so," she replied. "I feel terrible that we left before we knew they were safely on their way." She had another look around, and mented to the wizard as well.

"I do hope he's all right," she said aloud, to no one in particular. Their tight schedule meant they needed to keep moving, so they put their worries aside for the moment, and turned attention to contacting the Mentors.

They had just begun a conference on the matter when Nessie's brindled head and neck rose from the chilly loch to greet them. The travelers explained the current circumstances, and Nessie joined them in another attempt at reaching North and her sisters. Unfortunately, the results were no better.

"It is late and we need to rest," said Fianna.

"I can keep you safe beneath my barrier," replied Nessie, "but you might be more comfortable in a structure, for more protection from the elements. I know of a place that I believe you would find suitable."

"That is good thinking," said Jager. "I agree, Fianna, it's getting late. We can still try to reach North periodically."

They all loved Nessie's suggestion, and soon found themselves in a deserted but fairly well-preserved castle, within the protection of Nessie's shielding spell. Within minutes they all were fast asleep. Although they had planned to waken at intervals for further attempts at reaching the Mentors, exhaustion had other plans. They slept soundly until morning — when they were awakened by North.

CHAPTER 38

The Dragon of Salvation

"Oh, North!" gasped Celine. "It's so good to hear you. We were so worried."

"I am sorry that we were out of communication," replied North. "We did not mean to worry you so, but my sisters and I needed to go to assist West. We are back now, and should not have to leave again for a while. West sends her love."

"Oh! I understand," said Celine. "And thank you for relaying West's message! It's so good to hear from her." She drew Mutuum from her tunic. "Look! Our mission was a success."

"That is wonderful news, child," replied North, admiring the dazzling incant-baton. "I knew you would not fail. All of you should be so proud. And now we Mentors stand ready to help you with your next step. It is most appropriate that you are lodged in that castle, for it is from that very place that your next step must begin. But the time is not yet. For the moment, I recommend that you return to Nibiru."

"Oh! That changes things," said Jager. "We've made a list of things to do, but we can adjust it. What's happening?"

"Yes, this does change things," replied North. "But in a good way, as I believe you will agree."

"Well, that's a relief," said Jager.

"Yes, a relief for us all," said North. "It gives us time to reinforce our front and rear lines and get some needed rest. For you, Celine and the Dragons, Nibiru is the safest place at the moment. The Kerr Dragons are not needed just yet, and unless there is some crucial matter I am not aware of, I believe the rest of your action list can wait."

"What about TS 428?" Celine cried out. "What about the Earthers?! G.O.D. is about to harvest them! We can't let that happen!"

"I quite agree, child," replied North. "Fortunately, there have been several disruptions to the harvesting equipment installation, and it will be weeks before they are operational."

"Oh, how wonderful!" exclaimed Celine and Jager together.

Celine recognized the glow that now shown from North: when West had glowed in just that way, it had always signaled happiness.

"Now, before you travel the tube-chute to Nibiru, you must rest for at least one day. Alika and the others can remain with us until you are ready to depart. Perhaps they should stay here until the shield can be lowered; then they can be transported to Nibiru in our ship. I prefer that they travel in that manner, though I believe the youngsters may disagree."

"Understood, and thank you," said Ahimoth. "I am pleased to know we have at least one day to rest. I truly need the time to prepare." The others all agreed. "Regarding Alika and the others, I would prefer that they not travel the chute again, but I know we must discuss this further, and decide upon the best course of action."

North thanked Ahimoth and excused herself. After a brief discussion, the friends decided the Dragons would go fishing for their breakfast while Jager and Celine ate from their packed supplies. They also agreed to leave discussion of how to proceed with the youngsters until the next morning; they wanted the opportunity to give the matter as much clear thought as possible.

The couple enjoyed a chat and a simple meal, then decided to practice some spells from Prince Deet's grimoire. They concurred that the book was sure to contain spells that could prove highly beneficial when they least expected it. They opened up the ancient pages and settled down to study.

"Here's an interesting one," said Celine. "A spell to create an 'escape pod' when there is no place to hide. Sounds intriguing. And obviously a handy tool to have, especially when you consider some of the situations we've found ourselves in lately."

"That's for sure," said Jager. "Here, I'll try it first." He read over the spell a few times, committing it to memory. "Okay, I have it. Here goes."

He recited the incantation and flicked his incant-baton at an empty corner of the room. For a split second, nothing happened. But then, a remarkable phenomenon occurred: a couple of cubic meters of space in the corner he'd pointed to seem to fold in upon itself. There was no other way to describe what he and Celine were seeing. The most surprising part, though, was that they could now see into what appeared to be a new, different room, in the middle of the air before them. The outer edges of the opening seemed to spin around, shimmering. They couldn't help but grin.

"Wow!" laughed Jager. "That's really cool. It's kind of like the time-traveling spell, in a way."

"Yes, that's what I was thinking," said Celine. "Here, I want to try it."

Jager handed her Mutuum. She took her position and began to recite the incantation. But before she'd completed the first line, a powerful gust of wind plucked them up and flung them into a tunnel-like passage, similar to the tube-chute they'd traveled so many times now, but without the tube-chute's awful, churning, air-liquid mixture.

It was not until much later that they discovered that — unbeknownst to the Mentors — the little castle in which they'd take refuge had been hexed. Anyone performing magic could be plucked up and whisked away by the very vortex in which they now found themselves.

Buffeted and jostled by gusts of the strange wind that had brought them here, the couple sailed on down the dark "meta-tunnel" for what seemed like several minutes. Then, abruptly, the winds ceased, the tunnel disappeared, and they were dumped hard on a chilly, stone-slab floor.

Quickly regaining their bearings, they surveyed their surroundings. They had arrived in a cavernous room, like one of Earth's old Gothic cathedrals, or the great hall of an oversized medieval castle.

Both mented for the Dragons and Mentors, but their calls went unanswered.

"Celine, I get a very odd feeling here," said Jager, aloud. "Do you feel it? Hard to explain, but it's as if this place were stuck in time."

"Yes, I feel it," said Celine. "Odd for sure. I agree, there's a sort of 'stuckness' to it."

"It reminds me of what I've read about the Viking people," said Jager, and he explained briefly who they were.

They approached one of the windows lining the long wall to their right and looked out. "Wow! Look there!" Jager exclaimed. "I've only seen stockades like that in museums. I wonder where we are. Maybe this *is* a museum."

"But that wouldn't explain the delicious food I smell," said Celine.

"Ha!" laughed Jager. Their serious situation hadn't dampened his cheerful optimism. "You've got me there, Pumpkin. Come, the smell is coming from down that hallway." They made their way through a broad doorway and into a long, dimly lit corridor. Advancing cautiously, they came to a second chamber; spacious, but not so large as the one they'd left. This one was filled with candlelight, and the delicious aromas of herbs and cooking foods.

Near the far left corner of the room was a waist-high railing. Celine and Jager approached and discovered it surrounded a rectangular opening in the floor, about two meters long and a meter wide. It looked down into a shadowy room where several figures moved about. Seeing one of the figures begin to look upward, they quickly ducked back away from the rail, then crept forward to look down again, taking care not to show themselves. The cloaked figures below formed an interesting tableau, their shadows flickering in the firelight. It was as though one of the scenes from the Nibiru cave paintings had come to life.

A small fire burned in a bowl atop a raised pedestal. A softly chanting voice could be heard from someone out of sight. A garishly robed figure advanced to the little fire and sprinkled something into the flames; Celine recognized the aroma of dried oak leaves and rosehips. Examining the scene more closely, Celine noticed a dais just beyond the fire bowl. She shivered at what she saw resting atop the dais, covered in sheets of gauze: two bodies, a male and a female, lying side by side. She pointed cautiously, and Jager saw them too.

"What's going on?" she whispered.

"I don't know, but I don't like this," replied Jager. "I do know the spell that brought us here, though. Perhaps it will work to return us to the castle. Vin and the others will be worried when they discover us missing, and I don't see anything useful for us to do here."

"Okay. It's worth a try," said Celine, still with an eye on the figures below. Just then, a tall, lanky form moved towards the dais, but stopped abruptly and cast his eyes upward, scanning toward where the two hid. In an instant, Celine enacted her cloaking spell, rendering them invisible to the man's probing gaze. And not a moment too soon.

"That was too close," she mented. "I want to leave, but I feel we are supposed to see this. That we are meant to be here."

"Agreed. Let's stay for a while longer."

Apparently satisfied there was no one above, the tall figure returned to his rite, facing the dais. Three others joined him, praying in unison. Celine listened intently, but could not make out much of what they said. She noticed flashes of light from walnut-sized crystals arranged on the dais alongside the silent bodies — reflections and refractions of the dancing flames. She could see from the faint rise and fall of their chests that the veiled Humans were alive. Their clasped

hands also flexed or twitched slightly from time to time.

"I know what this is," gasped Celine. "I...I know what to do now. But first, we let them finish." Jager nodded, and they continued their secret vigil.

A second figure smiled down at the two on the dais and positioned crystals upon their foreheads. The crystals' purpose: to promote healing energy of the highest vibration, on a cellular level, flowing life back into injured bodies at the brink of death. Small fuchsite and hematite crystals were also placed in the hands, to restore spiritual health and absorb negative flows draining from the bodies.

Celine and Jager began to doze, lulled by the droning chant and perfumes of lavender and eucalyptus oils. Jager squeezed Celine tighter, fighting the drowsiness. More robed figures entered the chamber and gathered into three circles round the dais. Their deep, strangely angelic voices edged Celine and Jager further toward sleep. The sing-song continued; sprinkled herbs fell gently to the flames.

Mother Spirit of the light
Father Spirit of the night
Your children are suffering
The good, the might.
Please help our friends
in this deadly plight.

The power of the light
The power of the right
Your children are suffering

The good, the might.

Please cure our friends

Divine spirits of the fight.

The chant repeated until at last the candles were spent.

"Oh my," gasped Celine, shaking her head to clear it. "I've lost track of time. Do you know how long we've been here?"

"No, I don't," replied Jager. "This all has been very strange. Very."

"Fianna will be so worried. We need to get back to the others."

Jager nodded agreement, then gave the spell a try. Before they knew it, they were back in the castle.

"Wow!" said Celine. "Strange indeed. What do you think it all means? Could it be some sort of foreshadowing — maybe of what will happen to us when the Mentors activate their weapon? Whatever it was, we have to tell both Nessie and North what's happened. And right away."

"Absolutely," said Jager. "I can't answer your questions, but your guesses make sense. And this castle must have been compromised. We'll have to find somewhere else to rest until tonight."

They returned to Loch Ness and contacted North, who was adamant that she come to assist Nessie in erecting a more secure barrier. She told the two to refrain from using Prince Deet's grimoire or incant-baton again, for the moment. Not until she could confer with West.

When North arrived, she asked for the spell book and baton; Celine turned them over at once. "Thank you," said North. "I will return them shortly — after my sisters and I have performed a cleansing spell to ensure that these are not themselves compromised."

If Dragons had hair, it would have risen straight up on the back of Fianna's neck as she listened to Celine's account of what had happened. The Dragon had been beyond worried when she had lost contact with her Companion. And now she was beyond delighted to have the girl back, and to know that North and Nessie were bolstering the protective barrier.

Safe again, and with all their immediate worries put to rest, the friends enjoyed an afternoon of fun and camaraderie. They forgot, for the moment at least, about all the troubles behind them, and the those that might lie ahead. They talked and laughed for hours, then raced through the skies in a game of aerial Dragon-tag, shielded from the eyes of the region's Human inhabitants by Nessie and North's potent spells. Although the day had not begun well, it ended with everyone refreshed, ready to catch a few hours' sleep before another taxing journey through the Nibiru wormhole.

Though she did not look forward to the chute, Celine knew the journey would end with all of them back safely on Nibiru. Well worth the troublesome trip. She curled up between Fianna's ivory forelegs and fell almost instantly into a restful sleep. As usual, she visited dreamland — but in dreams more real than she had ever experienced. Vivid images and angelic voices danced across her mind, culminating in a complete performance — by who, she couldn't say — of the old familiar song of her childhood, The Princess and the Boy:

> The princess and the boy
> The princess and the boy

Where have they gone
The princess and the boy?
Some say together, some say not
Some say lovers, some say lost
The princess and the Dragon
The princess and the Dragon
Where have they gone
The princess and the Dragon?
Some say white, some say black
Some say for good, some say for bad
The princess and the prince
The princess and the prince
Where have they gone
The princess and the prince?
Some say up, some say down
Some say back, some say now

Her and he
Him and she
They and them
Where are they now?
Where could they be?

As the song's last words rang out in her dream, she awoke.
Fianna and the others were still sound asleep, so she tried
to sleep again herself. She found it impossible. Her mind

churned with too many unanswered questions. And how strange it was, she thought, that that dear old song would crop up in her dreams — and then persist, as it was right now, in her waking mind. But then again, perhaps it wasn't all that surprising, she thought. Not when she considered the song's significance, and its direct foreshadowing of her travels through time with Jager.

After a few minutes' musing, she gasped, annoyed at herself. How could she have missed it? The song's words were the same she'd heard sung in the tunnels of yesteryear, on their visit to Prince Deet! At the time, she'd been so caught up in managing an avatar and meeting the prince that she'd not paid attention to the words of the soft chanting close by. Not until she'd recognized a new verse had begun — one she'd never heard before. And then a second.

Re-listening to the new verses in her mind, Celine realized that not only must the past be visited, just as they had recently done, but they must visit the future as well.

The Dragon and the girl
The Dragon and the boy
They have come back
From the blackness of our world
Some say then, some say now
Our future will not disallow

Girl of the moon
Her Hunter from above
Salvation proof of

The Dragon of Love
Her and he
Him and she
They and them
They are now
They must be

Celine gasped again. Beads of sweat formed, then trickled down her face. How could she have been so blind? It was inevitable it would come to this, seeing as she was Fianna's Companion. She was Companion to the Dragon of Love! The Dragon of Salvation!

In her heart, the girl had known this to be the case. But she had kept her premonition to herself, not even sharing it with Jager. Now the truth of what Fianna meant to Nibiru — and the rest of the universe — stared her in the face. And she knew what she must now do.

Fianna was the one.

She was the Dragon of Love and Salvation.

Fianna was destined to save the universe, not she and Jager. Fianna would bring peace, to end the ages of unrest. Just as they'd hidden the true path to Mutuum's recovery, the prophecies hid the Dragons' true salvation, and the way to peace for all the universe. Hid them to await the proper moment of revelation.

Celine recalled what West had once told her: "Your legacy, my dear child, is every life you touch. So, make sure each touch is one of goodness and love — for then goodness and love shall return to you in the end. If you were to touch with hate and untruth, you would live out your days surrounded

by them. Do not forget these things." Now she realized West's words had held double meanings. She had always suspected as much; now she understood their meanings and import in full.

How very clever of the Mentors to create an illusion, she thought. To lead everyone to believe that her linking with Jager would hold the universe together. Everyone — Scabbage, Bryne and the Volac Forces included — had been fooled. So had she and Jager, for that matter.

Now Celine could see the truth. She realized how clever it had been for the Mentors to allude to the idea that a religion would save the universe. True, some religions had been great forces for good — for a time. But as time had gone on, so many formal religions and religious belief systems had also torn apart societies of every size and description. It seemed that some ill-intentioned person or group always managed to pervert them, and turn them from forces for good to agencies of evil.

And so, religions could not be relied upon to save the universe today, or in the future. They could fix a thing or two, maybe improve quite a lot, but they would not reverse the dwindling spiral of existence. Only love could.

"Yes! Ha! Love will," Celine laughed quietly. Love would save them. She smiled, watching her sleeping friends. Love and only love was the answer. Without it, there was no hope. And without hope, there was no life for sentient beings anywhere.

Thinking further on what she'd realized, she concluded that religion was too often used by evil forces, offering false hope. A carrot, so to speak, to lure, control and abuse people of good will. She and Jager were the guardians of the sacred spiritual framework that would make continued happy life possible. But first Fianna must save it, as only the Dragon of Love could.

The girl smiled, knowing that once she and Jager had played their part, Fianna could reveal who she truly was; who she and Vin were, and would be. They were the salvation. And their children would seal that salvation.

Looking again at all the signs, it was obvious to Celine that Fianna and her chosen mate were the keys. That is what she had alluded to and mentioned to Jager, back when they were studying one of the paintings in Vin's cave — the one that showed the two of them — herself and Jager — in death. It was an image they had never discussed with anyone else, or even among themselves, since that day.

She realized Fianna and Vin, together, were the hoped-for answer to a huge problem she and Jager still hadn't solved. It was a good solution, she thought, but it made her shudder. She knew she must not fail to meet the challenge that lay immediately ahead. And it would be the most difficult task of her life. She had to complete it, just as the painting predicted. The prophecies must come to pass, or the Dragons would cease to exist.

And, finally, she recognized she must keep these new realizations strictly to herself. Fianna and Jager must not learn of them. Not until the time was right. Their very lives depended on it.

CHAPTER 39

Celebrations and More Celebrations

The vortex snapped shut behind the band of travelers it had just deposited on Nibiru. Celine and Jager turned and grinned at one another, delighted to have returned their Dragon friends home in time for the big wedding day.

They joined right into the merriment that greeted their arrival. The huge throng of Dragons that had gathered in the courtyard to greet them leapt, trumpeted, fanned and flapped, cheering and laughing. They were celebrating something every one of them had dreamed of for ages. Today marked the long-awaited start of great things for Nibiru and her people.

"Augh!" groaned Ahimoth. "I hope I never have to make that trip again! But it was almost worth it, to receive such a wonderous welcoming."

"I'm with you on chute travel," said Jager, one arm around Celine. "And about the welcome, too. It's almost too much to take!"

King Neal managed to quiet the ecstatic crowd long enough to make an official statement of welcome. But then the cheering, dancing, hugging and nuzzling resumed, more boisterous than before. Dragon Hall and all the surrounding hills and valleys were filled with sounds of elated greeting and pure joy.

No one was happier that day than King Quade. When the travelers had arrived, he'd rushed forward past King Neal and Queen Dini to greet his precious daughter, Fallon, with the biggest Dragon hug he could muster. No one took offence, though, or chastised him for his rudeness to the Nibiru King. Instead, everyone shared in his joy and cheered all the louder — King Neal included.

Quade was the first to pay his respects to Fianna and her fellow travelers, bowing to Fianna with a foreleg forward in deepest respect and gratitude. And every Dragon present followed his lead.

As tradition dictated, a celebratory feast followed at once. And although the travelers were thoroughly exhausted, they took part in the festivities as long as they could. All but one — Ahimoth had insisted that Alika be bedded down long before the evening ended, escorting the young Dragon to the Nursery himself.

Late in the evening, the travelers sat together, chatting about the trip and the weddings soon to come. Chatting was a challenge, though, for Dragon after Dragon stopped by to greet them, and to express thanks for all they'd done. At last, when even Ahimoth could no longer keep from yawning, they all retired. Every one of them enjoyed the best night's sleep they could remember.

The next morning, everyone gathered again for a solemn ceremony: Fianna's coronation as Queen of Nibiru. And then the celebrations resumed, reaching a more joyful intensity than had ever been experienced on Nibiru.

Celine's heart was filled with pride and happiness for Fianna. Yet at the same time, she was deeply sad — an emotion she fought with all her strength to conceal. Her sadness rose from the realization that this day marked the beginning of the end of her Companionship with the great Dragon. To keep the tears at bay, she busied herself with preparation for the grand weddings that would take place the following day.

Next morning, the wedding preparations were still in full swing. But to everyone's surprise, the new queen, her mate Vin, Prince Ahimoth, Joli and the two Humans were nowhere to be found. It was as though they had been swallowed by a vortex, just as Fianna's parents had been, so many years before. There was no time for worry, though. Too much to be done! They would all appear in due time.

But as the appointed time for the ceremonies drew near, concern began to rise. There was still no sign of Fianna or the rest — and there couldn't be much of a wedding without the brides and grooms!

Happily, and to everyone's great relief, just a half-hour before the wedding service was to begin, the missing Dragons and their Human friends reappeared. They had been close by all along, but hidden behind a cloaking spell Jager had conjured. The friends had wanted to spend some time with each other before the weddings set in motion the trail of changes certain to come. The crowd cheered at the unexpected surprise.

With the last of the preparations complete, it was time for the big moment. There was a hush as the Dragon couples passed through the gathered throng to stand before Orgon the Wise, at the very center of Dragon Hall.

The service was indeed grand, and many joyful tears were shed. It had been many long years since there had been such a momentous occasion. The celebrations that followed went on for a full two weeks, and one and all had a wonderful time. Celine and the other adventurers joined in, but somehow managed to rest, refresh and restore as well.

One morning found the little group lazing about over a picnic breakfast in Linglu Glade, waiting for Fianna to join them. She soon touched down, her beautiful white scales glistening in the morning light.

The Dragon Queen greeted each of her friends in turn, then asked if Joli would accompany her back to Vin's cave-home. The friends thought this strange, and followed at a discreet distance. When they arrived at the cave, Joli and Fianna had already entered, so they settled down outside to wait and watch. After a bit, Vin ventured inside — it was his home, after all, and Fianna his wife — but he soon reappeared. He explained that he'd been asked, ever so politely, to wait outside for a little while.

"It will be okay, friend," said Ahimoth, guessing at what must be going on. "It is part of life. Fianna will be fine, for she is in capable hands. Come, let us take a flight down the valley. By the time we return, I am sure everything will be perfect."

And perfect it was. For when the two touched down again at the cave entrance, Joli was waiting for them.

"Come, Vin," she said. "Fianna calls for you."

Joli stepped inside, Vin following nervously. And there, nestled in her favorite spot, was Fianna. Everything was

indeed fine with her — and with the six glistening eggs that lay at her warm underbelly.

Celine and the others, still outside, cheered and cheered when Vin brought them the wonderful news.

ABOUT THE AUTHOR

Lorna J. Carleton makes her home in West Kelowna, British Columbia. A BC native, Lorna is a Safety Advisor for a major utility, while also working toward a university degree. She's dreamed of being an author since childhood, and made several attempts at novel writing. *Dragons of the Past* is her fourth published work, and the fourth book in the Dragons of Nibiru series. She drew inspiration for the series from observations of life over the years; chief among them were clashes among diverse cultures, and the struggles of former cult members to get on with their lives and find happiness. While continuing the book series, Lorna is also planning a vacation trip to the Pleiades Cluster—providing she can find suitable transport (technological or otherwise).

www.lornajcarleton.com